Home Blooms

A Hometown Harbor Novel

Tammy L. Grace

Home Blooms is a work of fiction. Names, characters, places and incidents either are products of the author's imagination or are used fictitiously. Any resemblance to actual events, locales, entities, or persons, living or dead, is entirely coincidental.

Published in the United States by Lone Mountain Press, Nevada

ISBN 978-0-9912434-2-6 (paperback)
ISBN 978-0-9912434-3-3 (eBook)
FIRST EDITION

Cover design by Kari Ayasha, Cover to Cover Designs
Interior Formatting by Polgarus Studio
Author Photo by Cook's Photography
Printed in the United States of America

ALSO BY TAMMY L. GRACE

Below you will find links to the electronic version of all of Tammy's

books available at Amazon

Cooper Harrington Detective Novels

Killer Music

Hometown Harbor Series

Hometown Harbor: The Beginning (FREE Prequel Novella)

Finding Home

Home Blooms

A Promise of Home

Pieces of Home

Tammy would love to connect with readers on social media.
Remember to subscribe to her mailing list for another freebie, only available
to readers on the mailing list. Follow this link to her webpage and provide
your email address and she'll send you the exclusive interview she did with all
the canine characters in her books. **Follow Tammy on Facebook at this
link, by liking her page. You may also follow Tammy on Amazon at this
link, by using the follow button under her photo.**

Dear Readers,

I can't believe I'm getting married in a few weeks. I never dreamed I'd find such happiness after my divorce from Marty. I figured my faithful dog, Zoe, and I would go it alone. Not only do I enjoy my new business at Harbor Coffee and Books, but I was lucky enough to meet the man I love, Jeff Cooper. He's a retired firefighter and helps his son run Cooper Hardware and has his own handyman business.

He has a wonderful family and a town full of friends who make me feel at home here in Friday Harbor. There is one exception—Brenda Murray, the resident man-eater, who has been breaking up relationships on the island for thirty years. She's a real piece of work, complete with flimsy, tight dresses and an attitude that won't quit. She's done her best to entice Jeff and discourage me. When her tactics didn't work she resorted to starting a fire at my shop.

Jeff's sister, Jen, is a good friend and does a fabulous job on my hair. I hired her daughter, Megan, along with Rachel, Kyle, and Hayley to help in the coffee shop. They're a fun bunch of young people and Hayley lives in the apartment above the shop. She and Jeff's son, Charlie, are dating. Charlie is a wonderful young man who loves my pie almost as much as his dad. Jeff's daughter, Ashley, was recently married and lives in Virginia. Jeff's brother, Jeremy, runs the family resort, where Jeff grew up and lives in a cabin on Mitchell Bay.

The unexpected news of learning Kyle was the result of one of Marty's many affairs turned out to be the catalyst that forced me to deal with my past. I love Kyle like he's my own son and with my help he met Marty for the first time a few weeks ago. And I finally forgave Marty and am ready to enjoy my new life.

Max, my best friend, came for my surprise fiftieth birthday party in July and has decided to move back to the Pacific Northwest. He lost his wife five years ago and I'm so happy he'll be moving nearby. He, along with my college friend and whiz of an assistant, Becky, are like family.

We're having the wedding at Linda's nursery. She's the owner of Buds and Blooms and Jen's best friend. It's going to be a gorgeous setting. And, Ellie from Sweet Treats is doing our cake. I'm leaving in a few minutes to pick up Linda for our trip into the city. We're meeting Becky to pick out my wedding dress. Hope I'll see you at the wedding!

Sam

ACKNOWLEDGMENTS

I appreciate the enthusiasm and the positive reviews from the first book in the series, Finding Home: A Hometown Harbor Novel. I'm grateful to know readers enjoy the island and the characters they meet while visiting a place none of us would mind calling home.

I'm thankful for Theresa, Linda, and Dana, who eagerly read the early drafts and offered ideas to help improve the story.

Kari at Cover to Cover Designs is so gifted and has a way of coming up with exactly what I'm looking for in a cover. Jason and Marina at Polgarus Studio always deliver exceptional and professional formatting.

I will forever be indebted to my family and friends for their support and encouragement as I work on the next chapter.

One

Holding crystal champagne flutes, Becky and Linda turned from gazing out the window of Rose's Bridal Boutique when they heard Sam ask, "Well, what do you think of this one?"

"Oh, oh, oh, I think this is it," squealed Becky.

"I agree, it's stunning," said Linda.

Sam twirled around and faced the mirror. This was the seventh dress she had tried on and as she took in every angle, she too thought it may be the one. The dress was a soft blush, with delicate embroidery and tiny shimmering crystals. It had cap sleeves and a flattering sweetheart neckline. The tea length silk skirt was unadorned, drawing all the attention to the captivating bodice, featuring a sheer back, covered only with the dazzling beaded needlework.

"You look gorgeous, Sam. It's my number one pick," surmised Linda, placing her glass of bubbly on the table and stepping over to Sam. With her fingertip, she touched the crystal beads. "The view from the back is striking."

"You're gonna knock Jeff's socks off," Becky said, rushing to Sam and grabbing both her hands. A tear trickled down her cheek, "You're beautiful."

Sam smiled. "I like it. It's my favorite, too. Don't cry, Becky, not yet anyway."

"What do you think about white flowers, Sam?" asked Linda. "White is always so elegant and with this whisper of pink in the dress, we could use pink as accents."

"Sounds fabulous, Linda. I'll leave it to you, since you're the expert in all things floral." Sam turned again and looked at the dress. She saw her old classmate and Rose's daughter, Maureen, examining her in the dress. "What do you think, Maureen?"

"I agree with your friends, you look lovely. The color and the style suit you, Sam."

Sam took one more look and a deep breath. "I'll take it. Could I be fitted today? And we need to pick out a dress for Becky, too. I was hoping we could find something in a darker mauve or pink for my maid of honor. We only have four weeks until the wedding, so I know I'm pushing the envelope."

"Sure, let me get Viv in here to get you fitted and she'll get the adjustments done this week. Becky, come with me and let's look at a couple of dresses I have in mind for you," said Maureen, as she guided Becky across the shop.

Linda had her sketchbook out and was busy drawing ideas for a bridal bouquet and arrangements for the ceremony. Viv arrived and began fussing with Sam's dress and pinning it. After what seemed like an eternity, Becky appeared in a deep mauve chiffon dress. The flirty skirt hit just above the knee. Becky cut a striking figure and the dress enhanced her trim waist and long legs. The bodice was ruched along the diagonal and crossed over in a V shape, with the same becoming shape duplicated on the back.

"Wow, Becky, you look terrific," said Sam.

"Gorgeous color, what do you call it, Maureen?" asked Linda.

"Well, it's technically called mulberry, but it's the perfect pinkish purple color that's so complimentary. It looks great on her," beamed Maureen.

Sam motioned Maureen over and whispered something in her ear. She nodded and trotted to the racks of dresses.

"Ya'll, I love it too. If you like it Sam, I think this is it," smiled Becky.

"I do. It's perfect."

Maureen returned with a handful of purple and pink dresses. She approached Linda and asked her to take a look. "Oh, these are all pretty, but I think Becky looks fabulous in the one she has on."

"Well, I think you need a new dress for the wedding and I insist you pick one out. My treat," said Sam.

"Oh, I couldn't—" began Linda.

"Yes, you can," interrupted Becky. "Go try some on and model for us."

Maureen cajoled Linda into a dressing room. She modeled for the group and on the fourth dress, a collective gasp resonated.

"That's magnificent," said Sam.

"Va va va voom," shouted Becky.

"It's very becoming. The perfect color for you," said Maureen.

Linda glanced at the mirror. The dress was a deep eggplant and looked terrific with her dark hair. It was tiered chiffon, with lace and beads inset across the torso. The dress had a V-neck in front and back and came with a beautiful lace and beaded shrug. Linda didn't wear dressy clothes much and protested that it was too lavish.

"Nonsense, it's perfect and you look gorgeous. I want you to have it. Please accept it with my heartfelt thanks," said Sam, as she approached Linda and hugged her.

Tears threatened Linda's eyes and she returned Sam's hug and whispered, "Okay, Sam. I love it."

Viv rushed over to check the dress and pinned only a few places.

"I think our work here is done, Maureen." Sam grinned as she glanced at her watch, "Well, I guess it isn't as bad as I thought, it's only one o'clock."

"Sam, go ahead and change, Viv has everything she needs and we'll have her take a quick look at Becky, but I don't think she'll need to do much."

Viv shuffled over to Becky and began tugging and pinning the dress. Sam changed and Maureen took the chosen gown and gently hung it on a padded hanger, encased it in a protective cover, and slipped Sam's information into the outer pocket. "We can have all of these ready for you to pick up by the end of next week."

"That would be wonderful." Sam gave her a credit card and she moved over to an antique desk and completed the transaction.

Maureen returned with a folder she handed Sam. "I'm so happy for you and wish you only the best. I was so sorry to hear you and Marty had divorced, but you radiate joy. Your Jeff is a lucky man," she hugged Sam.

"I appreciate all your help and the rush. Becky will stop by and get the dresses at the end of the week. Be sure and tell your mom hello for me."

"I will. She doesn't get out much, but she always enjoys hearing about our new brides. She'll be pleased to know about your wedding. Do send me a photo, if you can. I'd like to share it with Mom."

"I'll make sure you get one. Thanks again for the help and keeping us stocked in champagne this morning," laughed Sam, as they made their way out of the store.

Becky took her list out as soon as Sam unlocked the car. "Well, girls, it looks like the last thing on the list is the photographer. Linda is handling the flowers, and being the kind woman she is, agreed to let us have the ceremony and reception at the nursery. Ellie is doing the cake and the caterer who did such a fab job on your birthday said he could do the wedding. Jeff has the same band booked and now we have the dresses. I think we deserve lunch," laughed Becky.

Since they were already in the Queen Anne neighborhood, Sam drove them to her favorite French restaurant. They had dodged the lunch crowd and found the restaurant almost empty. They lingered over delicious salads and pasta and decided to share a piece of the decadent red velvet cake for dessert.

As Sam pushed her fork into the tender cake smothered in cream cheese frosting, she looked at her two friends. "I can't believe I'm getting married in a few weeks. Thank you both so much for all your help." She glanced at Becky, "I'm lucky to have had you in my life since college. I could not have endured the last few years without you. You are a wonderful assistant, but an even better friend." She slipped the bite into her mouth moaned with delight. "Oh, my gosh, this is good."

Becky and Linda both nodded as they took their first bite. "You may want to have Ellie make one layer red velvet," smiled Linda, licking a bit of frosting off her fork.

"Excellent idea. I have to finalize the flavors with Jeff. I think it's going to be fun to have a variety. I never considered it until Ellie suggested different flavors for each layer."

"It's going to be a beautiful wedding, Sam. And Jeff is beyond excited. I'm thrilled for both of you," smiled Linda.

"And I'm grateful for your friendship, Linda. I see why Jeff and his sister think so much of you. I'm glad you're part of my new life on the island and that I can call you a friend," said Sam.

The plate was clean, nearly pristine, when the three finished. Sam paid the check and thanked them again for spending the day with her.

"You don't have to twist my arm to take a day off and sip champagne and play dress up. Plus a wonderful lunch and cake—I think we should do this more often," joked Linda.

"I haven't had this much fun in years. But, I guess we better take Becky home and then get the ferry," said Sam, as she maneuvered through traffic. Becky lived only about a mile from the restaurant. She and Brad had a beautiful early 1900's house they had remodeled into a modern luxury home with gorgeous views of Puget Sound. After a quick stop at Becky's house, Linda and Sam set out for the two hour ride north to catch the ferry to Friday Harbor.

Sam glanced over at Linda continuing to draw in her sketch book. As she drove, she thought of her newfound happiness and how lucky she was to have met Jeff and finally feel at peace. *I can't believe this is all real. I feel like I'm dreaming and I never want to wake up.*

Two

The last time Sam had made this drive to the ferry terminal she had been escaping her life. Her divorce after twenty-five years of marriage had plunged her into a dark despair. After a year of hiding in her home, she decided her only chance for survival was to go somewhere new and do something different. She was fortunate to have the proceeds from the sale of her software company, so financially she was set, but emotionally she was running on empty. She never dreamed her decision to move to Friday Harbor and live in her vacation home would turn out to be the best choice she had ever made.

The last few months had been a roller coaster of emotions for her. She had bought Harbor Coffee and Books and her old love of baking had provided a much needed distraction. She had met Jeff, a retired firefighter turned handyman, and as they say, "the rest is history". She finally had the courage to open her heart to Jeff and discovered she loved him. Her old friend Max helped encourage her and threw her a surprise fiftieth birthday party and Jeff proposed with a stunning ring she had left with the jeweler in Seattle to be sized.

The coffee shop started as a new venture and something to distract her from her failed marriage, but had grown into a thriving business she enjoyed. She was fortunate to have found four young people to staff it. Hayley, who was dating Jeff's son, Charlie, had the most experience and lived in the apartment above the shop. Megan, Jeff's niece, and another high school student, Rachel, were both hard workers. And, the most surprising member of her team was Kyle. He was the grandson of the local theatre owner and unbeknownst to either of them, he was the result of an affair Sam's ex-husband had engaged in almost twenty years ago. He was terrific and she was sorry he would be leaving for college soon.

Not only did she love Jeff, but she also treasured the bonus of a family she had longed for since losing her parents. She loved Charlie, and Jeff's sister, Jen, who owned a salon and spa down the street from her coffee shop. Jeff looked out for Jen, who was raising Megan alone. Jeff's mom was sweet and his older brother, Jeremy, who ran the Harbor Resort with his wife, Heather, was happy for them. The only person in the family who gave Sam any doubts was Jeff's daughter, Ashley. Sam was thankful she lived on the other side of the country.

As they approached the ferry lane, Sam's thoughts were interrupted by the ring of her cell phone and she hit her speaker button.

"Hey sweetie, how are you doing?" asked Jeff.

"We're fine. Just getting into the ferry lanes, so we should be home soon. We got everything done and Becky's checking things off her list," she laughed.

"Good. I missed you today. I'll have dinner ready when you get back and tell Linda she has to stay."

She watched Linda smile and nod. "She'll stay. See you when we get there. Love you."

"Love you too, honey."

Sam parked her car and they opted to get out and stretch their legs on the deck. The breeze felt refreshing and as they sat on a bench, Sam asked to see Linda's sketches.

"Sure, they're not complete, but let me know what you think," she said, handing her the book. "I'm going to go get us a couple of drinks, I'll be right back."

Sam flipped through the book, amazed at the talent contained in the pages. Linda had drawn the entire ceremony scene, complete with chairs

7

and ribbons, plus the bridal bouquet and all the other flowers. She had sketched out the reception and table arrangements. It all looked like something from a fairy tale.

Linda returned with two iced teas. "These sketches are magnificent. I love everything you've done," said Sam.

"Good, I'm glad you like the ideas. I'm looking forward to this wedding. I get burnt out on weddings each summer, but this one is special. I want everything to be perfect, so you tell me if you don't like something."

"Yeah, like I won't like something. You're an artist, Linda. I'm so impressed. And Max is going to come early to help, so you put him to work doing anything you need."

"Actually, that would be a huge help. You're lucky to have such a great friend."

"I know. Max is the best and has been my friend through thick and thin. He's so excited for me and he loves Jeff too. He can't wait to walk me down the aisle to give me away."

"Speaking of love. I love my new dress. Thanks again for treating me."

"Don't mention it. For what you're doing, a dress is a drop in the bucket."

They heard the announcement to return to their vehicle and made their way downstairs. Sam drove from the landing and turned on Spring Street to take a quick look at the shop. The outside seating area was full of people and the inside was humming with activity.

"Wow, business is booming," said Linda.

"Yeah, looks like. I feel guilty leaving Megan and Kyle to deal with it, but I'm pooped, so dinner at home sounds good."

"I know. It's amazing how tiring shopping and eating can be," laughed Linda.

Sam pulled into her driveway and as they entered, they were greeted by three happy dogs. Her own golden retriever, Zoe, followed by Jeff's chocolate Lab, Bailey, and Linda's black Lab, Lucy, bounded into the garage. The dogs were way past excited, vying for attention and depositing wet kisses on Sam and Linda.

Jeff came around the corner and greeted Sam with a kiss of his own and a hug for Linda. "Ladies, as you can see, we're thrilled to see you. I have dinner ready on the deck."

"Sounds great to me. I hope Lucy was good for you today."

"The three of them played all day and they should be tired out from all the running around we did," said Jeff.

They moved through the kitchen out to the deck. Jeff had grilled steaks and veggies and made a huge fruit salad. They began discussing the wedding plans as they shared the meal.

"Charlie and I got measured for our tuxedos today, so that's done. I talked to Max and he's getting measured in the city and they'll coordinate with our shop to add it to the order. I also talked to Jennifer about the photographer. She thinks Ryan at Harbor Photography does the best job and he's available. So, if you want to take a look at his portfolio we can finalize it tomorrow," reported Jeff.

"That sounds good. We need to pick our cake flavors with Ellie too. She wanted us to stop by tomorrow after closing so we can taste a few. Today we had scrumptious red velvet, so I want one layer to be that for sure."

"I'll have no trouble tasting cake. It will be hard to decide though."

"Linda, show Jeff your sketches for the flowers. She did these sketches while we were trying on gowns today and on the ride to the ferry. They're incredible."

Linda passed Jeff the book. "Wow. I'm not surprised, but Sam's right. These are wonderful."

Linda beamed. "I'm glad you like them. I told Sam I'm so happy for you both." She paused and started taking the empty plates into the kitchen. "I hate to eat and run, but need to get back and get some work done."

"Leave the dishes, Linda. You've done plenty. Thanks so much for coming with me today. I had a great time." Sam hugged her.

"Me too," she said in a quiet voice. "Come on Lucy, let's go." The black Lab bounded over to her and they both made their way to the car. Jeff and Sam stood at the door waving as she drove away with Lucy's head hanging out of the window.

"She's such a sweet lady. I wish she could have what we have. And I happen to think Max could be the perfect man for her. Now, I need to figure out a way to get them together," pondered Sam.

"Aren't you the little matchmaker," teased Jeff, bringing her close. "Linda definitely deserves happiness and so does Max, so maybe your idea isn't so crazy." He grazed her forehead with his lips.

"I told her Max was coming early to help with the wedding preparations and suggested she use him for anything she needed. I know they'll get along well and I think if they spend some time with each other, it could work out," she grinned.

"You're such a cute conniver," he said, bending to brush his lips over hers. "Let's plan on breakfast at the Front Street Café tomorrow and then we can meet Ryan and decide on the photographs. And we can stop by and test cakes in the afternoon. I'll be at your house around eight."

"Okay, sounds like a plan. Thanks again for dinner," she said reaching up to kiss him.

"Come on Bailey," shouted Jeff. "See you in the morning."

Jeff and Bailey trotted to his truck and headed down the road to his house on Mitchell Bay. Zoe whined as she watched the two drive away. "I know, girlie. I wish they could stay too, but we're almost married and then they'll be here all the time."

Three

Jeff and Sam lingered over breakfast at the café. Jeff ordered the Sunday special of two pancakes, bacon, sausage, eggs, and potatoes. Sam decided to stick with oatmeal, since she had just been fitted and didn't want to risk gaining any weight. She had gained ten pounds since moving to Friday Harbor. Her appetite had returned along with the contentment she felt with Jeff. She could stand to add a few more pounds, but didn't want to spoil the beautiful dress.

Jeff had Ryan's portfolio out and they were looking at his work. He had done hundreds of weddings, along with portraits and other photos. They both admired his work and knew Linda's nursery would present a beautiful setting. They weren't having a large wedding party, only Becky and Jeff's son, Charlie, would be standing up with them, plus Max giving Sam away. They wanted to do some family photos though, especially with Jeff's mom. Since Sam didn't have any relatives, Jeff wanted to make sure she was included with his family and wanted plenty of pictures with everyone. Jeff's daughter, Ashley, would be arriving the day before the wedding. She had a new job and couldn't take much time off work, so would have to leave the morning after, but Jeff was excited to see her.

"So, what's your vote on photos—before or after the ceremony?" he asked.

"I'm sort of traditional and like the idea of after, and I don't think we'll be in a huge hurry, do you?"

"No, I think it should be fine. We can talk to Ryan about timing and see what he thinks. The guests can hang out and wait in the tent and take advantage of the free bar."

They paid the bill and set out for Ryan's studio. They had a ten o'clock appointment and were early so they stopped by the coffee shop to see how things were going. Hayley and Rachel were hard at work and the deck was full of tourists.

They opened the door to a long line waiting at the counter. Sam gave Jeff her things and slipped behind the counter to help. "Hey, you guys are swamped."

Hayley turned, "Yeah, it's been like this all weekend." Sam stood at the cash register and rang up orders while the girls hurried to prepare drinks. She delivered pastries and pie and made a couple frozen smoothies. When the line was looking manageable, Jeff tapped her on the shoulder and motioned to his watch.

"Darn, girls, we have to get to Ryan's, but I'll be back to check and help when we're done."

"We're fine, see you soon," said Rachel.

"I may have to schedule three people for the weekends. I'll have to ask everyone what they think. I never dreamed it would be quite this busy."

"I'm glad it's busy now. You've done an impressive job, but it will slow down after Labor Day," said Jeff, as they walked the few blocks to Ryan's studio. "I'll call Charlie and see if he can zip over and help the girls clear the tables and make sure the trash is dumped."

"That will be a big help. Tell him I owe him a pie," smiled Sam.

As they turned the corner, Ryan was arriving and unlocking the door. "Morning guys, how are you?" he asked.

"Great, Ryan. We appreciate you meeting us on a Sunday," said Sam, as she extended her hand.

"No problem. I have a wedding this afternoon, so this is perfect timing."

Jeff disconnected, gave Sam a thumbs up, and shook Ryan's hand, "Hi, Ryan."

"Come on in and let's see what we can do," he said, holding the door for them.

The front of the studio was covered in a variety of photographs. Sam and Jeff sat on a comfortable couch and Ryan offered to let them look at more photos in the stacks of books he had piled on the coffee table.

"We've seen your work and think it's outstanding and want you to do our wedding. We need to talk about timing and the types of photos and get your pricing," said Sam.

"Thanks for the compliment. I have several wedding packages, so let's talk about your vision for the day and we'll make it work."

Sam and Jeff explained they were leaning towards photos after the wedding and Ryan nodded. He suggested he do some photos of both the bride and the groom separately prior to the wedding, including some with the maid of honor and the best man and a lot of candid photos of them getting ready. He planned to get some shots of each of them with their parents.

Sam's eyes blurred with tears, "I lost my parents over thirty years ago and I don't have any other family or children, so I'd like a few photos of my friend Max, who's giving me away and my maid of honor, Becky. They're my family now."

Ryan's face softened, "I'm so sorry, I didn't know. I'll make a note to shoot the three of you. I'll get Jeff with his mom, kids, and siblings. We can get those all done before the ceremony and then do other group shots after the wedding. I'll follow you to the reception. We could also do a video of the wedding and the reception."

"Oh, I'd like that," said Jeff.

"Okay, let's see." Ryan was checking his pricing sheets and scribbling notes. "Here's a package that should work." He handed them a sheet. "So, the price includes the video and all the shots before, during, and after. It includes a quantity of prints for you and a digital CD of all the shots you choose. You can add on more prints for a discounted price listed at the bottom."

Sam and Jeff studied the sheet. They looked at each other and nodded. "That looks great, Ryan. Go ahead and book us," Jeff grinned. "We'll be at the nursery early, using Linda's house to get ready."

He nodded. "I'll book it out and I have an assistant coming with me. We'll be out at Linda's by noon to get things organized and ready. The setting is going to be beautiful, so I think you'll be pleased with the results. I appreciate your business. I'll be in touch," said Ryan as he stood.

"We'll talk to you soon," said Jeff.

Sam was busy writing out a check for the deposit and handed it to Ryan. "Thanks, I think it will be lovely."

They left the studio and strolled back to the coffee shop, hand in hand. The deck was crowded and Charlie was outside clearing vacated tables. Sam dropped her things in the back and went back to the register at the counter. Jeff helped Charlie outside and dumped all the trash in the dumpster.

"Did you get squared away at Ryan's?" asked Charlie.

"Yep, it was fairly painless," laughed Jeff. "We have to stop by Ellie's to taste cakes this afternoon. Do you want to come with?"

"Sure, sounds great, if Sam won't mind."

"Ah, she won't mind. It'll be fun. We're supposed to meet Ellie at one."

"Could Hayley come too? We were going to hang out when she gets off at one."

"Sure, bring her along."

"If you can handle this for now, I'll get our lunch. Then we can be ready to go."

"I can manage. We appreciate you helping out."

Charlie smiled, "I'd do anything for one of Sam's pies."

Jeff laughed as he went back to clearing tables and wiping them down. Sam came out a few minutes later with a frozen drink for him. "You make a cute busboy," she laughed.

"At your service," he grinned. "By the way I invited Charlie to come test cake with us and he's going to bring Hayley."

"Oh, fun. That will be a big help. I think it's going to be hard to decide on the flavors."

They looked up when they heard Megan's sweet voice, "Hey, Uncle Jeff."

"Hi, Megan. How are you?"

"I'm good," she said as she hugged Jeff. "Hey, Sam. We've been busy, so I thought I'd come by early for my one o'clock shift."

"Thanks, Megan. We stopped by to help this morning because the place was swamped. We're heading over to test some cakes at Ellie's, but we'll be back to check on things. I might ask Rachel to stay for an extra hour or two," pondered Sam.

"I'm sure she would. She's saving her money for school clothes, so she'd like the extra time," said Megan. "I'll go ask her." She scampered off the deck and made for the door.

Sam glanced at her watch, "I'll get my things and we can wander over to Ellie's." Megan returned and told them Rachel had agreed to stay and help so they had two hours to make their cake choices.

They opened the door to Sweet Treats, welcomed by the aroma of warm bread and sweet pastries. Ellie waved at them, "Perfect timing. I was on my way to flip over the closed sign. Come on in the back and we'll get started."

"Charlie and Hayley are joining us and should be here in a few minutes," said Jeff.

"No problem. I'll get the lights and turn the sign." As soon as she reached the door, Charlie and Hayley arrived. "Hi guys, go on in the back. I'll be right behind you."

Ellie had several pieces of cake set out on a stainless counter. As she made her way back, brushing flour from her apron, Sam said, "I had a wonderful piece of red velvet yesterday, so I definitely want to include it in my final selection."

"Sure, I have a piece for you to try here. I made several small cakes for the sampling plus some cupcakes, so we'll see what tickles your taste buds," she chuckled. "Here's the red velvet," she handed Sam a plate.

Sam's fork glided through the tender cake, draped in creamy frosting. "Mmm. To die for." She passed the plate to Jeff.

He forked a bite into his mouth. "Yum, it's a keeper."

"Okay, here you go Charlie, you can test it too," Ellie said, handing him the plate. Hayley and Charlie both took a big bite. With their mouths full and eyes bright, they gave Ellie the thumbs up.

Next they tried a lemon with a tart lemon filling, followed by a fluffy vanilla cake filled with fresh strawberries. A luscious chocolate filled with chocolate mousse caused both Sam and Jeff to groan with delight. They sampled a salted caramel chocolate cupcake, the chocolate mint, and the carrot cake. Ellie's last two cakes were a white chocolate with raspberry filling and a pumpkin with a caramel chai buttermilk frosting.

All four of the tasters were overwhelmed. "Ellie, these are all delicious. I was hoping this would be easier," groaned Sam.

"Well, let's talk about what you pictured the cake looking like? Did you envision a large tiered white cake or maybe a smaller tiered cake and a few side cakes? If you want a white tiered cake, we can leave most of the chocolates out," suggested Ellie.

"Oh, we can't leave the chocolates out," directed Jeff. "We love chocolate."

"Well, maybe we need to do a smaller tiered cake for the main attraction and a couple side cakes or cupcakes," proposed Ellie.

Hayley nodded in agreement as she went in for a second bite of the chocolate mousse.

"I like the idea," said Sam. "How about we choose three of the white frosted choices for the main cake and then let's do a variety of cupcakes? That way people can sample lots of flavors."

"That works," said Jeff, licking the last bit of chocolate caramel frosting from his fork. "So, we know we need one layer of red velvet with the white cream cheese frosting. I like the white with the strawberries too."

Charlie added, "And the white chocolate with raspberry is super yummy."

"I think that does it. I like all of those flavors. Now for the cupcakes. I know we have to have the salted caramel chocolate."

"And the lemon," both Charlie and Jeff said at once.

Ellie laughed, "Okay, I've got those two. Any other flavors?"

"Oh, you're going to want to shoot me when we're done, but how about two side cakes in chocolate, the salted caramel and the chocolate mousse? And then, we do cupcakes in lemon, carrot, pumpkin, and chocolate mint. That covers all of them and I hate to leave any of them behind," said Sam, ducking her head, as if fearful Ellie might throw something at her.

Ellie laughed, "I'm not going to hit you, Sam. We can do whatever you like. My personal opinion is it could be a bit busy. I think we should make a four tiered white main cake and add the lemon layer to it. Then, I'll make two smaller side cakes in the chocolate selections and let's leave out the pumpkin, carrot, and chocolate mint. You have plenty of variety. We can make those for your next occasion."

Jeff smiled, "Perfect. I think we're on a sugar high and can't decide, so your idea makes sense."

Ellie sketched out a rough image of the cakes and explained she was thinking of decorating the main cake with a simple design that would look like each layer was tiered. It reminded Sam of Linda's new dress and she liked the look. Ellie continued to explain she would use flowers featured in the ceremony and create a simple cascade of blooms around the tiers. The chocolate cakes would be smaller, with two tiers each and frosted in a dark chocolate shiny ganache frosting. The chocolates would be totally smooth and adorned with the same flowers, although sparingly, and topped with some spiky chocolate curls.

Sam nodded the entire time she was looking at the sketches, listening to Ellie. Hayley's eyes were wide with admiration. "Wow, Ellie, you make it look so easy. I enjoy baking, but I'm not sure I could ever do something so elegant. Sam's teaching me to make pies, but you make me want to learn how to do fancy cakes."

"Anytime you want to pop in and watch, let me know. It's fun and I can't wait to make this cake," smiled Ellie. "Okay, guys, let me box the rest of the samples. I have a feeling Charlie will make good use of them." She glanced over and saw his eyes brighten.

Sam asked, "Ellie, when will you have a price figured?"

"Oh, about that. I'd like to do the cake as my wedding gift to you both."

Jeff and Sam both shook their heads. "Oh, that's way too generous," said Jeff.

"Well, I insist, so if you won't accept it, you'll have to find another baker," said Ellie, with a dash of triumph, knowing she had played the trump card.

"Seriously, we would never consider another baker. It's just we would have chosen something much less extravagant if we knew your intention," said Sam, placing a hand on Ellie's shoulder.

"I know you would have," retorted Ellie. With a twinkle in her eye, she continued, "That's why I waited to tell you. I want you to have what you want and it's going to be my gift. It makes me a part of your special day, so no more argument. It's done," she pronounced.

Jeff hugged Ellie and thanked her. Sam was overcome with Ellie's kindness and pulled her close for a hug as they left. Charlie was beaming with his box of treats and made plans to share them with Hayley while they watched movies at his house.

Sam and Jeff made their way back to the shop to relieve Rachel. The shop was bustling with customers. They made a plan to stay in town and help until closing. Around five, they enjoyed a respite and Jeff offered to go and pick up dinner. Kyle and Megan took a much deserved break on the sofa.

"So, Sam, did you guys get your cake picked out?" asked Megan.

"We did. It was hard to choose, so we picked about six flavors. They're all yummy."

"Say, uh," Kyle hesitated. "Did you let Marty know you and Jeff decided to get married? I haven't said anything to him, but didn't want to let it slip if you didn't want him to know." This had been on Kyle's mind, since the announcement at Sam's party a week ago. He knew she didn't talk to her ex-husband and had contacted him only when she learned Marty was Kyle's birthfather. He didn't want to cause her any trouble, but thought Marty would be pleased for her.

"I haven't talked to Marty since he left after his visit with you. But, it isn't a secret. You're free to let him know about it. I don't communicate with Marty on a regular basis, so hadn't given it any thought."

"I know he feels bad about what happened between the two of you and I think he'd be glad you and Jeff are getting married. He told me you're a special person and he knows he blew it with you. I know he likes Jeff. He was impressed Jeff let him stay at his place when he came to meet me."

"You know, I actually believe he will be happy for me now. It was a good thing I met you and that Marty and I were able to talk when he was here. But, if he asks, he's not invited to the wedding," she chuckled.

Four

The only item on the wedding agenda for Monday was a video appointment with Sam's lawyer in the city. After much discussion, she and Jeff agreed it would be best to have a lawyer prepare a prenuptial agreement. Jeff had strong feelings that Sam's wealth from her company and both her homes, along with the coffee shop, should always belong to her, no matter what happened in the future. Neither of them anticipated a divorce, but Sam wanted to make sure Jeff's children received all of his possessions should something happen. She didn't need any money and wanted to make sure his kids understood this.

They had a video meeting Monday morning at Sam's house. Sam's lawyer, Nick Montrose, was the same lawyer she had used in her business and her divorce from Marty. He knew everything about Sam, but was in the process of going through Jeff's items.

In the event of Sam's death she wanted Jeff to have her house. He was leaving his cabin at the family resort to move in with her and she knew he would enjoy and care for her home. Her new will would provide for Max and Becky, but she wanted to add Jeff as the recipient of a large portion of her estate and her island home and cars. She still had two cars at the Shoreline house that would have to be transported to the island.

Sam was working on her list of assets, double checking things, when the bell rang. She found Jeff and Bailey at the door. Jeff greeted her with a long kiss and his chocolate Lab raced to Zoe.

"There's some breakfast stuff in the kitchen if you're hungry. I didn't bake anything, but there's some cereal and fruit," she offered.

"I'm good. I ate this morning and need to cut back to make sure I fit in my tux," he laughed.

"Yeah, me too. No more treats until the wedding," she shook her finger at him, with a sly smile.

"Well, I don't know about none," he whined. "Maybe just less. But, I will take an iced tea."

Sam's reminder dinged on her phone. "We can do this in the office," she said, reaching for her notes on the counter along with the teas.

She connected the video conference equipment and they sat at the table and watched the flat screen television waiting for Nick to appear. Moments later, the soft spoken gray haired man appeared on the screen.

"Good morning, Sam and Jeff. Are you ready to finish this today?"

"Yes, Nick. That's our plan," she said.

"I emailed you some draft documents a few minutes ago. Could you print them out and you two can look them over while we talk?"

Sam went over to the computer and printed out a set of documents for each of them. Nick guided them through the prenuptial agreement and they both nodded at the provisions and echoed their agreement.

"Okay, that was easy. We can finalize them and we could send the documents to you or you could come into the city and sign them," Nick offered.

Jeff interjected, "We'll come to you. I'd rather this was done in your office than working with a notary here. The island is very small and we don't need to be the center of attention."

Sam nodded her head in agreement.

Nick continued, "Okay. Let's move on to the wills and if we can finalize them, we'll get those done and have everything ready for you in a few days."

They went through Jeff's first and Nick had prepared everything according to Jeff's prior instructions. He wanted to make sure Bailey went to Sam and wanted her to have perpetual access to the Harbor Resort and his kayak slip. He also made provisions for a specific box and all it contained to be given to Sam, but everything else, as they had agreed, was given to his children or siblings.

Sam had argued with Jeff about her wish to leave him the island house and her cars, but in the end, he agreed. She also made sure Zoe was bequeathed to Jeff. Over his objections, she solidified her decision to leave Harbor Coffee and Books to Jeff. He finally concurred when she pointed out that his family would always be in Friday Harbor and he could let Megan take over, if she had an interest. Her last item for Jeff was her collection of wooden boxes from her father and his antique woodworking tools still in the shed at the Shoreline house.

Jeff gripped her hand and squeezed it hard. "That means a lot to me, Sam. "

"Well, guys, I think we can get these finalized and we'll have them ready for you no later than Thursday this week. Give Donna a call to schedule a convenient time and she'll notarize everything and get you copies. Best of luck to you both. I'm so happy for you, Sam," Nick winked before closing the connection.

"Let's choose a day and we can pick up your ring, get my wedding band, and do our paperwork. Maybe we could do dinner and make a day of it," suggested Jeff

"Sounds terrific. Plus, I could take you by the Shoreline house and show you the place and we could drive one of the cars home, if we have time." Sam looked at her calendar and they decided on Tuesday next week.

"It's a date," said Jeff, taking her hand. "Have I told you how much I love you?"

"I don't believe you have…not today, anyway," she giggled.

"I can't wait to be married to you," he kissed her gently and then with more fervor, as his hands ran the length of her slim back.

"Me too," she whispered.

"I need to get back to the cabin and continue packing. So, I'll see you when you get home from work. I'll cook something and have it ready," he said, kissing her once more.

"You're too good to me," she paused. "But, I love it."

* * *

When Sam arrived at the coffee shop she found Rachel and Hayley hard at work helping the mob of customers at the counter. Sam went in the back and starting getting organized for baking pies and brownies. She was having a hard time keeping pace with demand and had concluded if they ran out, they ran out. She was in the process of teaching Hayley how to bake pies, but by the looks of the steady stream of customers, Hayley was not going to have time to bake and make drinks.

Sam was making strawberry cream pies today and had to make an extra for Charlie. She loved the coolness of the cream cheese and whipping cream coupled with the sweetness of the strawberries. It was a perfect summertime pie. She put the brownies in to bake once the crusts were done. The beckoning smell of chocolate drew in more customers.

Sam kept busy all morning chilling the cream cheese mixture in the crusts, making the strawberry glaze, and slicing the fresh berries. She decided to make a trip to Soup D'Jour and took lunch orders from the girls, who looked like they could use the nourishment.

Sam relieved each of them and they ate in shifts in the back. As she was tossing the last of the lunch containers, the mail arrived. She glimpsed a large decorative envelope addressed to Mr. and Mrs. Jeff Cooper from Max. She rushed into the backroom, intrigued by the delivery. She pulled the tab and ripped it open, spilling the contents on her desk.

Inside she found a burgundy folder from the Rosario Resort on Orcas Island and a letter from Max. As she scanned it, she put her hand to her heart and gasped, "Oh, Max." He told them he knew they were planning a honeymoon to the wine country in California in October, but he wanted to give them two special nights in the private honeymoon suite at the historic Rosario Resort. He had booked them in for the night of their wedding and the following night, as his wedding gift. He wanted to make sure they knew about it, so they wouldn't make other plans. He would be staying at Sam's so would take charge of both their dogs and they could enjoy a few days alone, with no responsibilities. He included a private boat charter to Orcas Island, courtesy of Jeff's fireman friend, Steve.

Tears distorted Sam's vision as she struggled to read the letter. She and Jeff had such wonderful and thoughtful friends. She couldn't think of a more romantic place for a honeymoon. They didn't have any plans, since they both wanted to splurge and go to California for the grape harvest in October. They had booked a house in St. Helena and were looking forward to relaxing with garden massages, a hot tub on their deck, and lounging in front of the fireplace. Sam knew the tourists would dwindle by then and she could go without worrying about the shop.

She was so excited about Max's gift. She couldn't wait to get home and show Jeff. They'd have to call Max tonight to thank him. She was brought back to reality by the girls coming into the office to sign out for the day. Kyle and Rachel had arrived and were ready for their shift.

Sam asked Hayley to let Charlie know he had a strawberry pie waiting for him in the cooler. She took the other three pies out to the display case. As soon as she set them down, she heard orders for pie erupt from the counter. She began plating slices and an entire pie was gone in a matter of minutes.

The rest of the day progressed at the same brisk pace of the morning. Sam decided to bake a lemon meringue and an apple pie, since they didn't take as long as the strawberry. She worked in the back and came out to help when she had the apple pie in the oven. The swift tempo of the morning continued until closing. Kyle and Rachel worked their whole shift without a break.

They rushed to clean the machines and get the shop closed. Although tired, they both perked up when the tip jar was tallied and they went home with bulging envelopes, even after splitting it with Megan and Hayley.

Sam drove home completely drained of energy. Opening the door, she was greeted by the smell of grilled chicken. She was famished and needed to sit down. She put the piece of strawberry pie she snagged for Jeff in the fridge. He had dinner waiting on the outdoor table.

They sat on the deck to enjoy the evening and Sam hustled back to snatch the package from Max. "You've got to see this. It's from Max," she handed him the envelope.

She watched Jeff's eyes get big as he read the letter. He looked in the folder and said, "Wow." He read the letter again and shook his head. "I can't believe what a great guy he is. This is an excellent idea. Have you ever stayed at the Rosario?"

"No. I went to an event there once, but didn't stay. It's a beautiful property."

"Let's video with Max after dinner and thank him. And, with Steve taking us over to Orcas, we won't have to worry about the ferry schedule," said Jeff. "I'll book us a car."

Jeff cleared the table while Sam dialed Max on her tablet in the kitchen. Jeff heard Max's cheery voice, "Hey, Sam."

"Hi, Max." She motioned Jeff over. "We called to let you know your wonderful gift was delivered today. We're so excited and wanted to thank you."

"Yes, that was thoughtful of you," said Jeff, squeezing in to make sure Max saw him on the screen too.

"You're both quite welcome. I'm glad you're excited about it. I wanted to let you know I should be moving into the Shoreline house by the end of next week. My realtor has everything moving at warp speed, so I'll talk to Becky about the plan. I'll see you on August third, so I can help with everything."

"Great, Linda needs a helper with all the prep work at the nursery and the flowers, so you'll be spending most of your time there," Sam turned and winked at Jeff.

"Sounds terrific. The only thing I have planned is the hospital grand opening on Monday after I arrive. I can't wait to see you guys. I'll be in touch once I'm in Seattle. Talk to you soon," Max waved.

"I see why he's your best friend, Sam. What a classy guy," remarked Jeff.

"Yep, I'm surrounded by classy men these days," she grinned, as she went to the fridge and retrieved the pie. "I brought you a treat," she said, returning with the pie and a quick kiss.

"Mmm, I can't resist you or your pie, Sam," he smiled as he opened the box.

Five

The next weeks were a blur of activity. Sam and Jeff took a trip to the city, retrieved the ring, chose a wedding band for Jeff, signed their papers at Nick's office, and had a romantic dinner on the wharf. Sam showed him her home in Shoreline and he stood in awe with his mouth open during most of the visit. It was normal for Sam, but she knew it was a level of luxury that was anything but ordinary for Jeff. She did her best to make him feel at ease, but he was anxious to leave.

She had a Mercedes convertible she wanted to take back to the island, so she drove it and Jeff drove her SUV back to the ferry terminal. They caught the last ferry and were treated to a magnificent sunset on the crossing.

The shop continued to be busy and all four of her dedicated team of workers had agreed to work longer shifts to provide extra coverage during the middle of the day. Sam felt better about the shop, but was swamped with baking pies, all of which seemed to grow legs and disappear as soon as she put them in the case.

It was soon the weekend before the wedding with Max due to arrive on Saturday. Jeff had almost completed all of his packing and moving at the cabin. They added a few special pieces of his furniture he had made to Sam's house and he took over the smaller master closet. Photos of Ashley and Charlie through the years now decorated Sam's walls.

Sam was double checking the guest rooms to make sure things were set for Max and Becky and her family. Becky was arriving Sunday and Brad and the kids were coming in the night before the wedding. Max would be staying until the Tuesday after the wedding to watch the dogs while Jeff and Sam enjoyed their time on Orcas Island.

Sam's list of things to do was long, but as she sat in the coffee shop, early Saturday morning, inhaling the smell of warm pie crust wafting from the ovens, she felt calm. Everything was covered and she knew all their friends had things under control. A quiet knock on the door startled her. She looked through the glass and saw Rachel, and glancing at her watch realized she had been daydreaming for longer than she thought.

"Good morning, Rachel. Sorry I had you locked out this morning," she said opening the door. "Hayley should be down any minute now."

"I'm a little early, so no problem." She sniffed, "Your pies smell good."

"I came around five to try to get ahead of it. The pies have been popular with the tourists and I'm hoping not to be here tomorrow."

They heard Hayley's steps on the stairs. "Morning ladies," she said, as she made her way to the counter and starting turning on the machines.

The buzzer sounded on the oven and Sam went to finish the pies while the girls got organized for the day. Sam had coconut cream, chocolate cream, and banana cream fillings chilled and ready. She began whipping the meringue for a lemon pie as soon as she took the crusts out to cool. She hoped eight pies would suffice through the weekend.

As she worked she heard the door chime every few minutes and knew they were in for another busy day. Ellie's pastries were popular with the morning crowds and by the time she came out of the kitchen with four pies for the case, the deck was packed with people and most of the inside tables were full. The girls were churning out drinks as fast as they could.

Sam stepped in to man the register and they caught a break in the traffic around noon. Sam was busy wiping off the outdoor tables when a familiar, "Hey, Sam," caught her attention. She turned and grinned at her best friend, Max.

She dropped her rag and rushed to meet him. "I'm so glad to see you," she said, wrapping her arms around him for a giant hug.

"Me too. How's everything going?"

"Everything's on schedule. At last count we had seventy-five confirmed guests for the wedding. And we've been flooded with customers, which is good, but a bit tiring."

"The ferry was crammed with tourists today, so I'm not surprised you're busy. You can show me the ropes, so while you and Jeff are away for a couple of days, I can help out. I want you to enjoy your trip and not worry about things," he said, grasping her shoulders and looking her in the eye.

"I'll show you how to operate the register. That would be a big help. Hayley is learning how to do some pies, and if we run out of pie, so be it. I've decided I'm not going to worry and I'm not going to call," she said, with determination. "And we need to talk to Linda and find out what she needs you to do next week."

"Sounds good to me. How about lunch?"

"Let me call Jeff and see what he's got planned. Come on in and you can have a drink while we figure out the rest of the day."

Jeff needed a break and decided to drive into town and meet them for lunch at Lou's. After lunch Jeff took Max and put him to work at the cabin moving some boxes and then got him settled at Sam's. When Sam got home from the shop, she found Jeff asleep in the recliner and Max busy making dinner in the kitchen.

"Maybe you should live here instead of the Shoreline house. I could get used to having you around," she said, giving him a soft rub on his head as she passed by him.

"You both look beat, Sam. I thought you could use dinner at home tonight."

"I know. We've been working nonstop to get things ready and get Jeff moved in here. It'll calm down now." She poured an iced tea and plopped into a chair at the island. "By the way, I talked to Linda and she has lots of work, so you can go out to her place on Tuesday and you'll probably be there all week."

"Jeff said you brought the Mercedes home. If I take your SUV, you can drive the Mercedes next week. Does that work for you?"

"Sure, I've missed that zippy little car," she smiled. "I'm excited for Becky to be here tomorrow. It will be fun to visit."

"She'll have everything organized and done in a heartbeat," laughed Max, as he placed the rice and veggies in bowls to accompany the delicious smelling teriyaki chicken. "Go tell Jeff it's ready."

They were starving and polished off the meal in record time. Sam had pilfered two pieces of pie from her dwindling reserves at the shop for her two favorite guys. They enjoyed dessert and Jeff excused himself for the evening, hoping to get some much needed rest.

Sam fell asleep watching television with Max and he had to wake her to get her to go to bed. He suggested she sleep in and forgo her alarm so she could recover from the craziness of the last few weeks. "You don't want to be sick for your big day. So listen to you friend the doctor, and sleep all day, if you need it."

She mumbled, "Okay, Max. Love ya," as she stumbled into her room.

The next morning, Max was pleasantly surprised to see no sign of Sam. He checked the garage and found both cars inside. It was eleven o'clock when he heard her moving around and the sound of her shower. Becky had texted him that Jen was throwing a surprise shower for Sam at her shop today. Jen was waiting for Becky to arrive and had a plan to lure Sam to the salon. Becky would be at the salon when Sam arrived, so she asked Max to trick Sam and tell her she'd be arriving on a later ferry.

Sam joined Max on the deck with a cup of tea. "Well, I think you were right. I needed sleep," she said, with a glow in her eyes.

"Good, you look rested. By the way, I heard from Becky and she said she'll be on the later ferry today, so no need to rush."

"Okay. Do you feel like going into the shop so I can show you the register? Then we can grab some lunch with Jeff. We can take both cars and I'll stop at Jeff's and pick him up on the way."

"Sure, let's go. I'll meet you at the shop."

On the way into town, Jeff got a call from Jen. She was in a panic and said she had a pipe problem at the salon and was hoping they could stop by and help her. Jeff was in on the surprise and played along telling her they were on their way.

Sam quickened her pace and pulled the sassy burgundy convertible in front of Jen's salon. Jeff held the door for her and as Sam walked in she shrieked with surprise to find the salon full of women, including Becky, and decorations everywhere. She gave Jeff a stern look. "You knew, didn't you?"

"Who, me? Nah, I was coming to fix a pipe," he laughed and gave her a quick kiss. "Max and I are going to lunch while you girls have fun. See you later, sweetie."

Jen hurried to Sam, "You look a little stunned. I was hoping to succeed in a surprise shower and it looks like we did. Becky helped, of course. Come on in. We've got loads of food and I've got things organized for pedicures for everyone."

Sam hugged Jen. "This is so kind of you. I never dreamed of a shower."

The ladies gathered around Sam and Jen guided them into the spa area for pedicures. Becky made everyone play foolish shower games. They had a tasty lunch courtesy of Soup D'Jour and Ellie made a gorgeous cake decorated with a fondant wedding dress and fresh flowers. Megan and Rachel had taken a break from the store to come spend some time at the shower. Kyle and Max were minding the shop.

The gift table was crowded with packages wrapped in shimmering silver and white papers. Becky took charge and had her notebook out to record the gifts for Sam. The first package she opened was from Annie and it contained a lovely afghan she had made. It was knitted with a silky luxurious yarn and the subtle color reminded Sam of sea glass. "Oh, Annie, it's gorgeous and so soft," Sam said, moving to hug Annie.

Annie was all smiles, "I'm glad you like it."

Sam opened present after present and received beautiful frames and photo books from Hayley, a massage from Jen and Megan, the statue of a dog she had admired from Linda, a tea set from Kyle's grandma Rita, a set of Emile Henry pie plates from Ellie, snuggly pajamas from Rachel, and a manicure from Hayley's mom, Cheryl. Sam gasped when she opened Abby's package of sexy black lingerie. She reddened and laughed, "It's always those quiet librarians that are full of surprises." Abby shrugged and gave her a grin.

Becky presented Sam with her gift last. It was a wood and glass tabletop clock with a note that read *It's your time, enjoy.* Tucked inside was a gift card announcing a year's subscription to a wine club from Napa Valley.

Sam was overwhelmed with the generosity of her newfound friends on the island. She fought back the sting of tears in her eyes and thanked everyone for the wonderful surprise and the lovely gifts. The women finished dessert and the rest of the pedicures and when only Linda, Becky, and Jen remained, Sam was shocked to see it was six o'clock.

"Wow, it's late. I can't believe we've been here so long."

Becky added, "Max and Jeff are cooking dinner for us at your house. Linda and Jen should join us and we'll continue visiting. Plus there's no way Sam can get all this loot in her tiny car."

They all worked together to clean the shop and loaded the gifts in Linda's car. Becky had brought the dresses and she took great care in placing them in the car for the ride to the nursery. Becky stashed her luggage in Sam's car and Jen promised to meet them as soon as she retrieved Megan from the coffee shop.

Jeff and Max carted in all the gifts from Sam's shower. Becky busied herself unpacking in one of the guest rooms. Jeff got drinks for everyone and ushered Linda and Sam out to the deck. Jen and Megan arrived and joined the conversation on the deck.

Max and Jeff treated them to a wonderful dinner of grilled salmon, pasta, salad, and bread, topped off with leftover cake from the shower. As soon as he was finished Max asked Linda, "So, what time shall I plan on for Tuesday?"

"I'll be out early, so whenever you get there is fine. We're going to be getting the plants ready for both the ceremony and reception. We have a tent coming for the reception and are going to situate the wedding in the rose garden. Friday will be the busiest day, we've got chairs, tables, and the tent being delivered and will need everything installed. Plus I have to make all the flower arrangements on Friday, so they're fresh."

"Sounds like a big job. I'm sure it will be fabulous, if you're the director," he smiled.

"That's what I'm aiming for," she laughed. "Be sure and bring a long sleeved shirt, you'll be working in some plants with thorns. Speaking of all this work, I better get going," she said, heading towards the kitchen.

"Let me walk you out," volunteered Max.

Linda hugged everyone goodbye and left with Max following her.

As soon as they were outside, Sam whispered to Becky and Jen, "I think they'll be the cutest couple. I'm trying to think of ways to have them spend some time together while Max is here. I think he likes Linda."

"Oh, wouldn't that be the best," said Becky in a high voice.

"Count me in. Linda could use a wonderful man like Max," said Jen. "Shh, I hear him coming."

They cleared the deck table and got all the dishes done and Jen and Megan wished them all a good night as they headed home. Jeff followed them out and Max decided to turn in. He was planning to meet his doctor friend, Sean Doyle, for breakfast before the hospital ceremony.

Sam and Becky stayed up late chatting and going over Becky's charts and lists for the wedding. Becky was in charge of all the details and the only thing Sam had on her agenda this week was to get a pedicure and manicure on Friday and get her hair done Saturday before the wedding.

They hugged each other goodnight and Sam thanked Becky again for the clock. "I love my new clock, Beck. And, you're right, it's time for a new start and I couldn't be happier to spend the rest of my life with Jeff."

Six

Max arrived at Linda's at seven on Tuesday morning, dressed as instructed in a long sleeved shirt and jeans. He found Linda already hard at work in the rose garden. Lucy was at her heels and came bounding over to Max with a cheerful bark.

"Morning, Max. I have some gloves for you."

"Good, I didn't bring any." He put them on and she began to show him how she wanted the plants trimmed. Once they were groomed she wanted him to work on decorating them with white twinkle lights. As he looked at the rose garden, which he estimated to be at least an acre of plants, he figured it would take him all week. Linda took one side of the garden and assigned him to the other side. He spotted Linda moving through the plants with ease, while he seemed to be taking forever.

They took a break for some iced water and she was over half done. He was barely a quarter of the way through his side. "Well, Linda, I'm not sure how much help I'm going to be. Take a look at my feeble progress," he gestured.

"Oh, you'll get faster. I've been doing this for years and it's second nature. Once I'm done with my side, I'll help you with yours. Then I'll leave you to the lights while I check on the rest of the nursery. I've got staff covering, but I like to keep my eye on things."

34

She finished her water and headed back to trimming, her black Lab at her heals. Max loathed to admit it, but his hands were already growing tired. Linda finished her side before he was half done and came over to help him. The day was sunny and Max wished the clouds would take over and block some of the heat. He was sweating and tired. The fragrance of the blooms was the best thing about the work. They smelled terrific and Max began to notice the subtle differences between the scents of various plants. As they worked together, they chatted about Linda's layout for the wedding and Max's move.

"My house sold rather quickly, so I was able to get moved to Seattle a little over a week ago. I like being back in the Pacific Northwest. I didn't realize how much I missed it here," he said as he continued pruning. "And, to be honest, there were too many memories of my late wife in San Diego. I've struggled to move on for five years. I hope it will be easier here."

"I'm sorry about your wife. I can only imagine how difficult it is for you. They say change is good." She chuckled, "I wouldn't know much about that, since I've lived here all my life. I can't imagine not living here. The one thing I'm trying to change is to cut back on work a little. I need to figure that out. I'm not as young as I used to be and wouldn't mind some time to relax or do something fun." She thought for a minute, "Sam has inspired me and seeing her and Jeff find such love makes me think it might not be too late for me."

"It's never too late, Linda. I don't know your whole circumstance, but I agree with the part about Sam being an inspiration. Watching her transform made me realize I had to do something. She was a big catalyst in getting me to move back."

As they chatted and progressed through the lines of plants, they soon found themselves in the same row. Linda suggested they take a break and have some lunch before Max got started on the lights. She led him back to the house and they raided the fridge for sandwich fixings. She cut some fruit while he made sandwiches and they sat on the back porch and relaxed with Lucy at their feet.

"It's beautiful here. You've got quite the place," admired Max.

"I enjoy it. Sitting here is one of my favorite pastimes. Sometimes I get lonely out here, especially at night, but I've always got Lucy," she said patting the dog's head.

"I know what you mean about the evenings. That's when it hits me, too. I stay busy during the day, but miss having someone to share things with at the end of the day—a meal, a glass of wine, a conversation. I don't even have a pet," he sighed.

"Lucy's my best friend. I don't know what I would do without her. Jen's been a lifelong friend to me and I know everyone in town, but I don't socialize much. Jen and I get together once a month or so, but the rest of the time I fill with work. I know it's my crutch, but that's what I've done for years. Ever since..." she stopped.

"Go on, Linda," he urged, patting her hand.

"Well, it's silly. I hardly know you and here I'm baring my soul. But, I was going to say, ever since Brenda helped break off my engagement to my fiancé, I withdrew and hid behind work. Then when my dad passed away and my mom decided to hang it up and moved to be near my brother, I needed to work harder and it became my norm. I tried to date after losing Walt, but I think he was my one and only," she said in a voice so thin, he strained to hear her.

Max clasped her hand in his. "I know that feeling and I don't have any magic answers for you. I've decided I need to take a chance myself and I realize I'll never replace Lisa, but I can't continue to be alone for the rest of my life."

Linda nodded, her eyes wet. "I know. I need to think about the same thing." She sniffed and started collecting the dishes. Clearing her throat, she said, "Let's get you lined out on the lights and I'm going to work on some containers I want to place around the reception tent."

Max struggled all afternoon with the lights, determined to get them draped in a uniform manner. He only completed a quarter of the garden by the time the nursery closed.

Linda came to check on him as soon as she had closed and locked the gates. "How's it going, Max?" she hollered.

"In a word, slow," he laughed. "I'm trying to make sure these are perfect and can't tell until we can turn them on in the dark. How would you feel about dinner tonight in town and then we can come back and turn them on and I can see if they look okay?"

"Well," she hesitated. "Okay, I need to get cleaned up. I could meet you in about an hour?"

"Sounds like a plan. Do you like pizza? I've been dying for those pizza wraps since I was here last."

"Perfect, I'll see you at The Big Cheese in an hour."

Max jumped in the SUV and hurried to Sam's. He rushed in with a quick hello to Sam and explained he was meeting Linda for pizza and needed to hurry.

Becky raised her eyebrows at Sam and they both giggled. "Maybe my plan is working already," Sam whispered.

Max was out in a flash, freshly showered and looking handsome. He was patting all his pockets, making sure he had his wallet and went dashing back upstairs. He waved a goodbye and said he'd be late because they had to check on the rose garden after dinner.

Max arrived as Linda was getting out of her car. She had changed into black capris and a raspberry colored shell. Her hair was pulled back in a loose pony tail and shiny silver beaded hoops dangled below her ears. "You look lovely," Max said as he held the door for her.

As the whiff of garlic and dough drifted through the open door, she realized how hungry she was. "I'm starving and it smells like heaven in here." She led the way to a table near the window, with a blue reserved sign.

They each ordered salads and pizza wraps and Max took the waiter's suggestion and ordered a basket of wedges as an appetizer. Max shrugged when he left their table. "Not sure what they are, but pizza dough and garlic sound good to me."

"Oh, they're yummy. You'll like them." She smiled and took a long sip of her drink.

The place was busy, filled with vacationers. "So, you're not only incredibly talented and gorgeous, you're smart too. I see we had a reserved table. Your doing, I presume?"

"I called Tony when you left because I figured it would be full of tourists. He always holds a few tables for the hungry natives."

The salads and their wedges arrived, and as advertised, they were scrumptious. Linda quizzed Max about the new hospital and he reported he had been impressed and spent the whole day meeting people and touring every nook and cranny. "It's a state of the art facility. It rivals the big city for surgical suites and it should serve the island well. The only thing they can't handle is major traumas, but patients can be airlifted to Seattle in a matter of minutes."

"I need to stop eating these, or I won't have room for the wrap," said Linda, shoving her plate away.

"I know, but they're so good. You can always take it home for tomorrow, if you can't eat it all tonight," he said, as he shoved another wedge into marinara sauce.

"Tomorrow we need to see if we can get the lights finished. I've got the containers done for the reception. I know Sam prefers more casual flowers, so I'm trying to stay away from the typical floral stands for weddings. I'm going to use some blooming trees and a trellis for the front instead of formal flowers. Then Thursday afternoon we can work at the shop cleaning the flowers and getting things ready for the bouquets and ceremony flowers. We have a ton of bows to make, so you'll have something new to learn," she said, with a gleam in her eye.

"I have a feeling you're going to teach me lots of new things this week," he said, as their wraps arrived.

Max chose a wrap stuffed with pepperoni, linguica, salami, sausage, and Canadian bacon. Basically a heart attack wrapped in dough. Linda picked the barbeque chicken with red onion and tangy sauce. They struggled to eat them without making a mess as the cheese and sauce spilled out when they bit into them.

Linda cut a small slice from hers and asked the waitress to box the rest. She used a fork, but Max was determined to eat without utensils and went through a stack of napkins before he wrestled the last bite into his mouth.

"How about we stroll around the harbor until it gets a bit darker? Then we can test the lights," suggested Max, after he paid for dinner.

She nodded, "Okay, it's a pleasant evening."

He carried her leftovers and they wandered along the harbor, mixing with the tourists. They made their way to Sam's coffee shop. "I'll put the leftovers in the cooler and we can sit on the deck with a drink. I'll bring you a chai," he offered.

"You have a good memory."

Linda selected a table and Max soon returned with their drinks. A breeze drifted over the deck, carrying a trace of salt from the harbor. They discussed the dinner Max was hosting for the wedding party on Friday night. He had booked the posh Cliff House for the event. Since he had tricked Sam into thinking she was going there for her birthday dinner, but instead lured her to a surprise party at the nursery, he thought it would be the perfect place for a pre-wedding dinner.

"I want to make sure you can come to the dinner, so we need to get everything done before five," he warned.

"It could be tough, but I'll do my best. I want to be there." She paused and took a sip of her drink, "Tell me about your wife, Lisa."

"Lisa was terrific. A fabulous wife and mother to our two children. I met her at Stanford. She was from San Diego and we moved there. She was beautiful. Blond with gorgeous blue eyes. She was a dedicated pediatrician and worked wonders with kids. Lisa worked nonstop, until she got sick. She dragged me to more charity events than I ever thought existed. She was always doing something for a worthy cause. She took a break from working when we had the kids, but when they went to school, she started her practice," he smiled. He added in a whisper, "I miss her terribly and have had a horrible time getting over her death."

"She sounds like a special person, Max. I'm sorry to make you sad, but I'm glad you shared her with me," she patted his hand.

"I've been feeling better since I moved into Sam's house. The memories there are before Lisa, so it's not always staring me in the face like it was at our house. I was reluctant to leave her…I mean the house, but I think it was the right thing for me. Like I said, I need to go on and start a new life."

The sky was beginning to darken as dusk set in. Linda finished her drink and Max tossed their cups and retrieved her leftovers. They strolled back to their cars and Max followed Linda back to the nursery. It was dark by the time they arrived, but she had left a light on in the house and the bushes lining her entry path were wrapped in lights.

She opened the door and put her things away and guided Max to the rose garden. He had seen the power boxes earlier and with the help of a small flashlight plugged in the lights. Before he could extricate himself from the plants, he heard Linda. "They look terrific, Max. You did a wonderful job."

He hurried out of the roses and took a look. It looked like a professional job. "You ought to see how long it takes me to decorate a Christmas tree," he laughed. "They look good though, so hopefully, I'll be faster tomorrow. Let me unplug them," he said scurrying back into the plants.

They meandered through the gardens back to Linda's house. "Thanks for dinner tonight. It was fun," smiled Linda. "I'll see you tomorrow morning."

"Yes, you will. I had fun tonight, too," Max gave her a light kiss on the cheek. "See you tomorrow."

Max drove with a smile on his face all the way to Sam's. When he got there Becky was up, but Sam had gone to bed.

"Hey, Becky. I'm going to call it a night. I have to be to Linda's early tomorrow."

"How was dinner?" she asked.

His face brightened, "It was fun. We had a good time and made some progress on the rose garden today. I was thinking. Would you mind if one of the kids drove my car over when they come with Brad? I might be staying a little longer than I thought and it would make it easier."

"Sure, they could do that. I'll let Brad know."

As Max drifted to sleep, he began to imagine a new life and the woman in his dreams was a gorgeous brunette with dark eyes.

Seven

Linda and Max continued their efforts and he was able to develop a rhythm with the miles of green cords and by noon he had the entire rose garden wrapped in lights. He went to find Linda, who was busy working on some trees for the ceremony and reception.

"How about a lunch break?" he suggested. "I'm finished with the rose garden."

"Sounds like a good idea," she said climbing from a ladder. "I put a pot of soup together this morning and we can split my leftover wrap."

He offered her a hand and she gripped it. Hers was soft and warm and felt like it was made for his. "Do you ever get tired? I could barely crawl out of bed this morning and you're already making soup."

"Sure, I get tired, but I was up early and thought it sounded good. I'm always hungry at lunch," she smiled.

"I'm sure you are. All this work, hauling things and climbing ladders. You're unbelievable."

"Ah, it's not that bad. I like being busy," she said, as she led him to the farmhouse with Lucy trotting behind her.

They washed their hands and ladled steaming bowls of chicken noodle soup to go with her leftover wrap. They took their food to the porch and enjoyed another tasty lunch.

"Excellent soup," said Max, as he made his way back to the kitchen for a refill.

"The flowers for the wedding will be delivered tomorrow afternoon. So, we can finish what we need to do here in the morning and then go in and clean all the flowers. Friday I have extra help here to assist with the tent and chairs, so if my plan works, we'll be done in time for your dinner party."

"It'll work. You and Sam are alike in that regard. She's an awesome planner and organizer and gets more done in a single day than most people do in a week."

They cleared their lunch mess and stored the soup in the fridge and headed back to finish the trees. By the end of the day, Linda was feeling confident everything was ahead of schedule. Max heard his phone beep with a text from Sam.

"Sam's inviting us to dinner at her house tonight. What do you say?" asked Max.

"Sure. I need to shower, but I'll stop by as soon as I'm ready," Linda said, with a new brilliance in her eyes and smile.

Max got back to Sam's and ran upstairs to hop in the shower. When he came down and caught sight of the makings for grilled steaks and roasted potatoes his stomach rumbled. "Looks delish," said Max, giving Sam a hug. "Linda will be here as soon as she changes her clothes. Before she gets here, I meant to ask you about the arson investigation and Brenda. Is there anything new?"

"Last week Jeff heard Chief Malloy expects to have his investigation finished before the end of the month, but he's not divulging any information. I sure hope they have enough evidence to prove she started the fire at the shop. She hasn't been seen around town or at any events since the whole town shunned her at the Fourth of July Festival."

"She's such an awful woman. She caused Linda so much pain. Her fiancé's name was Walt and Linda told me how she has always felt he was her one and only. I hope justice prevails this time," Max said, shaking his head with disgust.

"On a brighter note, how was your day?" she asked.

"Great. We're ahead of schedule and Linda's pleased. Tomorrow afternoon we start working at the shop in town, cleaning all the flowers." He got himself a glass of lemonade. "Say Sam, I've been thinking about moving here to the island. What do you think?"

"Really?" she squealed with delight. "I would love, love, love it."

"Like I told you before, the more time I spend here the more I like it. I figure I could do something at the new hospital and continue to consult and lecture. I enjoy Jeff and his family and spending time with the two of you would thrill me."

"Not to mention a stunning brunette we know," teased Sam.

Max's face reddened, "Am I that transparent? Yes, I like spending time with Linda. She's the whole package, but I'm not sure how interested she is in getting involved. She told me she had given up on dating after losing her fiancé."

"You keep at it, Max. I think there's a spark there. Just give her time. If you move here and it works out with her, I would be even happier." She did a dance around the kitchen, "I'm so excited."

Jeff walked in from the deck in time to see the dance number. "Wow, I didn't know we were offering dinner and a show tonight," he grinned.

"Max told me he's serious about moving to the island. And," she stopped and looked at Max and got the nod. "He's interested in Linda."

"Damn, I was hoping you two would get together. Linda's a special lady. She deserves a class act like you, Max."

"Well, like I told Sam, I'm not sure she's interested in getting involved, but I'm going to give it a try."

"It might take some patience, but she's worth it," said Jeff.

The bell rang and the two dogs ran to greet Linda. Sam opened the door and led her to the kitchen. "Dinner will be about fifteen minutes. Come out and sit on the deck while we wait."

Becky joined Sam and Linda on the deck while Max and Jeff visited in the kitchen. The steaks were sizzling on the grill and the mouthwatering aroma made everyone hungry. Jeff and Max provided a bowl of chips and salsa to munch on while they waited.

"Max said you guys are ahead of schedule. So that's good news," said Sam, struggling to guide a chip loaded with chunky salsa to her mouth.

"Yes, we did a lot today and tomorrow afternoon we start cleaning your flowers. Are you set for meeting Pastor Mark out at the nursery on Friday to go through a rehearsal?"

She nodded and finished her chip. "He'll be there at three o'clock and it shouldn't take long. Max should probably come too, so he knows the drill," Sam smiled.

Max winked at Linda. "I'll see if my new boss will give me an hour off."

Linda laughed. "It means you'll have to work harder to get all the flowers done by three."

Jeff announced dinner was ready and placed a platter of steaks and a mountain of grilled potatoes on the table. Sam added a salad and refilled drinks. The group would have made termites proud at the speed with which they consumed the meal.

They retired to the fire pit and Sam delivered ice cream as they continued to visit well after the sun set. Linda and Max both started yawning when it was nearing nine o'clock. They looked at each other and laughed.

"I need to get home and rest for our big day tomorrow," she said, standing.

"I'm zonked too. You're a slave driver," he teased. "I'll see you out."

Max presented his arm as they made their way to the house. He accompanied her to her car and hugged her, breathing in the fresh scent of her hair as it brushed across his face.

She waved as she started her car and drove away. As she made the short trip home, she felt lighter. She had enjoyed spending the last two evenings with Max. He was thoughtful and attentive and if she didn't know better, she thought he may like her. She giggled to herself as she turned into her driveway. *I never thought I'd meet another man I could love, but being with Max is fun and has me looking forward to the next time I see him.* Glancing at the clock when she opened the door, she realized she was only a few hours away from seeing him again.

Eight

Max and Linda spent Thursday cleaning the nursery and getting all the trees and plants she planned to use moved to a staging area for final placement after the tent and chairs were installed. Max suggested they splurge and have lunch at Dottie's Deli since they would be working at Buds and Blooms in town.

"I don't go out to lunch much, since eating alone seems so pathetic. It's been fun having you for company this week," she said, as they munched on huge sandwiches and potato salad.

"I've loved spending time with you, Linda. It makes me realize what I've been missing all these years. I'm considering moving to the island myself." He paused trying to gauge her reaction. "And, if that happens, I hope you'll be willing to spend more time with me," he said, gazing into her chocolate eyes, noticing the subtle streaks resembling spun gold.

Linda blushed as she swallowed her bite and wiped her mouth. In a timid voice, she said, "I think I'd like that."

His face brightened. "Maybe you could help me find some homes to consider. After seeing Sam's I tend to favor a water view, but I'd appreciate your help."

"Sure, Jen and I both went to school with a local realtor. We can hook you up with her. From what I know, she's one of the area's best."

"I'd appreciate the help. I'll talk to Sam and see if she wouldn't mind if I stayed a bit longer and look at houses next week."

"I'll call Kellie and make an appointment for early next week. I get busier towards the weekends with weddings, but should have some freedom on Monday and Tuesday."

They collected their to-go drinks and rushed back to Linda's shop. The flowers had arrived and she began instructing Max on cleaning and trimming each stem. As the boxes were opened, an intoxicating fragrance filled the back room.

"Mmm, I see why you always smell so appealing," he grinned.

"I never grow tired of the scent of fresh flowers. Smells always evoke such strong memories. I associate roses with my mom. She loves them and their aroma always followed her."

They worked stem by stem and soon had buckets of gorgeous roses, peonies, lily of the valley, and greens. It was a sea of white, blush, and pinks. "Sam is going to love your selections. They're magnificent."

"I hope so. I'm excited to create something unique for her," she beamed. "I want to show you how to make bows, so you can start on those for me tonight." She selected several spools of filmy ribbons and showed him the technique of looping the ribbon and using florist wire to wrap the middle. She made him practice with some unpopular colors before she turned him loose on the real material.

She took a break and called Kellie. When she returned she let Max know they were set for tours on Monday at one. Kellie would meet them at Linda's shop.

Max was concentrating hard and finally completed one in an ugly military green color. He looked over at the pile of bows in front of Linda's station. "So far, I'm proving to be downright incompetent when it comes to decorations. Sorry I'm so slow."

Linda examined his bow. "You may be slow, but it looks good. It must be your surgeon's hands. Keep practicing and don't worry about speed. Remember, I've worked in this shop for over thirty years."

Max focused on his technique and finished three smaller bows. His neck and back protested and he got up to stretch. When he looked out the front window he was surprised to see it was after seven. "Wow, I can't believe how late it is."

She had been gathering candles and organizing glass bowls and looked at her watch. "Yeah, we better pack it in. I need to organize the troops early tomorrow out at the nursery and then I'm coming in to do the flowers."

"How about I help you put all this away and then let me treat you to ice cream before you head home? I'm not super hungry, but a scoop or two sounds good."

She thought for a minute and looked at her watch again. "You've got a deal," she smiled.

They cleaned up their mess and closed the shop before walking to Shaw's Ice Cream Parlor. Max went with a scoop of chocolate and a scoop of peanut butter cup in a waffle cone. Linda chose the chocolate chip and as she savored a bite said, "You know I've always wanted to do something and have felt awkward going alone. You don't have to do it if you don't want to," she faltered, "but, we have movies each Monday in the park. Would you like to go Monday night?"

"Count me in. I enjoy movies." He smiled as he caught a gob of chocolate ice cream before it fell from the edge.

"Terrific, they start as soon as it gets dark and show classics. They're showing several Cary Grant movies in a row and he's one of my favorites."

"Since we're looking at houses Monday afternoon, let's do dinner before we hit the movies," he suggested.

"You're going to make me want to take every afternoon off," she laughed. "But, it sounds like a plan."

Max finished his cone on the loop back to the shop. He followed Linda to her car and before she got in darted towards her and gave her a hasty kiss on the lips. "I had a wonderful time today. See you tomorrow," he waved as he jogged to the car.

All the way to Sam's he beat himself up over his amateur move with Linda. *I don't know what came over me. I wanted to kiss her and was afraid if*

I was slow about it, she'd turn away. She must think I'm a complete moron. I need to work on my technique. He chuckled. *Maybe I can practice at the movies on Monday.*

* * *

Friday morning Max was at the nursery early. He found Linda organizing a team of young men who were charged with erecting the tent, placing the chairs, and moving all the trees and plants to their final locations. The party rental van arrived and everyone scurried to help unload.

Linda gave Max a shy wave and motioned him over. "Good Morning. I'll be done here soon and will be heading in to the shop. I thought you could stay here and make sure things get placed correctly." She handed him a notebook with sketches and instructions for the positions of the foliage.

He looked it over and nodded as he perused each page. "I've got it. If I run into a problem or have a question, I'll give you a call. I'll come by the shop when we're wrapped up here. I've got to be here at three for the rehearsal, but I'm sure we'll be done long before then."

"I'm sure you will. I want to get the flowers done so I can make it to your dinner tonight. I'm looking forward to the swanky Cliff House." She raised her eyebrows and grinned.

"Me too. It should be fun." He looked away as he heard a worker call out a question. "Okay, I'll see you soon."

The men worked for hours and Max followed them around like a nervous new mother. The most time consuming part was running all the lighting inside the tent. Since the reception would start around dusk, Linda had ordered lighting and it proved to be a painstakingly slow installation process. He double checked everything to make sure it was exactly as Linda had instructed. Shortly before noon, he signed off and released the crew.

The gauzy tent fabric billowed in the breeze and the entry was lined with flowering plants and shrubs. All the tables and chairs were arranged in the tent and there were stacks of blush colored linens waiting to adorn the tables. The ceremony area was complete with rows of white chairs and a pretty vine and blossom covered trellis where the pastor would officiate. Max knew Linda planned to install the large bows she had made on the ends of the chair rows.

Max arrived with lunch to find Linda working on boutonnieres. He laid out the soups and salads. "How's it going?" he asked.

"Great. I've got the bouquets done and most of the centerpieces. The girls are going to finish them and I think we'll be set." She let out a heavy sigh as she closed the cooler door. "The busy week has caught up with me. I'm pooped."

They gobbled down their lunch, both tired from the long week of work. Max tossed their containers. "I'm going to take off and get ready for the rehearsal and dinner tonight. The nursery looks fantastic. I know Sam and Jeff will be pleased."

"You were a big help today and now I have time for some rest before dinner. I'll see you at the restaurant."

"I'll stop by and pick you up and save you another trip into town."

She vacillated between the more practical solution of driving herself and his kind offer, before agreeing with him. When Max left she felt a flutter in her chest. It had been a long time since a man had paid any special attention to her or went out of his way for her. She knew she hid behind her long hours and used her work as a convenient excuse for maintaining a solitary life. She caught herself daydreaming about what she would wear tonight and rushed to clean up her mess so she could get home and ransack her closet.

She tried on several outfits and found flaws with all of them, creating a pile of discarded garments on her bed. She plucked a couple more dresses from the back of her closet and tried on her last hope. It was an ankle length deep sapphire sleeveless dress in silk with a long filmy duster jacket. Linda couldn't find fault with it and caught herself smiling as she checked the mirror.

After rehanging every piece of clothing she owned, she flopped onto her bed for a nap before a hot soak in the tub. She was ready ahead of schedule, dressed, and waiting for Max. She kept pacing the floor, realizing she was nervous. *I don't know why I'm so jumpy. It's not like this is a real date or anything. I do like Max though. But I haven't been out with a man in decades. I'm sure I'm making more of this than I should, but he did kiss me.*

Her thoughts were interrupted by a bark from Lucy announcing Max's arrival. Linda patted Lucy on the head as she opened the front door. Max was coming up the steps and stopped to admire her.

"Wow, you look gorgeous." His eyes twinkled with wonder, taking in not only the stunning dress, but her beautiful long hair, released from her usual ponytail, styled into soft curves framing her face and cascading down her back. She wore a sapphire necklace and earrings the same blue as her dress.

"Thanks, Max. I like your suit, too," she took his hand. At the end of her walkway, she bent over and plucked a primrose and tucked it into the lapel of Max's jacket. "Now, it's perfect," she smiled.

Max opened her door of the SUV Brad had delivered today. He made sure her long dress was tucked in and shut the door. "Did you get some rest when you got home?" he asked.

"Yes, I indulged in a nap," she said with a hint of guilt. "Followed by a long soak in the tub. I feel like a new woman."

"Whatever you did, keep doing it. I should be taking you somewhere in the city, looking like you do tonight. I only hope the Cliff House is as glamorous as you."

"You're sweet. It took me forever to find a dress I liked in my closet."

They parked at the restaurant and Max ran around to open Linda's door. He linked her arm in his as they approached the hostess. She led them to their private room, with a superb view of the waterfront. Waiters set trays of appetizers near the bar.

Max was relieved they were the first to arrive. He showed Linda to her seat. Sam and Jeff appeared soon after and Sam raced across the room to Linda. "The nursery looks perfect. We were there for the rehearsal and I was so excited. It's magical," she said, leaning in to hug her. "Max said you went home to rest otherwise I would have burst into your house to tell you."

"I think it turned out well. Tomorrow it will look better when we get all the linens and centerpieces placed. I'm so glad you're pleased."

"And I must say you look spectacular tonight." Sam glanced up to see Max watching Linda. "I can tell Max is smitten with you."

"He's a wonderful guy. I've surprised myself this week and have enjoyed spending the day with him. He's talked me into dinner and lunch a few times and I find myself looking forward to seeing him each day. He told me he's planning to move to the island and we're going to look at houses on Monday." Her eyes were bright with excitement, "I mustered up the courage to ask him to go to Monday Movies," she blushed.

"Oh, we couldn't be happier, Linda. Max is one of the best. You two are perfect for each other. I'm so excited he's moving here and I hope you're able to spend lots of time together," Sam said, as Jeff's family arrived and she spotted Jen coming towards them.

Becky, Brad, and their children, Andy and Chloe, arrived soon after, followed by Ashley. Sam had met Ashley online a few weeks ago, but this was the first time she had seen her in person. Ashley gave her dad a huge hug and smile and Jeff guided her to Sam and Linda.

"Sam, please meet my beautiful daughter, Ashley."

Sam hugged Ashley, "We're so excited you're here, without a computer screen between us."

Ashley was stiff and didn't return the hug. "Will sends his best. He couldn't get away, but we're planning to be here for Thanksgiving."

"That'll be great, Ash. Our first Thanksgiving with Sam. I'm not sure she's up for it," Jeff laughed, as he put his arm around his daughter. "You remember Linda, but I want to take you over to meet Max. He's throwing the party tonight and is Sam's best friend from when they were kids."

Jen rolled her eyes when they left. "She's trying to be upbeat, but I think she's having a hard time with the idea of her dad getting remarried. So, if she acts weird or rude, just let it roll off your back, Sam. She'll come around eventually."

"I understand. Charlie said she always wanted her parents to get back together. Hopefully, she'll come to accept me," murmured Sam.

Charlie was guiding his grandma to the table. Her seat was between Charlie and Jeff and he helped her get situated and brought her a drink. Sam excused herself when she noticed Mary take a seat.

"Hi, Mary. How are you tonight?"

"I'm wonderful. And you look so pretty," she grasped Sam's hand.

"Ah, you're sweet. Honestly, I'm tired. Jeff and I have been working so hard these past weeks and I'm hoping I can stay awake tonight," she said with a quick laugh.

"It will all be worth it tomorrow. I'm so pleased for you both. Jeff is happier than I've ever seen him."

"Me too," she said, rubbing Mary's hand and raising her eyebrows in delight.

Charlie arrived with a drink and a snack for his grandmother and gave Sam a hug before she went to greet the others. Sam and Jeff mingled with his relatives and introduced Becky's family to the others. Soon, they heard a tap on a glass and Max asked everyone to be seated.

"I want to thank all of you for coming tonight. I never had a sister growing up and Sam was an only child so we sort of adopted each other. She's the best sister and friend I could have ever asked for and I'm so very fortunate to have her in my life. I'm ecstatic she has found the love of her life in such a fine man as Jeff. He has brought joy back to my friend. Please join me in a toast." He raised his glass and said, "To Sam and Jeff and the lifetime of happiness you both deserve."

Glasses clinked and cheers erupted, followed by waiters distributing salads and bread. Sam leaned over and kissed Max on the cheek. "Thanks," she whispered. The hum of conversation took over as each course was served. The whole table raved about the excellent food. Sam tried to catch a glimpse of Ashley and noticed she was laughing with her cousins, but each time she looked at Sam, her smile disappeared.

As soon as dessert was served, Jeff stood and turned towards Max. "We'd like to thank you, Max, for such a special evening. It means a lot to have everyone we love here with us tonight. We'd also like to thank all of you who have helped us in so many ways make this weekend so memorable." Sam scurried behind the bar and retrieved several bags and passed out exquisitely wrapped gifts to Becky, Max, Linda, Charlie, and Jen. "This is a small token of our appreciation. We love you," ended Jeff.

There were gasps and shrieks as packages were opened. Linda was flabbergasted to find a long weekend trip to Victoria, complete with a stay at the Empress Hotel and a tour of the Butchart Gardens. Max was overjoyed with a gift of a year's golf membership to the San Juan Golf Club and a note that read, *One more reason to move here!* Charlie shouted when he opened his gift of a ski trip to Whistler outside of Vancouver. Jen jumped up and hugged Sam and Jeff when she discovered her weekend of pampering in Seattle at the Fairmont Olympic, including every spa treatment she could imagine.

After the decadent assortment of cheesecake was devoured, the group started dispersing. Sam and Jeff waited by the door to wish everyone goodnight and remind them about photos tomorrow. Max settled the bill and took Linda's arm as they headed outside. Sam wrapped both of them in a hug. "Thanks for a memorable evening. We'll see you tomorrow." Jeff followed with an embrace of his own and waved goodbye.

When Max and Linda arrived at her door it was nearing ten o'clock. He led her to the door and took her key to unlock it. Lucy greeted them with enthusiastic barks. "Would you like to come in?" she asked.

"Are you sure it's not too late?"

"Oh, it probably is, but we could have a quick cup of tea. I won't be able to go to sleep anyway. I'm too excited about my gift." Her eyes were wide with enthusiasm.

"Well, I'll never refuse an invitation from a beautiful woman. Twist my arm," he joked, stepping in.

She filled the kettle and put her delicate tea service on a tray. "Let's sit in the old parlor, since we're having a fancy evening."

He carried the tray into the Victorian inspired room and placed it on the table in front of the settee. Taking a sip of her tea, Linda commented, "That was a lovely celebration. Thanks for including me."

"It was fun. And I can't get over our outrageous gifts. I've always enjoyed golfing and haven't been for quite a few months. I haven't looked at the club here, but now I'm more excited to move here. I could golf every day," he said, as a wide smile covered his face.

"I haven't been to Victoria in years and I'm excited to go." She brought the cup to her lips again and put it back on the saucer. "Would you think it too forward of me to invite you to join me? Maybe we could make a trip in September?"

"I'd love to," he said as he leaned forward, deliberately slow in case he caught a signal to abort. He grazed her soft lips and was greeted with an eagerness he didn't expect.

Unwilling to let go, he deepened his kiss and felt Linda's hand caress his neck to cradle the back of his head. With slow and purposeful movements he progressed from her lips to her cheek and then her neck, eliciting a shudder. He looked into her dark eyes, "I'm going to love living here."

Nine

Saturday morning brought a swarm of activity. Since they had decided to be married on Jeff's birthday, Becky went out of her way to make sure Jeff felt acknowledged on his special day. She made him one of her famous birthday breakfasts. Max scurried out after breakfast to help Linda with any final touches.

After helping Sam tidy the kitchen, Becky commandeered her family to load all the wedding favor boxes she had put together. Becky made sure everyone would go home with the photo coaster serving as their name card for the tables, plus an engraved pie server and glass mug. Since pie and coffee had brought Sam and Jeff together, she thought it was fitting. By the time all the items were checked off her master list, the Escalade was packed to the gills. She shouted a farewell to Sam and promised to meet her at Jen's salon later.

Sam stopped by the coffee shop to check on the crew on her way to Jen's salon. She found it busy, but under control. The shop was closing early so everyone could attend the wedding. "Hey Jen," she said, putting a drink carrier on the salon's front desk. "I thought I'd bring a few drinks to treat you and the girls."

"That was thoughtful," said Jen, as she took a frozen smoothie. "Let's get started on your hair. I talked Linda into taking time to let me do her hair today. She'll be here soon. And I just finished my mom's."

Sam sat in the chair and let Jen's magic hands take over. "By the way, I wanted to warn you," began Sam. "Jeff was adamant we sit Dr. Sean by you at the reception. I didn't want you to feel set up, so if you would rather he sit elsewhere, let me know."

Jen's eyebrows arched higher and a sly smile appeared. "Oooh, I think I can handle sitting by Dr. Sean. I wouldn't mind getting to know him better."

"Max said Sean likes it here and loves working at the hospital. Because of his background in trauma and emergency medicine they put him in charge of the emergency room."

"Kellie told me he bought a terrific place. It's on the east side with views of Orcas. She said it's an older place, but has been remodeled with a gorgeous deck. And it's only about six miles from the harbor area."

"Sounds like you two will have plenty to discuss," smiled Sam, as she turned to glance at the door. "Before Linda gets here, I wanted to tell you things seem to be going well with Max. He got home late last night after taking her home. I think he's quite taken with her."

"That's excellent news. It looked like they were fixated on each other last night. I haven't seen her dressed up like that in years. She looked so beautiful and so happy."

"I know he's on cloud nine. He mentioned they're going to look at houses for him on Monday and Linda invited him to the movie in the park, so they're going to dinner too. I could tell he was excited."

Linda and Becky came in the door as Jen was applying the finishing touches to Sam's hair. She had styled it in a low twisted chignon that she was accenting with small crystal jewels. She turned Sam around to face the mirror. "Do you like it?"

Sam stared at herself and turned her head to each side. "It looks fabulous. Exactly what I was hoping for," she smiled.

Becky and Linda hovered behind Sam to admire her. "Oh, Sam, you look so elegant," said Linda.

"Yes, it's gorgeous," agreed Becky. "Now let's see what you can do with this," she said fluffing her hair.

Sam said her goodbyes and told them she'd see them all later at Linda's.

By the time three o'clock came, Linda's house was full of chatter and excitement. The guys were using Sam's house to get ready and the women were helping each other with dresses and makeup. Ryan wanted to start the group photos before the ceremony, but he was at Sam's taking some candid shots of the guys and his assistant was snapping pictures as the girls fussed over each other.

There was a strict photo schedule to prevent Sam and Jeff from seeing each other before the ceremony. Jeff's group was first and Ryan took several photos of him with his entire family, plus individual shots with his mom, each of his children, Jeremy and Jen. The lush grounds made for an ideal backdrop and Ryan moved the groups to various areas to capture the colors of the gardens. Ryan finished Jeff's portion by taking some photos of Max and Becky with Jeff and added the dogs for an amusing pose.

After Jeff was safely hidden away in one of Linda's bedrooms, Sam made the trip outside for her photos. Max was waiting for her at the bottom of the stairs. When he saw her, tears filled his eyes. He grasped her hand, admiring her. "You're breathtaking," he said, kissing her lightly on the cheek.

"No crying," she said trying to keep her composure. "I've never put in so many hours on my face, so I don't want to ruin it," she joked.

He took her arm and Becky and Linda followed them outside. Ryan had them all laughing soon and in between planned scenes, took some candid shots of them giggling and teasing each other. Ryan included the dogs in photos with Sam and promised to take one of the bride and groom with their spoiled pets. Sam also asked him to take some of Linda and Max.

As Max put his arm around Linda for a photo, he whispered in her ear, "You look spectacular and the dress is perfect."

Max ushered Sam back into the house and ensconced her in the bedroom with Becky and Linda to keep her company. He went to watch the guests arrive and make sure things were going well.

The band was playing soft music as people arrived and were seated. The weather had cooperated; it was a flawless evening, with a delicate breeze and no rain in sight. Jeff and Charlie were hiding out in the gift shop waiting for their signal. Max took the opportunity to retrieve Linda and as they made their way to the ceremony he told her what a fabulous job she had done with all the flowers and the setting. He guided her to her seat where he would join her after walking Sam down the aisle, lingering as he left, holding tight to her hand.

As the band began playing the gentle instrumental, "A River Flows in You", Jeff and Charlie took their cue and made their way to the left of Pastor Mark and Max went to stage Becky and Sam. Zoe and Bailey had a place in the wedding and Linda had made sure their collars were adorned with pink and white flowers. They dashed along the aisle together and Bailey sat next to Charlie and Jeff. Zoe, with a little prodding, sat on the other side. Becky stepped forward with a huge smile and a beautiful peony and rose bouquet in shades of soft pink and made her way to the pastor.

Sam and Max stopped at the edge of the rose garden listening to the beautiful melody and watching Becky. For her entrance, Sam had chosen "Canon in D" and the guests rose as the first notes began. Max squeezed her hand, "Here we go," he said, as they began their march.

Linda had outdone herself on the bridal flowers. White peonies dominated the elegant full bouquet. Some flowers were gaping to their fullest, petals outstretched, and others were plump round mounds barely open. Green closed buds separated the snowy blossoms. She had tucked a few white roses tinged with the palest pink in between the fluttering peonies. Linda had captured Sam's refined grace in her creation.

As Sam looked towards the pastor, she fixated on Jeff. She felt herself relax when she noticed his smile and sensed Max's arm in hers. The band stopped playing when they reached the front. Pastor Mark looked at them and asked, "Who has the honor of presenting this woman to be married to this man?"

With a slight catch in his voice, Max replied, "On behalf of her loving family and friends, both those here today and those gone before, I do." He turned to Sam taking her hand and kissed her on the cheek and then turned her to Jeff and shook his hand. His job done, he slid into his chair next to Linda, clasping her hand.

Pastor Mark welcomed everyone and spoke of the joy evident in Jeff and Sam. He communicated a special love they had found and how blessed they were to be marrying each other. They exchanged their personalized vows, promising to love and treasure each other forever, followed by the presentation of the rings.

As soon as Pastor Mark said he could kiss his bride, Jeff seized Sam and pulled her into a long kiss, followed by a dramatic dip. Cheers and yelps erupted from the wedding guests. Pastor Mark presented the new married couple and invited all the guests to move to the reception tent where the bride and groom wanted them to enjoy dinner and drinks while they finished their photos. Sam and Jeff had picked a country tune for the recessional, "Bless the Broken Road", and the band began playing as soon as the pastor finished his announcement.

Jeff slipped his arm around her waist and they made their way along the aisle, with Zoe and Bailey at their heels. They stopped for hugs and well wishes at every aisle and eventually made their way to the rose garden where they were set to meet Ryan for the photos.

Charlie escorted Becky, followed by Max and Linda, and Jeff's mom and Ashley. The rest of Jeff's family brought up the rear and met everyone in the rose garden. Ryan had already started taking photos and as soon as the guests cleared out, directed the group back to the ceremony area to finish. They had a good time with each other and smiled as Ryan snapped continuously. Sam noticed Ashley kept her distance and forced a phony smile when she posed for a photo with her.

As promised, Ryan was fast and they were on their way to the reception in less than thirty minutes. The sun was setting and Jeff gripped Sam's hand, holding her back to let the others leave. "I haven't had a minute to tell you, but you're beyond gorgeous. When I saw you coming down the aisle, I knew I was the luckiest man alive. I love you," he said, as he bent to kiss her again.

"I love you, too. More than anything," she said, wrapping her arms around his neck. "This is the best day."

"We better get in there," he tilted his head towards the tent.

They linked hands and took the short path to the reception. The sun had slipped into the sea and the glow from the tent looked inviting. Sam gasped as she stepped in and saw Linda's sketch had come to life. Gorgeous centerpieces in pink hues made of peonies and roses adorned the head table. The ribbons shimmered in the candlelight from the pillars she had scattered in the flowers. Linda had decorated the guest tables with dozens of small candles and simple glass bowls filled with the same beautiful flowers. Containers of pink and white blossoms and flowering trees provided the perfect accents for the room. The band played as everyone mingled and served themselves from the buffet table, framed in sparkling ribbons and dusted with rose petals.

As soon as they were noticed, clapping and cheers broke out across the tables. The band announced a welcome and invited them to the dance floor for their first dance. Sam let Jeff pick the song and he chose "Then", a country song by Brad Paisley. As Jeff led Sam across the dance floor, he sang along with the chorus, knowing she was his whole world. Watching Sam and Jeff wrapped in each other's arms, Becky, Jen, and Linda were all crying. The song ended by the groom dipping the bride low and planting a long kiss on her lips. They broke apart to resounding applause and the band invited other couples to dance.

Jeff grasped Sam's hand and led her to the head table. Max and Linda had finished eating and volunteered to fill two plates for them, so they could relax. Sam glanced over at the cake table and Ellie's magnificent creation. The cake looked like silky fabric had been draped over each tier and was covered in glittering sugar. The pink flowers she had placed were the only decorations. The chocolate cakes were glossy and ringed with white and pink flowers, topped with a pile of spiky chocolate curls. She was pleased to see Ryan's assistant taking several shots of the cakes.

Max and Linda returned with their plates, piled high with food. Sam and Jeff took the opportunity to eat and after taking a few bites, realized they were famished. They could see the party was a success by the cheery faces of everyone gathered at the tables, snapping pictures with their phones and the disposable cameras Becky had added. Laughter and chatter filled the space and Jeff clasped Sam's hand under the table and squeezed. "This is an excellent party," he grinned.

Sam had been watching Ashley, noticing she was animated when she visited with her family and others, but the minute she looked at Sam, a veil of contempt shadowed her face. "Do you think Ashley is okay?" she asked Jeff.

"I'm not sure, Sam. I know she isn't being very nice to you and her body language speaks volumes, but," he brought her hand to his mouth and kissed it, "I think she'll warm up to you. She's probably thinking about her mom. I've tried to encourage her to see a counselor, but she isn't willing. I don't want you to worry about her. She'll come around."

Sam shook her head with sadness. "I know. I was hoping it would be different, like it is with Charlie."

"Charlie definitely loves you," he smiled. "And, much more important, I love you. We have the rest of our lives to figure it all out."

They were interrupted by Becky who said she thought it was time to cut the cakes. As they approached the cake table, the band leader handed Sam a microphone. "Thank you all so much for coming. I wanted to take the time to thank Linda for her outstanding work on all the details that have made this such a magical setting. I also want to thank my new sister-in-law, Jen, for her help with the wedding preparations and my maid of honor, Becky for everything she has done to make this a success. This exquisite cake is Ellie's masterpiece and we can't thank her enough for it. Lastly, I have to thank my dear friend Max for being here and walking me down the aisle on the happiest day of my life. "

She extended her hand to suppress the applause. "One more very important person I want to acknowledge is my husband, Jeff. Today is his birthday, so please join me in singing and light the sparklers at your table. Happy Birthday, I love you." She turned and kissed Jeff, as the sizzle and light of dozens of sparklers filled the tent. After posing for a few photos with the cake, they cut into the tiered cake and honored the long tradition of shoving it in each other's faces. They took care not to use big pieces and then took a slice of the red velvet and a slice of chocolate mousse to their table. Megan, Kyle, Hayley, and Rachel had volunteered to manage the cutting and serving of the cakes.

As the confection was being devoured and Ellie was surrounded by guests telling her how wonderful it was, Sam made her way to the dance floor. She nodded at the band and the lead vocalist asked Sam's friend Max to approach the dance floor to join the bride in a special dance at her request. The band played, "Because You Loved Me." Max smiled at Sam, both of them with tears in their eyes as they floated across the floor, swaying to the song that reminded Sam of all the times Max had been there for her. Towards the last verse of the song, Jeff asked Linda to join him in a dance. As the song ended Jeff took his new bride's hand and placed Linda in Max's arms.

Soon the band had everyone dancing in groups to funny songs like the "Chicken Dance". Jeff and Sam spent the evening moving from table to table visiting with all their friends and sneaking in a few slow dances. Each time Sam glanced at the dance floor, Max and Linda were on it, looking as if they were the only two people in the room.

Sam was touched when Kyle asked her to dance. As he took her hand he said, "I'm so happy for you and Jeff. I know finding out I was Marty's son had to be hard. You could have made it worse. But, instead, you've been so kind to me, treating me more like a son than you had to. I want you to know how honored I am to have you in my life."

Sam felt her eyes fill with tears as his words sunk in. "Thank you, Kyle. I'd be proud to have you as a son and I'm glad we stumbled upon each other." She hugged him tight. "I'm so excited for you to go to college this fall, but I'm going to miss you. You'll have to come and visit." They finished their dance and Kyle returned her to Jeff.

Soon it was time to throw the garter and toss the bouquet. Sam didn't want to part with the beautiful bouquet she had carried and was thankful Linda had suggested she make a small one for tossing. The band supplied dramatic music for both events and in the end, Dr. Sean caught the garter and Hayley caught Sam's bouquet. Jeff couldn't wait to tease his sister about Dr. Sean and rushed over to torment her. Jeff hugged the rest of his family and went to steal Sam away from Max and Becky.

"You guys should get going. We'll see you on Monday and I'll take good care of the dogs, so don't worry," said Max, as he gave them both a hug goodbye.

"We'll see you all soon," said Jeff, steering Sam away from them and out a side entrance. They made their way to Linda's house and changed out of their wedding clothes for the boat ride to Orcas Island. Bailey and Zoe were in the house with Lucy and after lots of doggie kisses and belly rubs, they left them; promising to see them soon.

When they stepped off Linda's porch, they gazed at the guests lined up on each side, holding sparklers to light the path to Sam's car. "Oh, how pretty," sighed Sam. She noticed Ryan and his assistant both snapping pictures from different angles. She felt like a princess as they strolled along the walkway. Sam's little car had been decorated with the traditional "Just Married" theme, but with vinyl static clings so as not to damage the finish. The guys Jeff volunteered with at the firehouse brought the old fire truck and provided an escort with lights and an occasional burst from the siren. Ribbons and cans had been tied behind the car and they rattled down the road as they headed to the marina.

Steve left the reception early to ready his boat for the trip and was waiting for them when they arrived. He offered to store Sam's car in the shop for the next few days and helped them load their bags into the boat. It was a clear night with the moon reflecting on the water and the glittering stars shone across the indigo sky. With Orcas Island being less than fifteen miles away, it didn't take Steve's express cruiser long to dock at the Rosario Resort. He helped them unload the luggage and waved as he headed home.

Jeff and Sam found the golf cart left for them at the marina and drove over to the mansion to check in. The staff was expecting them and had made the process quick and easy. They left with a key to the honeymoon suite and offers of assistance. Jeff opted to handle the luggage himself and drove over to the solitary building perched on a bluff above the ocean. He hauled the luggage and Sam carried a tote. Jeff opened the door and they were greeted with a fire burning in the sitting area and a glass wall exposing a fantastic view of the ocean. The resort had provided champagne, a basket of snacks and fruit, wine and beer, chocolate dipped strawberries, bottled water, and soft drinks.

"I can't believe we're finally here," said Jeff putting the luggage down. "Wow, what a room," he grinned, as he took in the huge bed covered in rose petals and wandered into the bathroom. "Sam, check this out," he hollered.

She came through the doorway and found a huge soaking tub nestled into a corner of windows revealing a private view of the water. A separate walk-in shower with multiple heads was situated next to the tub. Candles were lit on the granite surround of the tub and all across the polished counters. "They definitely know how to do romantic."

Jeff started the tub running and returned to take her in his arms. He covered her mouth and then traveled to her neck, depositing soft kisses along his route. His lips made slow progress upward to her ear and he whispered, "I've been waiting for this for a long time." He fingers worked their way into her hair and he began unpinning it, letting it cascade over her shoulders. As he continued kissing her neck he found the zipper of her dress and slowly drew it down to her hips and flicked it off her shoulders. It fell in a silky puddle at her feet.

He stood back, admiring her in the candlelight. "I remember those," he said, fixated on her lacy sheer lingerie. "I told you on your birthday, I couldn't wait to see you in them," he laughed.

"Well, Happy Birthday, Mr. Cooper," she said, as she slipped out of them and led him towards the tub.

Ten

Max stayed until the band and caterers had packed their gear and left. He and Linda were both tired and it was approaching midnight. He disconnected the main lights in the tent and was headed to unplug all the twinkle lights when she stopped him. "Leave them on for tonight. I like them and I can deal with them in the morning, when I'm not so tired."

"It is pretty," he said looking out towards the rose garden. "I think Sam and Jeff were elated tonight."

"I know they were. It was a wonderful wedding."

"I enjoyed dancing with you," he said taking her hand.

"It was my pleasure." She tilted her head up to meet his lips. As he kissed her he swayed to the nonexistent music and guided her around the floor.

"Let me take you home and I'll be out in the morning to help you clean everything," he linked her arm with his.

He whistled for Zoe and Bailey and loaded them in his SUV, kissing Linda goodnight at the steps. "I'll cook breakfast for you," she said, as she waved to him.

"It's a date. See you soon."

When Max got back to Sam's the lights were on and Becky and Brad were up talking about the wedding. The dogs bounded through the great room and plopped on Zoe's dog bed.

"Hey, Max. We were going to bed, but we can't stop talking about what a wonderful day it was. They deserve happiness. The last year has been so hard on Sam and now she gets to have a new life filled with joy and love," said Becky.

"I know. I think her best years are ahead of her. Everyone did an incredible job and I had a fabulous time, but I'm exhausted, so I'll see you two in the morning," said Max as he ambled up the stairs.

"Good night, Max. See you tomorrow," said Brad. "We better get to bed too, honey," he motioned to Becky and hit the lights.

* * *

The next morning Brad was up early loading the car with luggage. Becky offered to make breakfast before they left, but Max said he wanted to leave and get to Linda's. Brad suggested they eat in town while they waited for the ferry. "We'll see you soon and keep me posted on the house hunting and moving plans," said Becky, as she hugged him goodbye.

He made sure the dogs were fed and watered and drove out to Linda's. He tried the house first since she mentioned cooking breakfast and when he knocked, he heard her call out, "Come on in, Max."

He followed the smell of bacon drifting from the kitchen and found her at the stove. Lucy greeted him with a wagging tail and a nudge for a pet. "Good morning, girls," he said, as he nuzzled Lucy all the way into the kitchen. He stepped behind Linda and noticed her hair was back in a ponytail. He reached out and rubbed her shoulders and brushed his lips against the back of her neck.

"Good Morning, Max. Breakfast is ready," she twirled around and gave him a quick kiss. "Go ahead and pour us some juice from the fridge and I'll get all of this on the table."

She piled plates with bacon, eggs, fried potatoes, toasted bread from Sweet Treats, and fruit. "Mmm, this is all so good," said Max, taking another forkful of potatoes. "I shouldn't be hungry after all the food last night."

"Must be the dancing," she laughed. "We don't have too much to do today. The party rental place will handle the tent and tables and chairs. We need to pile the linens and I want to take Sam's bouquet to the shop and get it preserved and press a few of the pink peonies between glass panes for her to keep too. And we need to take down the twinkle lights, except for the rose garden. I decided last night to leave them up for the summer."

"That doesn't sound too bad," he said, as he took his last bite of toast and wiped his plate. "I'll help you do these dishes and we'll get started."

They made quick work of the kitchen duties and headed out with Lucy to clear the grounds. Max worked on the lights in the shrubs outside the tent and Linda took care of all the linens and lights in the containers inside. She came outside to check on Max. "I'm going to grab the ladder from the shed for the trees and I'll be right back."

"Okay, I'll help you if you hang on a minute."

"I'm fine with it," she said jogging towards the shed.

She wasn't gone long when he heard her cry out and a crash. He dropped the string of lights he was working with and rushed over. Linda was on the ground, "It's my right ankle," she said. "I tripped on one of those blasted power boxes for the lights and fell."

"Don't move. Let me take a look," he said kneeling beside her. He shifted her pant leg up and she winced. "At least it isn't a compound fracture," he said, probing her ankle with care. She flinched again. "It's hard to say, but it's either a fracture or a bad sprain. We need to get you to the hospital and find out."

"Oh, I don't want to go to the hospital," she groaned.

"Nobody does, sweetheart. I'll call an ambulance and we'll get it figured out."

"Oh, not an ambulance, how embarrassing. Could you just take me?"

"Let me call Sean and see if he can come out and take a look and help me get you in. I don't want you to put any weight on it." He reached for his cell and dialed Sean. He explained the situation with the speed of a surgeon and disconnected. He monitored Linda's pulse, but didn't have any equipment with him. He ran to the house and retrieved an ice pack and snatched some cushions from the porch chairs. He stacked the cushions and elevated her leg and put the icepack over the ankle.

"Sean said he's on his way. He sat behind her and propped her up to lean against him. While they were waiting for Sean the party truck arrived and Max explained Linda had a leg injury and they would need to carry on without them. He wanted them to stay away from the area she was in until they got her assessed and transported.

Sean came barreling down the road and ran towards them with his bag in hand. "Hey Linda, how are you doing?"

"I'm okay. My ankle only hurts when you touch it."

"Okay, let me take a quick look." He looked at the ankle and examined it, apologizing to Linda. "I think it's a fracture. Max, go get your SUV and we can load her in the back and you can drive her in. I'll meet you at the ER."

Dr. Sean stayed with her while Max maneuvered through the nursery, trying his best to stay on paths to get as close to Linda as he could. He jumped out and folded down the back seats, to clear a large spot for her.

Dr. Sean enlisted the help of a couple of the party rental workers so they could hold her as steady as possible and with relative ease they loaded her in the back. "Keep your legs straight, Linda," said Dr. Sean, as he stabilized her with a blanket and pillow from the car.

He shut the back and told Max to go slow and minimize bumps and he would follow him in and call ahead. Max led Lucy into the house, so she'd stay out of trouble while they were gone and found Linda's purse and tossed in on the seat.

He eased his SUV through the nursery and onto the road. Once he got on the pavement, he went faster, but the trip was painstakingly slow as he attempted to provide a smooth ride. When they arrived at the emergency entrance, a team was waiting with a gurney to help Linda.

They unloaded her and wheeled her inside. Sean let Max know he had called in an orthopedist to assess Linda. "I'm not sure if she'll need surgery or not, but we'll get the x-rays and once Dr. Brown arrives he'll make the recommendation. Come on back and you can get the forms filled out for her and keep her company."

Max was handed a fistful of forms and found Linda. They were giving her something for the pain and had taken an x-ray. He asked her all the questions and dug through her purse to get her insurance card. When he came to the emergency notification section, she hesitated. "Would you mind if I listed you?"

"Of course not. I'll fill in my information," he said. He finished it and handed her the clipboard to sign the paperwork. A nurse stopped by to check on her and Max handed her the clipboard.

She looked it over and pronounced it complete. "Dr. Brown has arrived and will be in shortly."

In a matter of minutes, Dr. Sean appeared with another man. "Max and Linda, this is Dr. Brown."

"Good morning to you both. Although, not so good for you, Linda. I took a look at the x-ray," he said, poking a button on a monitor. He took out a pen and pointed, "As you can see she's got an isolated lateral fracture of the fibula. The good news is I can fix it without surgery. I can put it back in place and we'll get you in a cast."

Linda's eyes were filled with worry. Max was holding her hand while Dr. Brown explained what was wrong. On the verge of tears she asked, "Will you have to knock me out to set the fracture?"

"Yes, but it's a light anesthetic and it's best if you're out, because it will be very painful, which is not good for you. It won't take long, but you'll have to stay overnight so we can keep an eye on you. You won't have to have any incisions or screws though. I'll go check on the schedule and see if we can get this done by this afternoon."

Max tried to reassure her, "You'll be fine and I'll stay right here with you."

Tears trickled down her face. "I know, I'm sorry, I'm a little scared."

Dr. Sean came in and said he had talked to Dr. Brown. "You guys need to know he's a top notch orthopedic doctor. You can trust him." He looked at Linda and pulled a chair over to sit next to her. "I know you're worried and scared. It's okay to be worried, but Max and I will be right here and I'll be in the room when Dr. Brown does it, so we won't let anything happen to you."

"I know," she said in a whisper. "I'm making too much of it. I'm worried about my work and Lucy and everything. And how I'm going to get up and down my stairs."

"I'll take care of Lucy. I'll bring her to Sam's with the other dogs and we'll be fine. I can help you figure out what to do about the stairs. We could talk to Jeff and see if you can stay at his cabin for a few weeks or we can turn your parlor into a temporary bedroom. Don't worry," he said leaning in to kiss her forehead.

Dr. Sean told them he had to leave, but promised to meet with Linda before she went in for the procedure.

"Now our Monday is ruined too. We were going to look at houses and do movies in the park," she shook her head.

"There are lots of Mondays left, so we'll go next week," he said, rubbing her hand. "If you give me Kellie's number, I'll call her and reschedule."

"It's in my cell phone," she pointed to her purse.

He found it and excused himself to go outside and make a call. "I'll be right back."

When he reached Kellie he explained what happened. She said she had several properties scheduled for him. He wondered if she would be available early in the morning, knowing he wouldn't be able to get Linda out until close to noon and she would need her rest. Kellie agreed to meet him at seven in the morning and show him the unoccupied properties on the list. She thought they could get through them by ten.

He returned to find Linda dozing. Dr. Brown motioned him to the door. "I've got us scheduled and since she had breakfast this morning, I'd like to wait and do it later this afternoon. It'll take about fifteen minutes to get this done and she'll be awake within an hour. Sean is going to join me and we'll be fine, so don't worry about your pretty lady."

"I know she's in good hands, doctor. Do you think she'll be able to go home by tomorrow afternoon?"

"Yes, I'd say early afternoon. I'll check on her tonight and again in the morning and release her around noon." He shook Max's hand. "Sean tells me you may be joining us here on the island."

"Yes, I'm going house hunting tomorrow."

"It's a wonderful community and I know you'll like it. We could use you around here too. I'll see you in a few hours."

Max heard his phone bleep. Sam had texted him asking about the dogs and telling him how much they loved their suite. He decided to step outside and call her with the news about Linda.

She answered on the first ring and he explained he was at the hospital with Linda waiting for them to set and cast her ankle. He heard Sam explaining it to Jeff in the background. "Tell Linda she can plan to stay at my house. We'll give her the bedroom downstairs and use one of the others. She'll only have a couple of steps into the house."

"Thanks, Sam. I'll let her know. She's worried about everything right now, so hopefully, that will take a load off her mind. I'm going to talk to the people at the flower shop and the nursery to let them know and try to ease her burden."

"Take care of her and we'll see you tomorrow afternoon. We're enjoying your honeymoon gift. It's been wonderful here. We're going bike riding today, but I'll call you later tonight to check on things."

When Max got back Linda was awake. "Hi, how are you feeling?"

"The pain is gone now. I feel groggy," she mumbled.

"That's the pain medication. I talked to Dr. Brown and he's got you scheduled around three this afternoon. He said it will be fast and you'll be awake within an hour. He also said I could take you home around noon tomorrow," he tried to sound upbeat.

"Okay. After I'm done, will you get Lucy?"

"Yes, don't worry. Who should I talk to at the nursery and the flower shop to let them know?"

"Oh, yeah. Talk to Lucas about the nursery. He can handle things there and Sara can handle the shop."

"Do you want me to call your brother or your mom?"

"Yeah, that would be good," she whispered, her eyelids struggling to stay open.

"Okay, I'll go make some calls and you rest. I'll be back before you have to leave. And I talked to Sam. They want you to stay at her house."

"Oh," she moaned. "I can't do that to newlyweds." And then her eyes shut.

Max left with her cell phone to make the calls to Lucas and Sara. He reached them both and explained the situation, making sure they understood Linda would most likely be unable to work for about six weeks. He asked Sara to preserve Sam's bouquet and press the flowers Linda had mentioned. Then he tackled Linda's brother, David.

Max explained he was a friend of Linda's and had been at the nursery when she injured her ankle. He let her brother know he was a doctor and she was in excellent hands in the new hospital on the island. David asked if he should come and Max told him he didn't think it was necessary and assured him he would call after the procedure with an update. He explained that Jen's brother, Jeff, had married his best friend and they had invited Linda to stay with them.

By the end of the conversation David sounded relieved and promised to let his mom know. He also told Max to let him know if Linda needed help and he'd make the trip to the island. Max learned he lived near Yakima and had recently retired, so helping would not be a hardship.

When he returned he found Linda more alert and reviewing her chart noticed they had cut back on her pain medication. "Hey, how do you feel?"

"I'm less dopey, I think. Did you get in touch with David?"

"Yes, he asked if he should come and I told him I thought you would be fine. He also said if you need help with the business, to let him know. He was going to let your mom know what was happening. I promised to call him as soon as you were done and let him know how things went. He was concerned."

"He's a good guy and it was kind of him to offer to come. I hope I don't need him, but you never know."

"I also talked with Lucas and Sara and they're prepared to manage things while you're recuperating. I told them it could be around six weeks or so and they both said not to worry."

A fresh tear stained the sheets. "What a mess," she said.

"It'll be fine. I'll do anything you need me to do and I think you should stay at Sam's. At least until you can maneuver better."

"I know. I hate being a burden and I'm going to go completely crazy if I'm off for six weeks."

"Oh, I talked to Kellie and she has a few properties she can show me, so if you don't mind, I'm going to meet her early in the morning and then come by here around ten. They don't like visitors before then anyway, so thought I might as well use the morning and see what I can find. I'll take pictures and we can go over them when I get here. Does that sound okay?"

"That sounds terrific. I wish I could go too, but I'm glad you're going. You'll like Kellie."

Max looked up to see Dr. Sean and Dr. Brown at the door. "Hi, Linda. I wanted to see how you were doing. They'll be by in a minute to get you ready for the procedure and Max will be waiting when you're done. It won't take long," said Sean.

"I'm ready," she said.

"Okay, Linda. I'll see you in the surgical suite and we'll get your ankle set and you on the road. You'll be fine," smiled Dr. Brown.

A nurse arrived and Max knew she would be wheeling Linda out soon. He placed his hand on top of her head and leaned in to kiss her. "I'll be right by your side when you wake up, sweetie. It'll be fine."

"I'll see you in a few minutes," she tried to smile.

The nurse released her wheels and guided the bed into the hall. Max held Linda's hand until they reached the surgical door and he kissed her once more. As the doors were closing he whispered, "I love you."

He opted to wait in the garden area outdoors and let the surgical staff know where he would be. As he sat he rebuked himself for telling Linda he loved her. *I should have waited, but she looked so scared and alone and I wanted her to know how I feel.* He decided he better call Becky and Jen while he waited.

They were both shocked and worried and made Max promise to call them later. Jen wanted to come to the hospital, but Max told her everything was fine and Linda would need her later.

He finished his calls and leaned back on the bench when he heard his name, "Dr. Sullivan," said a nurse. "Dr. Brown wanted you to know he's finished and your friend will be in recovery soon."

Max sprang from the bench and hurried inside to the recovery suite. Dr. Brown met him there and explained everything went well and they were finishing her cast. "I'll be back this evening to check on her and make sure she's doing well."

Max shook his hand, "I appreciate your help."

Linda was wheeled in with a bright white cast on her leg covering her entire calf. Max held her hand and waited until her eyes began to flutter open. "Hey, everything is fine and you're all done. Just rest and relax now," he spoke in a gentle and calm voice.

She nodded her head and closed her eyes. He asked the nurse for ice chips, water, and a ginger ale for each of them. When she returned, Linda was awake. "How about some ice?"

She nodded and he raised her head and brought the cup over, spooning ice into her mouth. She crunched it and swallowed, smiling. "That feels good," she said.

He continued to help her and urged her to drink. The nurse came in to check on her and told her she was doing well and they planned to move her into her room as soon as it was ready for her. Max told her he had talked to Jen and Becky and they both sent their love. As soon as they came in to move her, he dashed outside to call David, Sam, and Jen. He wanted to give them all an update and let them know Linda was doing well and would be home tomorrow. Jen volunteered to call Becky and update her.

When he peeked into Linda's room he was surprised to see four flower arrangements. "Wow, I guess when you're the town florist, you get service," he laughed.

"Aren't they pretty? The nurses said Sara delivered them." She pointed, "Those are from everyone at the shop, the next is Jen's family, then Becky's, and that ginormous one is from Sam and Jeff."

"How do you feel now?"

"Not too bad. I'm hungry, so they're going to bring me dinner. Or should I say the hospital's idea of dinner," she chuckled.

"It will probably be broth and Jell-O to start with, but you should be back to normal tomorrow.

"Have you eaten since breakfast?"

"No, I'll go get something when we get you all settled."

"Here she is now," Linda said as she glanced at the doorway. The nurse delivered a tray and uncovered the food. "You called it, Max," she laughed. It held crackers, broth, Jell-O, and juice.

"If you're a good girl, I'll bring you ice cream after dinner," winked the nurse.

Max helped Linda unwrap her utensils and get situated in the bed. She ate, realizing she was hungrier than she thought. Max talked about the houses Kellie had sent to him. Their heads pressed together, they looked at his phone to see the photos of the homes he would be visiting tomorrow.

Max removed her tray and made sure her water and ice were full and showed her how to work the bed and the television controls. "You look like you feel better," he said, bending over to kiss her on the cheek.

"I feel pretty good. I think I'll watch a little television and then go to sleep."

"Okay, I'll get you some crutches in the morning and bring them when I pick you up. I should be here around ten. I'll leave your cell phone here and you call me if you need anything. Do you want me to go to your house and get your things?"

"I'll call Jen and have her do it, she knows where everything is." She gripped his hand, "Thanks for taking care of me and staying with me."

"I meant what I said when they took you in today. I love you and I wouldn't be anywhere else," he kissed her again. "Now, you get some rest and I'll see you in the morning. Call me even if you don't need anything," he winked.

"I think I love you too, Max. This all feels so new, but I can't imagine my life without you in it. Maybe I'm on too many drugs," she smiled.

He kissed her hand, "Get some sleep."

"Okay, see you in the morning," she waved as he left.

Max stopped by Tony's for a pizza wrap and then retrieved Lucy before going to Sam's. After checking on the dogs and playing a game of fetch with all of them, he slumped into the recliner to watch television. He woke three hours later when he heard his cell phone.

"Hi, Max," said Linda. "Sorry to call you so late, but I needed to hear your voice."

"How are you?"

"Okay, but bored out of my mind, and tired. I'm going to sleep but wanted to tell you good night."

"I came home and fell asleep about seven watching TV."

"I'll see you in the morning and you can tell me all about the houses."

"I will. I hope I find one I like tomorrow. I'll see you soon, sweetheart." Max turned off the television and the lights and stumbled upstairs to bed. As he climbed into bed he thought of Linda. *She said she couldn't imagine her life without me. I feel the same way. I know it's fast, but she's been waiting for a long time and I'm tired of being alone. I hope she feels the same way tomorrow when the meds wear off.*

Eleven

Max got up early Monday and ran the dogs along the beach. He scarfed down some toast and rushed to meet Kellie at the first property by seven o'clock. The first house was a short three miles from Sam's. He pulled in front of an immaculate Cape Code style home.

Kellie was waiting outside and waved him over. "Hi, you must be Max," she said shaking his hand.

"I'm grateful you could meet me early today."

"How's Linda feeling?"

"Much better. I'm going to stop by when we're done this morning. I should be able to spring her by this afternoon."

"Good, give her my best." She had the door unlocked and guided Max into the entry way. She led him through the four bedrooms and bathrooms. It had been built in the 1970's and had been remodeled, but lacked something. Max loved the yard and the dock, but the house was not one he could see himself living in.

"The house is well cared for and the yard is wonderful, but I know it's not the one, so how about we move on?" suggested Max after a few minutes.

"Perfect. I like it when clients know what they want and don't want. Let's go a few more miles and see the one on Mitchell Bay Road. I think you'll like it."

Max followed Kellie and noticed this one was less than a mile from Jeff's cabin. He liked the idea of being in the vicinity of Sam and Jeff. He admired the modern design, sporting stone and wood, with a sloping metal roof. It was set back from the main road, giving it a secluded feeling complete with a gorgeous yard as big as a park.

Kellie unlocked it and from the moment he stepped into the entry he knew this was it. It was similar to Sam's in that it felt like a lodge, but was contemporary. It was built in the late 1990's and then remodeled last year. It showcased stunning views of the water from all the rooms in the rear of the house. It had an enormous open style kitchen with a curved granite bar and beautiful stone pillars throughout the home. It was all one level except for an upstairs loft suited to a child's room or perhaps an office.

Max thought it was a bit big, but couldn't see any other deficiencies. He loved everything about it and the manicured landscaping was spectacular. "Linda would get a kick out of this yard," he said, noticing the owners must have had dogs since it was equipped with a dog run and fenced area. "Kellie, I think this is the one. We can take a look at the others on your list, but this is what I had in mind."

She reached for her tablet, "Let's look at the virtual tour and photos of the other two before we go. This is the only home with this style, so these others may not be something you want to waste your time seeing." She flipped through the photos of the first home.

Max shook his head, "No, I like the exterior and the glass, but it is a bit too modern and cold inside." She loaded the next home she had in mind. He continued shaking his head and said, "No, I don't like that one either and I think it's too small if my family were to come and visit."

"Okay, you've saved us time. If you're interested in this one, I'll contact the owners and get the ball rolling."

"I'd like to take some photos while we're here to show Linda."

"Sure, feel free and I'll be here starting the process. I assume you want to offer something a bit lower than the asking price?"

"Yes, let me know what you think. I don't want to drag this out forever, so give me a call later after you've talked with them and see what you can work out. I sold my house and have the cash, so I'd like to speed it along and close quickly."

Kellie got on her cell phone and Max toured the rest of the house, taking pictures of each room and the yard. When he returned to the kitchen, Kellie was still on the phone.

He checked his watch and saw he had an hour. He was hoping to stop by the coffee shop and pick up something on his way to see Linda and he had to collect the crutches from the pharmacy.

Kellie put her hand over the mouthpiece. "I'll be in touch soon and I think I can save you a few hundred thousand off the asking price." She gave him the thumbs up and was still talking when he left.

Max purchased the crutches and stopped by the Harbor Coffee and Books to get drinks and treats for Linda. Hayley rushed to him. "How's Linda?"

"She's doing better. I stopped by to get her a treat and a chai. I'm going to head over to the hospital now and check her out today."

Hayley made two of the chai tea lattes and boxed some treats. "Don't dare try to pay for these. If I know Sam she would have delivered this to Linda herself if she were in town. I'll let her know what I did, so don't worry," said Hayley, as she handed Max his care package.

"Thanks, Hayley. Sam and Jeff will be back today. I'm glad since I think we'll need their help. I'll see you soon," said Max, as he darted for the door.

He pulled into the hospital with two minutes to spare. He balanced the drinks and treats and left the crutches for later. When he arrived at Linda's room, she was sitting on the edge of the bed, dressed, looking ready to go.

"Wow, you look good this morning," he said. "And I have a treat for you," he showed her the box and the drink carrier.

"Sounds great. I've been a good girl and the nurse told me I've done everything I need to get out of here," she motioned him over. "And Jen brought me some clothes and stuff, so I was able to get ready."

He handed her the cup and she took a long drink. "Oh, that tastes heavenly," she purred. She dug into the bag and pulled out an almond croissant. She savored a bite and closed her eyes.

Max joined her and selected a cinnamon roll dripping with icing. "So," he said, "I found a house I love. I told Kellie to get the ball rolling. It's perfect."

"You're fast. Tell me more about it," she urged, slipping more of the pastry into her mouth.

Max went on to describe the house and gave her the Mitchell Bay Road address, explaining it was near the resort Jeff's family owned. He brought out his phone and scrolled through all the photos. She oohed and aahed over the slate and wood floors and the beautiful wood ceilings. "What a fabulous kitchen. It all reminds me of Sam's style."

"Yeah, I thought so too. And check out the stone patio, complete with an outdoor kitchen."

Linda continued to look and raved about the yard. She didn't remember doing anything at the house, but wanted to see it in person. Dr. Brown's jolly voice interrupted them, "Good morning, Linda. How are you today?"

"Much better, thanks. I just need to learn how to maneuver with this cast," she pointed to her leg.

"I looked at the x-ray I asked for this morning and everything looks good. I don't want you to put any weight on your leg, so you'll need to use crutches and I'm hoping in about a month we can get rid of this bulky cast and get you in a walking boot. It takes time to heal," he said patting her thigh. "I'll have the nurse come in and show you how to use the crutches and then once they do your paperwork you're free to go."

"I'll take good care of her," said Max.

"I expect nothing less and I hope to see you around the hospital soon, Dr. Sullivan."

Dr. Brown held Linda's hand. "You take care and call me anytime if you need anything. And get in to see me in a month." He slipped her a card and jotted his home and cell numbers on it.

Max retrieved the new crutches and a couple of nurses demonstrated how to use them and had Linda practice in the hall. They showed her a video on how to use crutches on stairs, but told her not to go up and down more than a couple of them and made sure the crutches were adjusted properly. Max gathered the bag Jen had brought and loaded Linda's items in the car.

The nurse wheeled Linda out to the loading zone and Max helped her get in his SUV. They made a quick trip back to the pharmacy to retrieve her prescriptions and drove out to Sam's.

He parked in the garage and helped Linda with the steps into the house. He guided her through the house and towards Sam's room, trying to keep Lucy from blocking her way. "I feel awkward taking their bedroom. I could sleep in a chair, you know," she said, as she shuffled to the doorway.

"I've known Sam my whole life and I know she will demand you sleep in a bed, so let's get settled and when they get here we can talk about more permanent solutions."

Linda was tired by the time she got into the room and sat on the edge of the bed. Max got her situated with pillows to elevate her leg and turned on the television. He brought her a cold drink and sat on the other side of the bed. His cell phone rang and he saw it was Kellie. He had a short conversation ending with, "That sounds terrific. I can stop by this afternoon."

"Well, sounds like good news."

Max's eyes twinkled, "Yes, she said she talked with the owners. It's her listing so she knows them. She negotiated a deal for me and I can sign the paperwork. They were excited to have a cash offer and Kellie thinks we can get it closed in less than a month."

"Maybe we could take a ride over there when Sam and Jeff get here?"

"That sounds like a great idea. You take a nap and I'll putter around here and see what we can create for dinner later."

While Max was busy in the kitchen, he heard the dogs bark and they went tearing through the house. Either their owners were home or they were being attacked by squirrels. He heard the garage open and the two came traipsing in with their luggage.

"Welcome home," said Max, as he moved to hug them both.

"Is Linda here?" asked Sam.

"Yes, she's asleep on your bed. She doesn't feel right about taking your room, but I told her you wouldn't take no for an answer. I thought we may be able to figure something out, but for the first few days I'd like her to have some help."

"Of course. We'll talk to her and make her stay. It will be fun to have you both here," said Jeff.

Sam and Jeff went on to describe their stay and showed Max the pictures they had taken. They had hiked in Moran State Park, went for long bike rides and enjoyed the peace of the sanctuary provided by the resort. Jeff glanced at his watch, "In fact, we liked biking so much, we decided to make it a habit here at home. I have one, but I want to run into town and get a bike for Sam." He bent and kissed Sam and promised to be back soon.

Max asked to tag along so he could stop by Kellie's and sign the offer and talk her out of a key so he could show the place to Linda. Sam finished the dinner prep and took the dogs outside to play. After they ran and tumbled on the beach and shook all over Sam, she trotted with them back to the house. She heard some noise coming from the bedroom and darted down the hall to check on Linda. She found her struggling to reach her crutches. "Hey, let me help you," she said, as she placed them at her sides.

"It's good to see you, Sam. I appreciate you letting me stay here. I feel like such a fool," said Linda.

"Nonsense, it's not a problem. I feel horrible you're hurt. How're you doing?"

"Tired, but not much pain now. Although, I haven't done anything strenuous. I was hoping to take a ride over to see the house Max found."

"We'd like that. Jeff and Max ran into town and he was going to get the key from Kellie so we could all take a look after dinner," she smiled. "Max said it's right by the resort. Jeff said he thought a family from the city owned it, but he didn't know them."

Sam stood guard over Linda as she clunked across the floor. She got her situated on the deck with some iced tea and started the grill for the chicken.

Sam had finished plating the chicken and tossing a salad when she heard the boys arrive. Jeff bent over to hug Linda where she sat.

They chatted about the excitement of Max's new house and discussed Linda's situation. Sam and Jeff insisted Linda stay as long as necessary.

"Oh, I hate to be a burden to any of you," said Linda. "I don't know what to do. It's clear I can't be alone for right now. I need too much help," she dropped her eyes.

"We're happy to have you, so don't worry. You would do the same to help any of us," said Sam. After dinner they loaded Linda into Max's car and Jeff and Sam took their own because they planned to go into Friday Harbor.

They parked on the driveway made of pavers, staggered in an eye-catching pattern of earth tones. Max handed Jeff the key and he stayed behind to help Linda out of the SUV. Not only did the crutches delay Linda, but she stopped to look at plants and shrubs along the way. "Oh, this yard is something else. It's like you have your own private park."

"Wait till you see the back," he grinned, guiding her to make sure she didn't fall.

They arrived at the slate entry way and Max cautioned Linda about the one small step down into the house. Cherry hardwood covered the main pathways through the house and the kitchen housed matching cherry cabinets. Sam and Jeff had wandered off, so Max showed Linda the kitchen first. "Wow, the granite is perfect," said Linda, as she ran her hand over the smooth cool surface.

The formal dining room was adjacent to the kitchen and had floor to ceiling windows showcasing a stunning view of the bay. He led her through the open design to the great room, with a large stone fireplace. As she shuffled down the hall they found Sam and Jeff in the master bedroom. The bedroom was huge with a curved wall of windows looking into the backyard and beyond at the water. The bathroom was done in slate and granite with a huge walk-in shower and a corner soaking tub.

"Max, this is gorgeous," said Sam poking into closets. "It's big, but it has a cozy feel about it."

"Yes, it's a little big, but I fell in love with it. Plus when the kids come visit, I'll have room for them and if I'm lucky maybe some grandchildren someday."

They roamed through the rest of the house, checking out the additional bedrooms and bathrooms. There was a room designed as an office and one intended as a library, lined with bookshelves and outfitted with a fireplace. Linda skipped the loft, but the others tackled the stairs and hung over to wave at her below.

"Come outside, you guys need to see the patio and deck," motioned Max. "Kellie told me today all the outdoor furniture stays and it appears to be in terrific condition." Jeff ogled the built in grill and outdoor kitchen. There were six chaise lounges facing the water and a huge table with sixteen chairs. There was also an outdoor living room set on the stone patio adjacent to the great room. The kitchen area sported a granite bar with high chairs for additional seating. Several containers for flowers were stationed around the patio, but they were all empty.

Linda eyed the empty pottery. "You need some flowers in your containers, Max. I could help you with that," she grinned.

"Yes, you have free reign," he put his arm around her.

"It's a spectacular home, Max. I know a family from the city had it built as a vacation home, but I don't know much about it. A local firm built it and they do quality work, so I'm confident in the construction," said Jeff.

"I like how they incorporated an outdoor living area. And you'll get a breeze through the house when it's open." Linda gestured to the row of glass doors that could be opened or closed, depending on the weather. "What a perfect place to relax."

"I agree, Max. I can't wait for you to move in. And Becky will enjoy helping you coordinate everything. She's an expert and has all the contacts from my recent move."

He nodded. "I'll call her once we know a date. All my stuff is in storage. I'll have to get it all here and decide what works."

"We're going to stop and see Charlie and we should be home within an hour or so," said Jeff, as he took Sam's hand.

Max helped Linda back into the car and they drove along the narrow paved ribbon back to the main road and on to Sam's. He could tell she was tired and guided her into Sam's bedroom. "Let's get you ready for bed," he suggested.

At her insistence, he left her alone with a nightgown and told her to let him know if she needed help. After about twenty minutes he heard her, "Max, could you come here?"

He hurried and found her with her nightgown on and her shorts stuck on the cast. "Let me help you with those," he offered as he bent over and slid the shorts down past he cast.

She sighed and rested back on the pillows. "Could you hand me my notebook?" She watched him go through her bag. "I want to make a list of things I want you to check on at the shop and the nursery over the next few weeks. I have been fooling myself into thinking I could work part of the day, but I know I can't."

"Sure, I can do anything you need. I have nothing planned, so we can hang out here and you can send me on errands," he smiled.

They heard Jeff and Sam come in. Max hollered, "We're in the bedroom."

Sam and Jeff both came in and sat on the sofa. "We stopped by the shop and I stole a couple slices of pie for dessert."

"None for me," Linda said. "I'm used to working all day and without moving I'm going to gain weight, so I've got to cut back."

"I'll take some," smiled Max.

"And we stopped and got a movie, since we knew you two were going to miss the movie in the park tonight. We found *North by Northwest,* which is the one they're showing, so you won't miss anything," said Sam, as she slipped it into the player.

Linda smiled and grasped Max's hand. "How thoughtful of you guys."

"Okay, I'll deliver you some pie and then Jeff and I are going to hit the hay. Tomorrow, I can help you with a shower too, Linda. We'll get a system to keep your cast dry. I'm going to work in the shop and Jeff has a job to start, so you guys will have the run of the place tomorrow," Sam said, as she bent to give Max a kiss on the cheek.

"I'm working not far from here tomorrow, so if you need something, call. I'll be back before Sam and handle dinner," said Jeff, as he put his arm around Sam and led her out.

Sam delivered pie and cold drinks for both of them and found them glued to the movie, watching the opening scene on the busy streets of New York City. Sam extinguished the lights and headed to the guestroom.

Linda snuggled into Max, resting her head against his shoulder as they watched the classic Hitchcock film. When it was over Linda squeezed his hand, "This was nice."

"I agree. I could sit like this with you every night," he bent and kissed her on the lips. "But, you need to rest."

He helped her get situated and kissed her once more before shutting her door and making his way upstairs. Linda fell asleep savoring the gentle brush of Max's lips on hers and the warm feeling of sharing an evening with a man she cared about. *I can't say I'm glad to be hurt, but I can't deny how much I'm enjoying spending time with Max and letting him take care of me. I haven't cared for a man since Walt, but I know this feeling and it wasn't the drugs talking. It's serious.*

Twelve

Tuesday morning Sam helped Linda use a garbage bag to cover her cast and they worked on a method that allowed Linda to sit on the tile shower seat and wash her hair. She needed help getting out, but was able to shower by herself. Getting dressed was another hassle and Sam had to help her maneuver her legs into her panties and shorts.

"Whew, it felt good to take a shower, but what a work out," said Linda, once she was dressed. "Sorry to put you through nursing duties."

"Don't worry. Let's go out and get you some breakfast and then I'm going to head into the shop and get some work done. Max already left this morning with your lists. He's planning to bring back all the paperwork and your laptop so you can do your books at home."

"That'll keep me busy. I do all my own financial stuff and sign the checks, so I know what's going on. Lucas and Sara can handle organizing and running things, but nobody does the books."

"I'm lucky to have Becky. She's a wizard at that stuff. If you get in a jam, call her, she'd be glad to help." Sam made Linda some cereal and fruit and got her situated at the island.

"Go ahead, I'll be fine. Max will be back soon and he told me yesterday he wants me to start doing some exercises in your gym to limit my muscle loss during this ordeal. I'll be supervised soon enough," she smiled.

"Okay. Jeff will be home in the afternoon and he's going to get things ready for dinner. We're going to take a bike ride before we eat. If you need anything before we get here, give us a call."

Linda busied herself with breakfast and television until Max arrived. He reported back on Linda's list and handed her the laptop. "Here are all the reports you wanted and your checkbooks. But, before you start, let's get you going on a few exercises."

He adjusted the equipment in the gym and showed Linda what he wanted her to do, taking care not to involve her bad leg. "I'm used to a fair amount of physical activity, so this is a good idea. I'm afraid when this cast comes off, my leg will be out of shape."

He monitored her movements and guided her as she completed a routine. "By the way, Sara said to tell you Sam's bouquet is done and she has the flowers pressed like you wanted. I ran into Ellie and she said she put the small one year anniversary cake in Sam's freezer at the shop. She made them a special little red velvet cake."

"That's a good idea. When I feel better, we can take a trip to the shop and I'll collect the bouquet and put the pressed flowers in a frame for Sam."

"I also heard the local authorities are close to charging Brenda with the arson at Sam's shop a few months ago. It sounds like they have enough evidence to prove it was deliberate. She's standing by her story of thinking the planters on the deck were trash bins. I hope they convict her and teach her a lesson so she'll leave Sam and Jeff alone.

"I couldn't agree more. She's a heartless woman who enjoys causing grief for others. I think she's actually a very sad person and when she sees anyone happy it makes her jealous and then she acts out. I always hoped she would move away." Linda looked down, "I seriously considered moving from the island after she humiliated me by breaking off my engagement. But, I loved my home and being around my parents. Walt left, so that helped me not have to relive it, although his parents are here."

"I, for one, am glad you stayed so I could meet you. I'm even happy Sam got divorced from Marty and moved here. It's working out great for me," he laughed and kissed her forehead.

They finished in the gym and Max suggested Linda work on her books in Sam's office. He retrieved her computer and all the paperwork and set her up at the table. "I got a call from Kellie while I was out and my offer was accepted. She's going to rush things and thinks it will close around the beginning of September."

"How exciting. That reminds me, I want to treat you to some plants and flowers for your containers. When it's all yours maybe I could talk you into hauling some things from the nursery and I could work on them. You could help," she grinned.

"Sounds terrific. I'm going to call Becky and let her know and see if she has the time to help me coordinate moving all my stuff."

Linda worked for a couple of hours and hobbled out to the kitchen to find Max fixing lunch. As they were finishing, Jeff arrived.

"Hey guys. I finished early today. How are things going?"

"Linda's been working on her books and we did some exercises in the gym. I told Linda when I was in town I heard they were close to charging Brenda."

"Yeah, I heard the same from Chris and a couple of other guys at the firehouse. It serves her right. I hope she goes to jail and we won't see her again."

Jeff excused himself to change clothes and they sat on the deck to enjoy the afternoon. Jeff started some salmon marinating for dinner and prepped some veggies to grill. Soon the dogs went darting to the door and he knew Sam was home.

She greeted him with a kiss and stuck a box in the fridge. "I hope that's for me," he teased.

"Yes, I brought a pie home for everyone to enjoy."

"Let's go for a ride and I've got everything ready to throw on the grill when we get back."

Sam ran to change clothes and they hollered goodbye to Max and Linda and set out for a ride. They rode out towards Linda's nursery enjoying the sunshine and light traffic. Sam hadn't ridden a bike in years, but found she enjoyed it, especially with Jeff.

They turned around and were heading back to Sam's. Her head was down when she heard Jeff shout, "Watch out, Sam!" She saw a red car coming right at her. He shoved his bike into hers and knocked her to the shoulder where she tumbled over the edge and rolled. She heard a horrible thud and the crunch of metal. When she lifted her head and crawled up the embankment, she spotted Jeff sprawled on the grassy shoulder and his mangled bike several feet away. There was no sign of the red car.

She dashed to Jeff, clutching his hand and shouting at him. He had a gash on his leg and cuts on his face and head. She tapped his cheeks with her hand trying to wake him. "Jeff, Jeff, please can you hear me?"

She fumbled with her cell phone and dialed 911. She reported the accident and asked for medical help telling the operator Jeff Cooper had been hit by a car. She felt Jeff's chest and wasn't sure if he was breathing or not. She was afraid to move him, but tilted his head back to attempt mouth to mouth.

As she was doing this, she heard the squeal of tires and in moments Chris, a fellow firefighter, was at her side. "I heard it on my pager and rushed out here." He began to assess Jeff and continued the rescue breaths. Sam called Max and although shaken was able to tell him the highlights and asked him to call Sean Doyle to help Jeff.

They heard sirens and the police were the first to arrive followed by an ambulance and then Dr. Doyle. They moved Sam out of the way as they began working on Jeff. Chris came over and told Sam they had called for a helicopter to take Jeff directly to Harborview in Seattle. Sam knew it was part of the University of Washington and a top trauma center. She sank to her knees knowing this meant Jeff's condition was serious.

Max arrived next and talked with his friend, Dr. Doyle. He came over to Sam and helped Chris support her. "Sam, honey, I talked to Sean. He's going to ride with Jeff to Seattle. He thinks it is best to get him there so they can treat him quickly."

"Did he wake up?" she whispered, fighting the tears.

"No, he's still unconscious."

"Is he going to make it?"

Max hugged her close. "I don't know. But, Sean will do everything possible."

"I have to get there," she panicked.

"I know. I'll drive you. Charlie is coming too. Linda talked to Jen and she's going to stay here until we know more. She'll stay with Linda at the house and we'll go to the hospital."

Sam nodded, unable to speak.

They heard the sound of a helicopter and watched it land on the road. Jeff was swept up and Dr. Doyle jumped in with him and the chopper faded away towards the mainland.

A deputy approached them. "Mrs. Cooper, I'm Deputy Douglas. I'm sorry to intrude right now, but need to get your statement and then you can go to the hospital. First off, are you hurt?"

"No, not really. Jeff rammed me..." she began and then took a breath. "He said to watch out and I looked up and saw a red car headed right for us. He shoved me with his bike and I went off the shoulder and rolled down the embankment. Then I heard an awful sound and when I climbed from the edge I found him alongside the road and no sign of the car."

"Did you get a license plate or see the driver?"

"No, it all happened too fast."

"Tell me more about the car. Did it have two doors or four? Do you know the model?"

"It was a small two door and if I had to guess, just by the body line, I would say it was a Porsche and a bright red color."

"Okay, very good, Mrs. Cooper. I'll take your cell number and home number and I'll get working on this. We'll be in touch. I hope your husband is okay. We'll be working the scene and when we're done, I'll make sure your bike is returned to your house."

Max thanked the deputy and took Sam by the hand and led her to his car. When they got back to Sam's they found Charlie and Jen there. When Sam's eyes met Charlie's, she lost it and began sobbing. Charlie hugged her as they both cried.

Max told them what little they knew and suggested they get going since it was a drive from the ferry landing to Seattle. Sam threw some things in an overnight bag and hugged Jen and Linda goodbye. "I'll call when I know anything." Zoe and Bailey both whined, sensing her distress. She kneeled on the floor and hugged them both, tears streaming down her face.

Charlie sat in the back and they hurried to the dock. Luckily the ferry was boarding when they arrived. Max drove the car on and they decided to sit in the car for the hour ride. Sam and Charlie were both too nervous to do anything. Max kept checking his phone for texts from Sean, but there weren't any.

"Dad's in good shape. Do you think he'll be okay, Max?" asked Charlie.

"He's in terrific physical condition and that helps a lot in these situations. I'm sure they'll take care of the gash on his leg and then they'll have to run some tests to see about his head injuries. Usually head injuries take time to heal and the patient can be unconscious for hours, days, or sometimes weeks. But, your dad is strong."

The hour ride seemed to take days, but they finally reached Anacortes and then Max drove them at the highest speeds he dared. They made it to the hospital in just over an hour.

Max approached the desk and was pleased to find out they were already expected. They were directed to a small private waiting room and Dr. Doyle walked in. Sam ran to him. "Oh, Sean, how is he?"

"He's stable. They took care of the large cut on his leg and got it stitched. They ran some tests and found swelling in his brain, so they're treating that and monitoring him. There is also brain activity, which is terrific. He's on a ventilator, because he's not able to breathe on his own."

Sam began shaking and hugged herself. Max stepped over to put his arm around her.

"I know it sounds grim, but he's doing as well as possible. We'll know more as time passes. You need to be prepared since these types of injuries can take some time, so don't be discouraged if he remains unconscious. It's actually the body's way of healing. The brain needs to rest."

"Can we see him?" asked Charlie, his eyes filled with tears.

"I'll come and get you as soon as possible. It will be a few hours before they have him ready." He handed Sam a plastic bag, "I thought you'd want to hang on to Jeff's wallet and I was able to get his wedding ring off without cutting it. You keep it safe for him until he's up and around."

Max volunteered to go get Sam a blanket and some hot drinks for everyone. Sean followed him. "So, anything you didn't say in there, Sean?"

"Not much. It's quite serious. He's not responsive, so it's hard to say, but it's early. I'd tell her to go get some rest while she can, but I don't think she'd do it."

"No, I'm sure she won't. If anything changes, let me know."

"You bet. I'm going to stay until I know more and then snag a lift back so I can get to work in the morning."

Max returned with blankets and drinks and found Becky and Brad had arrived. Sam was curled into Becky and Brad was speaking in a low voice with Charlie. Max placed a blanket around Sam and did the same for Charlie.

They waited for hours speaking only in whispers and most of the time sat in silence. Dr. Doyle came back and offered to lead Sam and Charlie back to see Jeff. They both jumped at the chance. "Don't be scared by all the equipment. As he improves, things will be removed, but right now he needs it all."

He led them into a room where the lights were low and the whoosh of the ventilator was the first sound they heard. Machines beeped and Jeff lay motionless. He had bandages on his face and a fresh wound was visible on his shaved head. Sam took one hand and Charlie the other. She prayed he would squeeze her hand, but felt nothing. They spoke in low tones to Jeff and told him where he was and assured him they were there and he would be okay. Sam watched her tears splash onto the sheets of his bed, but couldn't stop them.

After several minutes, Dr. Sean came back and motioned to them. "You guys should go get some sleep and come back in the morning. They're going to monitor him tonight and watch the swelling. Right now, it's not getting any worse, which is an excellent sign. They'll want to get him off the ventilator as soon as they can, but he needs rest. This could take some time, so don't get discouraged," he gave Sam a hug. "I'm going to head back, I need to be at work in a few hours, but I've made arrangements to get access to Jeff's charts and updates each day. I'll pass on everything I know to Max. Jeff has the best neurologists with him and they'll take good care of him."

"I appreciate all your help tonight," said Sam, as they navigated the maze of halls to get back to the others.

Charlie shook Dr. Sean's hand and followed Sam into the waiting room. Becky's house was about five miles from the hospital and she already had things organized for them to stay overnight at her house. "Sam, you can stay as long as you need to, but you need to get some rest, so you're strong for Jeff."

"I know, but I feel horrible leaving him here so alone."

Max put his arm around her. "I know you do, but all you'll do is wear yourself out sitting in his room. Let's go to Becky's. We'll talk to his doctors tomorrow and see if we can work out a schedule. If they'll allow someone to stay at his bedside. If…" he paused, "and it's a big if, they allow it, you have to promise you'll let others help so you don't sit all day and all night."

Sam nodded her head. "I will. I just want him to be okay," she sobbed.

Charlie wrapped her in a hug, "Me too, Sam."

Max followed Brad to their house and Becky assigned rooms to everyone and hugged Sam and Charlie. "You guys try to get some sleep tonight. Things will look better tomorrow."

Sam checked her cell phone before climbing into bed and noticed she had a voicemail. It was from Deputy Douglas and he asked her to call at her earliest convenience.

Sam hugged her pillow to her. Her mind would not stop reliving the accident. Her throat ached from the effort it took to contain her sobs. She gasped as she lost the struggle and hoped the pillow would muffle the sound. As fresh tears soaked Becky's crisp pillowcase, she flashed back to when Jeff yelled at her on the road. She knew if he hadn't pushed her, she would have been the one hit. He had sacrificed himself to save her. *Please don't let him die.*

Thirteen

Max and Becky were talking in hushed tones so as not to wake Charlie and Sam. It was after three in the morning when they arrived at Becky's and Max was hoping Sam could sleep for a few hours. Shortly after nine o'clock Sam came downstairs. She was showered and dressed, ready to go. Charlie was not far behind her. Becky did her best to get them to eat some breakfast.

"I have an update from Sean and he said nothing has changed overnight. No increase in swelling and things are basically the same as they were last night. They've begun weaning Jeff from the ventilator. They would like to get him off of it today, if he does well. The longer he's on it, the more risk there is for other problems like pneumonia. He's maintaining right now and taking some breaths on his own, so that's all good news. I also got the approval to have one person in Jeff's room day and night. Becky and I can make a schedule to help you, Sam."

Sam nodded. "I need to call the deputy in Friday Harbor. He left me a voicemail last night." She found her cell and dialed, moving into the living room.

Becky asked Charlie, "Did you call your sister?"

"Yes. I told her I'd let her know if she should come today. I'm not sure what to tell her. She doesn't have a lot of time accrued at work and the ticket would be expensive, but if he..." he couldn't finish and stared into his half eaten breakfast.

Max grasped his hand. "I know Sam will pay for a ticket. Ask her to come out when she gets off Friday when she can stay for the weekend. Tell her to pick the flights and Becky will book it and have it waiting for her at the airport. I don't think she needs to rush out here. Usually these types of injuries take time and we'll know more each day."

Charlie looked up and nodded. "I'll call her and let her know. I just needed someone to decide for me." He took his phone and headed back to his room.

Max had called Linda earlier and also had spoken with Jen. Jen and Megan had stayed at Sam's and their plan was to stay with Linda until Max returned. Jen could help Linda get ready before she went to work each morning. He gave them the same update and Jen said she'd let her mom and Jeremy know the latest.

Max told Linda they were going to work out a schedule. Jen planned to spend her days off on Sunday and Monday at the hospital. He knew he couldn't convince Sam to leave, so he and Becky plotted a timetable that included Sam each day. According to Jen, Charlie had a couple of people at the hardware store committed to running things in the short term. They scheduled Charlie to stay for the rest of the week and had him going home Saturday night. Becky could cover any shifts needed since she was so close.

Jeremy offered to come and stay with Jeff anytime they needed. Max knew how hard it was for him to get away during the tourist season, which made his offer all the more touching. Max planned to go back on Saturday night, depending on how things were progressing. He knew Linda needed help and hated to leave her alone any longer than necessary.

Hayley had reported they had the coffee shop covered until Kyle had to leave for school. He was starting at the University of Washington and had to be there in mid-September. Rachel and Megan were both seniors and once school started at the end of August could only work weekends and after school. Max knew the shop would need some extra help until Labor Day, when the tourists left. He thought it might be best for him to go back to the island and help cover the shop and take care of Linda. He had a feeling Jeff would be in the hospital for several weeks; possibly longer.

Charlie returned and conveyed Ashley's plans to text him the flights. He would forward the information to Becky. "Thanks for your help."

"Not a problem. I checked the flights already. If you give me her number, I'll text the possibilities for Friday and get going on it."

Charlie nodded and showed Becky the screen with Ashley's information. Sam came around the corner, looking ashen and shaking. Max jumped out of his chair, "What's wrong?"

"The deputy, he, he," she stuttered. "He told me they identified the car from my description and found it with damage they matched to Jeff's bike. He said the lab will test to confirm, but the car is Brenda's."

"That bitch!" shouted Becky.

"She claims someone stole her car, but the deputy didn't sound like they believed it. He said they're going to continue the investigation, but asked me about past encounters with her. I had to explain the whole permit thing with the expansion at the shop and the stories from Jeff and his family about her hoping to be with him. He also knew about the arson and confirmed they were days away from charging her with that." She steadied herself on the back of a chair. "I can't believe she would go this far. I kept replaying the accident last night and realized the car was headed for me. Jeff yelled and rammed me out of the way or it would have hit me." Sam's shoulders shook as sobs racked her body.

Max got her to a chair and stroked her arm. Charlie was already on his phone with Jen. Becky was seething and paced her kitchen floor, finally deciding to step outside for some air, so as not to upset Sam further.

"Sam," Max said in a calm voice, "we need to focus on Jeff right now and getting him better. I know all of this is overwhelming, but the police will handle Brenda. Let's get to the hospital and visit Jeff."

She nodded and went to the bathroom to splash some water on her face. Max went over the schedule with Charlie and he confirmed he would leave after he visited with Ashley Saturday. "Maybe by then Dad will be awake and can come back to the island."

"I hope so, but like I said, be prepared for this to take time," cautioned Max.

Charlie nodded as Max's cell phone rang. "Hi, Jen," he answered. He nodded as he listened. "Wow, that's terrific. I know Sam will appreciate all the help."

Sam walked in as Max was saying goodbye to Jen. She gave Charlie a big hug. "What did Jen want?"

"She had some great news. Steve, Jeff's fireman buddy, reserved a boat and enough firemen to shuttle people back and forth whenever we need to go. He wanted you to have the convenience of being able to come and go and transport any of Jeff's family or friends who wanted to come without the hassle of driving all the way to Anacortes. He said he can dock at Shilshole Bay, which is only a few miles from the hospital."

Sam touched her hand to her chest. "How thoughtful. That will make it easier for everyone. What a great guy. Jeff's lucky to have such wonderful friends," she said, as her eyes filled with tears again.

Max snapped her out of it by telling her to get her things so they could head over to the hospital. Becky was staying home for the morning to make sure Ashley got her plane tickets and a hotel.

When they arrived at the hospital, Jeff's neurologist, Dr. Dawson, met with them. He explained about the swelling and was optimistic it had subsided slightly. He reiterated they would be working to get Jeff off the ventilator and he was hopeful that would happen today. He gave Max his cell and home number and told him to call if he needed anything and had ordered a recliner put in Jeff's room so those staying the night would be comfortable.

They all thanked him and while Max waited with Charlie, Sam was ushered back through the critical care unit to Jeff's room. He looked the same, with tubes running everywhere, but his pale face looked thinner. She sank into the chair and took his limp hand, squeezing it as tight as she dared. "Jeff, honey, it's me. I'm right here. Charlie and Max are outside and they'll come see you soon. We'll make sure someone is always here."

She slipped out to let Charlie and Max have a turn, but was back at Jeff's side within the hour. She decided to talk to Jeff like she would any other day and rambled on about Becky's house and told him Steve had organized a brigade of firemen to transport friends and family with a boat from Friday Harbor to the marina. She told him Ashley was coming in a few days and Jen would be with him on the weekend. She babbled nonstop for several hours, talking about their trip to Orcas Island and how much she loved him.

She fingered the sea glass earrings Jeff had bought her on their honeymoon trip. Max came in through the door, "Sam, how about we get some lunch and Charlie can sit with his dad for a bit?"

She eased her hand out of Jeff's and nodded. He forced her to leave the grounds and go to a small café a few blocks away. She had a cup of soup as Max explained he would be going back to Friday Harbor on Saturday. "Ashley will be here late Friday and Becky booked her into a hotel near the hospital. Steve is going to bring Jen over on Saturday when she's done at work and Charlie and I will go back. Jen will stay until Monday night and I can come back on Tuesday, if you need me."

"I hope he's better by then, Max. It's hard to see him so helpless. He's such a strong guy and always active, so seeing him in that bed is horrible. I'm terrified he won't wake up or if he does he'll have problems. This whole thing makes me want to find Brenda and beat her senseless."

"Sam, his signs are good. Like I told you, he needs rest and the brain needs to heal. He's lucky he landed on the grassy shoulder and not the road, his injuries could have been worse. I want them to get him off the vent and I'll feel better."

"I'm not going home until I know he's okay and I can talk to him. Could you ask Linda to put some more clothes together and send them with Jen on Saturday?"

"Sure, I'll be talking to her." They continued talking about what Sam needed done at the shop and she explained the ordering process to Max and told him Becky could handle all the reports and bookkeeping as long as he emailed her the daily reports.

Max paid the check and tried to set a slow pace back to the hospital. "Let's have Charlie stay the rest of the day and you can come back this evening and stay all night. I'll relieve you in the morning." He put his arm around her shoulder, "And, before you argue, let me remind you we had a deal that you would accept help."

"I know we did, but it breaks my heart to leave him." They walked in companionable silence until they reached the hospital doors. "Okay, Max. I'll go to Becky's and rest. After dinner I'll come back to relieve Charlie."

When they arrived at Jeff's unit, they found Charlie in the waiting room. "They asked me to leave while they take the ventilator out. That's good news, right?"

"Yes, that's fantastic news," nodded Max.

Sam wanted to wait and get the report on Jeff before she left and as she was checking her cell for messages, Dr. Dawson opened the door.

"One of you can go back in. We've removed the ventilator and he's doing well on his own. He's not conscious, but his breathing is fine. This is a big step in the right direction, guys."

Sam checked on Jeff before she left and thought he looked better without the tube in his mouth and was relieved to have the horrible hissing sound of the machine gone. She kissed his forehead and squeezed his hand, "I'll be back tonight. Charlie will be here until then. I love you."

Max drove Sam to Becky's. After some persuasion, she retired to her room to rest until dinner. Max and Becky went over a plan to keep everything running at the shop. He planned to email the daily reports to her and would handle ordering and help the kids, unless things changed and Sam needed him back. Becky worked on dinner and when Brad got home from work, they sat down to a home cooked meal of meatloaf, mashed potatoes and gravy, and biscuits. Sam looked rested and dug into the ultimate comfort food. She brightened as she shared the good news about Jeff getting rid of the ventilator.

"When ya'll get back to the hospital, tell Charlie to get right over here. I'll keep him a plate in the oven and then he can get some rest," said Becky, as she cleared the table.

Sam glanced at her watch, "I will. I'm going over and I'll see you guys in the morning."

"Okay, if you need anything, call me," said Max, as he hugged her at the door.

Charlie rang the bell about fifteen minutes later. "Sam said you made meatloaf," he smiled. Becky took his plate out of the oven and they visited with him while he devoured the food and took Becky up on her offer of seconds.

"I think he looked better today. Probably because that big tube was gone," he said, as he mopped up the last of the gravy with a biscuit. "I'm gonna call Hayley and then hit the sack. I told Sam I'd be there by eight tomorrow." Becky promised breakfast before he left and hugged him as he trundled to bed.

Max wished them a goodnight and pressed the button to dial Linda. She answered on the first ring. "Hey, how are you?"

"Doing well. How's Jeff?"

"He made progress today. They took him off the ventilator and he's breathing on his own. Still unconscious, but it's good news."

"Oh, that's good. Bailey and Zoe look so sad and miss them."

"I bet they do and I miss you."

"Me too. When are you coming back?"

"I'm going to leave on Saturday night. Steve is bringing Jen over and he's going to take Charlie and me back."

"Jen's been a big help to me. I feel bad she's had to stay with me."

"It's better she's keeping busy. I'm going to try to cover for Sam at the shop until she gets back, unless she needs me."

"Oh, does that mean you'll be baking pies?" laughed Linda.

"Uh, no. That would close down her shop in a heartbeat. Anyway, I'll be there to help at the shop and take care of you. I suspect Jeff will be in the hospital for several weeks and if I know Sam, she won't come home until he does."

"I wish my leg wasn't a mess and I could be a lot more help. Sara has been bringing me all the paperwork from the shop and the nursery each day, so I've been keeping busy, but I'd like to help Sam."

"We can take good care of her shop and her dogs and that will be a big help. By the way, she asked if you could pack her some more clothes and send them with Jen on Saturday."

"Okay, I'll get that done. Be prepared when you get back. Brenda and the hit and run are the talk of the town. Nobody believes her story about her car being stolen. I think all of her lies are catching up with her."

"Well, this should put her in prison for sure, especially with the arson charge too. What a psycho."

"They say if you wait long enough, people like her get their comeuppance. I guess it's time."

"Yeah, I hope it's over soon. Sam is doing better today, but she's going to wear herself out. Becky does a good job of making sure she eats, so she'll keep an eye on her." He yawned, "I better get to bed. You take good care of your leg and remember your exercises."

"Yes, doctor," she snickered. "I can't wait to see you on Saturday."

"Me too. I'd like to talk to you when you aren't under the influence of drugs and I can see your beautiful face. I love you, Linda."

"I love you too, Max. And I haven't taken my pain pills since lunch," she laughed.

Fourteen

They developed a rhythm over the next several days with Charlie taking the days and Sam the evenings and Max overlapping part of each of their shifts. Jeff's vital signs remained strong, but there was no change in his responsiveness. Becky made sure everyone was fed and rested and handled the business end of Sam's shop.

Friday brought steel gray clouds hovering in the sky and rain all day. As Sam stared out of the window of Jeff's room, driving rain slapped against the dark glass. Ashley's flight had arrived and Becky made the trip to the airport and got her checked in at the hotel a few blocks from the hospital. The hotel provided a shuttle service to the hospital allowing Ashley to come and go as often as she wished.

Becky tried to engage Ashley in conversation all the way from the airport without much success. But Becky could carry on a conversation with a fence post and was unrelenting. "Charlie said you started a new job. Do you like it?"

"Yeah, it's fine," said Ashley.

"What do you do?"

"Secretarial stuff."

"That's how I started with Sam. I enjoy organizing and keeping things running smoothly. It's important work."

"Hmm mmm."

"Charlie and Max are with Sam at the hospital, waiting for you. We've been covering your dad in shifts, but everyone wanted to see you."

"Okay."

"Here we are," Becky said as she pulled to the door. "You go on ahead and I'll park and see you upstairs."

Ashley got out and followed the signs to her dad's unit. She checked in with the nurse and was directed to the private waiting room. Upon seeing her, Charlie rushed to her and hugged her. "Hi, Ash. I'm glad you're here."

"Hi, Charlie. Can I go see dad now?"

"Sam's in there, but she said to bring you back when you got here. She likes to make sure someone is always with him."

Max suggested he take her back, since the staff knew he was a doctor and let him have more leeway. "How was your flight, Ashley?"

"Fine."

"Good. Here's the unit," he pointed to an all glass cubicle.

Sam stepped out and motioned Ashley inside. "Hi, Ashley," she moved to hug her.

Ashley dodged the hug and went around her into the room. Sam looked back and shook her head. Max took her hand and led her back out into the waiting room. They joined Becky and Charlie and chatted about the hardware store. Charlie had the store covered and planned to be back at the hospital on Tuesday morning. The four of them continued to visit for a couple of hours, until Ashley returned.

Her face was red and streaked with tears. Charlie got up to embrace his sister. "He's gonna be okay, Ash. He's doing better already."

With a look of utter contempt, Ashley turned towards Sam and pointed. "It's all your fault. My dad would have never been riding his bike if he wasn't with you. You did this. Everything was fine until you came along," she screamed.

"Ashley, that's not true," said Charlie, trying to touch her arm.

She flinched, locked eyes with him for a moment, then turned and dashed out of the room, slamming the door.

As Max made a move for the door, Charlie called out, "Let her go. She needs to walk it off." He turned to face Sam and held her by the shoulders. "Sam, none of what she said is true. Like we all know, she has never dealt with my mom leaving and hasn't faced reality. None of this is your fault." He hugged her close as she started to cry.

Becky and Max were at Sam's side, attempting to console her. "I'm trying not to let it get to me, but I feel like it's my fault too." She stuffed some tissues in her hand and headed out the door, "I'm going to go back and sit with Jeff. I'll see you in the morning."

Max decided to stay around in case Ashley returned. He didn't want Sam to have to face her alone right now. Charlie promised to text Max if he heard from his sister. After an hour, Max heard his phone chirp with a text from Charlie letting him know Ashley was back at the hotel for the evening.

Max drove through the streets, dark and wet from the unrelenting rain. Max arrived back at Becky's to find the house quiet and everyone in bed. He locked the door and tiptoed to bed. He hated to see Sam so distressed and knew Ashley's words had hit their mark.

* * *

Ashley did her best to dodge Sam all day on Saturday, making a point of being away from the waiting room and spending time with her dad during Charlie's shift. Max helped Sam through the decision of approving the insertion of a nasal feeding tube for Jeff. He explained it was to make sure Jeff could get nutrition until he was conscious. "It feels like he's not making any progress," she said in a weary voice. "If only he would wake up."

Max assured her he was taking steps forward, although it was difficult to see. He and Charlie left in the late afternoon, as soon as Jen called to let them know she had arrived. Charlie told Jen what had happened with Ashley and Jen decided to go to Becky's to see Sam and drop some things there before going to the hospital. Max had left the car at Becky's for Sam to drive.

Becky was making dinner when the taxi dropped Jen at the house. Brad led her, cold and drenched from the merciless downpour, into the kitchen. When Sam saw her she leapt from the chair and wrapped her in a long hug. "I'm so glad you're here."

She noticed Sam looked thinner and ashen. "Me too. I talked to Charlie and Max before I came here. Max gave me the latest update and Dr. Sean has been stopping by to see me each day and keep me posted. It sounds like Jeff is doing a little better, huh?"

"I guess. I'm so relieved he's breathing on his own. Everyone says to be patient and he'll wake up when he's ready, but I don't see much change."

"And Charlie said Ashley is being a real jerk to you. I'm so sorry, Sam. You have to believe me when I tell you; nobody thinks this is your fault. Plain and simple, it's Brenda's fault. You've been nothing but wonderful for Jeff, so as hard as it is, please try to ignore Ashley. I'm going to try to talk to her while I'm here and do more than suggest she see a counselor. It's been far too long for her to still be acting out."

"I know how hard it is to miss your parents and long for them, so I can relate, but it makes me feel horrible."

"I know it does. You keep doing what you're doing for Jeff. He loves you and when he opens his eyes, he'll want to see you," Jen said, as she hugged Sam again.

Becky interrupted, "Ashley's at the hospital now and Sam's going to go back around eight tonight and Ashley plans to go to her hotel when she leaves. She's on a morning flight home tomorrow."

"I'll head over now and see Jeff and hopefully talk some sense into Ash. Take your time tonight, Sam. I want to sit with Jeff anyway, so come later and get some rest. I'll be back in the morning to relieve you."

"Don't you want to eat first?" asked Becky, as she took a lasagna out of the oven. "You're cold and this will warm you up. Eat first and then I'll drop you at the hospital. Sam will take the car tonight and trade spots with you."

Jen eyed the casserole and breathed in the aroma. "Okay, it looks good and smells heavenly. I haven't cooked in weeks. Linda has been spoiling us and cooking for us each day. She makes delicious soups and they're easy for her to prepare. She's a little unsteady, but excited for Max to be home tonight."

"I'm glad he went back to help her. I know he missed her," said Sam, as she dished lasagna onto plates.

Taking a bite, Jen said, "She's enthusiastic about his move here. She's led a very solitary life and keeps herself busy with work, but not much else. I think she's afraid, but I can tell she's serious about Max."

Brad arrived as they were finishing and Becky gave him a quick kiss goodbye as she left to drop Jen at the hospital. Jen followed the directions Sam had given and found Jeff's room. The nurse led her back to see her brother.

Ashley was sitting with him and Jen caught herself gasp when she saw her big brother looking shrunken and helpless. Ashley looked up with tears streaking her young face. The two hugged, containing their sobs. Ashley left to allow Jen some time with him.

Jen sat and stroked his arm and hand. "Jeff, it's me, Jen. Mom and Jeremy are going to come and see you tomorrow," she whispered, knowing she couldn't talk without crying. She hadn't expected him to look so small. He'd always been big and strong and funny. She rested her head on the bed and kissed his hand. "Please wake up," she begged.

She was startled by a tap on her shoulder. The nurse asked her to step out for a few minutes. She found her way to the waiting room and found Ashley staring at the television. "Hey. What time do you leave tomorrow?"

"Early. I need to be at the airport by seven."

Jen sat by her and held her hand. "Ash, sweetie, I know you're upset and worried. But, I trust the doctors and know from talking to Max your dad's making progress. I think he'll be okay."

Ashley shrugged.

"I want you to listen to me for a minute. I know you're in a bad place right now, but I want you to see a counselor when you get back home. I love you and I want you to talk to someone about your feelings. I'm not sure you've ever dealt with your mom leaving you and Charlie."

Ashley looked down at the worn carpet, not meeting Jen's eyes.

"I know how much you've worshiped your dad and he's always put you and Charlie first. But, Ash, you're an adult now and he deserves his own life and happiness. Sam is what he needs. She didn't do this to him. If anything, she made him happier than he's ever been."

"But he wouldn't have been riding his bike," she blubbered. "Why couldn't Sam have been the one hit? She doesn't have a family, so nobody would care."

Jen narrowed her eyes. "If your dad heard you say that he would be heartbroken. Sam has all of us. We're her family and he wanted to ride his bike, Ash. Nobody made him do it. And riding his bike isn't the problem. Like I said, I want you to make an appointment with a counselor. I think there's a good chance your anger at Sam is linked to something else. It's important you deal with it. Promise me, Ash."

She shrugged, but lifted her head. "I'll look into it."

Jen hugged her. "That's a good start. But, I want you to make an appointment and go and if you don't like the first one, try another. This is important and Sam's going to be here. She's not going anywhere, so you're going to have to figure this out. She's been nothing but kind to all of us, including you."

Ashley looked at her watch. "I'm going to go back and say goodbye to Dad and get back to the hotel. I need to get to sleep."

Jen gripped her in a tight hug. "Promise me, Ash."

"Okay. I promise."

"I'm going to call you each day and nag you until you do this. You've wasted too much time already and need to resolve your feelings. I mean it, Ash."

Ashley stared at her.

"If I can't trust you, I'll call Will."

Ashley's eyes widened. "No, don't call him. I'll make an appointment on Monday."

Through misty tears, Jen watched her walk away, hoping she would follow through. *I'd like to get my hands on Amy right now. She'll never comprehend the damage she did to Jeff and her children. If someone had to get hit by a car, it should have been her. Now he finally has the woman he deserves. Please don't take him from us.*

Fifteen

Max opened the door to Sam's house and found Linda propped on the couch reading a book. "Hey, how are you feeling?" he asked, as he bent to kiss her forehead.

"Better, now that you're back. I've missed you," she said gripping his hand. "How's Jeff doing?"

"Not much change. I think it could be a long haul. Everyone is waiting for him to wake up. The doctors will know more when he's awake and they do more tests."

"Do you think there will be permanent damage?"

"It's hard to say. The tests they have done look good, but regardless, the recovery is going to be a long one."

"Poor Sam."

"Yeah, and Ashley went off on her on Friday night and told her this was all her fault."

"She's never wanted Jeff to have a woman in his life besides her. She struggled when her mom left. I think we all hoped she would grow out of it, especially now that she's moved away and is married."

"Jen's planning to have a talk with her and get her to see a counselor."

"Maybe it will work this time."

He squeezed in next to her and put his arm around her. "On a lighter topic, how about pizza tonight?"

"Sounds great. I've been behaving and staying off my feet as much as possible, so have been living on soups."

"Good girl. I'll call in our order and have it delivered. What else have you been up to?"

"Reading and bookkeeping duties. Also, I had a visit from Kellie and she wanted to know if I had an interest in selling the farmhouse. She has a new couple interested in it for a bed and breakfast."

"Wow. I didn't know you were thinking about selling."

"I wasn't. I told her no, but as I've been sitting here thinking about it, I'm considering it. Being injured like this makes me realize my house is going to be more difficult to navigate the older I get. Having all the bedrooms upstairs is not the best design. I'm not sure."

"Do you need to discuss it with your mom?"

"I would, but I don't have to. The house is mine."

"What about the nursery?"

"If I decide to sell the house, I'd keep the nursery, but do less out there and have Lucas manage it. I could work in the flower shop and oversee the rest. Lucas does a wonderful job and loves it like his own. I trust him completely."

"Sounds like you have a lot to think about. I'm sort of shocked you're considering it."

"I know. I surprised myself," she laughed. "But, what happened to Jeff hit me hard. Life's too short and I think I want to be open to more fun in my future and not focus every minute on work."

"Here, here," he clapped. "I like the sound of that. I could help you out in the fun department," he teased, brushing a tendril of hair from her face and kissing her lightly.

"When do you have to go back to the city?"

"I'm not going back, unless Sam needs me. It's a waiting game now and she has Becky, so I think she'll be okay. If something changes, I can be there in a heartbeat."

"Mmm," she said tilting her head to kiss him. "That's the best news. I'm happy you're home."

"Speaking of home. I wonder how the sale on my new house is going. I'll have to get in touch with Kellie and make sure things are moving along."

"I'm sure she's all over it. I was wondering how you'd feel about taking a ride out to the nursery tomorrow?"

"Do you have cabin fever already?"

"A little. I wanted to look around. Maybe you could help me go through some old boxes. If I sell it, I'll need to clean it out. If I don't sell, I'm bored, so it's a good time to get the job done. It's something I've been meaning to do for years, but never had the time."

"Sure. It's a date," he smiled. "I'll go get our dinner coming and you pick out a movie for tonight." He turned and watched Zoe leap from the floor and curl herself into Sam's leather chair. He shot Linda a questioning glance.

"I know. She's been so sad with Sam gone and started sitting in her chair. It soothes her, so I let her."

"Poor girl," Max said as he petted the golden retriever. "I know you miss her."

"I bet she doesn't come back until Jeff can come home," said Linda.

"Yeah, she won't leave his side."

They spent the evening stuffing themselves with pizza and watching two funny movies. Max helped Linda get settled for the night and promised a homemade breakfast before they started for the nursery.

* * *

Linda had improved her system for getting ready each morning and only needed help making sure her cast was covered in plastic before she showered. Max was determined to stay outside the bathroom door in case she needed help. "I don't want you to fall, so shout out if you need something."

It was slow, but she managed and Max relaxed and headed to the kitchen once she was wrapped in her fluffy robe. "I'm fine, honest. Go make your waffles and I'll be there as soon as I get dressed."

They decided to take the dogs with them and let them run around in Linda's backyard. Linda's leg hindered her normal speed, but they were on the road around eleven. Lucy led the other two dogs to the backyard and they began a game of chase. Max made sure they had water and went in to help Linda begin her task.

She gave Max instructions on where to find the boxes she wanted to start sorting and he brought them downstairs. She started making piles and used some plastic tubs to hold the items she wanted to save for her mom or her brother. They worked without stopping for several hours, only taking a break for lemonade.

"Whew," Linda said as she took a sip. "That hits the spot. I can't believe how much junk is here. I thought my mom cleaned all this stuff out when they moved, but I think she missed some boxes."

"I know from packing my house, you can accumulate a lot of stuff over the years. It's a real pain to pack it all."

"I want to finish one more box and we'll call it a day."

"How's your leg?"

"Not bad, I'm just getting tired of the awkward position I'm in while sorting."

They went back to work and she added several things to the container for her mom. She found an old photo album and decided to take the time to look through it, since she didn't recognize it. An envelope fell out when she flipped the cover. She opened the yellowed packet and discovered a newspaper clipping and a letter. It was from the *Chicago Daily Tribune* in 1960. It was an article about a man found dead in an alley. The man had known mob ties and was reported to have been killed with a blow to the head from a pipe or tire iron. Police suspected the death was related to his mob activities.

"This is weird," she said as she scanned the article. She took care opening the brittle letter.

"What is it?" he asked.

"I'm not sure. I found an old newspaper article from Chicago about a dead mobster. And this letter," she held up the fragile paper.

Max took the article while she read the letter.

"It's addressed to someone named Millie. It looks like it's from her parents. It says how sorry they are to see her and Joe have to run away, but they understand it's for their safety. I can feel the sadness as I read this."

Max handed her the clipping. "What else does it say? Is there a Millie in your family?"

"No, not that I know of. My parents were both only children and their parents died young, so we didn't have many relatives. It goes on to say they will forever suffer not knowing their grandchild and seeing their beloved daughter. They hope one day they can all be reunited, but want them to use the money to buy a new home somewhere safe. They know they can't know where it is. How horrible."

"That sounds intense."

"It sounds like Millie was pregnant, too. They agree they will only communicate in an emergency and use the system they discussed. It's signed, *We Love You Both, Mom & Jack.*"

She continued to flip through the photo book. She found several of her mom and dad standing outside a house she didn't recognize. Her mom was obviously pregnant in some of them. They were both so young.

"I'm going to have to ask my mom about this," she said, as she placed the letter and clipping back in the book and stuck it in her bag. "Let's call it a day."

Max called the dogs and loaded everyone into his SUV. "Tomorrow's Monday, so I was hoping we could go to the movies in the park. Are you game?"

"Sure, sounds fun. We'll need to take chairs and probably an extra one to keep my leg elevated."

"Sam has some in her garage that will work. How about dinner at Lou's first?"

"Sounds perfect," she said, as she reached for his hand.

He unloaded the dogs and persuaded her to take a nap while he worked on getting their dinner ready. He sent Sam a text to check on things while he sliced lemons and chopped garlic for a chicken and pasta dish. As he was rinsing his hands his phone chimed. *No change* was the response from Sam.

He shook his head as he added the garlic to the melted butter and oil. The savory smell filled the kitchen. He added the browned chicken breast. He set place settings on the deck table and made a pot of iced tea. As he was tossing the linguine into the chicken and sauce, Linda hobbled into the kitchen.

"Something smells yummy," she smiled.

"I know. It's making me hungry. I thought we could eat outside," he gestured.

She used her crutches and maneuvered into a deck chair. "I'm sorry I'm not much help. Once I'm mobile, I'll pay you back," she laughed.

"I'm counting on it." He kissed her as she set the bowl of pasta on the table. He poured their teas and added some garlic bread to the table.

She took a forkful, "Delicious. I like the lemon flavor."

"It's quick and easy. Did you get some rest?"

"Yeah, a little. I'm intrigued by the letter and want to call my mom tonight and ask her about it."

"Once I get the dishes done, I'm going to get some things at the market. That will give you some time to talk to your mom. And I can snag us some ice cream," he winked.

She grinned. "I'm sure you're going through withdrawals without Sam's desserts."

"I was eating too much, but I wish she was home," he looked out at the water. "I hope Jeff is himself when he wakes up. I've never seen Sam so full of life and to think it could all be gone breaks my heart."

She gripped his hand and they sat in silence, content to watch the last of the summer crowd drift by on kayaks. Max brought her hand to his lips and kissed the back of it. "I'm thrilled to be home with you."

He cleared the table and tidied the kitchen. He got Linda situated in the recliner with her leg elevated and an iced tea. "I'm going to stop by and talk to Hayley about the schedule at the shop. I'll see you in a bit and then we can talk about the mysterious letter."

As Linda reached for the cordless phone to call her mom, it rang. She didn't recognize the number, but answered.

"Hi, this is Marty, Sam's ex-husband. Is Max in?"

"No, I'm sorry. He'll be back soon. May I have him call you back?"

"Oh, sure. Kyle told me Max was staying at her place and I wanted to talk to him about an idea I had concerning Jeff's situation. I know Sam listens to Max and I wanted to offer to bring a lawsuit against the woman who hit Jeff, but need to speak to him about it."

"Okay. I'll have him call you. At this number?"

"Yes, and I'll give you my cell number, just in case."

She found a pen and a pad and wrote down the cell number. "I'll be sure he calls you right away."

She disconnected and dialed her brother's number. She knew her mom had a hard time hearing on the phone and wanted to explain everything to him with the idea he could talk to her mom and they could call her back. "Hi, David."

"Hey, how are you doing?"

"Much better. I'm staying at my friend Sam's house, since stairs are a no-no. But, I'm feeling good."

"Good news. Mom's here do you want to say hi?"

"Yes, but I need to run something by you first. I had a realtor approach me about selling the old farmhouse to a couple who wants to open a B&B. At first I wasn't interested, but have been giving it some serious thought. Anyway, I went out yesterday and had Max help me sort through some old boxes, in case I decide to sell. I found an old newspaper clipping and a letter in an old photo book. Judging from the car in the photos it looks like it must be the late 50's. What's weird is the letter is addressed to someone named Millie and the clipping is about a mobster found dead in Chicago. The letter is from Millie's mom and from the sounds of it her daughter and her husband are running away and can't tell them where."

"How strange. I've never heard the name Millie or anything about Chicago. I'll ask Mom and we'll call you back. Are you really thinking about selling?

"Yeah, I am. I'm not sure I want to work as hard as I have been and the income would give me some freedom."

"I hear ya. I'm enjoying retirement. We'll call you back soon."

Linda disconnected and pushed the power button on the remote. Surrounded by three dogs she watched a rerun of *NCIS* while she waited for Max to return and her brother to call back.

The dogs ran to the garage when they heard Max drive in. His arms were loaded with bags from the market and he hollered out a hello.

"Marty called for you right after you left and wants you to call him. He's thinks Sam should sue Brenda, but wants to talk to you. I've got his numbers in here. And I talked to David and he's going to talk to Mom and call me back tonight."

"That's interesting. I'll be right there as soon as I get all this put away."

He came in with a small bag and handed it to her. "I ran into Annie and she wanted me to give you this to borrow while you recuperate."

She opened it and discovered the complete set of *Downton Abbey*. "Oh, this will be perfect. I've wanted to watch this series, but never had the time." She handed him the note from Marty.

"I'll go call him on Sam's business line in the office and then we can put in the first disc."

While Max was talking with Marty, the house phone rang and when Linda saw her brother's number, she seized the receiver. "Hey," she answered.

"Are you sitting down?" he asked.

"Funny, David. What did you find out?"

"This is going to be shocking, I'm warning you." He hesitated, let out a sigh and continued. "Mom and Dad lived outside of Chicago for a short time. Dad worked as an accountant. He was doing the books for a bar. He discovered the bar was a front for the mob and they used it to launder money. Before he figured it all out, he mentioned some of the irregularities to the owner and asked some questions. He and Mom had gone to dinner in the city one night and when they were going to their car, a man Mom described as a thug threatened them with a gun and told him to keep his mouth shut about the books or he'd kill him and his family. Mom was pregnant with me at the time. Dad grabbed a pipe from the alley and hit the man, trying to disarm him." He paused and then in a quiet voice said, "He killed him, Linda."

She gasped, "Oh, my gosh."

"I know. Mom is pretty upset right now and it took everything she had to tell me this story. Anyway, Mom's real name was Millie and Dad's was Joe. Joe and Millie Flynn. Our grandfathers on both sides had passed away and our grandmothers both remarried men with money. Dad and Mom called their parents and explained the situation. Both our grandmothers got a large amount of cash together and wired it to Dad. They were afraid to go to the police, since back then the cops were in bed with the mob. They left the very next morning and drove out west. Mom's stepdad had connections and was able to buy them new identities."

"So, we had grandparents after all?"

"Yeah and aunts and uncles. The whole thing about them being only children was a lie."

"And they never contacted their parents again?"

"I don't think so. They never divulged where they lived. They bought the house and the land and started a nursery. Dad never wanted to work for anyone again and they tried to create a life different from their real one."

"Well, that explains why we never went on any vacations. I remember one trip to Disneyland and nothing else."

"Yeah. I think they were afraid for their lives for years."

"When she's rested, find out what you can about their siblings and email me. Do you think she's afraid of the mob now?"

"I don't think so. It's been over fifty years. I think they never knew how to unravel what had happened and found it easier to live the life they had created. I can't imagine it."

"This is unbelievable. I'm going to do some research. Tell Mom to call me when she feels like talking."

She rang off, in shock from the news. She was staring at the tablet where she had written *Joe and Millie Flynn*.

Max came in and said, "Well, that was an interesting conversation with Marty." He noticed the glazed expression on her face. "What's wrong?"

"David called. He talked with my mom and you won't believe the story behind the letter."

Max sat in the other recliner. "Tell me."

She recounted the story for Max. When she was done he stared at her, eyes wide with astonishment. "I don't know what to say. It's unreal."

"Tell me about it. I can't believe the life I've always had was a complete fabrication. I think they could have told us when we were older," she snapped, her anger bubbling to the surface.

"I don't know. It's hard to second guess them. The fear they must have had."

She shook her head. "I know. I get it when we were little, but after a few decades I think they could have trusted us."

"Only your mom can answer that one." He let her sit and watched as she wrestled with the news. "Do you want to watch the DVD or start it on a different night?"

"Later, I think. I'm too preoccupied to concentrate on anything. I think I'll get ready for bed and focus on researching tomorrow."

"Good idea. I'm going to go into the coffee shop once you're set in the morning and work a few hours. They're swamped and Hayley wants to try to bake some pies, but needs help covering the front."

He helped her up and got her settled in bed. As he turned out the light, she felt exhaustion overtake her and her eyes shut. The image of her dad, a kind and gentle man, killing a mobster in an alley was etched in her mind as she drifted to sleep.

Sixteen

With all the excitement last night, Marty's call had been forgotten. Over breakfast Max explained Marty wanted him to talk with Sam and convince her to allow him to file suit against Brenda. "Kyle has been communicating with him and keeping him in the loop with regard to Jeff's accident. From what Marty said, the police plan to arrest Brenda soon. Marty wants to make sure she pays for all medical expenses and any other related costs, plus some. I'm not sure what Sam will think, but I'll call her today."

He reminded Linda they had a dinner date and movie tonight as he left for the coffee shop. Her sole mission for the day was the Internet. She wanted to learn all she could about her real family and the events that transpired in Chicago.

By looking at archived news articles, she found out the man her father killed was the nephew of a low level member of the Chicago Mafia. The newspaper reported no leads in the investigation and they attributed the death to mob violence. None of the reports mentioned her father or an accountant.

She got a call from her brother around noon and he said his mom didn't want him to send any emails. He gave Linda their mother's maiden name, Mildred Kelly. He also passed on the names of siblings and where they had lived. "Mom is frazzled. She plans to call you later."

"Okay, sorry to have upset her. I appreciate all the information."

Linda munched on leftovers and continued combing the Internet for information. She found references to her mom's family and it looked like several of them had lived outside of Philadelphia. Her mom had been the youngest and if Linda's research was correct, she was the only living sibling.

Her dad had a younger brother and from everything she found, it looked like he was alive and lived in Nevada. She was itching to make some calls, but wanted to talk to her mom first. *I'm angry I didn't get to know my grandparents or aunts and uncles. I want to find my last one before he's gone. I know I shouldn't be mad at my parents, but I am. It would have been nice to have known my family.*

As she was trudging down the hall, Max arrived. He intercepted her in the kitchen. "I brought us some pie for snacks. Hayley is doing her best to keep the place stocked up." He put the boxes in the fridge and took in Linda. "How are you? Did you find out anything?"

"Mom is going to call me back, but I think I found Dad's brother in Nevada. All of Mom's siblings have died, but there may be some cousins. I want to make some calls, but David says she's nervous, so I want to check with her before I go further."

He poured them both an iced tea and suggested they sit outside and enjoy the rest of the afternoon before going into town for dinner. "Well, I talked to Sam today about the lawsuit. I think she's too tired to put up much of a fight. She knows Marty is brilliant when it comes to the law, so she told me to tell him to go ahead and proceed with whatever he thinks is best. I told her I tend to agree with Marty and think Brenda should certainly pay for all the costs associated with this horrific mess she caused."

"So, did you talk to Marty yet?"

"Yep. I called him and told him to move forward. He's going to have the paperwork messengered to Sam in the city and Becky can notarize it all. He wants to be ready to file the moment she's arrested."

"That woman is toxic. She has never had to suffer a consequence for her actions, so I hope this time she does." She paused as she took a sip of tea and gazed at the ocean. "For far too long I let what she did paralyze me.

When Walt left me, I was devastated. It might have been better had I left the island."

Max smiled at her, taking her hand in his. "I'm glad you didn't."

The corners of her mouth turned up for a moment, "You're sweet. But, I didn't trust my own judgment for years. I went to work with my parents and they urged me to consider going to college, but I was afraid. Months turned into years and pretty soon I was comfortable hiding from life by working."

"When did Walt leave here?"

"Oh, soon after the fling with Brenda was over. It was short-lived. I'm sure he was embarrassed, but it hurt so much when he never came to talk to me before he left. I haven't seen him since. His parents live in the southern part of the island and have always been friendly to me. I know they regret what happened. I don't see them often, but they're customers of mine. I know Walt got married and had kids. Last I heard he lived in California. I think his parents usually make a trip to visit, rather than him coming here."

"I'm sorry. I don't have much advice, except I know for a fact you can't change the past. I'm grateful you're part of my life and I'm excited you're thinking about some changes that will allow us to spend more free time together." He placed his hand on her thigh and leaned in to kiss her.

"Walt was a fool," he said as he brushed her hair back and kissed her again.

She chuckled, "Yes, he was. Thanks for listening." She finished her tea and Max helped her up. "We better get ready and head into town."

Max changed and loaded the chairs in the SUV while Linda got ready. She had been living in shorts and t-shirts, but chose a pair of capri pants she could fit over her cast and a feminine draped neck shell in a vivid purple. She grabbed a matching sweater to take for the movie. She was slow, but finally satisfied with her hair she emerged to find Max waiting on the couch.

"Ready to go? Sorry, I took so long."

"No problem. It was worth the wait." He helped her into the SUV, noticing the smoothness of her skin as he held her arm.

He parked at Lou's and went around to retrieve her crutches and open her door. Lou met them outside and led them to a table on the lower level deck. "How's the leg?" he asked.

"Doing better, thanks."

"I heard Jeff isn't awake. Is that right, Doc?"

He nodded. "He's doing about the same. Like I told Sam, these types of injuries can take time."

"I hope they hang Brenda for this. It's a damn shame, just when Jeff found the love of his life. Well, you kids enjoy," Lou said, as he placed the menus on the table.

They each wanted crab cakes and ordered a side of lobster mac and cheese to share. "I sure hope I get rid of this cast when I go see Dr. Brown in a few weeks," said Linda. "I'd like to get over and see Jeff and Sam, but it's too hard with the crutches."

"I know. I hope you get a walking boot when you see him. You've been behaving and not putting weight on it, so chances are good."

"I always behave," she smiled.

"I hope not," he looked at her with mischief in his eyes. "When you're back to a hundred percent, I plan to tempt you into some serious delinquency." He reached across the table for her hand.

"Sounds like one more thing to look forward to," she raised her eyebrows.

The waitress appeared with their meal and they unlinked hands to make room for the dishes. The crunchy brown top of the mac and cheese was the perfect contrast to the creaminess of the cheese shrouded pasta mottled with bits of succulent lobster. "Oh my gosh," said Max. "This is sinful."

"Mmm. I know. One of my favorites and I haven't had it in a long time. I forgot how big it was. There's no way I can finish my crab cake and this."

"And we have to save room for the dessert I have planned at home."

"Really?" she laughed. "You have dessert plans?"

He grinned. "Yes, and I insist you join me."

"Remember, I don't want to gain weight. All this sitting around is not good."

"A little won't hurt. Trust me," he winked.

"You're a bad influence," she smiled. "I'll box the rest and have it tomorrow."

He took a few more bites before the rest went in the box. Max settled the bill and helped Linda position her crutches. "Let's store our leftovers at Sam's shop and then we'll get settled in the park."

He made a quick stop to stash the boxes and then snagged a parking spot close to the park entrance. He unloaded the chairs and helped Linda maneuver over the grass. They positioned their chairs near the center of the screen on the main aisle so Linda could get out easily. Once she was seated, he jogged back to the car and brought the cold drinks he had picked up at the coffee shop and a spare chair for her leg.

Linda looked at her watch. "We have about half an hour before it starts."

"No problem," he said, as he took her hand in his and rubbed his thumb over hers.

"Did you talk to Kellie about your house?"

"With everything else, I forgot to tell you. She said everything is on track and I'll take possession the Monday after Labor Day. She also said the owners have agreed to let me have access for moving some things in whenever I'm ready."

"How exciting. Is Becky working on getting your belongings moved over?"

"Yep. She's scheduling it so my things will be delivered in a couple of weeks. Do you feel up to helping me decorate and pick out anything new I need?"

"Of course. I also want to make you some containers for your deck. If you're going to stick to your morning schedule at Sam's shop, we could use the afternoons to work on your house."

"It may slow down enough after Labor Day. With Kyle leaving and the girls going back to school, it will just be Hayley in the morning and she's trying to keep some pies and brownies on the shelf."

"I think Sam's going to have to find someone to help. Hayley can't work seven days a week."

He nodded. "I'm going to talk to Becky and see what she thinks about it. I can help until we know more about Jeff. Since they're seniors, Megan and Rachel get out of school early, but they can't work seven days a week either."

The lawn was soon covered with moviegoers and at seven o'clock the screen was filled with the opening scenes of jewel thefts in *To Catch a Thief*. As Linda took in the view of the harbor, the moon reflecting off the water, and the park trees wrapped in cheerful white lights, she glanced over at Max.

He was engrossed in the movie, but sensed her eyes on him. He turned and winked at her and gave her hand a squeeze, moving closer. "This is fun," he whispered.

She nodded. "I'm glad you came with me." She rested her head on his shoulder and watched the rest of the movie.

The film ended and the crowd began to collect their belongings and scatter to their homes and cars. Max and Linda sat, waiting for a lull in activity. Max had a tiny flashlight on his key ring and used it to guide Linda to the car. Once he had her seated, he went back and hauled the chairs.

"Great movie," he said, as he pulled away heading back to the coffee shop to retrieve the leftovers.

"Yes, it was. It's another one of my favorites. He's such a debonair guy and Grace Kelly is gorgeous. They make a stylish couple. I loved her in *Rear Window* with Jimmy Stewart, too."

"We'll have to add it to our list for a movie one night."

They pulled into Sam's garage and he helped her into the house. "Now it's time for some dessert. How's your leg feeling?"

"A little tired, but not bad."

"How about we get you settled and I'll bring dessert to you in bed."

"A new twist on breakfast in bed, huh?"

"Exactly. I'll start a fire in Sam's room and we can start that series Annie gave you." He helped her get situated and left her to change clothes while he put on shorts and a t-shirt and made them each a plate of pie.

He came through the bedroom door as Linda was slipping her nightgown over her head. "Do you need some help?" he asked, noting the cascade of dark hair against her well defined back and shoulders.

She turned, thankful for the low light of the television and the fire. "I think I've got it. What do you have there?"

"One piece of chocolate cream and one piece of apple. You get first choice." He set the plates on the nightstand and bent to help her get her leg under the sheet.

"That's a tough choice" she brushed his hand with hers.

He caught her eyes, bright in the flicker of firelight. He leaned in, clutched her smooth shoulder and her light floral scent drew him to the side of her neck. He burrowed into her hair, pushing it back and kissed her collarbone. He let his lips travel up and past the thin strap of her gown, giving it a tug with his teeth. It slipped off her shoulder and his hand smoothed over the silky fabric and the curve below it.

She gasped as his lips skimmed past the neckline of her gown. His lips were unhurried, deliberate in their advance to the other side of her neck, below her ear. She shuddered and he moved to cover her mouth with his.

He felt the urgency in her kiss. Her fingers dug into his back and then moved up gripping his shoulders, weaving through his hair to massage his scalp. Her hands relaxed and she held his head letting her thumbs rest under his jawline and they continued the hungry, probing kiss, until they were both breathless.

"Wow. I sure wish my leg was healed," she said, the gold flecks in her dark eyes dancing.

"You and me both," he smiled. "I thought you might need more convincing to have some fun, but I think you're ready."

She felt heat rise and cover her face. "I hate to say I'm eager, but I've been saving up for thirty years. I don't want you to think I'm like this all the time." The dimness of the room gave her the courage to go on. "I've only been with Walt. Not another since him. I'd stopped believing I'd find someone. Living here limits your choices, unless you're into summer flings with tourists, and I'm not."

Max clasped her hands in his. "I'm only teasing you. I don't think anything of the kind. I'm flattered a beautiful woman is excited to be with me." He brought her hands to his lips and kissed them. "I haven't been with a woman since Lisa and these feelings I have for you…they're the real thing."

She leaned in and brushed her lips against his. She touched her forehead to his, "I'm glad, because I feel the same way."

"How about we put in the DVD and eat some pie and we'll finish what we started in a few weeks, when you get rid of your cast." He kissed her forehead as he got up.

Linda chose the chocolate pie, but while nestled back against the pillows they traded bites with each other. After the first episode, they decided they were hooked on the show. Max took their plates to the kitchen and found the three dogs sacked out for the night.

He detoured to Linda's room on his way upstairs and found her already asleep. He covered her bare shoulders and kissed her on the cheek. *I've been thinking about asking Linda to move into my house with me. I'm not sure she'll do it, but maybe she'll consider it if she decides to sell her place. I'm way past falling. I love her and need her in my life.*

Seventeen

Max and Linda went through their routine in the morning and he left her once she was out of the shower. While waiting for her mom to call, she busied herself sketching containers for Max's new deck. Her cell phone rang and she grabbed it, expecting her mom, but it was Max.

"Did you forget something?" she asked.

"No. I have news."

"Do tell."

"Jen stopped in this morning and gave me the latest on Jeff. No change there, but she wanted us to know the police arrested Brenda first thing this morning."

"Good. She needs to pay for what she's done."

"Jen said they arrested her for the arson at Sam's shop and for the hit and run. They have a long list of charges and the bail is high."

"She'll get the money from her family, so she'll be out soon. She's the only one left on the island, but I think her brother lives in the city."

"I'm going to call Sam and I'll let Marty know so he can start his paperwork."

"How's work going?"

"Busy. In fact, here comes a crowd through the door. I gotta get back. I'll see you this afternoon."

She disconnected and went back to her sketches. She finished her ideas before lunch and put them in a stack for Max. She was looking through the fridge for lunch, when the house phone rang. It was her mom, so she hobbled over to her notes on her family before hitting the answer button.

"Hey, Mom. How are you doing?"

"I'm fine, Lindy Lou. I'm sorry I was upset. It was a shock."

She was relieved her mom had used her old nickname, thinking she must not be too distressed. "I know. It was a big bombshell. I'm sad we missed our chance to have a relationship with our aunts and uncles and cousins. I feel cheated."

Her mom sighed. "I know. You have to understand, we were afraid for our lives."

"I know, Mom. I understand. I wish you guys would have told us about this thirty years ago."

"We, we…" her mom hesitated. "We thought about it, but we didn't know how. We wanted to keep you and David safe. It sounds silly now, but we never relaxed."

"And you and Dad never got to see your parents again?"

"That was the worst part. I wanted my mom to see you kids. I know we cheated you out of grandparents and it breaks my heart," she began crying.

"The whole thing is so sad. I'm sorry I'm making you relive all of it. I know you must have been scared out of your minds. It's hard to believe Ed and Peggy Graham never existed."

Linda waited for her mom to respond, but she only heard sniffling.

"Say, Mom, I did a little research and I think I found Dad's brother, Michael, in Nevada."

"What? You found Mikey?" her mom asked in a choked voice. "I've always been too afraid to try to find anyone. Do you think it's safe to be poking around?"

"Yes, it's been fifty years. In looking around it looks like Michael is seventy years old. Are you okay with me calling him and seeing if he's interested in meeting us?"

"Oh, my. I don't know."

"I bet he'd love to see you, Mom."

"It would be good to see him. I guess give it a try."

"Okay, I'll work on it this week and call you guys back," she paused. "It'll be okay, Mom."

She rang off and zapped the leftover mac and cheese from last night. She looked over her printouts from the Internet and hoped Michael Flynn still lived in Carson City. She finished lunch and rehearsed what she would say. *Hi, Mr. Flynn, you don't know me, but I'm your niece. Joe was my father and I'm Linda. I was hoping you would be willing to meet us—that is my mom and brother and me.*

She mulled it over in her head. She thought it sounded lame, but wasn't sure how else to introduce the topic. *I need to quit overthinking it and call him. He could be happy to hear from me.*

She took a notepad into the great room and got comfortable in the recliner. She dialed the number and took a breath. It rang several times and then a generic answering machine clicked on. *Crap, I hadn't thought about a message. I don't even know if it's the right number.*

In a panic, she rattled off a short message saying she was hoping to contact Michael Flynn and left her name and number, saying she was a distant relative, not mentioning her parents. She also left her email address.

She punched the end call button as she heard Max come in. "I'm home," he hollered. A parade of dogs followed him. He stepped behind Linda and brushed her hair away to kiss the back of her neck. "How are you?"

"A little flustered. I left a message for my dad's brother. I hope he calls back."

"So, you talked to your mom?"

"Yeah, she was weepy and concerned, but agreed to let me pursue Michael Flynn, my dad's youngest brother."

"Wow. That's exciting news."

"Anything else on Brenda?"

"Marty said he would get the paperwork filed today and Sam sounded relieved, but worn out. She's having a hard time seeing a happy ending in all of this."

"I don't blame her. It would be a horrible situation. I wish they would keep Brenda locked up."

"She's already out on bail. Just as you predicted. The whole town is talking about it. Her family provided the cash bail and it was close to a quarter of a million. They tacked on every charge in the book."

"I bet that surprised her. I think she believes she's exempt from everything. They're going to have a hard time getting an impartial jury for her."

"Yeah, she may be wise to take a plea bargain. Jeff is so well liked and it's apparent the town is against Brenda."

"I think Marty was a total jerk to Sam, but I'm thankful he's helping her now. Brenda needs to rot in prison and lose all her money."

"How about we do something more pleasant for the rest of the day?" he smiled.

"What do you have in mind?"

He reached for her hand, "Let's go take a look at my new house and get some ideas flowing."

"Oh, fun. I did some sketches of ideas I have for your deck." She pointed to the pile of papers. "Take them and you can decide what you like. I need to get my cell phone in case Michael calls me back."

Max parked and helped Linda out. He carried her sketchbook and hurried to unlock the door. "So, I'm not much of a decorator, but I think you have a knack for it. You shout out some ideas for furnishings and art and I'll make a list."

"Only if you promise to be honest if you hate an idea. We may have different tastes. I'm better at doing yards than houses. Sam would do a better job for you."

"I want you." He moved to her and wrapped his arms around her, letting her crutches fall away. He smelled the same enchanting scent that drew him to her last night. "What is this scent? It drives me mad," he said nuzzling her neck.

She giggled when he reached her ear. "It's probably the jasmine shower gel I've been using."

He pulled himself away, "Don't ever run out of the stuff." He brought his lips to hers and felt her falter.

"Whoops," she said. "I better get my walking sticks back."

"I'll get them and leave you alone so we can get some work done."

"Do you think I'll be able to travel to Victoria in September?"

"Let's see, that would give you seven weeks if we choose the very last week of September. I think it may work. If you get a boot when Dr. Brown sees you, I would say yes."

"I was looking forward to going, so I hope it works."

"Plan on it and if it looks like it won't work, we can cancel and rebook it for later. It will give us something to look forward to."

She nodded and tottered towards the bedrooms. She started with the master. "All the window treatments remain, right?"

"Yes, most of them have blinds, but these are different," he said pointing to the fabric roman shades.

"I like them and they're neutral, so they'll work with any colors you choose for your bedroom."

"I need to get a new bedroom set. So, I'm open."

"I think a gray or brown would be a good base color and then we can accent it with something else."

"I was thinking dark furniture, so how about we go with the gray for contrast."

"Perfect. And your bathroom has both brown and gray in the slate, so the same theme can carry over in there. I bet you have some art that will work on these walls and with all the windows, you don't need much."

"I need my television and I think I do have some paintings that would look good in here."

Max scribbled notes as Linda moved to the next bedroom. "So, we should choose a base color and work from there. What do you think about sea glass colors?"

"I think that's what Sam called Hayley's apartment above the shop. It looked nice."

"I think we could do one in blue tones and the other in the green tones, they're both calm colors. The tile work and granite in the bathrooms are different, but both are neutral, so we can make it work." He jotted away on his pad.

"We could put some plants in the bathrooms. They all have plenty of natural light and they would brighten the space. I'll pick out a few for you."

"Only if you'll take care of them. I tend to forget plants," he said with a sheepish grin.

"Didn't you take an oath? Do no harm or something like that," she laughed.

"Yeah, but it doesn't apply to plants."

"The half bath here in the hallway has gorgeous brown and black granite. I think we should emphasize it and do everything dark brown and black," she continued.

He nodded. "Are you getting tired?"

"Nah, I'm okay for now. Let's look at the great room." They maneuvered to the main living area. "I think an area rug would work on the wood floor and then you could place your furniture on it. What's your furniture like?'

"Brown leather."

"That will look fabulous with all the open beam ceiling work and wood floors. We need an accent color to carry through this area."

"How about some dark green?"

"Perfect. It will look rich, especially with the hint of cherry throughout."

"I have a big wooden dining room set, which I think will work. I may need to find something smaller for the breakfast area. I have a desk for the library and a couch and with all those built in shelves for books, I'll be set. I don't have any grandkids yet, so could leave the loft alone and outfit it once they come along."

"There's a bathroom upstairs too, right?"

"Yeah, it's basic. Shower only, no tub."

"This will be fun once you get all your stuff delivered. We can see how it all looks. We've got a list to get started on things you'll need and then you can add to it. How about we sit on the patio?"

"Right this way," he said, stowing her crutches and gripping her around the waist. He helped her get settled on a lounge chair and slipped behind the granite topped outdoor island and returned with two bottles of iced tea.

"What service," she said taking one.

"I stashed these in the outdoor fridge earlier. I figured we may need a cold drink or two."

They had an hour or so before the sun would set and relaxed, taking in the view of the blue water against the tree lined coast. The water lapped the beach below and as they sat, silent, holding hands, the sun began its descent. Outdoor lights lit the patio and pathways as soon as the sun dimmed.

"Oh, Max, this is gorgeous," said Linda.

"It is. I haven't been here at night, but the view is incredible. Are you getting hungry?"

"A little, but let's stay right here. I want to enjoy the sunset."

"Let me turn on the fire. It's getting chilly," he said, as he stood and fiddled with the fire pit. Soon flames shot through the glass pieces lining the fire bowl. The flames danced against the backdrop of the apricot sky. The bright orb had slipped behind a dark cloud casting a golden ribbon of light across the water.

"What a lovely place to enjoy a sunset," said Linda, reaching for his hand.

He brought her hand to his lips. "It's perfect."

* * *

The rest of the week went by without a call back from Michael and nothing new from Sam. Linda and Max had a solid routine established and he filled his days at the coffee shop while she worked on books for the business and waited for the phone to ring. Max cooked dinner and they spent the evenings watching one or two episodes of Downton Abbey and playing with the dogs.

Friday night, as they were getting ready to eat dinner, Linda's cell phone rang and she recognized the area code for Nevada. She pounced on her phone. "Hello."

Max kept eating, listening to her end of the conversation.

"Yes, thanks so much for calling. This is going to sound strange, but I'm your niece. Your brother Joe was my father."

Linda nodded her head. "Yes, my mom is alive, but my dad died several years ago. It's a long story, but I called to see if you would be willing to meet us. My mom lives near my brother, David, in eastern Washington near Yakima. And I live on San Juan Island."

Linda furrowed her brow, intent on listening. "That would be wonderful. In person we could explain the whole story and why you couldn't know about them. I'm not able to travel now, due to a broken ankle, but I know Mom would love to see you. She's a bit nervous about all this, but was excited to know I thought I had found Mikey," she smiled.

She laughed. "Yes, she did call you that."

"Uncle Mike, it is. Yes, I have a pen, go ahead," she scribbled on her notepad. "I'll talk to Mom and David and get back to you."

She was all smiles when she disconnected. Max raised his eyebrows, "Well?"

"He's nice. He didn't ask many questions, but was excited to know Mom was alive. He said he hadn't seen her since he was about sixteen and he thought they had both died in an auto crash. He and his wife had been on a trip and got home today. Sounds like they travel by motorhome quite a bit." She paused and took a bite of her dinner.

"I take it he agreed to a visit?"

"Yes, he suggested they drive to Washington for a visit. He said they could plan something next month or Mom could visit them in Nevada."

"What do you think?"

"I think Mom would feel better if he came to see her. She's not much for travel and since he offered, I think it would be best. If I'm in a boot, maybe I could get over to David's place. Or, I could invite Mike and his wife here?"

"Totally your decision. I'll help you either way. If you get the boot, you won't be able to drive, but I could drive us over or you could fly."

"When we're done here, I'll call David and Mom and see what they think." She gobbled down the rest of her dinner, anxious to make the call.

Max neatened the kitchen, while she took a calendar and her notepad and shuffled over to the recliner. He peeked in on her when he was done and by the peaceful look on her face knew it was going well. He took the dogs to the beach to play ball and romp in the water.

When he led the three sopping wet dogs to the deck, winded and with tongues hanging out, he caught a glimpse of Linda through the office window. She was on the computer. He tried to wipe the dogs with a towel, which started a new round of games and then left them in the yard to continue drying.

His clothes were soaked, so he padded upstairs to change into something dry. He found her as she was coming out of Sam's office. "How'd it go?"

"Well, Mom agreed to a visit and she liked the idea of Mike coming to Yakima. I emailed him and told him a little about why Mom and Dad disappeared. David thought it might be fun for all of them to visit here together. Then I wouldn't have to worry about travelling over or the timing. So, I emailed everything to Mike and left the dates open. I told him the only week that wouldn't work is our Victoria week."

"We could change it if you need to," he offered.

She shook her head. "No way. I want to get over there before it gets too cool and see as many flowers in bloom as possible." She hobbled down the hall back to the recliner. She turned and he was there to take her crutches.

"Plus, I want to spend a few days with you somewhere special and I can't wait."

"I never argue with an attractive woman who wants to spend time with me," he said, as he helped her into the chair.

"I liked David's idea of them coming here. I'd like you to meet them."

"Hopefully, I'll have my house by the time they come."

"I haven't told them we're together," she looked at her lap. "I've never had to deal with this before, since I've never had a man in my life."

"Will they be upset?"

"No, I don't think so. I think they're used to me being…well, me. Alone."

"I bet they want you to be happy." He knelt on the floor and held her shoulders, leaning in for a soft kiss.

"I am."

He stood and linked their hands together. "You ready for another episode of our show?"

"Yeah, it's the last one of the first season," she smiled.

He lit a fire, brought the dogs in and they plopped on their beds in front of it. He put the DVD in and he and Linda spent the evening, content to visit a bygone era of servants and aristocrats, living together in a magnificent English manor, finding themselves on the brink of World War I.

* * *

Max was startled from a sound sleep at four in the morning. His cell phone was ringing. For a moment, he thought he was in the past, reaching for the phone, expecting a medical emergency. Through blurry eyes, he made out Jen's name.

"Sorry to wake you," she said.

"It's okay. What's wrong?"

"It's Brenda."

"What do you mean?"

"She's dead."

"How?"

"A car accident. Chris from the Fire Department called me and said she drove her car up near Mount Dallas and took a narrow dirt trail. She basically drove off the edge and fell all the way down. She died at the scene."

"Well, that sounds like an odd place to drive in the middle of the night."

"Yeah, Chris thinks it was a suicide. They'll know more when they do tests on her."

"She probably couldn't deal with her future. Linda says she's never had to account for her actions."

"Yep, she's right. She was facing prison, if convicted. I'm sure she couldn't deal with that."

"I'll let Sam know. I'll wait a couple of hours and call her."

"I was hoping you'd call her when Charlie's with her. Tell her I'll see her Sunday night."

Max disconnected and stared into the darkness. He knew he couldn't get back to sleep so he tiptoed downstairs to make some tea. The dogs were sleeping and Zoe pried open an eye, but shut it again when she saw him.

He put the kettle on and out of the corner of his eye caught Lucy dart down the hall. He followed and heard Linda call out his name.

He poked his head in the doorway, "I'm here. Sorry, to wake you. I'm making some tea."

"Oh, is everything okay?"

"I got a call from Jen I'll tell you about. Let me pour us some tea."

Lucy settled in at the foot of the bed and Max returned with two mugs. He gave her one and she patted the mattress and pulled back the sheets on the other side of the bed. He went around and slipped under them. He took a sip of tea and leaned back on the pillows.

"So, Jen called to tell me Brenda had been in a car accident tonight. She drove the dirt trail by Mount Dallas and went off the edge. She's dead."

Linda gasped and grabbed her chest. "Dead?"

He nodded. "She said Chris called to let her know. He thinks it was a suicide."

Linda shook her head. "As much as I think she should have paid for her actions, I wouldn't wish that on anyone."

"I'm going to call Sam and I should let Marty know, too," he sighed.

She gripped his hand. They finished their tea and Max shoved the sheets aside and swung his legs over the edge of the bed. "Stay," she whispered. "Please."

He put the mugs on the nightstand and slid closer to her. He wrapped his arm around her and cuddled her into his shoulder. He hadn't bothered to put on a shirt when he came downstairs. He felt her smooth skin and the gentle curves under her satin gown against his chest. As he rested his head atop hers, the scent of jasmine tickled his nose. He felt his eyes grow heavy and for the first time in five years felt content, as he snuggled closer to the woman he loved.

Eighteen

As the lavender light of dawn filtered into the room, Max slipped out of bed, letting Linda sleep. He crept upstairs, and used his cell to call Marty first and tell him the news. Marty was shocked and shared he had been contacted by Brenda's lawyer earlier in the week and from the questions he asked, thought they wanted to settle the lawsuit. He told Max he'd keep him posted on any further developments and thanked him for the information.

Next, he dialed Sam. It went to voicemail and he left her a brief message asking her to call. He figured she was in with Jeff and silenced her phone.

He took a shower and on his way downstairs, peeked in on Linda. She was sleeping, looking peaceful in the soft morning light. He shut her door and continued to the kitchen to start breakfast.

As he was gathering the ingredients for waffles, his cell rang. It was Sam.

"Hey, how's Jeff this morning?" he asked.

"No better, no worse. What's new with you?"

"Well, I have some news. Is Charlie with you yet?"

"Yeah, he just got here and I checked my messages."

"Good. There was an accident last night up by Mount Dallas and it was Brenda. She drove off a dirt trail and she died at the scene."

"She's dead?"

"Yeah, she is. Chris was there last night and he called Jen and she called me around four this morning. Chris thinks it was a suicide."

"Oh, my gosh. She truly was crazy."

"I think so. I called Marty and let him know. He said he's already had conversations with her lawyer about the suit and he thought they wanted to settle, so he'll let me know if anything comes of it after this latest news. He also said to send you his best."

He heard her take a huge breath. "I don't know what I feel. I can't deny I was hoping to never see her again, but I was also hoping she would go to prison. Suicide seems a bit too easy for me right now." Her voice was tired and she sounded worn out.

"I know. There are no rules about how you should feel. I wanted you to hear it from us first. Jen will be there tomorrow."

"How's the shop doing?"

"Busy. I'm going in each morning after I get Linda settled and helping the girls. School starts soon, so I may have to go in a little earlier. Linda's getting used to the cast and doesn't need as much help as she did, so it will work out."

"If it gets to be too much, work with Becky and hire another helper. How's your house?"

"Wonderful. We went over this week and Linda helped me make lists of things I need and then we started a fire and sat on the patio to watch the sunset." He paused. "It was magical."

"I think she's perfect for you."

"We booked the trip to Victoria for the end of September. If you're not home by then, I'll get Jen or Charlie to stay with the dogs."

"Man, I hope we're home by then. I don't know how much more of this I can take. I want him to wake up. I'm getting discouraged."

"Try not to. I know it's hard. He's going to need you when he's fully awake more than he does now. So take care of yourself."

"I know. I will."

"Hey, I almost forgot. Linda is thinking about selling her house. Kellie approached her with an offer from a couple who wants to start a B&B. I can't believe she's considering it, but she says her injury and what happened to Jeff has made her realize she needs to do something besides work."

"Amen to that."

"So, I know it's fast, but I'm thinking about asking her to move in with me, when my house is ready. What do you think?"

Sam voice brightened. "I hear joy in your voice, so I think it's the right thing. Do you mean get married?"

"I'd love to marry her, but I thought it might be best if I suggested she stay in one of my spare rooms until her ankle is healed. Then we could see how it goes. I don't want to pressure her. I'm sure I want to spend the rest of my days with her, but I don't want to overwhelm her with marriage. We'll see how our trip goes and if she agrees to stay with me, I'll ask her to marry me when it feels right."

"How wonderful. I'm sure she'll say yes. I wish we could all be there having fun instead of sitting in a hospital."

"So do we. Sean keeps us informed and everything looks good as far as Jeff's tests go. Try to be patient."

"I will. I better get going and I'll let Charlie and Becky know the latest."

"Call if you need me to come. Linda is hoping to get rid of her cast in a couple of weeks and wants to make a trip over to visit Jeff."

"Oh, I'd love to see you guys. Give her our best and hug my Zoe girl."

Max disconnected and slipped down the hall to see if Linda was awake yet. He opened the door a crack and saw her sitting against the headrest. "Hey, sleepyhead. You're up."

"Hi, it's late, huh? Thanks for letting me sleep in. I was going to take a shower. You probably need to get to the shop."

"As soon as you're done. I called Sam and gave her the news. She said to give you a hug and was excited to hear we plan to visit when you get your boot."

"How'd she take the news about Brenda?"

"I think she's numb right now. She said she thought suicide was too easy."

Linda nodded her head. "Yeah, I know what she means. I was looking forward to seeing her in an orange jumpsuit, sitting behind bars for many years to come. But, obviously, she was unwell. I always thought she was wicked, but not mentally ill. I do feel bad for her family."

"Marty said the family lawyer had already contacted him earlier in the week and it sounded like he wanted to settle the lawsuit Marty filed."

"They'll want to hurry it along now. They don't like bad press and I'm sure they would like to put this behind them."

He helped her out of bed and guided her to the bathroom. "I'll wait here until you're out and then we can have breakfast. I'm making waffles," he smiled.

"Sounds yummy. I'll be quick."

Once she was ready, he finished the waffle batter and sliced fresh strawberries. He poured glasses of juice and made a pot of tea. Linda shuffled in as Max put a stack of waffles, the berries, and a warm pitcher of syrup on the island.

He helped Linda into a chair and they each took a steaming waffle, dripping with butter. Max topped his with some berries and Linda spooned some of the plump berries into a small bowl.

She bit in to the crusty edge and groaned with delight. "These are the best."

Max smiled. "I was tempted to add whipped cream, but thought better." His cell phone chirped and he scrolled to a text. "Wow, Becky said the movers can deliver my stuff on Monday afternoon."

"That's quick. Are you ready?"

"Yeah. Kellie warned me there's a risk to moving in before it closes, but she also said she knows the owners and doesn't see a problem. They're anxious and she said the property has no liens, so it should be straightforward."

"Well, it would give us something to do, that's for sure," she smiled.

"That'll be the best part. We can spend our afternoons organizing the new place."

"And I promise to get an earlier start, so I can get my exercising done and get showered before you leave for work."

"Speaking of work, I need to get moving," he said, as he gathered the dishes.

"I'll do the cleanup. It'll give me something to do while I wait to hear back from Uncle Mike." As she shuffled over to the sink, she smiled, "That felt good to say Uncle Mike."

Max made her agree to rest her leg when she was done and he promised to return with dinner. "Call me if you need me," he said and kissed her goodbye.

Linda finished the dishes and went back to her nest in the recliner. Using the list she made for Max, she opened her laptop and began searching for an area rug and bedding sets for all the bedrooms. She found two possible rugs and several bedding options. She marked them all for Max to review. As she was searching she kept checking her inbox for news on what she had come to think of as her family reunion.

While she was online, an email from Kellie arrived. She read through it, and realized she was going to have to make a decision about selling the farmhouse. Kellie wasn't pushy, but wanted her to know the couple was interested and she hadn't been able to find them anything else they wanted. She mentioned a sum much larger than Linda had imagined and told her she needed a firm answer from her by Labor Day. Kellie thought the deal would close before the end of October, if she agreed to sell.

She replied back and told Kellie she would give it serious consideration. She needed to think about it and also see if she could find a small place in town, so she could downsize, but promised an answer, one way or another.

She spent the rest of the afternoon running the numbers on her businesses. She knew with the influx of cash from the sale, she'd have no problem finding a place and she could pay Lucas more to manage the nursery and concentrate on the flower shop. If she wanted, she could cut back her hours and increase Sara's salary to cover running the store. *There's so much to think about. I've never had to deal with so much change at once, but it's sort of exhilarating, in a scary way.*

Max returned with take out from the Jade Garden. He set out the selections on the deck and told her Brenda's death was the talk of the locals. "Everyone was shocked. Not too many people had anything good to say about her, but they were stunned by the news. There's a lot of speculation on what will happen with her business and it sounds like the lawsuit is common knowledge. I played dumb, but Sam and Jeff sure have a lot of support in the community."

"Jeff and his family are well loved and although Sam's only been here a short time, she's loved like a local."

Max offered Linda more fried rice and shoveled some onto his plate. "So, what else is new?"

"Well, I heard from Kellie today. She wants a decision from me on selling the farmhouse. I have until Labor Day."

"What do you think?"

"I'm thinking I'll sell. It's a big change, but the price she gave me is way more than I thought it would be, so it makes sense to move on it. I need to work on finding a smaller place in town."

"So, you're thinking about having Lucas manage the nursery and you'll work at the shop in town?"

"Yeah. I'll have Sara do more there too and maybe cut back to three days a week."

Max turned to face her and grasped her hand in his. "I think it would be wonderful for you to have more free time. I can think of ways to fill it," he said with a wink. "And I've been doing some thinking of my own."

"What about?"

"Us."

She put her fork on her plate, curiosity penetrating her stare. "And?"

"Well, hear me out before you say anything. But, I'd like you to think about moving into my house, if you decide to sell yours. You'll need help until your ankle heals, so it makes sense. Plus, I love you, Linda. Until I met you grief had taken over all the space in my heart. I never thought I'd get a second chance at having a beautiful woman in my life, who brings me happiness. And I don't want to do anything to spoil what we have going, but I'd like you there every night when I go to sleep and every morning when I open my eyes. I was smitten with you when you first delivered those flowers to Sam's shop and my feelings for you have only grown." He reached for her hand and squeezed tight.

She smiled a slow smile, her eyes misty with tears. "I never thought I'd find another either. I'd resolved myself to being alone…forever. But, I have to admit, it's easy to be with you and I love having you in my life. We've definitely got chemistry. There's just…" she shook her head.

"What is it?"

"Stupid, really. My own worries about what people will think. It's a small town, one I've lived in my whole life. What if people think I'm a floozy?"

He suppressed a smile, realizing she was serious, "I don't think anyone will think any such thing about you. What would you think if someone you knew was dating a guy she liked and needed a place to stay and moved in?"

She hesitated, "I'd think she was lucky to find him."

He smiled, "There you go. That's what your friends will think. Are you worried about your family?"

"Maybe, a little. I don't know, I think it's a lot of change, for someone who hasn't changed in years."

"Tell me," he held her hand tighter, "what would you say if you didn't have to worry about anyone thinking anything?"

"I'd say I love you and I'd move in.

He leaned across the table and kissed her. "Think about it. No pressure."

She leaned closer, rested her head on his shoulder. "I will."

"You could think about it as a temporary solution. Your ankle won't be healed for months. What better friend to move in with than a doctor?"

She laughed, "You make a good argument, Dr. Sullivan."

They went inside and she showed him the items she had picked out for his house. He scrolled through and nodded his approval. "I like all of it. You pick whichever you think is best. You have a better eye."

"But it's your house. You need to choose."

"I want you to think of it as your house, too."

She smiled, letting the warmth of being with Max wash over her. She had been alone for so long and wasn't used to the idea of sharing her thoughts or decisions with someone else. But, she thought they were meant for each other, like warm tea and honey. Deep in her heart she knew she wanted to live with him. She'd never met a man like him. Correction, she'd never let herself meet a man like him. She did her best to escape any chance of living, using her work as an excuse to avoid invitations.

Max was taking tomorrow off to stay home and do some household chores. He and Linda spent the evening racking up reward points on his credit card by buying the items she had selected for the new house. Before turning in, she checked her email one more time, hoping for an update from Mike or David, but after pushing the send and receive button repeatedly, found nothing new in her inbox.

* * *

Max used his day to change the sheets, do laundry, clean all the floors and scrub the bathrooms. While he was busy with chores, Linda met with Lucas and Sara. She had invited them over to explain what she was considering for the nursery and the flower shop.

They were both excited to take on a new role and willing to do all she had envisioned. They were young and single, focused on growing their careers. Linda had complete faith in both of them and gave them each a packet of salary information she proposed and asked them to look it over and let her know their decision in the next few days.

The projects for the upcoming week consisted of checking on Max's delivery at the new house and Linda getting her hair cut. Max had a meeting at the hospital to discuss a consulting job the same day as Linda's haircut, so they planned to meet for lunch after they were done.

It took the movers all afternoon to unload the furnishings for the house. Max stayed to supervise them, but insisted Linda stay home with her leg elevated and save her energy for afternoons at the house. She heard back from Lucas and Sara while Max was tending to the delivery. Both of them agreed to her terms and were excited to make their new responsibilities permanent. They were pleased with the generous salary and bonus based on profits she had proposed.

Feeling confident about them and knowing she wanted to work less, her decision to sell was all but finalized. She was anxious to talk to Jen on Thursday and get her take before she decided about moving in with Max. *Then if I decide to do it, I'll have to tell Mom and David.*

As she thought of her family she opened her email and found one from David. It was short and to the point, letting her know they were working on a date with Mike and would get in touch as soon as it was finalized.

She felt herself relax as she read the email again. It had been nagging at her, but as if a weight had been lifted, she felt the tension in her shoulders ease. Her plan was to let David and her mom, plus Uncle Mike stay at the house out at the nursery. There were plenty of bedrooms and she thought her mom would enjoy seeing the house. She made a note to get the house cleaned before their arrival.

* * *

Max spent mornings at Harbor Coffee and made a habit of picking up lunch before he collected Linda. They worked every afternoon at his new house and were making small dents in the mountain of boxes and furniture.

Thursday morning Max drove Linda to Jen's salon and helped her out of the car and through the door. Jen heard the door chime and dashed over to them. She enveloped Linda in a strong hug, "I'm so glad to see you. I feel like I haven't seen you for months." The intensity of Jen's embrace caused Linda to teeter on her crutches. Max reached out a hand to steady her.

"And, Max, how great to see you. Kellie tells me you're already moving your things into the new house. I can't wait to see it." She engulfed him in her arms.

He noticed dark circles under Jen's bloodshot eyes. "You look tired. Are you taking care of yourself?"

"I'm okay, but worn out from working and spending so much time with Jeff. I can't get anything done at home and it's hard to concentrate."

"How about you and Megan come over for dinner tomorrow night? I'll cook," he smiled.

Linda reached for Jen's arm, "Yes, please come. I'd like to have time to visit."

Jen's smile eased the strain in her tired face. "We'll be there. Does seven work for you guys?"

"Perfect. And we can take you on a tour of the new house when you have the time," beamed Max.

Jen sighed, "That sounds like fun." Tears filled her eyes and threatened to overflow.

"Sweetie, what's wrong?" asked Linda.

Jen shook her head. "I'm worried about Jeff. It's been a month and the thought of doing something normal made me think of how much I miss him." She took a breath. "I thought he'd be further along by now. I guess I expected more. I'm worried about Sam, too. She looks like the life has been drained out of her."

"We're planning to go over as soon as Linda gets a walking boot. We hope that happens at her appointment in about ten days," he said.

"I wonder if you ought to go this weekend with Jen?" suggested Linda.

"I could. You're going over Saturday, right?"

Jen nodded her head. "Yeah, Steve's taking us over around noon and he'll bring Charlie back here. Megan's coming with me and we come home on Monday."

Max looked past Jen at Linda and she nodded. "That works fine. I'll meet you at the marina on Saturday."

She hugged him again.

He patted her on the back. "We'll see you tomorrow night for dinner. I've gotta get to the hospital for a meeting."

He kissed Linda as she made her way to Jen's chair. "I'll meet you at the coffee shop around one and then we'll have lunch."

Jen got Linda settled into her chair and began painting on the color she had mixed. "How's your leg feeling?" she asked, as she made sure each long strand was coated.

"Not too bad. I'm ready to get rid of this cast."

"What else is new?"

Linda smiled. "Actually, a lot. I've been dying to visit with you."

Jen raised her eyebrows. "Spill it."

"Well, first, Kellie emailed me and said she has a firm offer for the house at the nursery. A new couple wants to do a bed and breakfast and I need to give her an answer by Monday."

Jen nodded. "I knew she had someone interested. Are you thinking you'll sell?"

"Yes, I've decided to sell it and let Lucas manage the nursery. I'm also going to let Sara take over more at Buds and Blooms and cut back on my hours."

"Wow. I'm sort of shocked. I can't imagine you giving up the house."

"I know. I'm not sure I can explain it, but it feels like the right move and the right time. I want to work less and I think not living out there will force me to cut back." She lifted the cape and tapped her cast. "And this has shown me the house is not the best arrangement, especially as I get older, with all the bedrooms upstairs. Plus, it's too big for me."

"How exciting. Then you can find a smaller place."

"That's what I was thinking, until Max asked me to move in with him."

"Shut the front door," Jen said, dropping the brush into the color bowl and twirling the chair around. "He asked you?"

Linda laughed. "Yes, a few days ago. He said it makes sense because I need help with my ankle plus he said he loves me and I make him happy. I'm …you know, nervous."

"What? He's perfect. Handsome, kind, a doctor, and he clearly worships you."

"No, not about him. I love him. You don't think people will think I'm, you know…"

Jen rolled her eyes. "Oh, for cripes sake. It's the twenty-first century; nobody cares who you live with." She turned the chair to look her in the eye. "I think it's wonderful you love Max and he loves you. I didn't think I'd ever meet the man who could tear you away from your work."

Linda smiled. "I know. We have fun together and it's great to have somebody to do things with. And Jeff's accident impacted me. Between that and my broken ankle, it was the nudge I needed to quit thinking about cutting back and do something. I'm glad you think I should do it, too."

"Sam and Jeff will be overjoyed," said Jen with tears in her eyes.

"I know. Part of me feels guilty for being happy with all their troubles."

"Don't say that. They love you both. It's what Sam hoped when Max came for the wedding."

Linda's eyebrows shot up. "Wow, she wanted us to get together?"

"Oh, yeah. She was scheming the whole time," Jen grinned.

Linda sighed as Jen went back to work with her brush. "And there's one more bit of news you don't know."

"Man, you have been busy."

"This is weird. Max and I went out to the house and I had him help me sort through some old boxes, in preparation for selling it. Anyway, I found an old news clipping and a letter. As it turns out my mom and dad lived near Chicago and my dad was an accountant. He found some goofy stuff going on in one of the accounts and he later learned it was a bar owned by a mobster. Dad had asked some questions and they sent one of their guys to threaten him and Mom when they were leaving a restaurant. She was pregnant with David at the time. Dad hit him with a tire iron and ran away. But, he killed him."

Jen gasped. "That's unbelievable. Your dad? He was like the nicest guy ever."

"I know. So, they were both freaked out and got money from their mothers and fled the area overnight. They came here and started over and acted like they were in the Witness Protection Program. They didn't trust the cops in Chicago, which at that time makes sense. So, they told us we didn't have any relatives and bought the place and started a nursery. Mom said Dad never wanted to work for anyone else and living here they were sure they could spot someone new who paid them any attention."

"Wow," Jen said, as she stood frozen to her place, brush in the air, hanging on every word.

"The best part about this is I found my dad's brother, Mike. He lives in Nevada and after I talked to Mom and David, she calmed down and gave me permission to contact him. He's planning a trip to see them and then they're all going to come here to see me."

"That part sounds terrific. Your poor mom. I bet she was upset, huh?"

"Yeah, she was knocked for a loop. She's nervous about it, but I think she's lived in fear for so long, she doesn't know any better. I was upset with her when I first learned about it. I thought she and Dad should have told us about it. It's been over fifty years."

"What a tough spot to be in for them. How scary. But I'm glad you have an uncle you'll get to meet." Jen got back to Linda's hair and finished covering it with the thick cream. She piled it on top of her head and clipped it to keep it out of her face.

"Yeah, that's the best part. And I'll get to introduce them to Max." She giggled and continued, "They'll wonder what's happened to me. Selling my house, cutting back on work, and moving in with a cute doctor."

"I bet they'll be thrilled for you."

"I hope so. Then I've got to get the house cleaned out and ready. And, with my ankle, that's going to be a problem."

"Hire some movers and don't worry about it. We'll all help you with whatever you need. I told you I was struggling to get things done so I hired someone to clean my house. I met a new client a few weeks ago and she's been helping me. She's the new secretary at the high school, but was looking for some extra work for the summer. Her name is Regi, short for Regina; I'll give you her number. She does a great job."

"Okay. I'll call her. Is she still doing it with school starting?"

"Yeah, but she's cut back. She does it after school and is looking for a weekend job. She's ambitious."

"I should say so. We should tell Max about her. He was thinking he's going to have to hire someone else for the shop with Kyle leaving. Maybe Regi could work the weekends."

"That's an excellent idea. She's ultra-responsible and everyone at the school says positive things about her."

The timer dinged and the two continued chatting as Jen rinsed her hair, trimmed it, and styled it. Linda glanced at her watch. "Even with all our visiting, I have time to stop at Buds and Blooms before I meet Max."

"I'm going to get my lunch, so I'll walk with you and make sure you don't fall."

"Okay, I'll let you. I haven't been by since the accident, so I wanted to see how it was going."

Jen kept a close watch as Linda navigated the sidewalks and crossings to her flower shop. She hugged her goodbye and held the door for Linda before she continued on her way to Soup D'Jour.

The familiar aroma greeted Linda as she maneuvered to a chair at the front counter. Sara came out from the back and when she saw Linda bolted around the counter. "Wow, you look great. I'm so glad you stopped in."

"I had to get my hair cut today, so I wanted to stop in and see how things were going." She looked around the shop, nodding her approval. "It looks busy."

"We've got two weddings this weekend, so we're cleaning flowers. After this weekend, we don't have many more on the books. As usual, the tourists will leave, and so will all the weddings."

"Yep, that's how we know summer is over. Would you put together some fresh flowers and I'll take them with me? I miss having them around. I'm meeting Max in a few minutes."

Sara nodded and hurried to the cold case. She returned with a beautiful selection of fragrant flowers in a plain glass vase and a bow made with the same whisper pink ribbon Linda used for Sam's wedding.

"Gorgeous," she said as she turned the vase and admired the blooms. "With the glass, I better have you carry them. Do you mind?"

"No, not at all."

They ambled down the street to Sam's coffee shop and Sara helped Linda get settled at a table where she placed the vase. "Take care and stop by again when you can."

"I will. I hope to be back working a bit in October, but I'll keep you posted."

Hayley brought Linda a drink while she waited for Max. She sipped an iced tea and looked at her watch. She glanced to the door as she heard the chime and recognized a man she didn't expect. He was older, but she knew the gait and the smile. It had been three decades, but her heart fluttered when she saw him.

She ducked behind the flowers, hoping he wouldn't see her. He stepped to the counter and ordered a drink and a piece of pie. With his cup and plate in hand, he scanned the room, looking for a seat. His eyes locked on the flowers and then glanced to Linda.

His eyes flashed recognition, and then apprehension. He smiled at her. The same melt your heart grin he had always had. She felt her mouth go dry and her face redden. *Crap, crap, crap. I have no idea what to do.*

"Hey, it's you, isn't it?" he asked, as he approached her table.

"Hi, Walt. Yep, it's me."

He set his cup and pie on the table and took a step to hug her, expecting her to stand.

She pointed to her leg. "I've got a cast, so I'm stuck in the seat."

"Oh, no. I hope you're okay." He bent and hugged her and she closed her eyes. The feel of his cheek on hers and his strong arms took her back. He held her tight, reluctant to release her. "May I join you?"

She nodded and moved the vase. "I'm expecting someone in a few minutes."

"I won't be long. I can't believe I ran into you here. My mom took a fall and I'm here visiting and helping them out."

"I'm sorry to hear that. Is she okay?"

"She'll be fine, but it'll take some time." He looked at her, his eyes crinkled as a slow smile spread across his face. "It's been a long time, but you're still the most beautiful girl on the island."

Linda felt her heart race. She stammered, "Uh, I uh, don't know about that. But, despite not seeing you for thirty years, I would recognize you anywhere."

He stared at his plate and took a bite of pie. "About that. I've been a complete fool. I should have apologized to you years ago, but instead I ran away and the more time went by the harder it was for me to call you. I can't believe I did what I did. I know I hurt you and I'm sorry."

Linda stared at him. She wasn't prepared for this conversation. "It's been hard," she whispered.

He reached across the table and held her hand. "I know. You of all people didn't deserve it. I was an idiot. Mom and Dad told me what happened to Brenda."

"Yeah, she hadn't changed much. She continued her ruthless pursuit of any and all men on the island and lately it had escalated when she became obsessed with Jeff Cooper."

He nodded his head. "That's what I heard. Mom said his new wife owns this shop."

"Yes, her name is Sam and she's become a wonderful friend of mine. She's from Seattle, but vacationed here as a child. She and Jeff fell in love while he was helping her work on remodeling this shop. They're a great couple and I'm sickened by Brenda's actions... Jeff is in a coma!"

"I had no idea she was such a nutcase. I'm sorry I ever fell for her. I have no excuse and feel worse that I left and never apologized or tried to contact you. I was too ashamed to face you. My parents thought I was nuts and haven't let me forget it since. To be honest, I've avoided coming to the island. This is my second trip home in all those years. Usually my parents come to visit me in California."

"Where do you live?"

"Roseville, outside of Sacramento. I work for a corporation that develops shopping centers. Mom tells me you're always working. Running the nursery and the flower shop."

"Yeah, I've been doing it for several years." She paused and took a breath. "Since we're being honest, that's how I tried to get over you. I threw myself into work after you left. I was crushed and embarrassed. So I hid at the nursery with my parents. They got older and after Dad died, Mom moved near David and I stayed and took over everything and started working more at the flower shop. I enjoy it, but I'm ready to cut back."

He nodded, shoved his plate away. "I'm sorry I caused you such pain. I'm thinking about moving back here to help my parents. I know I'll never convince them to leave. And I recently divorced, so I'm feeling lost and I think I need to come back."

"Sorry to hear that. I'm sure it isn't easy for you."

"You never married, huh?"

"No."

He glanced at his watch. "I need to leave and meet with Mom's doctor, but I'd like to get together while I'm here. Are you free anytime this weekend? I could stop by the house.

"Uh, well, I'm staying at Sam's place. My old house isn't designed for crutches and a cast."

"I'd like to take you to dinner. How about Saturday?"

"Um, I don't know."

He slid out of his chair, took a card from his wallet, and handed it to her. "Think about it and give me a call and let me know. For old time's sake." He bent and kissed her on the cheek and went out the door.

Man, if I had two good feet, I'd kick my own ass. How can feelings from thirty years ago come rushing back and erase all the crap I went through losing him? I can't believe I'm even considering dinner. He's still so charming and I loved him so much. I want to go to dinner, but do I tell Max?

Nineteen

She got through lunch with Max and when he asked if she was feeling okay she said she was just tired. He drove them back to Sam's and ordered her to take a nap. She lay in bed, staring at the ceiling. She felt stupid. She hated the fact she had enjoyed visiting with Walt. She couldn't bring herself to say anything about him to Max. Her mind exhausted, she fell asleep and didn't wake until it was time for dinner.

Max had gone shopping for their dinner party tomorrow while she was resting and was busy making a chef's salad. He had brought home some crusty bread from Ellie's bakery and was toasting it with garlic and butter. Linda wandered out and leaned against the wall, watching him. He was talking to the dogs while he chopped the veggies. He started on the cheese and slipped the dogs a few slivers. As she watched him she witnessed the kind and loving man he was. She knew she had to tell him about Walt.

She couldn't move quietly and the clunking of her crutches made him look. "Hey, how are you?"

"Much better." She plunked herself in a chair and watched him cook.

"We tried to do too much today."

"Yeah. And I never asked you about your meeting at the hospital."

"It was good. They want me to work as a consultant. The offer they made is a good one. I would get to do the things I like the best, including some training and mentoring. I'd like to do it, but wanted to talk to you about it first."

"That sounds like what you were hoping to do. Why talk to me?"

He leaned across the cool granite and held her hands in his. "Because, I think we have something special. Something that could blossom into more and I want you to have a say in decisions about what I hope is our life."

A tear slid down her cheek and her lips quivered. "Oh, Max."

He stroked her hands with his thumbs. "What's wrong?"

She shook her head and more tears fell. "That's so sweet. And I'm such a...jerk."

He furrowed his brows. "You're not a jerk. What are you talking about?"

"Today while I was waiting for you in the coffee shop, Walt came in and we visited. He's here because his mom is ill."

"Okay, but I'm still lost."

"Well, I liked talking to him. It felt like when I was young. He invited me to dinner this weekend and part of me wants to go. I haven't seen him since high school. He finally apologized for what he did and for not calling me. I can't explain it. It was good to talk to him."

Max smiled. "I see. He was a big part of your life for a long time. I'm not surprised. You were going to marry him. It's natural you feel something for him."

"I feel so guilty that I'm considering having dinner with him. I don't know what to do. I didn't want to betray you."

He tilted her chin up with his finger. "Having dinner is not a betrayal. I think he's a jackass for what he did to you, but that's your deal to sort out. I love you and I want you to be certain. I trust you to go to dinner with him."

She reached up to hold his face with her hands. "Thank you. I think I need to do this and catch up with him. A lot of old feelings came rushing back. When he apologized it was like all the hurt was washed away."

"Promise me this," he paused. "If you decide you want to get back with him, be honest and tell me." His dark eyes were serious and intense as he studied her face.

She sensed the hurt and fear. "I don't think that's going to happen. But I promise. I'll tell you everything."

He kissed her and turned away struggling to hide the sadness he felt. He gathered the rest of their dinner and the plates. They sat at the island and neither said much as they picked at their salads. He cleared the dishes while she scanned the television channels in search of something to watch.

He shouted from the kitchen, "I'm going to the beach to run the dogs. Be back soon."

Before she could say anything, she heard the trampling of feet and the door shut. *The last thing I wanted to do was hurt Max. But I didn't want to see Walt again without saying something. What a mess I've made.*

With the television selection lacking, she picked up her laptop to send Kellie the email on the sale of her house. As she composed the email she opened another window and typed a quick note to her brother asking him to break the news to her mom about the house. She thought her mom would understand, but wasn't in the mood to talk. She finished the email and her finger hovered over the mouse. She closed her eyes and clicked the button.

Max came in with two cups of tea and sat on the couch. "What are you working on?"

"I sent David an email asking him to break the news to mom that I'm selling the house and I sent Kellie my decision." She took a sip of the warm tea and let out a breath. "I hope I'm making the right move."

"Change is good." He wiggled his eyebrows at her. "That's how I met you."

She smiled and reached for his hand. "Oh, by the way, Jen told me about a new secretary at the high school she thinks may be interested in working at Sam's shop on the weekends."

"That would be a relief. I was beginning to worry about how to staff it. Kyle leaves soon and without him, it's going to be hard. I'll talk to Sam about it while I'm there and make sure she's okay with the idea."

"I'm glad you're going to see her and Jeff. I wish I could come."

"We'll go back when you get rid of your cast."

Linda's laptop dinged. She glanced at the screen and found a reply from Kellie. She clicked it open and laughed as she read it. "Kellie is excited and put a whole row of smiley faces in her response. She'll make sure it closes before the end of October."

"We'll have to get busy packing your stuff. What about all the furniture?"

"Most of it stays with the house. There are a few pieces I want to keep and Mom and David may want some of it, but the majority of it stays."

"That makes it easier."

She closed the lid on the laptop and finished her cup of tea. "I'm going to call it a night."

"Are you sure you'll be okay while I'm in Seattle?" He moved to help her out of the chair.

"I think so. I'll call someone if I have any real trouble, but I'm getting better at maneuvering and from the looks of your shopping excursion, I won't need any food." She smiled as he put the crutches under her arms.

"Tomorrow will be fun. Jen needs the distraction."

"I agree. It will be fun to visit with her and Megan."

Max went ahead of her and turned on the bedroom light and pulled down the sheets. "Do you need any help?"

"I'm okay. If I get stuck, I'll yell for you."

"By the way, I forgot to tell you, you look beautiful. Jen did a great job on your hair."

She plopped onto the bed and he took her crutches. He sat beside her and wrapped his arm around her shoulders. Her head bent to his chest. "You've had a stressful day."

She nodded. "The house decision has been hard. And seeing Walt was awkward. Plus, my leg is tired."

"I know, honey. You rest and we'll have a better day tomorrow." He bent toward her and found her lips. "I love you, Linda."

She smiled and turned toward him. "I love you back."

* * *

Linda wanted to get ready on her own, in preparation for Max's absence. It took her hours, but she finally emerged from the bedroom, dressed and ready for the day. When she got to the kitchen she noticed a sticky note from Max. He had taken the dogs for a run on the beach and left a box of fresh pastries from Sweet Treats.

She glanced at the clock and saw it was close to eleven. She retrieved Walt's card from her pocket. She punched in his number and felt her heart speed up.

He answered and her mouth went dry. "Hey, Walt. It's Linda."

"I'm glad you called."

"Will dinner work for you tomorrow?"

"You bet. I'd love to see you."

"I can't drive, so how about you stop and get something and come here. I'm staying at Sam's out on Hidden Cove."

"Perfect. Mom and Dad can give me directions. They're pleased I'm going to see you."

"Give them my best. Walt, you know this is just dinner between two old friends, right?"

"Oh, yeah. I've missed you and when I ran into you the other day, I realized how much."

"Okay. I'll see you tomorrow. Say around six."

"I'll be there. Can't wait."

Her hands were shaking as she hit the end button on the phone. *I hope I'm not making a big mistake.*

She picked a fresh cinnamon roll from the box and poured herself a cup of tea. While she nibbled she opened her email. She clicked on one from David. Her eyes darted over the screen and she smiled. He had explained the sale of the house to her mom last night and they were both excited for her. He told her they were looking at the middle of October for a visit, but would finalize the dates soon.

She typed a response thanking him. She told him she planned to let the family stay at the old house when they came to visit. She wanted David and her mom to take any furniture they wanted.

She looked at her calendar and realized it was only a few weeks until she and Max would be taking their Victoria vacation. That is, if things were still on with Max and she didn't wreck everything by reliving her youth with Walt.

She caught a glimpse of the dogs running towards the house. Max was several paces behind and they all clambered onto the deck. He opened the doors and the dogs dashed for their water bowl. Max went to the fridge for lemonade and slid into a chair.

"Whew, they can motor," he said, catching his breath.

"Looks like you had a workout."

"When did you get up?"

"Around nine, but it took me two hours to get ready. I wanted to try it alone."

"Good. I told Ellie and Hayley you'd be alone this weekend. They both said to call if you need anything. And Jeremy and Heather are right down the road."

She gripped his hand. "I know. Remember, I've lived here all my life. Trust me, I'll be fine."

"Just be careful."

"I promise. Also, Walt is going to come by here for dinner tomorrow. I don't want to go into town."

"Okay. Call me tomorrow night and let me know how it goes."

She nodded and gripped his hand and squeezed.

"While you were sleeping, I called Sam and asked her about hiring someone. She was fine with it, so I called Jen and she gave me Regi's number. I'm going to meet her today after school at the shop."

"Do me a favor and ask her if she's interested in working at the house, as well, helping pack and clean over the next month or so."

"I'll do that. I might ask her to help us on my house too, so we can get it all done."

They spent the afternoon in the kitchen. Linda watched while Max did the prep work for dinner. He was chopping all the veggies and cheese for the taco bar he was planning. They snacked on leftovers and chatted about their upcoming trip to Victoria.

Around three Max left to meet Regi and pick up a pie he had ordered for dessert. Hayley was proving to be a capable baker and had been working hard to make sure Sam's reputation for delicious pies was intact.

Linda rested in the recliner and watched television. She felt her eyes grow heavy and awoke with a start when she heard Max return. The dogs followed the trail of fresh pie and danced around Max as he made his way to the kitchen.

"How'd it go with Regi?"

"Great. She's interested and wants to work weekends. She also said she'd help us with all the moving at both places. She's trying to earn extra money and can work after school and weekends. If you're feeling like it, she offered to stop by and take you out to your house so you could show her what you want done tomorrow."

"Wow, that's fast."

Max dashed from refrigerator to stove, getting the meat seasoned and starting the rice. He was rushing since he had less than an hour to get everything ready.

"Yeah, she'll start working weekends at the shop in two weeks, so she wanted to get as much done for us while she has the time. I told her I'd be gone this weekend, so she suggested she work with you. You can give her a call and let her know."

"Okay. That will keep me busy while you're away. I heard from David and Mom is fine with me selling the house. It sounds like they're planning to visit in October, so that will work well."

"I'm looking forward to meeting them." He retrieved glass bowls for the salsas and dumped chips into a couple of wooden bowls.

"I wish I could help you."

"It's okay. I stayed too long visiting with Hayley and Kyle. They're both great kids."

"Sam's lucky to have them. How old is Regi?"

"She's close to forty. She has an interesting story."

Linda raised her brows with an inquisitive look.

"She and her high school sweetheart took a trip here and loved the island. They went their separate ways after graduation, but made a promise to each other. If they were both available, they would meet back here for their fortieth birthdays."

"So romantic," said Linda. "So, is he here?"

"Not yet. Their birthdays are a few days apart in December and she told me she had been a school secretary and decided to put in for a job here and get settled, hoping he comes."

"So, they haven't talked in all these years and she doesn't know if he'll come or not?"

"That's right."

"Wow, that's trust."

"Yeah, pretty brave of her."

Max began blending margaritas as the doorbell rang out. The dogs ran to the door and when Bailey caught sight of Jen and Megan, she bolted to greet them. After playing with the dogs, they found their way to the kitchen.

"Smells terrific, Max," said Jen, sniffing the spicy scents coming from the stovetop.

"We're all set. I'm pouring some margaritas. They're virgin in honor of Megan and Linda's medication, but we could add something if you'd like?"

"No, they're fine as is." She took the festive drinks and carried them to the island.

Max finished setting out all the fixings for the tacos and added the rice dish. "Dig in guys."

They loaded their plates and sat down to a lively discussion about Max's new house, the sale of Linda's house, and all the latest news from the chairs of Jen's salon. When Max shared he had talked to Regi, the conversation quickly turned to her story.

Max piled topping onto a second taco and said, "I liked her and she's excited to work at the shop. It will take a load off everyone to have the extra help. I don't think Megan and Rachel want to work every weekend."

Megan nodded. "We don't mind helping Sam out, but it will be good to have some free time."

"She's going to take me out tomorrow and get started on my house. She wants to work all weekend and Monday, since it's a holiday," said Linda.

"She's a hard worker and very reasonable. She's been a big help at my place. And when she told me about her life, it brought me to tears. What a love story; and now her daughter is in college. It's unreal and amazing," added Jen.

"What daughter?"

"Well, she has a daughter. Regi and Cam, her boyfriend, came here right after high school graduation. Cam was from a wealthy family who had big plans for him. He was going back east to an Ivy League school. It sounds like they didn't think Regi was good enough for him. She said they were in love and had a romantic week here on the island. As it turns out she became pregnant and never told Cam. In fact, they both figured they would never see each other again and that's why they made the pact to meet back here to celebrate their fortieth birthdays, if they were unattached."

"Wow, she didn't share all of that with me today," said Max.

With a faraway look in her eyes, Megan said, "How totally romantic."

Jen glanced at Megan and furrowed her brow. "Well, it isn't exactly a story to be proud of. Having a child is a big deal and I don't think her life has been as romantic as it may sound."

"I know, Mom. Geez, I think it's neat that she came back for him."

Linda nodded, "I agree. I hope Cam returns for her and she isn't left waiting for nothing."

"So, she hasn't had contact with him? She came here completely on faith based on a promise she made over twenty years ago?" asked Max.

"Yeah, that's how she explained it. Her daughter is in college and that's one of the reasons she's working so much. It sounds like their life hasn't been easy and I respect her for providing for her on her own. She could have gone to him or his family when things got hard and asked for money, but she didn't. She said she didn't want Cam to feel a duty, she wanted him to love her." Jen paused and took a sip of her drink. "I shouldn't have blabbed so much, so don't act like you know all of this."

"Oh, I won't. Mum's the word," Linda said.

They finished visiting and Max and Megan did the dishes while Jen and Linda sat on the deck to catch the last sunlight of the day. Soon Max and Megan joined them and served pie for dessert.

"Mmm," Jen said taking a bite of the sweet berry pie. "Hayley is giving Sam a run for her money."

"Yeah, she told me she enjoys baking. She's working hard to make Sam proud," said Max.

"Speaking of Sam. Did you tell her you're coming with us to visit?"

"No, I thought I'd surprise her."

Jen nodded as she plucked the last bite from her plate. "She'll like that."

Max's phone beeped and he read a message. "Listen to this. Sam texted to say they're making plans to move Jeff into the rehabilitation unit. She said he started coming around today and they want to get him started on therapy as soon as possible."

Jen hugged Megan and they both had tears running down their faces. Jen swiped her hand under her eyes. "Do you think that means he'll be okay, Max?"

"I think it's a promising sign. I'll know more when I see him tomorrow and can talk to the doctors."

Jen's cell rang out. She fumbled with her pocket and answered, "Hi, Sean."

Max and Megan gathered the dessert plates and helped Linda up and they left Jen to finish her conversation, which sounded to be about Jeff.

Jen came in and handed the phone to Max. "Sean wants to talk to you."

Max took the phone and went into the great room. Jen and Megan loaded the dishwasher and tidied the kitchen.

"You guys are too good to me. I wish I could do a bit more," said Linda. "Megan, would you mind playing with the dogs while I finish talking to your mom? They love the attention."

"Sure," Megan said, as she crouched to herd the dogs out of the kitchen.

In a hushed voice, Linda said, "I wanted to tell you I ran into Walt yesterday after my haircut. I was waiting for Max at Sam's shop and he came in for coffee."

"Holy cow. I heard he was back in town because of his mom, but I hadn't seen him. What's he look like?"

"Oh, about the same, with gray hair and less of it. The thing is, he asked to join me and apologized for what he did."

"Damn straight, he was a complete asshole."

Linda hung her head. "He's coming over for dinner tomorrow."

"No, you've got to be kidding. Did you tell Max?"

"Yes, of course. He told me he understood I had a history and he was a big part of my life."

"He's just being nice." Jen bent over with her elbows on the island to look at Linda. "Linda, don't fall for him. Max is ten times the guy Walt could hope to be. I know you loved him, but it's been a long time."

Linda's eyes watered. "All those old feelings came rushing back over me. I'm not sure why I said yes, but I need to see him."

Jen shook her head. "Be careful."

Max came around the corner and handed Jen her phone. "Well, the news is optimistic. He's been very responsive today and they're running more tests, but everything looks good. He's going to need a lot of therapy to regain his strength and they plan to remove the feeding tube soon." He paused and put his arm around Linda. "I'm so happy for Sam. This will lift her spirits."

"We better hit the road. I need to pack and get to the shop early for a few appointments before we leave." She moved to hug Max. "Thanks for dinner and for coming with us to see Jeff."

Jen and Megan both hugged Linda and Jen whispered in her ear as she was leaving, "Remember, you have the best guy in the world right here and he loves you."

Twenty

Regi rang the bell at ten, right on time. Max opened the door and did his best to hold the dogs back from licking her to death. "Sorry about the dogs. They miss Sam and Jeff."

"No problem. I love dogs and these are cuties," she said, as she nuzzled each of them.

Linda was getting off the couch as Max led Regi into the great room. Linda waved, "Hi, Regi. So nice to meet you in person."

Regi's long legs carried her across the room and her stunning grey eyes and perfect smile greeted Linda. "I'm glad to be here. Are you ready to head to your house?"

"All set. Max helped out by delivering a load of boxes and all the supplies, so we should have everything we need. He also packed us a lunch," she pointed to a cooler.

"I'll get that and we'll be off," said Regi.

Max engulfed Linda in his arms, crutches and all and kissed her hard enough to suck the breath out of her. He rested his forehead against hers and said, "I love you. I'm going to miss you."

"I love you, too. I'll call you tonight and get a report on Jeff and Sam. Give her a hug for me."

He bent and kissed her again, softer, but longer. "I'll see you Monday."

Regi had seen their embrace and trying to give them privacy waited around the corner until she heard the thump of Linda's crutches on the hardwood. "Let's get you in the Jeep. Take care, Max."

Regi helped Linda into her old Jeep Cherokee. Despite the blotchy and faded paint, it was pristine inside. Every surface looked polished and the upholstery and carpet, although worn, were spotless.

"I'm excited to see your place. I've heard the nursery is spectacular."

"I'll miss seeing it every morning. Where are you living?"

"Oh, I rented a condo by the high school. It's small, but has a great view of the harbor."

"I know the ones you're talking about. And so close to work."

"Yeah, I walk, which is convenient. Plus I like my job."

"The principal there is a terrific guy. I went to school with him and everyone loves him."

"It must have been wonderful to grow up here."

"It was. It can get small, but I enjoy it."

"Your Max is a great guy."

"He is. I'm lucky to have met him. He's actually Sam's best friend. You'll love her when you meet her."

"He told me he fell in love with you from the moment he met you at Sam's shop."

Linda's head swung around to face Regi. "He said that?"

"Yep. He told me he'd been lonely for several years after losing his wife and had resolved himself to being alone, but when he met you, he knew you were the one."

Linda smiled. "He's terrific."

"He probably told you I moved here with the hope of meeting my old high school boyfriend, Cam. I'm not sure what's going to happen, but decided I might as well do it." She paused and then added, "I've been waiting a long time for him, so I hope he comes back."

"It's a wonderful story. Max mentioned you made this pact for your fortieth birthdays."

"Yeah, forty sounded pretty old back then. Now, it doesn't seem so. I have no idea if he'll show up or remember the promise we made. I haven't seen or talked to him since he left for college."

"Here we are." Linda pointed to the long driveway leading to her house.

Regi parked and bound her long blond highlighted hair into a pony tail and went around to help Linda out of the Jeep. "Max was right, it's beautiful."

"I think so," she handed Regi the key. "Go ahead and open the front door and we'll get started."

Linda gave Regi instructions on getting to her bedroom and bathroom and asked her to pack everything in those two rooms. Linda used sticky notes to mark items on the lower floor to indicate if they were staying or moving. The two pieces of furniture she wanted to take were the china hutch and her desk, which had been her father's. She labeled both of them so Regi would box their contents. She also made a list of the other rooms and what she knew needed to be done in each of them.

When Regi finished the bedroom and bathroom, they took a break and lunched on the porch. As they finished, Regi's phone chirped. She glanced at it, smiled, and tapped out a reply.

"It's my daughter, Molly. She's getting set for college at UW and checking on me. She wanted to come this weekend for a visit, but I told her we need to save on expenses right now."

"Oh, if we had known, we could have had Steve bring her back when he drops off Max and Jen."

Regi's eyes brightened. "Do you think he would do that?"

"I know he would." Linda glanced at her watch and dialed her phone. She asked Max where they were and he said they were nearing the city. She explained about Regi's daughter and asked him to call when they got to Seattle and they'd work on getting Molly to where she needed to be.

Regi rubbed her hands together while Linda was talking. "Wow, I can't believe everyone is so friendly. I'll call her right now and get her moving. Where should she go?"

"He docks at Shilshole Bay. She can look for the boat with Friday Harbor Marina on it. I'll tell Max to wait for her and make sure she gets there."

Regi was already on the phone explaining the opportunity for Molly to get to the island if she could move quickly. She went through the instructions and told Molly to hurry and get moving, giving her Max's name and describing him.

"She says she'll leave in a few minutes and take the bus. It will take her about half an hour to get there. I hope he can wait."

"That sounds fine. Let me call Max back and explain it." Linda told him about Molly's arrival and asked him to wait until she boarded and to make arrangements with Steve to transport her back to the city when he returned for them on Monday.

"Well?"

"It's all set. Steve is bringing Charlie, Jeff's son, back with him today, too. So Molly can join them and go back on Monday. Max said Steve will be back before we're done here, so he'll make sure Molly gets to your condo."

Regi took Linda's hands. "I can't tell you what this means to us. We're on a tight budget and visits are low on the priority list."

"No problem. I'm glad we got in touch with her and can make it work."

Regi rinsed the lunch dishes and repacked the cooler. "I'll get started on the kitchen."

Linda gave directions and packed some of the lighter items and Regi worked on the rest. It was three o'clock by the time they finished in the kitchen and Linda suggested they call it a day.

On the way back to Sam's, Regi asked, "Where are you going to move?"

"Well, Max has asked me to move in with him. He recently bought a home not far from Sam's and I'm considering it."

"So, you're not sure?"

"I think I'm sure. It's all such a big change."

"I don't know either of you very well, but I can tell he loves you and cares about you. He wanted me to be sure and take care of anything you needed while he was gone. He seems perfect."

"He is. I think I'm a little scared."

"I understand, but I hope you say yes," she laughed. "He told me about his house and it sounds gorgeous."

"It's spectacular with a stunning waterfront area and outdoor patio. I love it and I love him, so I'm leaning that way."

Regi turned into Sam's driveway. "So, tomorrow and Monday I'll bring Molly with me and we'll get as much as we can done on your house."

"Sounds like a plan. I left you a list on the table of the other rooms and what you need to do. Be sure and bill me for Molly's hours, too. She'll need to head back in the afternoon, so don't stay too late Monday. And you may want to go to the pancake breakfast on Monday in the park. It starts at six in the morning and it's yummy, plus a good place to meet lots of locals."

"I'll see if Molly wants to go. Do you want me to keep this key?"

"Oh, yes, please do. Hold onto it and we'll get together when Max returns. In fact why don't you plan to join us for pizza Monday night at Sam's house? We'll make Jen come, too, say around six."

"Really? That sounds fun." She came around and retrieved Linda's crutches and helped her to the house. She undid her hair and the breeze shuffled the golden strands around her face. Regi had the look of not working hard to look fabulous. She wore little makeup and her flawless skin and thick hair emphasized her effortless beauty.

Regi promised to see her Monday and waved as she drove away.

Linda collapsed into the recliner and felt her eyes close. She was exhausted from the work at the house, but excited to have a new friend in Regi. She was smiling as she drifted off thinking of the uninhibited joy she had seen on Regi's face when she knew her daughter was coming to visit.

* * *

The dogs nudging her hand, looking for dinner woke her after five. "Oh, crap, I slept too long."

She rushed to get her crutches and banged into the mudroom to serve kibble to the three hungry pooches. Then she hurried, as fast as her crutches would go, to the bedroom. She put on a clean shirt but knew changing pants would take too long, so left her jean capris on. She retouched her makeup and ran a brush through her thick hair. A spritz of perfume and earrings were the extent of her preparation.

She checked the clock and let out a sigh. Five minutes to spare. She thudded down the hall and as she rounded the corner, the dogs began barking.

She made her way to the front door and opened it to find Walt on the step with a huge bouquet of flowers. "Hi, Walt. You didn't need to bring flowers."

He stepped in and kissed her cheek. "They're beautiful and they reminded me of you. Let me put them somewhere and I'll make a trip back for our dinner."

She shut her eyes, taking in the familiar earthy scent of him. She led him to the island. "You can leave them here."

He dashed out and came back with several bags. "I stopped by Lou's and he got carried away." He fussed over the dogs as he unpacked dinner.

"Wow, you have enough to feed a dozen people."

"I know, I couldn't decide so ordered lots of things, plus I brought some dessert from Ellie's."

She pulled out a chair and he hurried over to take her crutches and help her into the chair. She took some lobster macaroni and cheese and a crab cake, plus a helping of homemade coleslaw. He loaded his plate with the same and added fish and chips.

"How was your day?" he asked.

"Good, I worked out at the old house. I'm selling it and trying to get things packed and ready to move."

"Wow, I can't imagine you not being at the house. What about the nursery?"

"I'm keeping it, but cutting back and letting someone else manage it for me. Once I get rid of this thing," she knocked on her cast, "I'll concentrate on working a few days at the flower shop."

"Oh, this is good. I've forgotten how much I missed Lou's," he said, biting into a crab cake.

"It's always delicious, just like when his dad ran it when we were kids."

His phone beeped and he looked at it with disgust. "Sorry, it's my ex-wife." He ignored it and shoved it away.

"Does she live in California?"

"Yep, she has the house and the kids and I get to pay for it all."

"Oh, sorry, I shouldn't have asked."

"No, no. It's the way it is. I'm angry about the whole thing."

"How's your mom doing?"

"Better each day. She has to stay in rehab for a couple more weeks and then they'll send her home. How about your mom?"

"She's living over near Yakima with David and his family. She's coming for a visit in a few weeks."

"So, where are you going to live after you sell your house?"

"I'm not sure yet. Um, I've been seeing a man and he's asked me to, uh," she stammered and paused. "To move in with him."

"Wow, do I know him?"

"I don't think so. He's Sam's best friend and moved to the island recently. His name is Max Sullivan."

"So, I guess I'm too late, huh?"

Linda blushed. "Too late?"

"I had this idea, fantasy, I guess. After we talked the other day, I had my hopes up that we could give it another try." He shrugged. "Guess my timing sucks."

His phone chirped again. He swiped it off the table. "I'm so tired of her shit," he said, as he slammed it on the granite.

"Anyway, I was kidding myself. Thinking about old times and how much fun we had and how beautiful you are. Hoping for a do over." He reached for her hand and gripped it. He leaned in and found her lips.

She closed her eyes and lost in the familiarity of his touch, gave in and let the kiss deepen. She sensed his hands on her back as he caressed her shoulder and felt his hand slide over her collarbone.

She took in a sharp breath and her eyes popped open. She pulled away and shook her head, "I can't do this."

She looked into the same gentle brown eyes, streaked with barbs of olive green, she had known so long ago. "I used to fantasize you'd come back. First I was angry and humiliated, but secretly hoped you'd come back to me. But that was decades ago. I waited around over half my life. Now I know I wasted those years. Truth is I gave up on finding anyone. Waiting for you and dealing with the humiliation crippled me. I never thought I'd find someone like Max. He's an extraordinary man and I love him." She paused, "Sorry, but what we had is over."

He looked down, held her hand, and shook his head. "I'm the one who's sorry. I tossed you away and went on to marry a real winner. I think I knew when I married her it wasn't right, but I didn't want to hurt her. Anyway, we should have divorced long ago, but we kept having kids, thinking they would solve our troubles. Truth is, she's nuts and got involved with her latest crazy religious group and decided I wasn't part of her plan, so she wanted a divorce. I miss the kids, but not her. Sometimes I think this is payback for what I did to you."

She shook her head. "I think it's life and sometimes things don't work out the way we think they're supposed to. I loved you for a long time and then I came close to hating you for several years." She looked into his eyes, "I never thought I'd say this, but I'd like to be your friend, just your friend."

He grinned. "I don't deserve you, but you'll always be my friend." His phone rang as he moved to hug her. He looked at the screen and shook his head in disgust.

"I better take this even though I know she put him up to calling me since I didn't answer her texts. It's my son," he said, irritation lingering in his voice.

Linda nodded as he answered the phone and moved to the end of the kitchen. He returned a few minutes later, apologizing for the call.

"Man, this house is something else. Jeff was always a great guy and it sounds like he found a terrific wife in your friend, Sam. How's he doing?"

"Actually, Max left today with Jen to visit him. He started coming around yesterday, so Max decided to make the trip and check on him. He's a doctor and has been communicating with Jeff's doctors whenever he can to get information for Sam. I'll be talking to him later tonight and hope he has good news. Sam hasn't left Jeff's side since this happened and Max was staying here to watch the dogs. Then when I broke my ankle I came to stay."

"Does Max know we're having dinner tonight?"

"Yes, he does. He understands you were a big part of my life."

He nodded as he stared at her. "Yeah, I always thought we'd be together forever. And we would have if I hadn't been such an idiot."

"Okay," she laughed. "We've established you were a boob and threw away the best woman in the world. I forgive you. Now, I'm moving on and you need to do the same. Your life sounds pretty complicated. Maybe you need to get things straightened out and calmed down before you decide to move or find someone new."

He nodded. "Yeah, you're right. It's not going to be easy and I need to concentrate on my parents right now. Would you be okay if I moved back?"

"Yeah, I'd be fine," surprising herself how fine she would be. What she had felt for Walt was a lifetime ago.

He gathered their plates and put the leftovers in the fridge. "I need to get going, so I'll leave these desserts with you. Share them with Max, okay?"

"Are you sure?"

"Yeah. You let me know when you get moved in with him and maybe we can get together. I'd like to get to know him."

She smiled. "I'll do that." She reached for her crutches and he moved her chair as she stood.

"You deserve nothing but happiness and I'm not worthy of your forgiveness." Walt looked at her with tears in his eyes.

She moved to hug him. He held her for a long time and squeezed her tight as he whispered in her ear, "You know I'll always love you."

She nodded and wiped her eyes with the back of her hand. He released her and she watched from the door and waved as he got in his car.

She locked the door and hobbled to the kitchen. She sliced a piece of cheesecake and put the box in the fridge. She dialed Max as she slipped another bite of the creamy dessert in her mouth.

Max answered with, "Hello, sweetie, how are you?"

"I'm wonderful, how's Jeff?"

"Doing well. We talked to him today. He's weak, but alert. They're moving him to rehab on Tuesday. I talked to his doctors and they're optimistic he'll make a full recovery, with time. We had him sitting up today, but not for long."

"That's terrific. I bet Sam is relieved."

"Yeah, she looks so much better now. How'd your dinner go?"

"It was fine. We visited and he left a few minutes ago. He wants to meet you and get together after I move in and get settled."

There was a long pause. "Did I hear you correctly? You're moving in?"

"Yep."

Max let out a sigh. "I'm thrilled. I've been worried all day you might decide to go back to Walt."

"Nope, I'm all yours. I waited around for Walt for years and after visiting with him tonight, realize I wasted those years. That is, until I met you. I'm not sure how this will work, but I love you."

"I love you, too. I can't wait to see you Monday."

"I invited Regi for pizza and thought you could ask Jen and Megan to come over. And we could talk to Regi about your house so she can get started on it."

"Okay. How did you guys do at your place?"

"She's a fast worker and she's going to have Molly help her tomorrow and Monday, so I'll know more Monday night."

"Molly's a sweet girl, you'll like her."

"Tell Sam and Jeff hello for me and if I get rid of my cast next week, we'll make another trip over to see Jeff."

"I will. Get some rest and I'll see you Monday."

Linda disconnected and got ready for bed. She slipped under the covers, feeling at ease, although tired from her eventful day. She rested her head on the pillow and exhaled. *I can't believe I waited so long for Walt. I'm glad I had dinner with him tonight, but sad it took me this long to realize he's not the guy I was waiting for. Maybe when we were eighteen it would've worked, but not now. My heart belongs to Max.*

Twenty-One

Linda slept in on Sunday and woke feeling relaxed and more rested than she had for a long time. She knew part of it was the sense of closure she felt from seeing Walt last night. He had meant everything to her and when he was gone, her whole life had slipped away with him. She kept an ideal picture of him in her mind, but last night's encounter had allowed the rose colored glasses to be removed and she saw Walt as he was; complete with all his flaws and the obvious anger he held for his ex-wife. She thought he'd have a hard time meeting someone new until he dealt with the chaos in his life and his obvious bitter feelings.

She stretched as she got ready to get out of bed, considering the beauty outside the bedroom deck, knowing she wasn't going to waste a moment of the next thirty years of her life longing for the past. She was done mourning what could have been and being a victim. She was going to follow her heart and let the love she felt for Max bloom into a new beginning.

She spent the day puttering around the house, planning and dreaming about living with Max. At the same time, she was rehearsing how she would tell her mom and brother. She knew she was overthinking it, since they both wanted her to be happy, plus she could throw in the excuse of her ankle.

She was thinking about eating some leftovers from last night, when she heard the dogs barking and running full speed through the house. She

182

shuffled to the front door and peeked out to see Regi and a young woman on the step.

Opening the door she smiled, "Hi, Regi. Come on in. The dogs are excited and will maul you with kisses, so be warned."

"Oh, we love dogs," said Regi, as she bent to pet all three of them. "This is my daughter, Molly."

"Hi, Molly, so glad to meet you," said Linda, balancing her crutches to extend her hand to the tall beauty with hair the color of cinnamon and captivating steel blue eyes. "Thanks for helping me get here for a visit. It's been fun."

"Sorry to barge in on you without calling, but we were on our way home and thought we'd stop by so you could meet Molly and we could update you on our progress," said Regi.

"No problem, I'm happy for the company. In fact, I've got a ton of leftover food from Lou's. How about you guys stay and visit?"

"We don't want to trouble you—" began Regi.

"No trouble at all. Max is gone and I'd appreciate the company."

Molly and Regi took care of heating all the food and setting the table on the deck. Regi chatted while she worked and Linda learned Molly was the recipient of an academic scholarship at UW and had a job working in the library. Since the job required some training, they offered the student workers the option of moving into their rooms early in August, which worked out well with Regi's move to the island.

"What are you studying, Molly?" asked Linda.

"I'm interested in microbiology and hoping for a career in research."

"Wow, that sounds terrific and ambitious. We'll have to introduce you to Kyle. He works at Sam's and is starting at UW this fall. If I remember, he's studying marine biology or oceanography, but you may be in some of the same classes."

"That would be great. It would be nice to know someone. It's a big campus. It's been fun working in the library, meeting a few people before school starts."

"We'll make a point of stopping in the coffee shop and see if we can catch Kyle. I told Molly I'll be starting work there in a couple of weeks. I'm looking forward to it," said Regi, as she took the last of the food outside. "I think we're ready, let's eat."

"Sam's place is so beautiful. I can't believe the view," said Molly, as she gazed out at the water.

"She's got a gorgeous spot. I miss her though," said Linda. "But her husband is doing better, so we're hoping they'll both be home before long."

The conversation drifted to the accident and Brenda. The high school was a good source of local information and Regi was well versed in the story. "What a horrible person she must have been to seek to hurt Jeff and Sam like she did," remarked Regi.

"Yes, it's been quite the ordeal. Jeff and his family are so kind and well-loved here and so is Sam. I was shocked about Brenda's accident, which I believe was a suicide. I don't think she could face the consequences of her actions," said Linda.

"Everyone at work thinks she killed herself and nobody has anything good to say about her. Looking at this beautiful island, I would have never guessed such sinister things could happen," said Regi. "But I'm pleased to hear Jeff's doing better."

As they finished dinner and passed around the leftover cheesecake, Regi told Linda they had made progress at her house and thought they'd finish tomorrow morning.

"Oh, terrific. Max gets his house next Monday, but we've been moving things in already. I'll be staying with him and will be taking some of the items you have boxed. Do you want to plan on working at Max's after school for the next week or two?"

"Yeah, I'd like to get it done before I start working weekends at the coffee shop, so that gives me all this week, plus one more weekend and the week after to finish."

"When he gets home tomorrow, we'll figure it out. You're coming for pizza, right?"

"Yeah," she hugged Molly to her. "I'll need the distraction after my girl leaves tomorrow."

Molly rolled her eyes. "She still thinks I'm her baby."

"Moms are like that," smiled Linda. "My mom thinks I'm her baby, too."

"UW is bigger than the towns we've lived in. Now she's in a huge city and all alone. It makes me nervous," Regi said as her eyes filled.

"I'll get our dishes cleared," volunteered Molly, as she took a pile into the kitchen.

"I think Molly will be fine. And you're only a quick boat ride away, if you need to get there," assured Linda.

Regi nodded. "I know. It's just she's all I have and we've been so close. I'm having a hard time letting her go."

"I can only imagine. I don't have any children, but I know it wouldn't be easy to see them leave."

"I hope I haven't made a big mistake moving here."

"I can relate. I've decided to sell my family home and cut back on work. Now I'm moving in with Max and I'm hoping it's the right thing, but not sure. I haven't had much change in my life, until now."

"For what it's worth, I think you're going to be happy. Max is a sweet man and he adores you."

Linda grinned. "Speaking of romance," she lowered her voice. "Does Molly know the reason you moved here was to meet Cam on your birthday?"

Regi shook her head. "No, I didn't tell her, since I'm not sure what will come of it and I don't want to add to her stress." She glanced towards the kitchen where Molly was working at the sink. "This sounds terrible, but I never told her about her dad. I told her I got pregnant and chose not to contact her father because he had moved away. I thought about telling her, but it never seemed like the right time and now I don't know what to do. If things work out and Cam comes, I'll tell her, but since he doesn't know either, it's complicated." Regi felt her cheeks redden as she stared at the water.

"It sure is. You've got a lot to deal with. I hope it works out for you, but either way, I know you'll enjoy living here," Linda said, as she patted Regi's hand. "And you've got a beautiful daughter."

"She is. She looks a lot like Cam's sister and she has his eyes."

Molly popped out of the kitchen to collect the remaining dishes. "Almost done," she smiled.

Regi got up to help her finish and Linda gathered her crutches and thumped after them.

"Molly, that was sweet of you to do all the cleaning," said Linda.

"Thank you for the dinner," she glanced at her mom. "Do you think we could go and stop by the coffee shop and see if Kyle is working?"

"Sure, if he's not there tonight, we'll stop back by tomorrow."

"It's a cute shop, you'll like it," said Linda. "I'm not sure if you have a lot of contacts in Seattle, but Sam's friend, Becky and her family live in Queen Anne and I know she would do anything to help, if you need it. Let me give you her contact information. Sam's been staying with her the whole time Jeff has been in the hospital."

"That would be cool. I don't know anyone in Seattle," said Molly.

"How kind of you to think of her. It would put my mind at ease a bit, knowing someone was close by."

Linda scrolled through her phone and found Becky's information. "She's Sam's super assistant and knows everything about everything. I'll let her know I passed on her contact information."

"Mom can give you my information to share with her, too."

"Okay, kiddo. Let's get a move on so we can get some rest before tomorrow. We need to have you to the marina by one o'clock."

Regi and Molly both moved to hug Linda. "Thanks for everything," said Molly.

"I'll see you for pizza tomorrow night." Regi waved as they climbed into her old Jeep.

Linda waved goodbye and herded the dogs back into the house. As she watched them drive away she hoped things worked out for Regi and Cam didn't disappoint her. *She's taking a big leap of faith to come here based on a twenty year old promise.* The three dogs watched her and whined, as if in agreement.

Twenty-Two

Max got home around four and arrived with a huge bouquet of bright flowers for Linda. The dogs were running in circles with excitement as he swept Linda off her feet and deposited a long kiss on her lips.

"Wow, that's some homecoming," she laughed. "The flowers are beautiful."

"I was at the market in Seattle and they reminded me of you. I'm thrilled you decided to stay with me. I can't wait," he kissed her again.

"How's Jeff doing?"

"Much better. They have him settled in the rehab unit. He's responsive, and although he's confused with some words, he's making sense. He's very weak and tires easily. It'll be a long road, but everything points to a full recovery. Sam looks so much better. I'm relieved."

"That's wonderful news."

"She's excited you're moving in. She wants to be home so bad."

"I bet. I can't imagine the horror she's been through."

"So, what's our plan tonight?"

"I ordered pizzas and Charlie and Hayley are coming plus Regi. And you knew Jen and Megan will be here. They'll all be here around six. Charlie is staying on the island this week, now that Jeff is doing better."

"Sounds good. Do we need to make anything else?"

"Nope. Big Tony's is providing everything and Hayley is bringing dessert. Jen and Megan will bring the order."

"So, what else did you do this weekend?"

"Not much. Regi and Molly stopped by and we had dinner last night. Molly's a sweet girl. I suggested they stop by the shop and visit with Kyle, since he'll be at UW, too. And I gave Molly Becky's information in case she needs something. I texted Becky and she told me she'd invite her and Kyle to dinner soon."

"Sounds like Becky. She's doing better now that Jeff's out of the woods. We all are," he yawned.

"And I heard from David and Mom today. They've been talking to Uncle Mike and have it worked out to be here the first weekend of October. So, that's the week after our trip to Victoria. Do you think we can make it work?"

"Sure. And you think they'll stay at your house?

"I think so. I'll let them decide, either there or at your house."

He moved closer to her and took her in his arms. "You mean our house."

She smiled and kissed him. "Yeah, our house."

"If you don't mind, I'm going to take a quick nap. I'm zonked and that way I'll be able to stay alert and visit tonight."

"Sure, I'll wake you in about an hour. Sweet dreams," she reached for his hand and squeezed. "I'm grateful you're home. I missed you."

He squeezed back as he turned for the stairs, "Me, too."

Linda dialed Sam, planning to leave her a message, but was surprised when she answered. "Hi, Sam."

"Oh, it's good to hear from you. How are you?"

"I'm great. Max told me the good news and I wanted to call and tell you how happy I am for you and Jeff. I'm so relieved he's doing well."

Sam let out a sigh. "I can't tell you how much better I feel since Jeff started improving. The first time he opened his eyes and I asked him if he knew who I was and he smiled, it was the best day. I asked him if he wanted anything and he asked for a piece of my pie." Her upbeat voice radiated relief and happiness.

"Oh, how wonderful. I'm thankful he's so responsive. You must have been scared out of your mind."

"I was. I had started getting depressed, thinking he was never going to recover or if he did, he'd be a—" she faltered, "a vegetable."

"Oh, sweetie, don't worry about that now. Max thinks all things point to a positive outcome."

"I know. We're so lucky and blessed. Speaking of, Max tells me you've agreed to move in with him in his new house. We couldn't be happier for you."

"I feel a little uneasy about it, but I know I love him."

"He's serious about you. I know he had abandoned hope after Lisa died and he's like a new man since he's found you. And you're a big part of why he decided to move to the island. I can't wait till we can get back there and spend time with you. I'm delighted my best friend found such a wonderful lady."

Linda's voice caught, "That means so much. If I get rid of this clunky cast next week, we'll hop a ride over to visit you and Jeff. Let me know if I can bring you anything or a special treat for Jeff."

"I will. He's not able to eat real food yet, but we'll see how it goes next week. They think he'll be in rehab for somewhere between one and two months. Thank God I've got Becky here. She keeps me sane and takes care of me."

"Maybe you'll be able to scoot home for a day or two once he's more settled. Zoe and Bailey sure miss you two."

"Yeah, it may work out down the road. I'm trying not to think about two more months, but take it a day at a time. I'm lucky you're there to take good care of the dogs."

"I'll let you go, but tell Jeff hi and give him a big hug from me. We invited Charlie and Hayley to join us for some pizza tonight and Regi is coming, too. You'll like her."

"Sounds fun. Wish we were there, but we'll be home soon."

Linda disconnected and reached for the dogs. She held Bailey's face and looked in her eyes and said, "Your dad is going to be fine and he'll be home soon."

* * *

Jen and Megan arrived balancing bags and boxes from Big Tony's. Jen also supplied some champagne and sparkling cider and Hayley baked a pie and some brownies. Regi's arrival produced dog treats from Ellie's bakery and a couple bottles of wine.

Linda introduced Regi to Charlie and Hayley. Hayley smiled and said, "We met when she stopped by with Molly to see Kyle."

"I'm glad she caught him. I thought since they'd both be at UW for their first year, it would be good for them to meet," said Linda.

Regi added, "Yeah, they found out they live next door to each other. Molly's in Elm and he's in Proctor. She works at the Suzzello Library and he's got a job as a barista in the café in the Art Building and the Suzzello, so they'll see each other. Pretty cool, huh?"

"Kyle's a good guy," said Max.

"Your friend Becky already got in touch with Molly. She wants to plan a dinner party and have her and Kyle come," said Regi.

Linda laughed. "Yeah, Becky is a master at organization, so I'm not surprised she's already coordinating an event. Sam will be there, so Molly will get to meet her."

They wanted to squeeze as much out of summer as possible, and decided to eat on the deck. Jen, Megan, and Hayley got everything ready outside.

Hayley came into the great room and announced, "Dinner is served."

They gathered around the table crammed with pizzas, garlic cheese wedges, and salads, amid flickering candles. Jen passed around glasses of bubbly for all and Max raised his glass. She noticed Bailey under the table with her head on Charlie's lap.

"Tonight feels like a bit of a celebration. I'm delighted to see Jeff doing so much better, which brings a new light to Sam's face." He looked at

Charlie, "Jeff's a wonderful father and I know you must be so relieved." He glanced at Jen and Megan, "And a terrific brother and uncle. I know you can't wait to get him home. So, here's to Jeff."

They all clinked their glasses and sipped. Jen stood and cleared her throat. "I'd also like to make a toast. To Linda and Max. We're thrilled about your new house. We love you both."

Linda touched her hand to her chest and glanced at Max. He turned to her and brushed her lips with his. "And I love you," he whispered, as he brought his head around to meet her ear.

"Let's dig in," said Jen, passing the salad. The table erupted into chatter and the non-stop passing of plates. Hayley completed the delicious dinner with a box of frosted brownies and a lemon meringue pie she made, using Sam's recipe.

"Oh, my gosh, your desserts look fabulous," said Regi, eyeing the mile high meringue.

"Sam's the master of the baking, but she started teaching me before Jeff got hurt and I've been doing my best to stock the store with her pies while she's gone," said Hayley.

"I've been eating her mistakes," laughed Charlie.

"Let me take a picture with my phone and send it to Sam. She'll be impressed," suggested Max.

Hayley's cheeks reddened with all the attention, but she posed as he took a few pictures and texted them to Sam.

The group had no problem polishing off every crumb as they oohed and aahed at the delicious ending of their feast, Max's phone beeped. He looked at the screen and smiled. "Sam says the pie looks perfect and she wishes she could taste it in person. She said Jeff threatened to lick her phone."

Regi offered to clear the table and do the dishes and Megan volunteered to help. Charlie suggested he start a fire in the fire pit and they sit by the beach.

Jen helped Regi and Megan with the kitchen duties so they could enjoy the fire with everyone. They had all settled in on the cushions and Max said, "I've been thinking about giving Kyle a little going away party next weekend. It will be his last weekend here, before he leaves for college. What do you guys think?"

"I think it's an excellent idea. He's an irreplaceable young man and we'll miss him," said Jen.

Hayley, Charlie, and Megan echoed Jen's thoughts and agreed it would be fun.

"I'm going to try to talk Sam into coming back for the day," said Max.

"Oh, how fun. Kyle would like that," said Linda.

"I thought we'd do a barbeque here at Sam's on Saturday night."

"Hopefully my cast will be off, so I can do something to help," said Linda.

"We can close the shop early, since the tourists will be gone and everyone can come," suggested Max.

"I'll make some desserts," volunteered Hayley.

"Perfect. I'll handle getting the meat and Charlie can help grill," said Max.

"Sure thing. I'll bring the drinks, too," Charlie said, as he patted Bailey, who was stuck to his side.

Regi said, "I'm not much of a cook, but I can do some snacks."

"That works. I'll do some side dishes and salads," added Linda.

Jen said she'd help Linda with all the side dishes and anything else she needed.

"Sounds like we have it covered. Do you think Molly would be able to join us?" asked Max.

"I'll check. I know her weekends aren't as busy, so it may work out," said Regi.

"If I can get Sam to come, she could share a ride with her," said Max.

Regi turned her watch toward the light from the fire. "I'll let you know for sure, but I better call it a night. I've got to get some stuff done at home and it's back to school tomorrow."

The party dispersed soon after Regi left. When Charlie and Hayley closed the front door behind them, Bailey's nose was pressed against the glass and she whined. Zoe and Lucy both snuggled up to her and then they all turned and trotted to their beds by the fireplace.

Max had started a fire while everyone was leaving and he and Linda burrowed into the couch, under Sam's soft blanket. "That was fun and you had a great idea for Kyle's party," said Linda.

"Yeah, plus the relief I feel knowing Jeff is better."

"I've been thinking about how to tell my mom and David I'll be moving in with you," said Linda, as she rubbed the end of the blanket between her fingers.

"And what did you decide?"

"Nothing, yet. I'm trying to decide if it's better to tell them before they get here or talk to them when they arrive."

"I think it may be best to tell them ahead of time, so you can stop worrying about it and they can have time to adjust, if they need it. Do you think they will be upset?"

"I don't know. I'm probably worrying too much. I was thinking of telling them now, but sort of hate to email them."

"How about email and tell them you have some exciting news and ask for a good time to talk on the phone or Skype?"

"I don't think David does Skype, but I could suggest it."

He rubbed her hand with his thumb. "I think it's going to be fine. I bet they'll be happy for you."

"You're right. I feel like a kid again, looking for Mom's approval."

"Speaking of parents, I haven't told my parents either. They're both in a senior living facility near my older brother, in Florida. They're both fine, but it's a place with incremental care for seniors, so they have everything they need now and in the future. I did email both of my kids and they couldn't be happier."

A smile lit up her face. "I'd like to meet them. Will your parents be shocked?"

"Nah, surprised and elated, but not shocked. They've been hoping I would find someone, so they'll be pleased. They were excited I was moving here. I think they've always hoped I would get together with Sam."

Linda's eyebrows shot up. "Seriously? I guess that makes sense since you've been so close all your lives. How come it never happened?"

"Oh, I don't know. It's never been like that between us. I've always felt like her protector, a big brother. I love her, more than my own brother, but not romantically. Not that people haven't accused us of being involved, but it's never happened. Marty was jealous of us at one time."

"He had a lot of nerve, since he was the one who was having affairs. What a jerk," said Linda.

"Yeah. I think he got over it and he's changed since he and Sam got divorced. I know he realizes he let the best woman he'll ever know fall right through his fingers."

"She's better off with Jeff. They make such a perfect couple and the added bonus is we like them both," she smiled. "I can't wait for them to get home."

"Yeah, we could have lots of fun together. I hope I can get Sam home for Kyle."

"I think she'll do it, as long as Jeff is doing well."

"I'm going to mention it to Jeff first and if he tells her to come, she'll do it."

"Ah, you're a sly one, Dr. Sullivan."

He leaned over and kissed her. They spent the rest of the evening wrapped in each other's arms, watching the flames dance in the fireplace as the last of the light faded away.

Warmed by the fire and the feeling of Max's arms around her, Linda felt herself getting drowsy. As her eyes fluttered and closed, she was composing the email she planned to send to her family in the morning.

Twenty-Three

Linda knew Max was right. She had to tell her family so she'd quit worrying herself about what they would say. As her finger hovered over the mouse button, she hollered out to Max, who was in the kitchen, "I'm sending the email."

"Do it," he shouted back, "and then we'll have some of my famous waffles.

She sniffed the air and inhaled the toasty aroma coming from the kitchen. She closed her eyes and hit the button. "Now, it's done," she whispered.

She thumped into the kitchen and took a chair at the island, ready for breakfast. Max delivered some tea and put the pitcher of heated syrup between them. Linda cut into the warm golden squares and released the pooled butter. She bathed her forkful in a puddle of syrup and brought it to her lips and groaned. "These are the best."

"Thank you. They're my signature breakfast dish," he smiled.

"So, do you want to work at the house this afternoon?"

"Yeah, I've got to work at the coffee shop this morning and I'll grab us lunch and then stop by for you. Regi is going to meet us there when she finishes at school.

"I ordered all the stuff on the list, so it should be arriving this week. I called Nate, our delivery man, and if he gets anything for us at the new house, he'll call me or leave word at the coffee shop or my flower shop, so we'll know."

"The beauty of a small town," said Max.

She grinned, "Yeah, you sacrifice a little privacy, but get extra service. He offered to bring my stuff over from the house in his pickup."

Max finished his breakfast and gave Linda a quick kiss goodbye. "I've got to get a move on, but I'll see you around one."

Linda straightened the kitchen and scrutinized the deck flower pots. When she came in she checked her email and discovered a response from David. He said they were excited to hear her news and he would do his best to set up Skype and plan a call tonight.

She typed back a quick response and knowing they'd be working late at the new house, set the call for eight o'clock. She wanted Max to be available so she could introduce him.

She went to do her exercises, hoping to work off her nervousness. She also hunted through Sam's recipe box and picked out a few side dishes for Kyle's party. By the time she was done, it was close to noon. She packed her tablet and her lists, so she'd be ready for Max.

When he arrived he suggested they take the dogs, so they would get used to the new dog run and the yard. He loaded them and helped Linda get in. "Kellie worked her magic and we have the phone and cable scheduled this afternoon, so we'll have television and Internet available, I hope," he said.

"Oh, good. We have lots to get done in less than a week."

"Yeah, but I'm sure we can do it."

Max unloaded the dogs first and got them situated outside. He unpacked new bowls for food and water and filled them while Linda maneuvered to the house.

They ate a quick lunch from Dottie's and then started tackling the boxes that were stashed all over the house. Linda was busy organizing the kitchen, when her cell phone played a soft melody.

She checked the screen, "Hi, Kyle."

"Hey, Linda. Nate's here and said he has some deliveries for you at the new house. Are you going to be there?"

"Yep, we're here all afternoon."

"Okay, I'll let him know. Do you guys need any help tonight?"

"If you're around, Max could use some help with the furniture. I can't do much and Regi is coming, but we could use some muscle."

"I'll stop by when I leave here at five and help."

"We'll see you then." She heard Max talking to the cable installer and she continued to dig through boxes.

Linda finished her third box and heard the doorbell. Max came running from the master suite. "Coming," he hollered.

He opened the door to find Nate stacking several boxes on the steps. "Hey, Max. Kyle said you guys were here, so I brought a load. I'll help you get them inside."

"Linda said she had some packages coming, I guess she wasn't kidding," he laughed.

Regi rushed through the door as Nate was turning to leave and they collided. Regi rocked back and teetered on the edge of the step, but Nate was quick and grabbed her before she could topple over.

"Sorry, Regi, I didn't see you. Are you okay?" he asked, his arm fixed around her.

"Yeah, it's my fault. Sorry. Uh, thanks for catching me," she said, looking at his arm.

He followed her eyes to his arm and his face reddened. He abandoned his hold on her. "Sure, see you tomorrow. At the school." He waved goodbye to Max and jogged to his truck.

"Come on in Regi, you sure you're okay?" asked Max.

"Oh, yeah. I was in a hurry and wasn't watching where I was going," she said, as she stepped into the entry. "Nate brought quite a load, huh?"

"Yeah. Let's find Linda in the kitchen."

She followed him and they found Linda perched on a stool, working on the cupboards. "Hey, Regi."

"Hi, how about I help you finish in the kitchen?"

"Sounds good. And Kyle is going to come over around five to help with the furniture we need to move."

Max went back to check on the cable. Regi was a fast worker and had several boxes done and emptied by the time Kyle arrived. Linda had unearthed the area rug out of the boxes Nate had delivered and they positioned it in the great room and moved the furniture around it. Then Kyle helped Max arrange the furniture in the bedrooms.

Linda and Regi had the kitchen finished by the time the two announced the bedrooms were ready. Linda glanced at her watch, "Hey, Max. We better get going. I promised David I'd call around eight."

"Okay, I'll hurry," he said, as he turned to Kyle. "Thanks for the help, Kyle. We couldn't have done it without you." Kyle waved goodbye from Rita's massive car, which seemed to take days to disappear from the driveway.

Regi wanted to stay and organize the boxes Nate had delivered and promised to be back tomorrow afternoon. Max scurried around the house turning out the lights and checking all the doors. He collected the dogs and managed to get them all home with half an hour to spare before the call.

He offered to make a quick dinner, but Linda said she was too anxious to eat. She went into Sam's office to connect to Skype, so she'd be ready to make the call. She'd told Max she'd shout out for him when she was ready.

Lucy sensed Linda's mood and placed her head in Linda's lap. As she let her hand glide over the silky fur, she relaxed. "I know, I'm being ridiculous. I can't believe I'm getting so worked up about this." Lucy's big brown eyes registered understanding and she licked Linda's hand.

She connected the call and soon heard the blip and saw her brother on the screen. "Hi, David. I can see you. Do you see me?"

"Yeah, we can see you. Mom's right here."

He moved over and Linda noticed her mom waving. "Hi, Mom. I see you. Isn't this cool?"

She heard her mom ask David if she had to press a button to talk. "Oh, heavens, this is like science fiction."

"So, what have you guys been doing?"

David answered, "We've been talking to Uncle Mike on the phone. He's a kind man and he and his wife are excited to visit. They're going to make the trip in their RV and then we'll all drive over to catch the ferry. So, what's your news?"

"Well, I wanted to tell you before you came for your visit. I've met someone special. You remember the man who called you when I broke my ankle? His name is Max Sullivan and he's a doctor." She caressed Lucy's warm ears.

"Yeah, I remember him. I thought he was just your doctor."

"We met each other through Jeff Cooper. Jeff married a lady named Sam and she's Max's best friend. They grew up together in Shoreline. Anyway, I met him a few months ago. He lost his wife to cancer about five years ago and has been living in San Diego. He decided to move here to be closer to his friends. We've been dating and it's serious."

"Oh, how wonderful? You're getting married, right?" asked her mom.

"No, not yet. He's invited me to stay with him, since I need help with my ankle and need to find a new place when mine sells. I said yes." She stared at the screen looking for any reaction, but they both sat, unmoving. "And, more than that, I love Max. He's been wonderful and we're taking it slow. I want to make sure this will work."

David looked at his mom. "Isn't that great, Mom?"

"Yes, he sounds like a nice man."

"He is, Mom. He's the best. I ran into Walt last week and we had dinner. After talking with him, I realized I'd let the loss of him define the rest of my life. I'd been waiting, I think for him. But, I know now he's not the one for me and realistically never was. I've been hiding from life for a long time and with Max, I finally feel like I'm me again. We've been working on his new house. It's down the road from Jeff's cabin."

"I know Walt hurt you, honey. I'm sorry and I'm glad you found someone special. I'd be happier if you were married, but I understand the times are changing," her mom shook her head.

"We're happy for you, Linda. Sounds like Max is a terrific guy and we can't wait to meet him."

"He's here now. I can have him come on the call."

David glanced at his mom. "Nah, let's wait. This isn't the best way to meet him. We'd rather see him in person."

Linda was quiet.

"Are you there?"

"Yeah, I'm right here. You'll need to decide if you want to stay at the old house when you come or you're all welcome to stay with us at Max's. I've got some things at the house you guys need to look over and decide if you want. You can take them with you or ship them back."

"That sounds great. We'll talk to Uncle Mike and see what he thinks and let you know on the arrangements. How's your leg?"

"Doing well. I hope to get rid of the cast next week and that will make it easier to get around."

"We'll see you soon, honey," waved her mom.

Linda said her goodbyes and disconnected the call. Lucy waited at her feet. "Well, it could have been worse. Could have been better, too. Maybe Mom will come around."

Lucy waited for her to get her crutches and led her to the kitchen. Max was making them salads for dinner. "Hey, you're already done?"

She nodded. "Yeah."

"So, it didn't go so well?"

"It was okay. I knew my mom would be less than pleased I was moving in with a man. She's pretty old fashioned. David's voice sounded sincere. I think he'll talk to Mom."

"I guess I better call my parents. Now I'm worried," he smiled. "But not too much."

"They decided to meet you in person instead of online. I think Mom is overwhelmed. It's a lot of change, with the news about Uncle Mike, me selling the house, and then moving in with you. She's not used to that much change in such a short time."

"Give her some time. I'm sure when she sees how happy you are, she'll approve." He put the plates on the island along with some of Ellie's crunchy bread he had slathered in butter and garlic and broiled until it was browned. "Let's eat and then you need to get some rest. You look worn out."

They ate in relative silence until Max steered the conversation to the new house and how beautiful it was going to look once they got done. Linda's demeanor became animated and energetic as she talked about the plants she wanted to put on the patio and how much she liked the dog run area for Lucy.

"I was thinking," he said, as he reached for another piece of bread. "If you get your cast off next week, and if we get Sam to come for Kyle's party on Saturday, maybe we could ride back with her on Sunday for a visit."

Linda's eyes sparkled, "That would be terrific. I miss Sam and feel horrible I haven't been able to see Jeff."

"Okay, I'll work on it tomorrow. I'll call Jeff and Becky before I talk to Sam, so they can help convince her."

Linda pushed her plate away. "I'm beat. If you don't mind, I'm going to call it a night."

He moved to help her and drew her close. "It's going to work out. I promise. Don't fixate on what your mom thinks right now." He bent and kissed her. "I love you."

She nodded and buried her head in his shoulder.

* * *

The rest of the week was spent readying the new house. Nate volunteered to transport the desk and china hutch Linda wanted to take from her old house, along with a few boxes of photos and mementos, and the rest of her clothes and personal items.

Regi proved to be a huge help and by the end of the weekend, she had everything unboxed and placed in the house. Since Max had a truckload of books, he decided to take the library and left the actual office for Linda. With Regi's help, she outfitted it with her old desk and hung colorful floral prints and photographs. Max had plenty of furniture and a leather sofa and chairs went to his office, while she took the matching loveseat for hers. It was near the master suite and looked out on the yard and water, presenting a stunning view from her desk.

David called on Sunday night and reported he had talked with his mom and she had come around to the idea of Linda staying with Max. He confirmed Linda's suspicions that she had been knocked for a loop ever since Linda found the letter and hadn't come to terms with reliving that part of her life. Then finding Uncle Mike had been emotional and she was overcome with Linda's news.

"Mom's not as tough as she used to be, Lindy. She's been obsessing about her and Dad not telling us sooner about the whole hiding out thing. She knew you were upset with her for keeping it from us. It's a lot for her to take in at once. I think she's worried about Mike's visit, too."

"I know. I thought it was too much. But I'm so excited, and didn't want to surprise her when she got here."

"I know she's delighted you've found someone. She told me now she can stop worrying about you."

Linda felt tears sting her eyes as the words pierced her heart. "That's sweet. You guys will like Max."

"I'm sure we will. I'm glad you're done waiting around for Walt. He never deserved you."

"Now I know it, too."

"I think Mom would like to stay out at the old house. I think knowing it's going to be gone is also weighing on her."

"There's plenty of room, so I'll make sure it's ready for you guys. You're not bringing Mike's RV are you?"

"Nah. He was game for it, but I told him we'll take my Tahoe. It's plenty big for the four of us and maneuvering a big RV on the ferry is not the easiest task."

"Good. We have plenty of cars, if someone wants to explore on their own. Max and I are going to Victoria the weekend before, so I won't be around. I'll have my cell phone, but won't use it in Canada unless it's an emergency. We get home Monday of the week you're coming. Sam and Jeff gave me the trip as a thank you for helping with the wedding."

"That sounds like fun. You two enjoy yourselves and don't worry another minute about Mom. She's pleased you've found someone. She needs some time to adjust to all the new things going on. She might be weepy about the house, but don't let it get to you either."

"I'll try. We'll see you in a few weeks."

"I can't wait to meet Max and see you. Love you, Lindy Lou."

Twenty-Four

Monday morning Linda went with Max to his appointment to take possession of the house and sign all the paperwork. They decided to stop by the coffee shop for a quick visit and then head to Sweet Treats for a celebratory pastry.

They found Hayley behind the counter finishing a drink for a customer. She gave a quick wave. Max led Linda to a table and went to the counter to fetch their drinks. "How's it going this morning?" he asked.

"Busy, but not like summer. It's been steady, nothing I can't handle. But, I need to bake some stuff."

"Morning, Hayley. Max," said Nate, as he carried in a couple of boxes and handed Hayley the electronic gizmo to sign.

"There you go, Nate," she said, as she scribbled her name and handed it back.

"See you later," he said, making his way to the door. He stopped when he noticed Linda and sat down with her.

Max turned his attention back to Hayley. "After I take Linda home, I'll come in so you can work in the kitchen. We're going to stop by Ellie's and then I'll drop her at home."

"That would be a huge help. Today's your big day, huh?"

He couldn't disguise his happiness, grinning from ear to ear. "Yeah, I'm officially a homeowner."

"That's exciting for you guys." She finished making both of their chai lattes. He paid her and headed to their table, seeing Nate leaving.

"Does Nate have more deliveries for us?"

"Not yet. He was asking a few questions about Regi. He's attracted to her and wanted to know what I thought. He's a sweet guy."

"Did you tell him she's hoping to meet her long lost love here?"

She shook her head, "No, I told him she wasn't seeing anyone I knew of here. He sees her on his daily route by the school and didn't think she was with anyone, but was afraid to ask the other secretaries, since they thrive on gossip. He thinks she's nice and pretty," she raised her eyebrows.

"Don't get the guy's hopes up. Regi is determined to wait for Cam."

"I know, but who knows if he'll come here." She took another sip of chai. "I'm not sure she should waste her life waiting."

Max clasped his hand over hers. "Do you think he'll ask her out?"

She nodded. "Actually," she paused. "I told him we could have them both over for dinner at the new house, sort of a thank you."

A slow smile stretched over his face as he chuckled and shook his head. "You are trouble." He leaned in and kissed her. "Lovely, but trouble."

She laughed. "What? They'd be good together. And it wouldn't hurt her to live a little."

"Mmm hmm. Let's go get our treat and then I need to get back here to help Hayley."

They waved goodbye to Hayley and made the slow trek to Sweet Treats. Max opened the door to let Linda step in first.

Alerted by the string of bells on the door, Ellie glanced from the counter and hollered out, "Hello, you two. I haven't seen you in ages."

"I know. My cast has had me more confined than usual. But, Max just signed for his new house and we thought we'd celebrate," smiled Linda.

"Oh, how exciting. You guys have a seat and I'll bring you a basket of goodies."

Ellie bustled around behind the counter gathering a selection of twists, donuts, croissants, and a cinnamon roll. They were the only customers in the shop, so she pulled up a chair to join them.

"Oh, wow, these look tasty, but one is plenty," said Linda, as she eyed the basket.

"Eat one and take the rest home for a snack," Ellie said, placing a pink box on the table for them.

Max dug in and took the cinnamon roll, oozing sweetness. "You don't have to twist my arm."

"How's your ankle doing?" asked Ellie.

"Better. I go to see Dr. Brown tomorrow and hope to get the cast off and get a walking boot. I'll be so glad to get rid of these clunky things," she said, gesturing to the crutches leaned against the next table.

"And Jen said Jeff is doing so much better." Ellie put her hand over her heart. "I'm so relieved."

"I know. If I get rid of the crutches, Max and I are going to sneak over for a visit."

"And did you get Sam to come to Kyle's party this weekend?" Ellie asked Max.

"Yeah, unless something changes with Jeff. He helped convince her it would be okay and Becky volunteered to hang out with him. So Steve's going to bring her home on Saturday and we're going to go back with her on Sunday. We need to see if Regi will stay at our place with the dogs on Sunday night."

"Are you guys going to be able to move in this week?"

Max looked at Linda. "That's the plan. We've been working with Regi's help, so we're about finished."

Linda nodded, as she finished her almond croissant. "We need to finish a few things and go to the store and get groceries, but we're close. We'll be staying there by the weekend for sure. That way Sam can have her house back when she's here Saturday."

The bells jingled and Ellie slid her chair back. She gave Linda a quick hug and dashed back to the counter.

Max boxed the rest of the yummy treats and retrieved Linda's crutches. They waved to Ellie and thanked her for the goodies.

"After the doctor tomorrow, maybe we could do some shopping and stock the kitchen. Then Wednesday, we could work on getting the rest of our stuff from Sam's house and let Regi concentrate on cleaning it Thursday and Friday," suggested Linda.

"That works for me. Then the house will be ready for Kyle's party and Sam." He pulled into his driveway and jumped out to get Linda's door. "So, we'll plan to spend Wednesday as our first night here."

"I'm excited. I love the house," she said, gazing at the landscaping as she clomped up the sidewalk.

Max opened the door and waited for Linda. They went into the kitchen to put the box from Sweet Treats away and found a huge bouquet of flowers from Linda's shop on the island, along with a bottle of wine. Max plucked the card from the flowers and smiled as he read it and moved to the fridge.

"Wow," he shouted. "Kellie filled the fridge as our closing gift. Along with the flowers and wine, what a cool idea." He peered into fridge and noticed a huge variety of condiments, plus all the staples, along with fruits, veggies, meats and fish.

"How thoughtful of her. Now we won't have to go shopping right away."

"I'll call her when I get to the shop and thank her."

"Gorgeous flowers, too. Sara did a fabulous job on these," said Linda, as she bent to sniff the purple freesias and creamy stock, nestled between snapdragons and lilies.

"I better get back. You'll be okay until I get back?" he asked.

She assured him she'd be fine and positioned herself in her new office to get some bookwork done. She spent a few hours on spreadsheets and bill paying and fixed a snack of fruit and cheese, along with another croissant. The house was much more luxurious than she was used to, but as she sat at the island eating, she knew it wouldn't take long to get acclimated. It felt like home already and the comforts it offered helped alleviate the guilt she felt for selling her farmhouse.

Regi arrived before four and the two of them tackled organizing the items they planned to store in the garage. As Linda pointed to boxes to be shelved, she said, "So, Max and I want to have you over for dinner next week. We wanted to thank you and a few others for helping us out. Kyle is leaving on Wednesday, so we thought maybe Tuesday night. Nate's going to join us, too.

Regi heaved a box onto the shelf. "Tuesday works for me. What time do you think?"

"Let's say six, but come early if you'd like."

"What could I bring?"

"Nothing, we're treating all of you. So, all you need to do is come and relax and visit. It'll be fun."

"Okay, I'll be here."

"I also wanted to get on your schedule for Thursday and Friday and see if you could work on cleaning Sam's house to get it ready for Kyle's party. We'll be out of there on Wednesday."

"Yeah, that works. I'd planned to work all week here, but I think we're about finished, so I'll go to Sam's whenever you need it done. That reminds me; Molly said she can come to the party on Saturday. She's off at noon and can stay Saturday night."

"Perfect. I'll text Sam right now and let her know Molly can meet her. And next on the list is my old house. Although, if it's too much, say so and I'll get a service in. My family is coming to visit the first weekend in October and I want to get it cleaned and ready for them."

"How about I start on it and see how it goes and if I begin running out of time, you can get a company in to finish. If I work after school each day, I should be able to do it."

Linda nodded. "And one last favor. Max and I are planning to return to Seattle with Sam on Sunday and stay the night. Do you think you could come here and housesit and stay with the dogs?"

"Sure, no problem. They'll be okay here while I'm at the coffee shop, right?"

"Oh, yeah. They've got a huge fenced area and they'll be fine. We need someone to stay with them at night and watch the house for us."

"I may not be able to go back to my little condo after I get used to this place," she laughed.

"You're welcome to visit anytime. We've loved getting to know you."

"Same here. I've enjoyed it and the work has helped pass the time. I wasn't sure about my decision to move here, but meeting all of you has made it easier."

"It's a great place to call home. Although, I know how hard change can be. And I'm sure you miss Molly."

Without warning Regi felt tears spill over her cheeks. "Sorry," she choked out. "It just hits me at times. It's been the two of us forever."

"Oh, sweetie, I'm sorry to bring it up."

She shook her head. "No, it's not your fault. She's been on my mind and this happens quite often," she sniffed.

"You'll see her at Thanksgiving, right?"

"Yeah. She's not that far away. I mean I'm lucky. Lots of parents have their kids going to college all the way across the country. It's so quiet without her and I worry about her. But, we talk every day."

"That's good. I can only imagine how you must feel."

"I'll be okay. I know it's an adjustment."

"Well, we need to do our best to keep you occupied and you need to work on living your new life."

They both heard Max's car outside the garage and within minutes he came through the house and found them. "Hey, how's it going? I forgot to take a garage remote, but wanted to test it out."

"Regi is going to clean Sam's and start on my house. She also said she could stay here Sunday while we're in Seattle. And I haven't asked her yet, but if it goes okay Sunday, I'm going to see if we can con her into staying here when we go to Victoria at the end of the month."

Regi chuckled, "It won't take much to get me to stay in this beautiful home. You might have trouble getting me to leave."

Max laughed. "Sounds like you've got Regi roped into everything. How about I make dinner for you two ladies?"

"That sounds perfect, do you need help?" asked Linda.

"No, but you can sit and visit with me," said Max, depositing a kiss on her lips as he went back in the house.

"You're a lucky gal. He's a terrific guy."

"He is," she smiled. "I'm so thankful I met him. I spent about thirty years of my life hiding and waiting. It wasn't until I met Max that I felt like I was alive and not just going through the motions. I've had more fun in the few months I've known him than I have for all of my adult life."

Regi frowned. "What do you mean hiding and waiting?"

"Let's go inside and I'll tell you my story," motioned Linda.

They finished stashing the boxes and since Max had started a fire, settled into the couch in the great room. Max followed with a glass of wine for each of them. "Since Linda's no longer on medication, I figured you could indulge in one glass while you wait for dinner. I'll call you when it's ready."

"So," Linda said. "I grew up living on the island and in high school fell in love with a local guy named Walt. We planned to be married after high school, but right before the wedding, Walt became involved with Brenda."

"You mean Brenda that ran over Jeff and killed herself?"

"Yep, the same one. She was an awful woman and Walt was a stooge for falling for her charm. Anyway, we called it off and he and Brenda were an item for a few short months. They split and he moved away, without a word. Needless to say I was devastated and focused all my energy on work. I never tried to date. I was embarrassed and now I can admit I was waiting for Walt to come back. So, thirty years of my life went by and I met Max when Sam moved here around Memorial Day."

Linda took another sip of wine and watched Regi staring into her glass.

"Anyway, you know Max is a fantastic guy. Neither of us was intent on seeking a relationship but, as luck would have it, we found each other. The funny thing is Walt came back to the island a few weeks ago because his mom has been ill. I ran into him in the coffee shop and all those old feelings came rushing right over me. I agreed to have dinner with him. But, while we were visiting, I realized he wasn't the guy I thought he was all those years ago and I had spent the better part of my life alone because of him." She paused. "No, because of me. I had the power to do whatever I wanted, but I let his betrayal define me and secretly hoped he would come back to me someday. Now I realize what a waste it was. I'm fortunate I met Max. I wish I had known all those years ago what I know now."

"Do you think I'm wasting my life waiting for Cam?"

"I'm not sure. I don't know Cam, but I think you have a lot to offer and you deserve happiness. I think it's quite romantic—the promise you made each other. I'm not sure if it's realistic all these years later. And I worry you could be making the same mistakes I made. I ignored any chance I had at a relationship and I'd hate to see you do the same thing."

Regi nodded. "I hear what you're saying. It was pretty easy to put relationships aside when I was raising Molly. I've always worked hard to support us and went on a few casual dates, but used her for an excuse." She stopped and swirled the wine in her glass. "I think I've been waiting to be forty, thinking Cam would come back and we'd be together and everything would work out."

"And I hope it does. I truly do. I just don't want you to dismiss someone wonderful, who could be the right guy for you because you're trapped in the past and focused on the hope for you and Cam to be together. He may not be the same guy you fell in love with."

Tears welled in Regi's smoke colored eyes. "Yeah, I know. He could be entirely different or married or not show up. I know it makes no sense. But, I would feel disloyal if I didn't try this and at least see what happens."

Max poked his head into the room. "Dinner's ready."

Regi helped Linda with her crutches and they admired the meal Max had ready for them. They enjoyed the glazed salmon, rice, and steamed veggies he had prepared.

"Wow, this is heavenly. I'm usually too tired to cook when I get home from work," said Regi, spearing another forkful of the salmon. "What's in the sauce?"

"It's a simple soy sauce and brown sugar glaze."

"Delicious," said Linda.

"And we have ice cream for dessert. Kellie stocked the freezer, too."

Linda looked at her watch. "The poor dogs will be missing us."

"While I was cooking, I was thinking about running out to Sam's and picking them up and bringing what we need for tonight. What do you think about staying here tonight?"

"I'm pooped, so I'm all for it. I'll write down a few things I need for overnight and then we can get the rest tomorrow after the doctor." She snatched a sticky note and scribbled out a quick list and handed it to Max.

"I think I'm more eager to stay than I thought I'd be. Now that I'm here, I don't want to leave," said Max. "I'll go now and when I get back we'll have some ice cream."

While chatting with Linda, Regi cleared all the plates, packaged the leftovers, and did all the dishes. "I appreciate you sharing your story with me, Linda. And I'm going to think about what you said. I know a lot can change in twenty years."

"And you've never seen him since or searched for him online or anything?"

She shook her head. "No, I've thought of it, but I'm afraid. I think I'm hooked on the idea of the big romantic gesture. If I looked and found out he was happily married, I'm not sure I could handle it."

"Sounds like you've built your future on him."

She shrugged. "I guess I have." They heard Max's car pull into the garage. "I'll go help him unload."

"And I'll get some bowls ready for our dessert."

The dogs bounded in and began their investigation of the place with their noses to the ground. Regi carried in a couple of small overnight bags and Max trailed with three dog beds. He put Linda's things in the blue bedroom and asked Regi to take his things to the master.

Linda took orders for ice cream and managed to fill three bowls by the time Regi and Max returned. "Kellie gave us the good stuff from Shaw's, not store ice cream," she said, handing Max his cookies and cream and her chocolate. "And here's your vanilla, Regi."

Regi yawned as she finished her last bite. "Dinner was scrumptious. Thanks for letting me share your first night in your new home. I need to get home, but I'll get Sam's place done for you by the end of the week."

"Here, I have a spare key. You can drop it by when you're done," said Max, retrieving a key ring from his pocket.

"Will do. You guys have a great night and I'll see you later. I'll be working at the shop on Saturday, but will be at the party." She bent and hugged Linda goodbye.

"See you Saturday," said Max, as he followed her to the door and made sure she got in her Jeep.

Max noticed Linda struggling to stay awake as they sat on the couch watching the fire dance before them. He took her hand and led her to her bedroom. "You need to sleep."

"Sorry, I'm so tired."

"No problem. You get yourself in bed and I'll see you in the morning."

He put the dessert bowls in the dishwasher, made sure the dogs had water and were bedded down for the night, and then settled into the couch to enjoy the fire. The place looked amazing. Linda had a done a fabulous job picking out some new things and blending them with his existing furnishings.

He wandered into the kitchen to turn off the lights and make sure everything was put away. He glanced at the family pictures Linda had thoughtfully positioned on the sideboard in the dining room. When he had talked with his kids and told them about Linda, they told him they could tell how happy he was and were glad for him. His eyes stopped at the last picture he had of Lisa, before she became ill. She was on the beach near their house in San Diego, smiling at him as the wind blew through her thick hair. Before she died, she had told him she wanted him to remarry and love again. It had taken him five years, but he knew Linda was the one. He whispered, "You'd like her." As he smiled back at the photo, he knew she would approve.

Twenty-Five

Linda was outfitted with a walking boot at Dr. Brown's office. He was satisfied with her healing and prescribed physical therapy for her and wanted her to increase her level of activity to help strengthen her calf muscle. She was instructed to wear the device at all times, except for sleeping.

Linda's first steps in the boot were faulty. "My foot feels so stiff." Max gave her his arm for support.

"Take it slow," he said, as he guided her to the car. "It'll get easier."

"I never thought I'd miss those blasted crutches," she said.

"Physical therapy will help with the movements." He opened the door and she positioned herself in the passenger's seat. "Do you feel like going by Sam's to get the rest of our stuff?"

"Yeah, it'll be fine. Just feels different and awkward."

He drove out to Sam's and packed the rest of his clothes and helped Linda gather all of her things. They boxed the food left in the refrigerator and made sure the garbage was emptied throughout the house.

"It's a good thing Regi's going to clean here. I thought I could do it, but I'm not as mobile today as I hoped to be. And we forgot to tell you last night, but Molly's going to come over with Sam and go back on Sunday."

"Good for her. I know Regi will have the house ready for the party. You'll be doing better by Saturday, don't worry."

215

"I hope so. It doesn't hurt, but it feels like my foot doesn't move anymore."

"That's normal. You go to therapy tomorrow and Friday. I bet you'll notice a difference after a couple of treatments."

Max packed their stuff into the car and locked the house. By the time they got back to his place it was past lunchtime. They were both hungry, so Max heated the leftovers from last night and they devoured lunch on the patio.

"I want to call my parents tonight and tell them the news. I told you Peter and Brooke are both thrilled about you. I planted the idea of them visiting for Thanksgiving and they're both going to put in for some vacation time and try to make it happen."

Linda beamed and grasped his hand. "That makes my day. I can't wait to meet them."

He squeezed her hand. "I need to get to the shop as soon as we finish here. You'll be okay?"

"Of course. I'm going to try to put all my things away and get a bit organized. I want to fill those empty containers with flowers this week, so I'll have Lucas deliver the supplies I need and that will give me plenty to do."

"Promise to take it slow and don't overdo it."

"I'll behave. Remember to talk to Kyle about coming over for dinner on Tuesday. Tell him to bring his Grandma Rita if she's free."

"Will do," he said, as he moved to kiss her goodbye. "I'm so glad you're here. I'll be home before dinner. I want to try out the grill tonight."

* * *

The rest of the week was spent getting ready for Kyle's barbeque, finishing a few things in the new house, and getting accustomed to physical therapy and the regimen of exercises she had to do at home. Lucas delivered a load of supplies and helped Linda maneuver the containers around. By the end of the week she had them looking magnificent, overflowing with colorful blooms.

Saturday morning they splurged on breakfast at the Front Street Café and then stopped by the market to buy a few things for Kyle's party. Regi had the place gleaming and everything looked perfect. With no rain in the forecast, it promised to be a flawless evening.

Linda used Sam's recipe for baked beans and got those going in a slow cooker. Max worked on getting the tri tip and chicken marinating in bags. Linda prepped all the ingredients for her spinach salad and made the homemade dressing, waiting to drizzle it on the greens, so it wouldn't get soggy. Then she put potatoes in another slow cooker to bake. Ellie was taking care of the bread and bringing some cupcakes, Jen would bring another salad, and Hayley had dessert handled.

"It smells delicious already," said Max. "I think we're about done here for now."

Linda looked at her watch. "Yeah, we can come back around four o'clock. Sara is going to deliver some flowers for the tables, so we need to meet her and take care of any last minute needs. Sam should be here by then."

Max grinned. "I've missed her."

They went back home and Linda did some exercises and then took a nap, before getting ready for the party. The doorbell rang out while she was finishing her hair. She heard a familiar laugh as she came to the entry and saw Lucas with Max.

"Lucas, what are you up to?"

"Hey, Linda. I had a delivery for you two," he gestured to the front steps. There were half a dozen mammoth size pots containing gorgeous mums in deep fall colors.

"Oh, they're magnificent. Who're they from?"

Max handed her a card. "My parents."

"How sweet. I think they'll look grand out front if we place them along the walkway and a couple near the steps. You know what I mean, right, Lucas?"

He nodded, already moving to place the copper containers. He was done in minutes and waved a goodbye as he hopped in the nursery truck.

Linda opened the card. As she read both sides, Max watched her eyes fill with tears. He moved to her and put his hand around her shoulders. "Everything okay?"

She nodded. "Your parents wanted to welcome us to our new home and me to their family. They said they've been waiting for your heart to be made whole again and know from your conversations you've found the love of your life," she paused and cleared her throat, "for the second time. They hope we can visit them soon. It's signed, Brian "Sully" and Maggie."

"I told you they were pleased," laughed Max, as he held her close. "Wait till they meet you."

She wiped her eyes again. "They sound wonderful. I'll give them a call to thank them. Maybe I'll take some photos of the front area with the mums and send them along."

"They're okay on the computer, so you can email them. They'd like that."

"Let me hurry and fix my face and then we'll be on our way."

Max loaded the dogs and brought two beds with them, since he knew Sam would want to keep Bailey and Zoe tonight. Linda emerged, all repaired, wearing dressy black capris and a blouse the color of ripe watermelon with a ruffle neckline resembling flower petals. A black pashmina drifted over her shoulders and a beautiful silver hair clip rested at the back of her head, securing the hair she had pulled back from each side. Silver filigree earrings hung from her exposed ears and matched the necklace she wore.

Max heard the thump of her boot and gazed at her. "Wow, you're stunning."

"Ah, you mean you're stunned I'm not in sweats or shorts," she laughed. It feels good to be out of the cast and I'm ready for a celebration."

They pulled into Sam's driveway and Sara was right behind them with the delivery. She put the flowers on the deck tables and the island. Max made sure the fire pit was ready, so they could light it when the sun went down. Linda worked in the kitchen readying the food and the three dogs stood watch.

Zoe's ears perked up and like a heat seeking missile she zipped to the door. As the door opened, Zoe flocked to Sam, forcing her to the floor. She jumped into her lap and shoved her head onto her shoulder, buried in Sam's hair. Her tail was wagging and thumping the floor. Linda stood in amazement as Zoe licked Sam and blanketed her with her body.

"You've been missed," Linda said, hurrying to Sam to try and help untangle her.

"I can't tell you how wonderful it is to be home." She took Linda's hand and steadied herself. She turned and Molly was at her side with another hand.

"Hi, Molly, so glad you were able to tag along," said Linda.

"Me, too. I appreciate the offer."

Zoe stuck to Sam like a bodyguard. She managed to put her purse and overnight bag down and then went into the great room and sat in her recliner. Max came in from outside and spotting Sam, smiled as he rushed across to greet her with a kiss and a hug. "We've missed you so much."

"How's Jeff doing today?" asked Linda.

"Good. He's making some progress in rehab. They have him getting dressed and learning to eat again. He does eight hours of therapy a day. Sometimes, he doesn't accomplish much, but he's getting there. Sunday is his one day off from therapy. How's your ankle?" Sam continued to pet Zoe and Bailey had joined in on the action, both of them covering her while she sat in the chair.

"Much better. I got rid of the cast this week. The boot is awkward, but easier and I can remove it to sleep. Speaking of that, I can't thank you enough for letting me stay here."

Sam waved her away. "Don't mention it. It put my mind at ease knowing you guys were taking care of the dogs."

"Yeah, Zoe has taken to sitting in your chair. She's missed you so much."

Sam bent her head to the dog and rubbed her face with hers. "I think we'll be home in November, if all continues to go well."

"We'll take good care of them until you're home. They like the new place and are taking advantage of the huge yard," said Max.

"Oh, and Steve said to be at the marina around ten tomorrow and he'll give us a ride and then be back on Monday afternoon."

"Regi is going to stay at our house and take care of all of our girls while we're gone."

Sam was dodging wild licks from all three and laughing. "I think we should let them stay here with me tonight. Lucy, too. I'll bring them to your house in the morning."

"I'll make sure I'm up and will make a Sweet Treat run. You can come over early and eat and check out the house," said Max.

"I'll be there. I've been dying for one of Ellie's chocolate croissants."

The bell rang out and Max opened the door to Charlie, Hayley, Jen, and Megan. Sam extricated herself from the dogs and went to hug everyone hello. She gushed over the two pies and decorated brownies Hayley had made.

Jen, who had tipped her hair in purple in honor of Kyle's new college colors, deposited her salad in the fridge and Charlie carried two coolers of drinks out to the deck. As she passed by Sam, she pushed her fingers through the back of Sam's hair. "Your hair is so long. Lucky for you I stashed my tools in my car. I'll give you a color and cut tonight when the party's over."

Sam engulfed her in a hug. "That would be fabulous. I need my hair done, but have been consumed with Jeff's care and haven't had time."

The doorbell signaled the arrival of the rest of the guests. Sam was showered with affection as she embraced Kyle, Rita, Rachel, and Ellie. Regi followed and Kyle introduced her to Sam.

"I'm so pleased to meet you. How was your first day in the shop?"

"It was fun. I worked with Kyle and Rachel today and Hayley was baking in the back. There's a lot to learn, but we had a great day."

"She's a natural," added Kyle.

"I'm a coffeeholic, so that helps and it's such a cheery place. I'm going to like it. I appreciate the chance, Sam."

"I'm thankful for the help. You're a godsend. And your daughter is lovely. We had a long visit about UW on our ride over. I heard she already met Kyle when she was here."

"Yeah, it's great they'll know each other. Their dorms are next to each other and Kyle will be working some shifts where Molly works."

"And Becky has invited us for dinner next weekend after I get settled in," said Kyle.

"Yeah, she is so nice," said Molly.

Max offered to take Regi's platters from her and the bag she was carrying. "I'll put these in the kitchen."

"I need to put the chips and salsas in some serving dishes, but the rest is set." She and Molly followed him into the kitchen.

Charlie volunteered to help Ellie with her signature pink boxes filled with cupcakes. He wiggled his eyebrows, "I'll take care of these."

Everyone laughed. "No testing," hollered Ellie.

Max had the meat grilling and invited everyone to sit on the deck. Charlie passed out drinks and the group chatted nonstop, munching on appetizers, while the smell of grilling meat promised a delicious meal.

As soon as dinner was on the table, Max stood and toasted Kyle, wishing him luck in college. Everyone added their own twist to the toast, touting Kyle's work ethic and academic prowess, assured of his success at UW.

Sam was last. "Kyle, I'm blessed to have you as a part of my life. Thank you for all your work at the shop and I know you'll do exceptional things in college. But, more important, I'm thankful learning about you caused me to let go of my past sadness and anger and be brave enough to trust again. Life is definitely too short, so learn from my mistakes. We love you and we'll miss you and expect you back at work next summer."

Kyle rose and stepped to Sam, hugging her tight. He let her go, but kept his arm around her and raised his own glass of tea. "Thank you all so much. I've loved being here and although I've known you all for just a few months, I feel like we're a family. Especially you, Sam. You've been wonderful to me and although our relationship is hard to explain, I hope you don't mind if I tell people you're my second mom."

Sam shook her head, tears streaming down her face and hugged him again. "I'd be honored," she whispered.

"Let's eat, everyone" Kyle said, squeezing Sam's hand as he let it go and went back to his seat.

The visiting continued as they dug into the scrumptious meal, followed by Hayley's tasty desserts and Ellie's cupcakes, adorned with the signature purple and gold colors of the Huskies. Max and Linda served tea and coffee and suggested they gather by the fire pit to enjoy the rest of the evening.

Regi and Jen insisted on doing the dishes. Once they had things done, they squeezed into the seats surrounding the fire. Sam slipped a small box, wrapped in purple paper and decorated with gold ribbons, out from behind her cushion. "Kyle, everyone chipped in and wanted to give you a little gift to help as you start your new journey."

He opened the box and discovered dozens of prepaid gift cards for eating out, the bookstore at UW, stores for outfitting his dorm room, and coffee. It also included a certificate for free transport on Steve's boat anytime he could get away. The fire lit up the grin on Kyle's face.

"Wow, this is the best. Thank you so much. I know I'll be back for Christmas for sure."

"Anytime you're free, call the number on Steve's card and he'll arrange a ride," said Sam.

"We have a little something for Molly, too," said Sam, as she pulled an oversized purple bag from under the table.

"For me?" said Molly, her voice high with surprise.

"Yep. A little something to get you ready for UW," said Sam.

Molly opened the bag and pulled out shirts, sweats, a jacket, gloves, a hat, lanyards, all emblazoned with UW logos, plus a gift card to the bookstore.

"Wow, this is so nice," said Molly, her eyes wide in disbelief.

Regi hugged her daughter to her. "I told you these were some wonderful people." She mouthed her thanks to Sam.

Ellie made her way to Kyle. "We're gonna miss you," she said, as she hugged him. "I've got to get going. Early baking tomorrow. Stop by the shop for a treat on your way to the ferry next week." She kissed his cheek.

He hugged her. "I'll do that."

Rita asked Ellie if she'd mind dropping her at home so Kyle could stay as late as he wanted.

Rachel gave Kyle a shy hug and told him how much she'd miss working with him. "We better get going, too," said Charlie. He shook Kyle's hand and wished him luck and Hayley engulfed him in a huge hug.

Jen stole Sam away to work on her hair and everyone else savored the warmth of the fire and the easy conversation. Around ten o'clock, the partygoers started leaving and Sam's hair was restored back to its usual beautiful color and style.

"I'm so proud of you and I'll see you for dinner at Becky's next weekend," promised Sam, as she hugged Kyle goodbye.

Sam made sure Jen, Rachel, and Regi took the table flowers home, since she'd be leaving tomorrow. Lucy was busy running through the house with Bailey and Zoe and didn't notice when Linda told her goodbye.

Sam let her feet sink into the plush carpet and collapsed into her chair. Zoe covered her feet and the other two dogs snuggled next to her. The party had been uplifting and together with Jeff's recent progress, made her realize how much she loved her life. She knew leaving tomorrow was going to be hard. She couldn't bear to see Zoe and Bailey so distraught, but with warm fur tickling her toes and a few quick wet licks from the dogs, she felt herself relax. "We'll be home soon, girls."

Twenty-Six

After a yummy breakfast of calorie laden croissants, Sam did her best to contain her tears as she hugged the dogs goodbye. The threesome set off to meet Molly at the marina. When Sam parked, Molly was already there, waving at them and chatting with Steve. She was sporting her new hat and jacket.

They climbed into Steve's boat and enjoyed a peaceful trip through the water, dotted with green islands. When they docked, they saw Becky waving and shouting at them. She decided to meet them and after dropping the three of them at the hospital, talked Molly into running by her house.

"This way you'll know where it is when you come for dinner," explained Becky. She pulled into the driveway. "I'm going to haul these bags in while I'm here." Molly offered to help and on the way back Becky showed her the bus stop a few blocks from her house.

"I've got a bus pass, so that should work out. I'll check the schedules. Do you know if Kyle's bringing a car to school?"

"I don't know, but I doubt it. I bet it's more of a hassle to have a car on campus than it's worth."

"Yeah, it's pretty easy to get around without one. I'll find out this week. He told me to stop by at the end of the week and check out his dorm room."

Becky pulled into the loading zone. "I'll see you on Sunday. Call if you need anything, Molly."

"I will," she waved, as she bounded into the building.

Becky stopped by the market on her way back home. She planned to make a yummy dinner for everyone and give Sam some time with Max and Linda.

* * *

When they arrived at Jeff's room, they found him dressed in sweats and a t-shirt, sitting in a wheelchair. Linda stifled a gasp. He was so thin and instead of Jeff's normal strong and capable stature, she saw a withered man. He was much grayer than he had been and his gaunt face was in need of a shave.

His eyes sparkled at the sight of Sam. "Hi sweetie," she said. "Look who came with me."

Max swooped in for a hug. "Hi, Jeff. You're looking good."

"I'm making a little progress. I wish it would go faster."

Max moved to make room for Linda. She was blinking fast trying to stop the tears threatening to spill from her eyes. She stooped and wrapped her arms around Jeff. "I'm so glad to see you," she said, her voice cracking.

"Don't cry, Linda. I'm doing much better."

She nodded and pulled a tissue from her pocket. "I know. I'm sorry to be so emotional."

Max put his arm around her. "Thanks for letting us steal Sam away last night."

"She needs to get out of this place more often," Jeff said, as he stroked Sam's hand. "How are the girls?"

"They're fine, but they miss us."

"I miss them, maybe we can sneak them in," he grinned.

Max asked Jeff a few questions about his appetite and therapy sessions. He shared he had been eating some soft food and the therapy was tiring. Sam explained the wound to his leg caused some issues and the traumatic brain injury had impacted his ability to walk and maintain balance. Speech therapy and physical therapy were the main focus of his rehabilitation sessions. They also worked on general strengthening, since he had been bedridden for so long.

"He also has some trouble maintaining a long conversation and sometimes mixes up words," she said.

"Yeah, I don't always make sense," he said.

Max patted his hand. "You're doing great. These types of injuries take time to overcome. You'll be relearning some things. Try to be patient."

"I want to go home," said Jeff, with tears in his eyes.

"We don't have much longer, sweetie. It will go by fast, I promise," said Sam, gripping his hand in hers.

Jeff noticed Linda's boot. "What's that?"

"Oh, I got this a few days ago and got rid of my cast."

Jeff frowned at her. "Why?"

Linda looked at Sam and her slight nod told her to continue. Linda explained about her fall the day after their wedding and her time in the cast and now she was in therapy three times a week and hoped to be rid of the boot next month. "So, maybe I'll be done with it, by the time you get home." She smiled and he smiled back.

He looked at Sam. "Did I know about her leg?"

"Yeah, I think you forgot."

The nurse bustled in with some equipment and a tray of lunch. Most days Jeff had to eat in the dining room, but Sundays were a day of rest from therapy and the group activities. "Hey, Jeff," she said, in a booming voice. "I need to check you out and then I've got some yummy soup and Jell-O, plus a chocolate pudding for you."

"Hi, Maura. These are our best friends Max and Linda," introduced Sam.

"Pleased to meet you." She directed her attention to Jeff. "How are you feeling?"

"Okay," he said. "Hungry."

"Good deal," she bent to inspect his feet and legs and proceeded with her vital checks. "You'll have to rest today. Rosie said she's gonna work you hard tomorrow."

Jeff rolled his eyes and laughed. "She's tough."

Sam explained Rosie was one of Jeff's therapists and she was always able to get Jeff to work hard.

Maura completed her chart and slid the tray onto his wheeled table and adjusted it so he could reach it. "Okay, we're all set. Call if you need anything."

They visited with each other while they watched Jeff concentrate on removing the covers from his food. The laborious process was painful to watch. It required all of Jeff's focus to guide the spoon into the food and then to his mouth.

Jeff's lunch took the better part of two hours and he looked exhausted when he was done. He was determined to transfer himself into his bed to rest. He managed it, using Max's arm to steady himself only once. Max suggested they get a bite to eat while Jeff rested. They drove to a bistro in the University District and enjoyed homemade soup and sandwiches.

"What do you think, Max?" asked Sam. "Is he going to be okay?"

"From talking to Sean and seeing him today, I think so. I know it seems slow, but he's basically starting over. I think he's very determined, which is good."

"He's weak, so I'm hoping now that he can eat he'll get stronger and gain some weight back."

"He's made quite a bit of progress in the last week or so. Imagine what he'll be like in a month. Plus, the hospital is one of the best for brain injuries and all the therapy work is going to help."

"Yeah, I think it's all catching up with me."

"What do you do all day while he's in therapy?" asked Linda.

"I do some of it with him and then just wait. I try to read and sometimes I go to Becky's."

"Would you consider taking a few days and coming home once a week?" asked Linda.

"I don't know. I'd feel horrible leaving him here." Sam shook her head. "I'm not sure."

Max added, "I think it may do you a world of good and the harder he works, the more tired he's going to be. I bet he sleeps when he's back in his room anyway."

"Yeah, he's worn out at the end of the day. Especially, after dinner. I sit and talk and visit with him, but he drifts off."

"Maybe talk to him and see what he thinks about the idea. You could make sure you're here for the weekend, since Sunday is his free day. But, maybe you could come home on Tuesday and Wednesday. I know, it's not my place, but I don't think it's good for you to sit in here all day," said Linda, as she patted Sam's hand.

Sam nodded. "I don't want him to feel alone."

Max took the ticket and dug into his wallet for his credit card. "If you're worried about someone being here, we could schedule it and rotate some people through. Jen, Becky, Charlie, me. We could all do it and then before you know it, he'll be released."

"I'll give it some thought and talk to Jeff."

They arrived back at the hospital to find Jeff napping. They visited in hushed tones and talked about the upcoming visit to Victoria and filled Sam in on Linda's family drama in Chicago. Sam was shocked at the story, but was glad to learn Uncle Mike was going to be on the island for a visit. They also shared the reason Regi had moved to the island and explained Molly didn't know about her dad.

"Holy cow," she whispered. "I've been missing all the good stuff."

Jeff's voice interrupted their huddled murmurs. "What good stuff?"

"Oh, you're awake. Sorry, if we disturbed you," Sam went to him and kissed him.

"You didn't. I was awake."

"Linda and Max have been filling me in on all the lively island happenings we've been missing. I'll let her explain about the letter she found."

They spent the next few hours rehashing all the excitement for Jeff and after he finished his dinner, they left for Becky's. "I'll be back later tonight," waved Sam, as they left him to watch some television.

Becky had fixed chicken, garlic mashed potatoes, and roasted veggies, plus a salad and rolls. They enjoyed a leisurely dinner and Brad shared his experience dropping off Andy and Chloe at college. They both attended schools on the east coast and Brad had taken the time from work to go with both of them and visit his family while he was there. He had returned last night.

"Oh, I forgot to tell you guys Marty called to let me know he has the settlement worked out with the Murray family lawyer. They're, of course, covering all the expenses, plus lost wages, and will continue to pay for all Jeff's medical needs in the future. They're liquidating her house and her business and are giving us their undeveloped land parcels as part of the settlement and providing a cash sum to offset Jeff's pain and suffering. He said the family has no plans to return to the island and they want to put all of this behind them."

"Wow that surprises me, based on how Brenda always acted. Maybe the rest of her family isn't quite as caustic as she was," said Linda.

"What will you do with the property?" asked Max.

"I don't know. I need to look into it a bit more and see what is possible. I was thinking it may be best to donate some of it for something, maybe a park. I haven't told Jeff all of this yet and I'm not sure how he'll react."

"Does he know Brenda caused the accident and she's dead?" asked Linda.

"He doesn't remember the accident itself. As you saw today, he doesn't remember some things, like your ankle. I told him Brenda was the one who ran us down and she died in an accident, which in all likelihood was a suicide. He became agitated when I mentioned her, so I haven't brought it up again."

"Does Marty think it's a good settlement?" asked Brad.

"Yeah, he's satisfied with it and said her brother has been easy to deal with. They're mortified, to say the least. I'll have Marty contact you to work out any financial details."

They all raved about the home cooked meal Becky had prepared and indulged in a piece of a decadent chocolate mousse cake Brad had picked up for dessert. As they were finishing dessert, Sam said she wanted to get back to the hospital and check on Jeff. Linda and Max opted to stay, since Linda had been on her foot most of the day.

* * *

Steve would be at the dock at noon, so they had a quick breakfast at Becky's and took their bags with them to the hospital. Jeff was already in a therapy session when they arrived and they watched him using parallel bars taking some halted steps. Sweat was pouring down his face, but he was determined to finish the length and Rosie was cheering him on as he worked to put one foot in front of the other.

While they were watching Jeff, one of the other therapists pulled Sam away for a chat. She returned a few minutes later and said, "They want me to try to get some photos and items that will remind Jeff of home and bring them so they can use them with some of his therapies. They want to hang pictures in his room. They say it helps patients remember things and motivates them."

"We can put together anything you need," volunteered Linda. "Pictures of the dogs, the house, Jeff's family and friends. I can work on that when we get home."

"That would be wonderful. And I'm going to talk to Jeff about your idea of me getting home one or two days a week and see how he reacts. When he isn't in therapy he's so drained, he's sleeping. So it may not be as impactful to him. We'll see."

Jeff got to the end of the bars and then collapsed into his wheelchair. He looked up at them and gave a shy wave.

"They'll bring him back to his room now, so we can meet him there," motioned Sam.

When he was wheeled in, he was met with a large lemonade Sam had ready for him. He smiled and took a big gulp. "That hits the spot," he said.

"You're looking good out there," said Max, clapping him on the shoulder.

"Trying to get out of this place," smiled Jeff.

"Do you want to get in the bed to rest?" asked Sam.

"Nah. I'll sit here for a bit. I have another session with the speech therapist soon."

Max glanced at his watch. "We better get to the marina."

Sam made a move to get her purse. "I'll give you a ride."

"No, you stay here and we'll catch a cab. It's not very far. We'll be back to see you guys in a few weeks. If you need anything, let us know," said Max, as he hugged Sam tight.

Linda bent to give Jeff a gentle hug and a kiss on the cheek. "I'm so pleased you're doing better."

They noticed Jeff's eyes were wet. "Thanks, thanks for coming here," he said. "I love you guys." He wiped his eyes with the back of his hand.

Max leaned in and hugged Jeff. "We love you, too. Keep up the good work."

Max carried their bags and Linda embraced Sam as they said goodbye. "I'll send you the photos this week," she promised.

"My camera's in my office and it has a bunch of pictures from our trip to Orcas he might like."

"Will do. Talk to you soon."

As they made their way downstairs and got in the back of a cab, Linda said, "I guess I wasn't prepared to see him like that. I'm not sure what I expected."

"He actually looks good for what he's been through." He gripped her thigh. "He's going to be okay. Maybe not quite as active as he was used to, but I think he'll regain everything."

The cab dropped them at the marina and they walked to the pier, spotting Steve's boat. "Hey, guys," he waved. "How's Jeff doing today?"

"Good, he's doing lots of therapy and looks good," said Max, heaving their bags over to Steve.

It was a sunny day and they sat back and enjoyed the view as Steve guided the boat out of the marina and into the open waters. Once they were underway, Max talked to Steve and explained the idea they had planted in Sam's head about trying to get home once a week, for a break. Steve was agreeable to the plan and said he could work out any schedule needed. The only barrier would be bad weather.

In less than two hours they were back home. They stopped for a quick lunch at Dottie's before going to Linda's therapy appointment. While Linda was at therapy, Max strolled over to the market and selected some steaks, potatoes, salad fixings, and a cheesecake for tomorrow's dinner party. When she was finished they made the drive out to Sam's and found her camera and took some of Jeff's old family photos so they could get copies made.

Tuesday Max worked at the coffee shop and took the framed photos with him, so he could get copies made. Linda spent the day selecting photos from Sam's camera and talking with Ryan about the wedding photos. He offered to print anything she wanted along with some of the wedding shots. She emailed him several photos and had Max run the family photos over to Ryan's office.

Max arrived home with a loaf of bread from Ellie's. Linda had already made the salad and had the potatoes ready to bake. The steaks had been marinating all day and were ready to throw on the grill. Linda had placed some glass hurricane lamps on the table outside and had it ready with place settings.

Max opened a bottle of wine, while Linda layered butter and garlic on the fresh bread. He checked his watch and turned on the fire pit. The dogs dashed for the front door, announcing the arrival of a guest.

Max opened the door to Kyle and Nate. "Hi, guys, come on in." Nate was out of his usual brown uniform and dressed in jeans, his short dark hair wet from a shower. His pale blue shirt enhanced the color of his eyes.

They followed Max into the kitchen and he fixed an iced tea for Kyle and Nate chose a beer. Max took the steaks and led them out to the patio. Max put the meat on the grill and they gathered around the fire pit.

"What a spectacular view," said Nate.

"It's my favorite place," beamed Max. He turned when he heard Linda's voice.

"Everyone's out here," she said, with Regi following her.

Regi was dressed in jeans and a peacock blue blouse that looked perfect with her blond hair. She was carrying a glass of wine and took the empty seat next to Nate. The dogs circled around her, tails wagging.

"We haven't had a chance to talk to you since we got home. Did everything go okay?" asked Max.

"Yeah, we were fine," she said, as she gave each dog a rub. "I didn't spend much time out here, though. It's gorgeous and whatever is on the barbeque smells fantastic."

"I'm grilling some steaks."

Linda placed a stack of plates and a tray of snacks on the small table near the fire pit. "I've got chips and salsa and cheese and crackers."

"Sounds terrific," said Nate, getting up to help himself. "Could I bring you some, Regi?"

"Um, sure. I'll take a few."

"Are you ready for your big move, Kyle?" asked Linda.

"Yeah, I think so. My grandma is pretty sad, that's why she stayed home tonight. She's trying to be excited, but I know she'll miss having me around."

"She's not the only one," smiled Max.

"I'm excited to start school. My mom is going to help me get my room ready. And I have my tickets to visit Marty over Thanksgiving."

"I've never been to New York City, I bet you'll have fun," said Linda, taking her seat between Kyle and Max.

"Yeah, I'm excited. Mom wasn't thrilled, but I think she's coming around to the idea and Marty has been super cool."

"Well, she's had you to herself for a long time. And you'd be tough to share," smiled Linda.

"I guess. It'll be weird not to have Thanksgiving with Mom and Grandma, but I'll be spending Christmas break here and Marty said Thanksgiving is a great time in the city. He lives in Manhattan."

"There's so much to do and see, it'll give you an excuse to go back," said Max.

"Have either of you been to New York City?" Linda asked, looking at Nate and Regi.

Nate and Regi both shook their heads. "Not me. I've barely left the island," laughed Nate.

"Me either. Sounds exciting though."

Max checked the steaks and announced it would be a few more minutes. Linda went to retrieve the rest of the food and Regi followed to help. By the time they returned, Max had the steaks on the table and the men were making their way to their seats. Linda made sure Regi sat next to Nate, with Kyle taking the head of the table.

After all the dishes had been passed and the plates were full, Max made sure everyone had a glass of champagne or sparkling cider and raised his glass for a toast. "Thanks so much to all of you for your help in getting the house ready. We couldn't have done it without all of you pitching in to help. So, here's to all of you."

They all took a sip and dug into the tender steaks and fluffy potatoes. "Oh, this is good," said Kyle between bites.

"I agree. Totally yummy," said Regi.

"I won't get another good meal like this for a long time," said Kyle. "I don't think the food on campus will be all that good."

"Molly said the restaurant in her building isn't too bad. You're next door, so you'll have to try it out," said Regi.

Linda glanced at Nate. "Molly is Regi's daughter. She'll be a freshman at UW and is living in the building next door to Kyle."

"Wow, I didn't know you had a daughter. That's great. Have you two met?" he asked Kyle.

"Yeah, over Labor Day and Sam's friend, Becky, invited us both to dinner this weekend. Plus, Molly works in the library where I'll be pulling some shifts in the coffee shop."

"Well that's cool you'll both know each other. It's always good to have a friend in a new place," said Nate, as he piled more salad on his plate.

"I'm glad she'll know someone. I'm pretty nervous about her being on her own. Do you have kids, Nate?"

"Nope, never been married, no kids."

"We've got a delicious looking cheesecake for dessert. Is anybody ready?" asked Linda.

Nate stretched and patted his stomach. "I'm going to have to wait a bit."

"Me too," said Regi. "How about Nate and I clear the table while you guys visit with Kyle?"

She and Nate were already in motion, gathering items, amid the protests from Max and Linda. "No, you two are the guests tonight," said Linda.

"Oh, we'll be fast," said Nate.

As they cleaned plates and loaded the dishwasher, Nate asked Regi if she had been exploring the island and what she had seen.

"I've been working, so I haven't seen much. And now with me working weekends at Sam's shop, I don't have much time for fun."

"That's too bad. There's a lot to see here and on the neighboring islands."

"I bought a book when I first moved here, but haven't had the time yet to see some of the sites."

"Well, if you find some time, I'd be glad to show you around. I've got a little boat and like to go out in it. Since the shop closes early on Sunday, we could make a plan for a Sunday afternoon."

Regi's head was in the dishwasher. *He's a nice guy. Say something. Would it hurt to have him show me around?* She finished and stood, closing the door and pressing the button to start the load.

"I'm working on Linda's house in my spare time, so I won't have a free Sunday until I'm finished out there. But, when I'm done, I'd like that."

Nate grinned. "Anytime, just let me know."

The two rejoined the group and visited by the fire, watching the yellow orb slip away to be replaced by a star filled indigo sky. After cheesecake, Regi said she needed to get going.

She hugged everyone goodbye and told Kyle to keep an eye on Molly. Kyle hugged Max and Linda and promised to keep them posted on his achievements at college and his trip to New York.

"Well, Nate, you doing okay?" asked Linda.

"Yeah. I mentioned to Regi I'd be happy to show her around the island and she said when she was done with your house, we could do something," he said with a shy smile. "I like her. I hope she isn't just saying that."

"She is working on my house. She's a bit of a workaholic, I think. But she'll be done by the end of the month, so that's only a couple weeks away. She's at the shop every weekend, so you can make sure and check in with her as it gets closer. She's going to be staying here and watching the dogs for us the last weekend of the month."

"It's so hard to meet people here. Most everyone my age is married. I hope it works out with her." He shrugged. "I guess time will tell. I better get going." They waved goodbye as he climbed into his pickup.

"He's a good guy. I hope she gives him a real chance," said Linda.

Twenty-Seven

The days leading up to their Victoria trip were filled with activity. In between Linda's therapy she worked on the photo project for Jeff. She and Max made a trip out to the resort and took pictures of Jeff's cabin and the grounds along with Jeremy and Heather. She snapped some pictures of the hardware store, Charlie, Jen, Megan, and the coffee shop. They stopped by the assisted living facility and took some pictures of Mary. She was elated to be helping with the project.

With Ryan's expertise and help she put together a variety of photos and got them in the mail for Sam in care of Becky. She printed out two sets and saved one, since some of the pictures were so good, especially those of Jeff's mom.

Linda's leg and foot were feeling better each day. She could tell therapy was helping. She wanted to be strong for the trip, so she was working extra on her home exercises. She squeezed in a hair appointment with Jen and made sure the house was stocked with food for Regi.

Max spent his days at the coffee shop and shuttling Linda to and from therapy. The hospital had called and wanted a start date for his consulting position. He promised to be there in the middle of October.

Regi was making progress at Linda's and took to her barista duties like an old pro. Because of her work at the school, she knew lots of people and was at ease chitchatting with the locals. She noticed Nate made a habit of stopping by the shop on the weekends, always during a lull. He'd order a drink and sit and visit.

Linda and Max finished their packing in time to gobble down some pastries at Ellie's before the sailing boarded for Victoria. Charlie and Hayley were going to handle getting Max's car back to the house. The ferry wasn't full and they had a relaxing trip and arrived in Sidney in less than two hours.

They took a taxi to the Empress Hotel. "I haven't been here for years, like I bet over thirty," said Max, as they took in the sites of the area.

"It's been a long time for me, too," she said, gawking at the Parliament Building.

Max tipped the driver and they both gazed at the iconic ivy-strewn brick as Max wheeled the luggage into the lobby. They knew they were early for check-in, but the pleasant clerk checked on their suite and told them it was ready. She presented them with an envelope and their keys and rang for a bellman to take their luggage.

As they left she gave them each a warm chocolate chip cookie and a bottle of water. "Enjoy your stay and if there's anything you desire, please let us know."

Max bit into the cookie. "Mmm. I like this place already."

Linda laughed and took a bite of her cookie while they waited for the elevator. They arrived at their suite as the bellman was opening the door. He showed them the amenities of the elegant suite, complete with a parlor and fireplace, and a gorgeous view of the Inner Harbour.

"Wow," she said. "What a view."

"The room is something else." Max opened the envelope and found their tickets to Butchart Gardens, Linda's spa treatments, his golf outing, and Afternoon Tea. The four and a half days they had were packed with things to do.

"Shall we take a look around and get some lunch?" asked Linda.

"Sounds good to me. I suspect we'll spend most of tomorrow at the gardens, so we may as well look around at the shops while we have the chance."

They took light jackets with them and set off to explore Government Street. They wandered in and out of souvenir shops, picking out small gifts. They found a pub for lunch and continued for a few blocks. Linda spied a tea shop and couldn't resist a stainless steel teapot she thought would look great in the kitchen. She also selected a variety of teas to give Sam, one with a hint of maple.

On the way back to the hotel, Max spotted a chocolate shop and dragged Linda with him. They were giving away free samples of some of their chocolates and Max invested in a couple of boxes of the sea salt caramels and a box of rich truffles.

They decided to travel one more block and visit the Parliament Building. They went on a short tour and admired the rotunda, artwork, and the legislative chamber. They both liked the reception hall where they discovered a wooden floor and beautiful stained glass windows. The library was filled with ornate woodwork and a reading room with an intricate coffered ceiling. The architecture and materials used both inside and on the massive exterior were striking. It was a building rich in history and design.

When they arrived back in their room, Linda plopped onto the couch and put her leg on the back. "Did you get worn out?" he asked.

"A little. I guess we put on more miles than I'm used to."

"Maybe we should eat dinner at the hotel and rest your leg for the gardens tomorrow. I know that's the place you're most looking forward to visiting and you'll need all your strength to walk through them. It's over fifty-five acres." He settled next to her and pressed the remote to turn on the television.

"I know," she grinned. "I can hardly wait."

"If you get tired we can get a wheelchair."

She frowned at him. "I don't think so. We'll take it slow."

"Whatever you say," he leaned in and kissed her. "You're the boss."

She snuggled against him and lulled with the sound of the television droning, she shut her eyes.

When she woke, it was dark outside and the lights along the harbor were illuminated. She glanced over and studied the gorgeous domed

Parliament Building outlined in white lights. Max came out of the bedroom and admired her at the window.

"How are you feeling after a nap?"

"Much better. I'm enjoying the view."

"Do you feel like going downstairs to dinner or shall we order room service?"

"Let's go. It'll take me a minute to change and I'd like to get a few pictures," she said, as she made her way to the bedroom.

She changed into some wide legged black pants and an electric purple silk tunic and quickly repaired her hair and makeup. She was back in the parlor in less than twenty minutes, ready to go.

"You look magnificent." Max put his suit jacket on and offered her his arm. "Shall we go?"

She linked her arm in his and they travelled downstairs to the Empress Room. They were led through the Victorian inspired décor and shown a table for two at the window, overlooking the water. After the waiter removed the crisp white napkin from her wine glass and placed it in her lap, Linda took in the room, before looking at the menu. The room dripped with opulence, from the hand carved wooden ceiling to the tapestries and crystal chandeliers throughout the room.

"I'm glad we didn't do room service," she smiled, looking at Max over the flickering candle on the table.

"It's magnificent, like the rest of the place. Very nostalgic."

They studied the menu and she chose chicken and he selected a rib eye. They started with crisp salads strewn with pecans and cranberries, dressed in lemony vinaigrette. They enjoyed the calmness of the regal setting and watched activities in the harbor while they waited for their entrees.

The meal was delicious and the wait staff attentive. They passed on dessert and went outside to take some pictures across the street. On their way back to the hotel, Max stopped at the horse drawn carriage tours and took a brochure. Then they asked another couple to take their picture in front of the Empress.

"I think we should squeeze in a carriage tour," said Max.

"It looks fun. Maybe Sunday we could book one. We could do it when we finish Afternoon Tea at the hotel. That's the only thing we have scheduled."

"I'll get it reserved. So, tomorrow the bus leaves for the gardens a little before nine and we can either take the three o'clock or the five o'clock back here."

When they opened the door to their room, a fire glowed in the fireplace, a plate of fresh cookies was on the side table, and foil wrapped chocolates dotted their pillows. "I think I could live here," smiled Linda.

They watched some television and nibbled on the cookies. It was after eleven when Max asked, "Would you feel more comfortable if I slept out here on the sofa bed?"

"Don't be silly," she blushed. "I appreciate your chivalry, but I think we can manage to share the mammoth bed in there."

"I don't want to rush things, so how about if we agree to sleep together, just sleep."

She chuckled. "If only my mother could hear this conversation. Seriously, I'm fine with it. I think we'll both know when it's time to take the next step."

Max brushed her cheek and turned her lips to his. Her hands found the back of his neck and their kiss deepened, leaving them both breathless. "I'm ready whenever you are."

"I'm going to do my exercises and get to bed," she got up, holding his hand in hers. "I'll see you in a few minutes." She let his hand drop as she went to the bedroom.

Max turned off the television and the fireplace and got ready for bed while Linda was in the bathroom. She emerged in her oversized t-shirt and sat on the edge of the bed to remove her boot and do her exercises. He helped her with the resistance bands and then they both popped a chocolate from the pillows and slid into the crisp sheets.

She reached for his hand, "This was a lovely day, Max. I'm glad you're with me."

"Me, too. Sweet dreams my sweet girl."

* * *

They selected a room service breakfast of oatmeal and pastries and met their bus outside the lobby. Although the morning was cool, the day promised sunshine. They arrived at the gardens shortly after they opened and Linda was already snapping pictures as they entered the pathway.

They strolled along the sidewalks and marveled at the beautiful reds, golds, and russets of the maple leaves throughout the garden. The walls of dahlias were breathtaking and showcased the variety of blooms in purple, orange, fuchsia, and white. Some of them were soft yet spiky, like sea anemone, and others full and lush. They lined the first pathway, for what looked like miles.

Next they encountered lush beds of snapdragons standing watch over bright lobelia plants. Along the path they encountered gorgeous chrysanthemums in deep purple, copper, white, and yellow, plus one of Linda's favorites, the graceful hydrangea in a stunning periwinkle blue.

They strolled through a thriving forest to arrive at the rim of the Sunken Garden. Max heard Linda's intake of breath. "Gorgeous," she sighed. It was slow going as they took the steps down to the garden. From above, the trees and bushes looked like miniatures, but once they were at the bottom, the garden was full size. Groomed beds held fall flowers with colorful shrubs interspersed among them. One side of the path was ringed with towering trees, turning orange and yellow, offset against the vibrant green grass.

Max took Linda's picture among the colorful fall asters and begonias the size of saucers. Each time he thought he found a favorite color, a new more resplendent bloom emerged around the corner. He led her to a garden bench to rest while they enjoyed the stillness of the colorful garden.

He gripped her hand and brought it to his lips. "Are you enjoying yourself?"

"Oh, yes. It's unbelievable."

A passerby offered to take their picture and they posed on the bench, surrounded by fall blooms. To save steps they decided to press on to the

Rose Garden and the Japanese Garden and have a late lunch on the way back, rather than backtracking to the restaurants.

Although it was the end of the season, the roses were spectacular. They strolled through a rose covered arbor running the length of one side of the garden. As they entered the garden, roses were displayed climbing over archways, as trellis decorations, in beds, and hanging in baskets. Full blooms in brilliant pink, deep crimson, blush, yellow, peach, lavender and white were showcased. Low green hedges separated areas of the garden and trees were intermingled with the vibrant and fragrant bushes.

They sat on another bench and savored the fragrance. "Makes my rose garden look pretty small, huh?"

"It's quite impressive. Yours is a petite version."

"I want to come back in the summer and see this in all its glory."

"Let's do it. See the fun you can have when you aren't working so much," he laughed.

She reached for his hand. "I'm beginning to."

They left the roses and made their way to the Japanese Garden. They were immediately sheltered in tranquility. The deep reds of autumn were everywhere and plush moss made a carpet for the falling scarlet and orange leaves. Lacy Japanese maples were reflected in the clear waters of the stream running through the garden. They stopped on the small wooden bridge and marveled at the vibrant colors mirrored in the water, dotted with water lilies.

"Peaceful, huh?" asked Max.

"I've never experienced anything like this. I think this is the best season for this garden."

They linked hands admiring the ponds and listening to the gentle trickle of water. As they exited, they stopped at the Star Pond and smiled at the fountain ringed by frogs spewing water. They made their way to the Italian Garden, housing neat, symmetrical beds of fall plantings. The walls of the buildings around the garden were covered in verdant plants, bleeding hearts, and delicate fuchsia. Max took Linda's picture as she posed along the wall, surrounded by the greens and pinks of the blooms.

"How about lunch?" he asked.

"I'm starved," she said, as they made their way to the restaurant and selected homemade soup and chicken salad sandwiches from the cafeteria style menu. They indulged in a piece of strawberry shortcake with fresh whipped cream.

"Oh, I feel better now," said Linda. She checked her watch and it was minutes before three o'clock. "I don't think I can hurry to the bus, so what do you say to spending our time looking at the last garden and checking out the gift store for some souvenirs?"

"Sounds good to me." They followed the path to the Mediterranean Garden, which was a showcase of less dramatic, but hardy plantings. It didn't take long to go through and Max could see Linda was moving slower.

They stopped at the gift store and found several unique items. Max bought a couple of books showcasing the garden throughout the seasons and glass coasters made from pressed flowers caught Linda's eye. After they completed their purchases, Max suggested they sit outside the coffee shop at a table and wait for the bus.

He treated them to lattes and they scrolled through their pictures. Linda had over four hundred photos on her camera and Max had about two hundred. "Good thing I have a big card in my camera. I don't want to forget a thing about this place," she said.

Max was thumbing through his books and showed Linda a picture of springtime at the gardens. "Check out the tulips. One of Sam's favorites."

"Beautiful. Maybe we can talk them into a trip if Jeff is doing well. I think any season would be magnificent. Spring flowers are so cheerful and the roses in summer would be unforgettable. We may have to come more than once."

He flipped the page to Christmas. "Oh, wow. Check out what they do for the holidays." He showed her the photos of the lights and decorations.

They finished their drinks and meandered out to the bus loading area. The bus arrived minutes later and they chose their seats. There were very few people on the bus and Max saw Linda nod off as the bus turned out of the gardens. He knew she was exhausted from the day.

The noise of the airbrakes startled Linda, and she woke as they stopped in front of the Empress. "You doing okay?" he asked.

"Sorry, I fell asleep. I'm pretty worn out. But it was a lovely day," she smiled.

He carried their items and followed behind Linda, noting her deliberate movements with her injured leg and the slow pace she set. "What do you say to dinner in the room tonight? We could do room service or I could scout out a restaurant and get us takeout."

She nodded. "I think that's a good idea. I'm beat."

He lit a fire and she changed into sweatpants and a t-shirt and he left in search of dinner. He asked the concierge for some ideas within walking distance and found a steakhouse only a couple of blocks away at the corner of Fort and Wharf. He enjoyed a glass of wine in the bar while he waited for their dinner.

He returned in less than an hour and found Linda snuggled on the couch reading. "Dinner is served," he held up the bag of food. I stopped downstairs and borrowed some real plates and silverware, so it'll be easier to eat."

They gathered around the small table near the fire and he sorted out the boxes. "I chose a teriyaki chicken and a honey mustard salmon, so we can share them or take your pick."

"Let's split them, they both sound and smell yummy."

He transferred the food to plates, squeezing in the giant twice baked potatoes smothered in crumbled bacon and cheddar cheese. He unearthed salads and a bottle of wine from the bag.

"Wow, this looks great," she said, taking a forkful of the steaming potato. "Mmm, terrific."

He used the corkscrew provided by the hotel and poured them each a glass of wine. "Here's to a perfect day," he said, as he raised his glass to her.

"I agree. It was all I hoped it would be and more. I can't wait to get some of these pictures printed and framed."

"Tomorrow, you'll be able to relax with your spa day while I'm golfing. I catch the shuttle at ten and should be back around three."

"I'm looking forward to a massage, especially after today. I need to check in around nine-thirty. From the list of treatments on my schedule, I'll be there most of the day. Sam provided for a massage package, facial, scalp treatment, manicure and pedicure. They include a spa lunch."

"You deserve all the pampering you can get. It'll be good for you."

They finished dinner and the wine. Despite her exhaustion, Linda was determined to do her leg exercises. With Max's help she did her normal physical therapy routine and then flopped into bed.

* * *

They slept in the next morning, both wakened by the wake-up call Max had requested. They opted for a room service breakfast and Max dropped Linda at the spa while he continued outside to wait for his golf shuttle. He was treating himself to a day of golf on two championship designed courses at a beautiful facility about twenty miles from the hotel.

Linda's day of beauty began with a spa ritual of a few minutes in a sauna, followed by a trip to the steam room and a mineral bath. Then she lounged on a chaise, ensconced in a fluffy robe fresh from the warmer. They provided cucumber water and herbal teas while she waited. Next she was ushered into a softly lit chamber filled with soft music and a fire in the fireplace. She met her technician, Nora, who asked about her ankle.

Linda was treated to an exfoliation, followed by a bath in rose water and a relaxing and soothing massage. Once the massage was done, Nora added rose oil to the moisturizers she worked into her skin, wrapped her in plastic, and placed warm towels over her body. She then went to work on her scalp massage and infused her hair with oils while stimulating the top of Linda's head and relaxing her neck and shoulders. Nora then wrapped her hair in another warm towel and left Linda to relax.

The fragrant oils combined with the warmth of her cocoon were like a sedative. Linda relaxed and closed her eyes, content to let the calmness wash over her like the tide on the beach.

Nora returned and worked quietly as she removed the towels and plastic and massaged the remaining oil into Linda's skin and hair. She was gentle with Linda's ankle and foot, but gave her a through massage and concentrated on the reflex points in the feet to release tension.

"How do you feel?" asked Nora, as she moved her stool.

"Wonderful, thank you. My leg feels great, too."

"Oh, that's good to hear. I'm going to step out and retrieve your lunch and when you're finished, Camille will be in to do your facial."

She returned a few minutes later with a plate of fruit, a fresh salad topped with chicken, and an orange and cranberry scone. Iced tea and cucumber water were also provided. Linda wrapped herself in her robe and sat in a comfy chair by the fire and nibbled on her lunch, finding it tasty and fresh.

She ran her hand over her leg and noticed how silky and smooth her skin felt. As she finished her lunch she heard a light knock on the door.

"Linda, it's Camille, are you ready for me?"

"Yes, come in."

Camille repositioned Linda on the table and adjusted it to raise her head. She also swung a lighted magnifier around and placed it near her face. "Just relax, Linda. I'll be applying several different products starting with a light exfoliator, followed by proteins and antioxidants I'll massage into your skin. Then we'll finish with a hydrating masque and a moisturizer. If anything irritates or bothers you, let me know."

Linda closed her eyes and felt the smooth brush strokes as Camille went to work. In about an hour, Camille finished spreading the masque and told Linda she'd shampoo her hair while it dried. She used a shampoo infused with rich hints of coconut and lime. She wrapped Linda's hair in a warm towel and began rinsing the masque from her skin.

Camille applied the last layer of moisturizing cream and pronounced Linda ready for her manicure and pedicure. She released her hair and sprayed it with another product to speed the drying and leave it soft and shiny. She explained another technician, Deb, would be arriving to complete her treatments. She also gave her some sample sizes of the products she used on her face, letting her know they were available for purchase.

Linda thanked Camille as she left and introduced herself to Deb. Deb moved Linda to another area around the corner and seated her in the pedicure throne, complete with a heated massage chair and a large spa for soaking her feet. Deb knew about her ankle and asked Linda to let her know if there was any discomfort.

"Today has been a day filled with absolutely no discomfort," she laughed. Deb handed her an iced tea and turned on the jets in the warm water and Linda noticed lemons slices floating in it.

Deb let her feet soak and then applied a citrus scrub to exfoliate, followed by a warm lemon butter masque to moisturize her feet. She kneaded and applied pressure to the reflex points in her feet, as Nora had done earlier, and Linda felt her body slacken. Linda chose a dark plum color for her toenails and watched as Deb expertly applied the coats of polish. Deb guided her feet into a nail lamp to dry the polish.

While Linda's toes were drying Deb invited her to select a nail polish and began her manicure, first dipping her hands in warm paraffin and wrapping them. Linda didn't normally wear nail polish, so she chose a nearly clear color. Deb made quick work of massaging her hands and shaping her nails before applying the prep coat. She worked quickly and guided Linda's hand under the LED lamp in between the coats. She finished by wiping each nail with a cotton wipe soaked in a residue remover, and applying a dot of oil to her cuticles.

"I can't believe they're dry and ready to use right after you're done," said Linda. "I've never had gel polish before."

"It's popular and it wears for a long time without chipping. You'll like it," said Deb, as she put away her tools. "Well, I think you're done for the day. Would you like to have a drink in the lounge or head back to your room?"

"What time is it?"

"It's a bit after four."

"Oh, my, that's hard to believe. I need to get back to the room, but thank you." She changed into her sweats and stopped at the desk on the way out and signed for her services, applying a generous tip.

When she opened the door to the suite, Max was back, propped on the sofa watching television. He glanced from the show he was watching, "So, how was the spa?"

"Delightful. I haven't felt this relaxed in years. My leg doesn't hurt a bit. I need to fix my hair and change clothes. Do you have an idea for dinner?"

"I was thinking we should try the Bengal Lounge while we're here. They have a buffet, but also á la carte items."

"Okay, I'll dash in the bathroom and get ready. How was golf?"

"It was terrific. I played both courses. It was gorgeous and fun. I need to make a habit of using my golf membership when we get home. I've been so busy I haven't thought of it, but now I'm in the mood."

"Did you have lunch there?" she hollered from the bathroom.

"Yeah, they have three restaurants and I had a beef dip on the terrace overlooking the golf course. It was delicious, as was the soup. How about you? Did they feed you?"

"Yes, it was actually pretty good. I was expecting a carrot and a slice of cucumber, but I had a nice chicken salad, fruit, and a warm scone. "

Linda changed into a long black skirt that hid her boot and topped it with a white silk blouse and threw her black pashmina over her shoulder. As promised, the hair treatment had left her hair shiny and smooth, so a quick finger tousle was all it needed.

Max gazed upon her standing by the fireplace as he emerged in a coat and tie. "I dare say you're prettier today than ever." He swooped in and engulfed her in a strong hug, daring to smudge her lipstick with a lingering kiss.

She used her finger to rub his lips and remove most of the colored gloss. "You look quite handsome yourself." She took his hand in hers as they walked to the elevator.

The Bengal Lounge, true to its name, sported the skin of a tiger mounted over a fireplace. It was full of dark wood, lush green plants, and animal prints everywhere. They were shown to a leather sofa, accented with oversize tiger print pillows, to enjoy drinks by the fire while they waited for a table. They both indulged in a signature cocktail. He chose a Bengal Tiger, a fruity rum drink with a splash of apricot brandy. She went with the classic Empress 1908, which consisted of tea, infused with vodka, lemon juice, sweet syrup and frothy egg whites all mixed together and served in a sugar rimmed glass.

"This room reminds me of the *Jungle Book*," said Linda.

Max laughed. "Exactly."

"It seems like we're in a far-away land. And look at all the statues of exotic animals."

Big band music filtered throughout the dark and masculine lounge. They sipped their drinks and Max described the panoramic views he had from the golf course. He told Linda he took a bunch of pictures while golfing. He was paired with a vacationer from California.

The hostess interrupted their conversation and led them to a cozy table by the window and near another fireplace. They sat in cushioned wing back chairs and selected an appetizer to share. Linda chose their fish and chips and Max selected a smoked pork chop. After dinner they succumbed to share a piece of lemon meringue pie, accompanied with fresh raspberries.

Max took the first bite. "Good, but doesn't hold a candle to Sam's."

Linda sampled a forkful and nodded her head. "You're right. I think she makes the best pie I've ever tasted."

They finished the dessert and lingered over tea. "So, I heard the museum is another must see place while we're here. The shuttle driver gave me two complimentary tickets, if you want to go. They're open late tonight."

"I'm game. My leg feels good."

Max signaled for their check and helped Linda with her wrap. They made their way across the street to the museum and found it to be busy with a special showing in the theatre, but the museum was sparsely populated. They took a map and set out on a recommended tour.

They covered the two floors of exhibits noting the natural history galleries were their favorites. Linda also liked Totem Hall where intricately carved totem poles were on display. They encountered very few people on their tour and were able to get through it in less than two hours.

It was close to ten o'clock when they returned to their room. Once again they were treated to chocolates on their pillows and cookies on the table. They cuddled on the sofa, enjoying the night view of the harbor as the fire crackled.

"I haven't had this much fun in years," said Max, turning to kiss her. His lips traveled to the side of her neck and as he inhaled the scent of her hair, he whispered, "You smell so good."

She laughed as his breath tickled her ear. "I should, I've been rubbed, scrubbed, oiled, soaked, and moisturized."

"You're perfect," he murmured, his lips finding hers again.

Her lips parted as the kiss deepened. She felt his hand on her back and as he released her, he continued to graze her neck with his lips, depositing gentle kisses as he plunged deeper and she felt his warm hands under her blouse. She let out a gasp as she felt the buttons give way and his mouth moved under the satin and lace covering her breast. She felt the stubble on his cheek against her tender flesh.

"Max," she whispered.

"Mmm hmm."

"It's time."

"For what?" he murmured.

"The next step."

He righted himself and looked at her, the firelight reflected in her dark eyes. "Are you sure?"

She nodded and placed her hand in his. "Yes."

He led her to the bedroom. Tonight they skipped her therapy in favor of a different form of exercise.

* * *

Linda was on the verge of waking and heard rain. She cracked open an eye and sensed the soft light of dawn. She blinked her eyes several times and listened again, noticing Max was gone. She propped her head against the pillows and realized the sound of rain was actually the shower. She looked at the clock and saw it was just past seven o'clock. She stretched and used the pillows for a backrest.

It feels right, being with him. I'm not sure what will happen next, but I'm not sorry about last night. She smiled remembering the romance of the evening and the easy way they had loved each other.

The bathroom door opened and steam wafted out. Max came out looking ready for the day. "Good morning," he smiled. "I hope I didn't wake you."

"No, I've only been up a few minutes. How'd you sleep?"

"Like a baby. Probably something to do with a Bengal Tiger," he grinned.

She laughed as she got out of bed and tousled his hair as she passed him to get to the bathroom. "I'll be out in a jiffy."

She put her hair up while she took a quick shower. She surveyed her face and touched her hair, noticing it was smooth and glossy. She decided to invest in some of their shampoo and the spray. Her face was velvety smooth from her treatments yesterday. She finished getting ready and met Max in the parlor.

"Feel like some breakfast?" he asked.

"Yeah, something light, since we're doing Afternoon Tea at noon."

"I found a bakery not far. We could walk if you're feeling strong."

"Yeah. If I get tired, we can take a cab back."

The fresh morning air infused the quiet streets as they made their way the few blocks to a bakery and café.

Max squeezed her hand, "I love you, you know?"

She returned the squeeze. "I do. I love you back."

"I hope you're okay about last night."

"Last night was wonderful and special; totally romantic." She blushed. "I'll admit, I feel a little guilty, especially when I think of my mom, but I'm not sorry. It felt right."

"I knew it would be special, and it was. I couldn't be happier."

They arrived at the old family owned restaurant and decided to split an omelet with fresh fruit and homemade cinnamon raisin bread. As they enjoyed breakfast they chatted about the beauty of the area.

"Is there anywhere else we need to go or do we need to buy any other gifts?"

"I need something for Regi. I was thinking a basket of products from the spa would be fun for her. I don't think she indulges herself much and I'd like to treat her. I was going to add a gift card to Lou's and the movies, too. That way she can treat herself or maybe invite a friend." She raised her eyebrows over her cup.

"Sounds like something she'll enjoy. And you're right about her. She works constantly and is focused on saving her money."

"She's a good mother. Christmas could be interesting this year, with her and Cam. I thought she and Nate got along well at dinner."

"Yeah, and it sounded like she was open to spending some time with him. I think he deserves to know more about her situation, but that's her call," he shrugged.

They had a couple hours to kill, so they took the long way back and ducked into some shops. After all their browsing, Linda's leg was feeling good and strong, so they continued past the Empress to Beacon Hill Park. The two spent an hour, holding hands, strolling through the gardens and admiring the lakes and statuary.

By the time they circled the park, Linda was getting tired. They made it back to the hotel minutes after the Tea Lobby opened. They were shown to a table overlooking the Inner Harbour. The room, like the entire hotel, evoked a feeling of a bygone era, decorated in floral chintz and thick rugs. The hand-carved wooden tables, made from the original floor, held fine china cups rimmed in gold, a variety of plates and flatware, and fancy linen napkins. They chose to sample a variety of teas and enjoyed the green tea and white tea, but ultimately selected the signature Empress tea.

"This place reminds me of *Downton Abbey*," she said.

"You're right. All the elegance and charm."

A tiered serving tray was loaded with finger sandwiches on a variety of breads and croissants, fresh baked scones with jam, ripe strawberries and clotted cream, and a decadent layer of mini desserts. A pianist filled the room with soft classical music while they enjoyed sampling all the delicious treats.

"What's your favorite?" asked Max.

"Oh, that's a hard question. I think I like the egg salad on the croissant and it's a toss-up between the devil's food cake and the lemon meringue tart."

"I think I liked the smoked salmon sandwich and I'm with you on the desserts, those are the best, plus I like the shortbread cookies for dipping in my tea."

"It feels so fancy. Very fun. I've never done it before."

"Here's to a trip of first times," he said, lifting his tea cup and leaning over to kiss her.

They finished the food and commented it was a good thing they decided to walk before tea. After one more cup of tea, they signed the check and stopped in the room to get their jackets for the carriage ride.

They met their driver, a beautiful young lady named Tilly, who got them situated into the plush velvet seat, covered their legs with a thick blanket, and presented Linda with a bouquet of red roses. "These are from your sweetie. Now sit back and enjoy the tour. I'll point out places of interest, but if you have questions, give us a shout."

Linda sniffed the roses. "Mmm, the fragrance is wonderful. Thank you."

Max put his arm around her and planted a long kiss on her lips. "You're welcome."

The horse got under way and they lunged forward. Tilly pointed out the Parliament Buildings and the museum. She drove them to Beacon Hill Park and took them through it, talking about its history and the fact it was a city owned park. They continued past St. Ann's Academy, a former Catholic girls' school, and now a national landmark. The slow pace of the horse and the clippity-clop of its hooves made for a relaxing ride.

Tilly took them to view the stunning Olympic Mountains and through James Bay and then back to Government Street to meander the streets around Chinatown and Olde Towne. The tour concluded as they passed by the Empress and rounded the corner to their starting position near the Legislature. Tilly suggested she take their picture in the carriage and they posed with her beautiful black horse, Inky. It was four o'clock when they left Tilly, with a liberal tip.

After relaxing in the room, they enjoyed a light dinner at The Veranda, a casual outdoor restaurant located below the Empress sign, revealing a panoramic view of the harbor and surrounding area. They each enjoyed a Tiger Cub; a non-alcoholic version of the cocktail Max had last night. After sharing an appetizer of sesame chicken, topped with toasted coconut, they split a huge cheeseburger.

As the crowd was light, there was no rush to leave and they stayed late into the evening, enjoying the view between the vine covered arches and the light jazz music. "This has been a perfect trip. I'm sorry to be leaving tomorrow," said Linda.

"It's been lovely. But real life awaits us." He took a sip of his drink. "Speaking of, I'm going to start working at the hospital the third week of October. I told them I would plan on working Tuesdays and Wednesdays, but wanted to see if that would work for you."

"With my leg feeling better, I want to get back to the flower shop. I think I'll plan on going back around the same time. I'm going to schedule myself to work Tuesdays through Thursdays. That will leave us the long weekends, in case we think of something to do."

"Terrific. After having so much fun golfing here, I'm going to book Thursday for golfing each week, until the weather makes it impossible."

"I bet Sam will be anxious to get back to work when they get home. Jeff, too. Do you think he'll be able to work?"

"I think he'll be doing lots of therapy for several months, but I think working at the hardware store would be doable, a few hours here and there. I think it will be longer before he can do the remodel jobs he's used to doing."

Before they knew it, the restaurant was closing. The outdoor heaters kept the area so comfortable, they hadn't noticed the lateness of the hour. They meandered back to their room and Linda did her therapy before snuggling into bed, resting her head on Max's shoulder.

"It's our last night," she whispered. "Do you feel like making it a memorable one?"

In answer, he turned to her, greedily kissed her and with the deftness of a magician, slid her silky chemise off and flung it to the floor before the kiss ended.

Twenty-Eight

They got home before three o'clock and spent time playing with the dogs, opening the mail and reading emails. Max fell asleep watching television and Linda planned to let him rest until they went to her therapy appointment.

Sam let them know Jeff loved the pictures and it helped him with memories. David emailed to confirm their arrival on Friday afternoon. Linda planned to take them to Lou's for dinner and called to reserve a large table. Jen texted and wanted to know all about the trip. She wanted to have lunch tomorrow.

Regi left a note saying all went well at the house and reported Linda's house was done and ready for her family visit and would only need a quick once over to get it ready for sale. She had a huge smiley face at the end of the letter and told them she'd be moving her stuff into the spare room later in the week. Linda laughed as she finished reading.

She texted Jen back and confirmed lunch tomorrow at Soup D'Jour and wrote back to David to let him know she had dinner reservations for Friday evening. She and Max would meet them at the ferry.

Linda organized all the souvenirs and gifts and then it was time to wake Max for the ride to the hospital for therapy. She gently tapped his shoulder. "Hey, sweetheart, it's time to go. Maybe we packed a little too much in last night."

He grinned, "You don't hear me complaining."

While she was in her session, Max stopped by the specialty department and confirmed his schedule with his boss, Dr. Craig Anderson. He showed him his office and told him he would be sharing his administrative assistant, Sylvia, who would help him with any items he needed for his workspace or exam rooms. He also showed him the state of the art classroom, which was more like a small theatre, and introduced him to Eric, the technology guru.

Linda was coming out of the patient door when he stepped into the waiting area. "Ready?" he asked.

"Yep. She said I'm doing well and gave me a few new exercises to add at home."

"Let's get take out tonight. How about pizza wraps?"

"Okay and then I have to cut back on the fun food. I can't remember when I've eaten so much."

"Technically, today is a vacation day. So, this will be our last splurge. Then it's salads and fish for the rest of the month. I promise."

"I'll believe it when I see it," she laughed. She called in an order on their way to the car.

They lit a fire and savored the warm dough of the wraps. While they ate they discussed the options of cooking for Linda's family versus eating out. Linda thought they should cook, but Max was concerned it would wear Linda out, so they reached a compromise. They'd treat them to the Cliff House on Saturday night and Linda would do a Sunday brunch at Max's. They'd eat out the rest of the time or get takeout.

"You'll want to spend time with Uncle Mike instead of worrying about dinners."

"Yeah, I want everything to be, you know, perfect."

"It will be. We can stop by the market and get some snacks and ice cream. Then on Friday night we can invite them back here for dessert. We can do breakfast at Ellie's on Saturday or the Front Street Café, whichever you think."

Linda nodded. "You're right. I'm overthinking things." She tossed the takeout containers and stopped to deliver Max a kiss goodnight. "I'm beat. I'm going to call it a night. See you in the morning."

"I'm worn out too, despite my nap. I'll play with the dogs and then I'm going to hit the hay."

* * *

The next day they delivered their gifts from the trip. Linda had lunch with Jen and presented her with a beautiful scarf and hat she had found at a woolen goods store. "Oh, how cute." She plopped the soft hat on her head and flipped the matching purple and green scarf across her neck. "Soft and yummy. Now I can't wait for it to get cold."

Linda told her about the trip and showed her some of the photos on her camera. "This is a project for me. I want to go through and pick out some of my favorites and get them framed. Maybe make some notecards out of some of the garden shots. It's all so beautiful."

"So, how was the hotel?"

"Fabulous. The spa was to die for. Our room had a fantastic view of the harbor and a fireplace."

"Romantic, huh?"

"Very. In fact, Max and I made love for the first time. It was magical."

"Oh, oh, oh," Jen squealed as she hopped up and down on her chair.

"Shh, I don't want the whole town to know."

"I'm so excited for you. He's such a great guy for you."

"He is. You know I'm not into meaningless flings, so this was a big step."

"I know, sweetie. I won't say a word. I know how much this means to you."

"He's the one, Jen. I guess there's a reason for everything and if I hadn't been stupid enough to wait around for Walt or whatever I was doing, I may not have met Max."

"Things happen when they're supposed to, right?" She patted Linda's hand. "You deserve all the happiness in the world."

They finished their lunch and hugged each other goodbye.

Linda met Max at the coffee shop. He had handed out the dessert cookbook they found for Hayley, a box of chocolates for Rachel, and a pretty sweater for Megan. Charlie stopped by and they gave him the red Canada hoodie they had chosen for him.

Everyone loved their presents and they spent some time chatting about the places they visited. Linda reminded him they needed to stop by and give Regi her gift. Linda texted her and found out she was already home for the day, so they stopped by the condo.

Regi greeted them at the door and led them into her small, but tidy living room. "Did you guys have fun?"

"We had the best time. It was a beautiful place. You need to visit someday."

"It's on my list," she said.

Max handed her a gift bag and told her they wanted to thank her for watching the house and the dogs.

"Oh, you didn't need to get me anything." She took the bag and untied the ribbons. She lifted out a huge basket filled with a variety of lotions and potions from the spa. She opened the card and discovered the gift cards. "Wow, you guys are way too generous."

"You deserve it," said Linda. "You'll love those products. I splurged on some of them myself."

"I haven't been to a real movie in a long time."

"We can't stay long, but wanted to get your gift to you while we were in town," said Max.

"I'm glad you stopped by. Here are your keys," said Regi, as she twisted both Linda's key and Max's off her ring.

"Perfect. I'll get in touch after my company leaves. We should get rid of a few more pieces of furniture and then you can give it a quick once over."

"No problem. I can do that after school."

They thanked her again and headed for the market. They loaded the cart with snacks for company, plus all the ingredients for the brunch Linda was planning. After salmon and salads they watched a movie by the fire.

* * *

Friday arrived and Linda and Max were waiting on a bench for the ferry to appear. It pulled in right on time and they watched the cars disembark. Linda spied David in a green Tahoe and waved frantically. As she glanced at the passenger, she put her hand over her mouth. Uncle Mike looked exactly like her dad. Linda motioned David down the street and he found a parking spot right next to Max's car.

Mike's smile was infectious. "You've got to be Linda," he said, gripping her in a bear hug. "And this is my wife, Diane."

A petite woman, with shoulder length gray hair and baby blue eyes, smiled. She took Linda's hands in hers. "I'm so pleased you found your uncle. You have no idea how happy this has made him, dear."

Linda felt tears leaking down her face. "I'm the one who's over the moon. Thank you both for visiting." She linked her arm in Max's. "This is my boyfriend, Max Sullivan."

Max shook hands with Mike and earned a hug from Diana. "You two make a gorgeous couple," she said, releasing him.

David and Peggy were waiting to the side. "Mom, this is Max Sullivan."

"So happy to meet you, Mrs. Graham. We're glad you could all make the trip."

"Lovely to meet you, too."

David and Max shook hands. "Hi, David. We've talked on the phone, but nice to put a face to the voice."

"You too, Max."

"Let's head over to Lou's and have some dinner. I'm sure you're all hungry," suggested Linda.

Lou greeted them at the door and led them to a table he had reserved. "Hey, Mrs. Graham, good to see you."

"You too, Lou. How's your family?"

"You probably knew my dad died last year," he said, with misty eyes. "But, my kids are doing great."

"Yes, I'm sorry about your father. He was a dear man. Are your kids on the island?"

"No, the last one went to college this year. So I'm living in my empty nest now, but they come home for visits. And money, of course," he laughed.

Lou took orders for drinks and everyone got settled. They made their selections and chatted nonstop until the food arrived. On their way to the table, David had whispered to Linda and let her know he and his mom had told Mike and Diane the whole story about how they came to live on the island with false names. She was thankful the topic wouldn't have to be revisited anytime soon, especially for her mom's sake.

After dinner, they strolled through town and Linda showed them her flower shop and Sam's coffee shop. Peggy hadn't been to the island for years, so Linda pointed out Jen's salon. "She said to stop by if you want your hair done while you're here."

Peggy touched her hair. "I might do that. She's always been such a considerate girl."

They split up on the way home and Max drove Diana and Mike, while Linda rode with David and her mom. They took them by the new hospital and explained Max had been asked to work there as a specialist and consultant a couple of days a week. They continued out of town to Max's house.

Everyone remarked about how beautiful the yard was and gasped when they walked into the house and observed the stunning view and huge patio. The dogs were going crazy, bouncing around all the new visitors. Mike laughed and kneeled to pet and talk to the eager trio. After bribing them with treats, Linda got them to sit on their beds, with their tails doing double time.

Max served ice cream to everyone and started a pot of coffee. They gathered in the great room and enjoyed the fire, while they continued visiting.

"We've got the old house ready for you. All the beds have fresh sheets and we stashed some snacks and essentials in the fridge," said Linda.

"Thank you, dear. I'm excited to see it one last time," said her mom.

"You've got a magnificent place here, Max," commented Mike. "Especially the outdoor living areas."

"It was one of the things that attracted me to the house. Linda is making brunch on Sunday and if the weather cooperates, we'll eat outside and enjoy it."

"Oh, that sounds marvelous," said Diane, as she collected the bowls and carried them to the kitchen.

"So, we made reservations for dinner tomorrow at the Cliff House and thought we could spend tomorrow exploring the island a bit. We could meet for breakfast and eat lunch or a snack while we're out and about. Does that work for all of you?" asked Linda.

They nodded. Mike smiled, "Sounds about perfect to me."

David noticed his mom was tired. "I think we're all bushed. We'll head out and plan to meet you in the morning."

"Let's say around nine at the Front Street Café," said Linda.

They hugged each other goodbye and Peggy touched Linda's cheek as she was leaving. "I'm so pleased you're not alone. You look wonderful."

"Thanks, Mom. See you in the morning." She and Max waved from the driveway as the Tahoe disappeared.

Max took her hand and led her back to the door. "I think that went well."

She nodded. "Yeah. Mom told me she was happy for me. I think it's all going to be okay."

* * *

After breakfast, they all squeezed into David's Tahoe for sightseeing. They started from town and drove to the lighthouse at Cattle Point and stopped at the American Camp Park, where they ran into Rachel. She was about to lead a tour and invited them to join.

After hiking around the park, they drove on to the lavender farm and made a stop at Lime Kiln to watch for whales. They stared out at the water and after only a few minutes were rewarded with a showing of a pod of orcas. Mike and Diane had never seen a whale and were in awe. "Unbelievable. What a humbling experience," he said, as he watched them glide by the shore.

Max had brought a picnic lunch from Dottie's Deli and suggested they stop at the Harbor Resort to eat and say hello to Jeremy and Heather. They pulled in and with the tourist season over, had their pick of parking spots. Jeremy was outside and looked over, recognizing Linda. "Hey, Linda. What brings you by?"

"My family's here and we're on a tour and thought we'd stop here for a picnic."

"Is that your mom?"

"Yeah, and David. Plus my Uncle Mike and Aunt Diane visiting from Nevada."

With a big grin, Jeremy stepped over to David and shook his hand and gave Peggy a gentle hug. "I haven't seen you guys in years."

They introduced Mike and Diane, who remarked on the beauty of the resort. Linda explained Jeff had married Max's best friend, Sam. She also recapped the horrific accident and Brenda's involvement and ultimate suicide.

"Wow, sounds like a lot of excitement for what looks to be such a quiet crime free place," commented Mike.

"It's been shocking and horrible for Sam and Jeff. They're both wonderful friends."

They invited Jeremy and Heather to join them at a picnic table and shared Dottie's huge sandwiches and salads. "What a peaceful place," remarked Diane. "We may have to plan a vacation here," she said, nudging her husband with her elbow.

"I'd love it. Are you two ready for some house guests this summer?"

"You bet," Linda smiled. "We'd be delighted to have you anytime."

"You're all welcome to visit us anytime. Carson City is beautiful and only about thirty minutes from Lake Tahoe. If you've never visited, it's awe inspiring."

Max looked at Linda. "Sounds terrific and I've never been there."

Linda nodded. "We'll definitely plan a trip."

They finished lunch and started out for the alpaca farm. They also made a quick loop into Sam's property to show them her home. The alpacas were a big hit and they enjoyed watching the graceful and gentle animals as they wandered through the grounds. Max treated Diane and Peggy to colorful hand knit alpaca sweaters.

Max noticed Peggy was moving slower and looked pale. "Are you feeling okay, Peggy?"

"I'm fine," she snapped. "Just more walking than I'm used to."

He and Linda had planned to stop at English Camp and a local vineyard on the way back to Friday Harbor, but he whispered, "I don't think your mom is feeling well. Maybe we ought to skip the next stops."

Linda nodded and went to help her mom to the car. Max took them back to town where he and Linda retrieved his car and they agreed to meet back at the Cliff House for dinner at seven.

When they got home, Max asked, "Do you think your mom is okay?"

"She says she's worn out and not used to this much activity. Why, what do you think?"

"She's short of breath and her coloring isn't good. Does she have any heart conditions?"

"Not that I know of. Do you think she should see a doctor?

"I'd feel better if she did. I could do an exam, if she's open to it."

"I'll go call David and see what he thinks."

Max played ball with the dogs and sat on the patio, taking in the sun. He had a cold drink ready for Linda when she returned.

She shrugged. "He asked her again and she got agitated and said she was fine. She's going to take a nap and they'll see us at seven."

"We'll see how she's doing at dinner. It could be nothing."

They finished their drinks and Linda put together a breakfast casserole, plus Sam's overnight French toast and then changed for dinner. Although they dressed separately, their choice in clothes complimented one another. She wore the same black and pink dress she had worn when she and Max danced together at the Harbor Resort. He emerged wearing a soft pink dress shirt paired with a pink jacquard tie and a black jacket.

"I remember that dress," he said, as he gathered her close. "You're as beautiful as ever."

She kissed him. "Are you ready to go?"

He nuzzled her neck. "I'd rather stay here, just the two of us."

She laughed and pulled his arm. "Let's go, we don't want to be late."

They arrived and were led to their table, where the other four were already seated. "Do you remember this place, Mom?"

"Oh, yes. It's the fanciest place around, I bet." She looked perkier and her color had returned.

They chatted and made their selections. Mike and Diane told them all how much they had enjoyed the trip around the island. "Do you do any fishing, Max?" asked Mike.

"No, I don't, but I know it's a popular hobby here. I've decided to commit to golfing once a week."

"Only thing better would be golfing twice a week," laughed Mike.

Their meals arrived and everyone raved about the food. Their selections included trout, salmon and halibut and they all praised the talents of the chef. Max noticed Peggy didn't eat much.

Linda recommended the molten chocolate cake for dessert and everyone but Peggy succumbed to the temptation. They served it with vanilla bean ice cream.

Max and Linda were glad they elected to share one, since they were stuffed when they got to the bottom of the bowl. "Yummy, huh?" she asked, looking at Mike.

"Very," he said, scooping the last bit of ice cream and fudgy filling into his spoon.

David tried to give his mom a bite of his, but she refused and said she was full. Much to Mike's dismay, Max made sure he received the bill for dinner and after a lot of wrangling, agreed to let Mike leave the tip.

It was after nine when they left the restaurant and Linda invited everyone back to the house, but Peggy said she was tired, so they said their goodbyes and planned to see each other in the morning for brunch.

"Mom looked better, but she didn't eat much," said Linda with worry in her voice.

"Yeah, I noticed. How old is your mom?"

"Let's see, she'll be seventy-nine."

Max was quiet as he drove to the house and into the garage. He talked Linda into sitting by the fire pit on the patio with a glass of wine. There was a chill in the air, and the fire felt wonderful.

"You think something's wrong with her don't you?"

"I think she needs an examination to rule out a few things. She could have a blockage in her heart, or an issue with her blood pressure, lots of different things. And, she may be right, she could simply be overtired."

Linda stared out at the dark water, the moonlight bouncing off the low ripples. "I'll try to talk to her again tomorrow."

* * *

The group rang the bell at Max's late Sunday morning. Max had put the dogs outside, so their exuberance wouldn't overwhelm Peggy. "Welcome, come in," Max said, opening the door.

"How is everyone this morning?" bellowed Mike.

"We're terrific. Linda's in the kitchen and I've got everything on the patio."

Diane and Peggy followed Max out to the patio and David and Mike stopped by the kitchen. "Something smells delicious," said Mike, giving Linda a peck on her cheek.

"Almost ready," she said, moving to the oven. "How's Mom doing today?"

"I don't know. She gets pretty pissed off when I ask her about it. She says she feels better today," said David, stealing a strawberry out of the fruit salad.

"Maybe the trip has been harder on her than we thought?" suggested Mike. "She's a bit emotional about the house and I think she misses your dad more than ever."

"I hope that's it. Max thinks she needs to get a thorough examination and fears something could be wrong with her heart."

"He ought to know. But, she's stubborn," said David. "She's got a family doctor she likes at home. I'll get her in to see him when we get home this week."

"Make sure she goes. I'm a bit worried."

They helped her carry out the food fresh out of the oven and the accompanying fruit salad and frosted cinnamon rolls. Max had poured mimosas, and the table was piled high with bacon, the two overnight casseroles, fried potatoes with onions, and caramel muffins.

"What a feast," remarked Mike, adding a cinnamon roll oozing with cream cheese frosting on top of his plate.

"Did you figure out what pieces of furniture you wanted to keep from the house?" asked Linda, while passing plates around the table.

David scooped up a huge portion of the French toast casserole. "Yeah, I want to keep Dad's gun cabinet and Mom picked out a few pieces. I thought we'd arrange to have them shipped home."

"The house looks lovely, Linda. You've done a great job," smiled Peggy, eating her fruit salad.

"I'm pleased with it and I think it will make a special B&B. It's too much for me to maintain though."

"I told Uncle Mike you could give him a tour of your nursery today."

"Sure, I'd like to. I haven't been out there since I hurt my ankle. It's been feeling a lot better, so I'm going to go back to work at the flower shop in a couple of weeks."

She gripped Max's hand and held it between their plates. "I decided to cut back on work so we could do more things and enjoy ourselves," smiled Linda.

Mike raised his glass. "I'll drink to that. Diane and I have been travelling for years. I retired before I was sixty and we've had a grand time together."

The feeding frenzy waned and Linda let them know she also had a pie for dessert. "Holy cow, I don't think I could eat one more thing. Maybe later this afternoon," said David, as he pushed his chair back.

Max started clearing the table and David and Mike pitched in and let the ladies relax. While they were busy in the kitchen, Max slipped into the library and retrieved a card. "Here, David. This is my business card from the hospital and on the back I've written the name of the top cardiac specialist in your area. If you can convince Peggy to go in for an exam, I'd feel better. And I'm happy to help in any way."

"I appreciate it. I'll talk to her on the way home and get her to see her regular doctor and I'll ask him to refer her to this guy. I hope it's the trip making her tired, but I agree, she should have a workup and then we'd all feel better."

They finished in the kitchen and Linda offered to go with Mike and Diane out to the nursery to show them her pride and joy. The others decided to stay on the patio and bask in the sunshine.

Linda relished the opportunity to have Uncle Mike to herself and peppered him with questions about her dad and their family. He told her he was a teenager when he was told Joe and Millie had died in a car crash.

"It was heartbreaking. I loved Joe so much and Millie was the perfect addition to our family. Sorry, I can't get used to Peggy and Ed, since I never knew them after they changed their names." He shook his head. "The whole thing is gut wrenching. I can't begin to imagine the fear they felt to take such drastic measures. And my mom was on board, too."

"Did they have a funeral?"

"We had a service, but no caskets. She told us it was complicated to transport their bodies and they had been cremated instead. I never suspected anything. Mom was totally distraught. I guess they may as well have died, in her eyes, since she couldn't see them again."

"I'm sad we missed out knowing our real family. Part of me is angry we didn't know anything until now." She didn't disguise the thin edge in her voice.

Diane, who had a permanent smile on her face, piped up from the back seat. "Well, I'm thrilled you found the letter now. At least we'll be able to keep in touch and visit."

Linda nodded. "I know. I sound like a big brat, but I feel like my entire life has been a fabrication. It's hard to accept and I know it upsets Mom, so I feel guilty if I say anything."

"I learned a long time ago we can't go back and living in the past is a waste of time. So, like Diane said, I'm going to focus on what we have now and make the most of it. I wish it had been different, but it wasn't," said Mike, patting her knee.

They pulled into the driveway and she directed him to park near the gift shop. They spent a couple of hours traversing the different areas of the nursery and visiting. Mike and Diane marveled at the selection of plants. "Your climate is much more conducive to growing than ours in Nevada. We have lots of pine trees, but it's dry."

"We're lucky here. We have pretty terrific weather and it makes growing lots of things easy. We're towards the end of the season now, so you'll have to come back in the summer and see it someday."

"We will. You can count on it," smiled Mike.

Diane admired a copper dragonfly on a garden stake and Linda insisted she take it, with her compliments. "You'll have a cheerful memory of my nursery in your yard."

"Thank you, dear. That's sweet and I'll think of you each time I see it."

They returned to the house and found the other three snoozing on the lounges. Two pieces of pie were missing and they tiptoed from the patio to the great room, so they wouldn't disturb them.

"So, how do you guys think my mom is handling the news of me living with Max?"

"She hasn't said anything negative, if that's what you mean. The only comment she made is how content you look," said Mike.

"Yes, dear," added Diane. "You needn't worry. I think she's pleased you have found such a fine gentleman."

"That's a relief. I know I've stressed her with the old letter I found and selling the house and then Max."

"Well, honey, it's all good stuff. So, don't fret about it."

They looked up to see Max. "Did you guys enjoy the tour?"

"Oh, yes. It's marvelous. Linda is so talented," said Diane.

Max moved to sit by Linda and put his arm around her. "That she is."

"How's Mom?"

"She was tired. We all were and fell asleep in the sunshine. I tried to pry a bit more by asking about her activities at home and from what she said I'm convinced she needs to get a workup."

"I know I'll feel better when David gets her to the doctor," said Linda.

"How about we treat you two to dinner tonight? What sounds good?" asked Mike.

"We've got a good pizza place, Chinese, and a great deli. Any of those are delicious, but you don't need to treat us," said Linda.

"Yes, it's our pleasure," said Mike.

David and Peggy came in, both looking refreshed. "Sorry, we fell asleep on you guys," he said.

"No problem. We've been discussing dinner and our plan to treat you all to dinner in town. Linda was telling us we have pizza, Chinese, or a deli. Which one sounds good to you?"

"How about Chinese, Mom?"

"That's fine. Whatever sounds good to all of you. I'd rather get it to go, though."

"Okay, I'll call in an order for delivery." She solicited their special requests and called in the order.

Later, as they were finishing dinner, a gust of wind blew the paper plates and clouds rolled in. Max turned off the fire and they gathered everything and moved inside. As he secured the glass doors drops of rain the size of quarters plopped onto the stone patio.

"We should get going, before it gets any worse," said David. They made plans to meet at the coffee shop in the morning before the ferry arrived.

Max pulled David's Tahoe into the garage so they wouldn't get wet. Linda put her arm around her mom as she led her to the garage. "I know you don't want us to fuss over you, but Max is one of the top cardiologists in the country and he thinks you need to see a doctor and get a thorough exam. Promise me when you get back to Yakima you'll go without a fight."

"Oh, Linda. I'm fine," she waved away the notion.

Linda took her by the shoulders. "I mean it. Do it for me, please," she begged.

"All right. All right. I'll go."

"Call us when you know anything," she kissed her on the cheek, as she released her to David.

"See you all in the morning," waved Mike.

Linda and Max watched them leave from the end of the walkway and held hands as they hurried back into the house. They doused the lights and listened to the rain pelt the patio and slap against the windows. In the light of the fire, Max slipped his arm around her and she nestled into his shoulder.

"She promised to go to the doctor and let us know what he says."

"Good," he kissed her head. "Now, listen to the rain and rest."

* * *

The showers had subsided, but the clouds were dark and heavy in the morning, with fog clinging to the ground. They met at Harbor Coffee and enjoyed Ellie's pastries and hot beverages, before heading to the ferry lanes.

Mike engulfed Linda in a hug. "I'm grateful you found me and we were able to see your beautiful home and meet all of you. You have to promise to stay in touch and come visit us."

Tears streaked Linda's cheeks. "I will. Thanks so much for coming. You remind me so much of my dad."

"That's a high compliment. He was my favorite brother." He wiped a tear from his eye. "I miss him terribly, but couldn't be happier to have a niece I love."

Linda hugged Diane, David, and her mom. Max received hugs from everyone and as they drove onto the ferry, he and Linda waved from the dock. Doubt crept over her as she watched the ferry disappear into the vapor grabbing at the pale silver water.

Tears trickled down Linda's face. Tears of happiness in finding a piece of her past she had missed; tears of sadness for her dad and mom and everything they abandoned for safety; and tears for the fear in her soul that this may have been her last visit with her mom.

Twenty-Nine

The next week brought an update on Peggy. Her family doctor had agreed she needed a complete cardiac exam and sent her to the specialist Max had recommended. When Max got home on Friday he found Linda in her office finishing the shipping arrangements for the furniture and boxes going to David's house.

"Hey, sweetie. I heard from your mom's specialist in Yakima." He caught the flash of fear in her eyes and noticed she was holding her breath.

He moved around the desk and leaned against it. "It's going to be okay. He diagnosed her with small vessel coronary artery disease. It's treatable with medication and lifestyle changes. No surgery."

He heard her exhale. "It's serious, though?"

"It can be. He'll monitor her and have her in a few times a year to check on her and run tests at least once a year, maybe twice. She'll need to watch her cholesterol and increase her exercise."

She moved from her chair and hugged him. He felt her entire being collapse into him and sobs heaved her body. "It's okay, honey. She's going to be okay."

He felt her nod her head. "I know," she blubbered.

"You've been wound tight with worry. Just let it all out." He gently patted her back and moved his hands to knead her shoulders and neck. They were rock hard with tension.

"I think you need another massage at the Empress."

He heard a laugh among the sniffles. He plucked a handful of tissues from her desk and handed them to her.

She blew her nose and gulped in air. He led her from the office out to the couch and brought her a cup of warm tea with honey. "Here, drink this and we'll watch another episode of *Downton Abbey*. You can call your mom tomorrow."

She nodded and wrapped her hands around the cup. He covered her with a soft blanket and went to fix a tray of leftovers for dinner. Then he popped the disc in and felt her relax as they exchanged the drama of real life for the shenanigans of the servants and a risqué indiscretion of the lord of the manor's first born daughter.

* * *

The sale of Linda's house was complete in mid-October. She met the new owners, Ben and Sherrie Clark, and took an immediate liking to them. They had innovative ideas and were full of energy. Although a bit sad to leave the only home she had known, her spirits were lifted knowing the house would be cared for and full of activity.

She had been released from physical therapy and now did exercises on her own at home. Max helped her each evening and she had regained most of the strength in her leg, walked without her boot, and could drive.

Max started his job and she went back to work at the flower shop. She enjoyed the bustle of the shop and visiting with her regular customers. She had missed being able to create and relished the opportunity to use her floral design skills. They were two days away from Halloween and she had several orders for holiday themed arrangements.

She and Max met for lunch on Tuesdays and Wednesdays, since they were both in town. Today, they were meeting at Dottie's for sandwiches. When Linda came through the door she spotted him at a table.

"How's your day?" she asked.

"Good. It's great to be back, doing what I love. And I heard from Sam. She's planning to come home tonight and stay for a couple of days. She said Jeff is doing well and he wanted her to take a few days and relax. Steve's getting her now and she was hoping we could take the dogs over."

"Tell her we'll bring the dogs and dinner," suggested Linda. "I'll get something on the way home and meet you at our house around five. Then we can drive out to Sam's."

Max texted Sam and waited for a response while they split a sandwich. His phone chirped and he smiled as he scrolled through the text. "She says she'll see us at the house."

There was a chill in the air and Linda wrapped her warm scarf around her neck and flipped up the hood on her jacket. Max linked his arm in hers as they took the long way back to work. He dropped her at the shop and continued to the hospital.

She finished some arrangements and chatted with Lucas on the phone about the trees they would be getting in for Christmas. She busied herself with decorating the shop with harvest décor and pondered what to order for dinner. She and Max had cut back on eating out and had been sticking with their fish and salad resolution, for the most part. She knew Max loved pizza wraps and decided to treat him.

She made a call to Big Tony's and placed an order to have ready around five o'clock. She also put together a festive arrangement with pumpkins and fall leaves for Sam. She called Max when she was a few minutes from home and he said he had the dogs loaded and ready to go.

She pulled in and transferred the arrangement and the bags of food into Max's SUV. He was coming out of the house as she put her seatbelt on. He sniffed when he opened the door and grinned. "Do I detect Big Tony's?"

"I knew it would make your day," she said, leaning over to kiss him.

They drove out to Sam's, Zoe and Bailey both shaking with excitement when they turned into her driveway. They noticed lights on in the house and the garage door open. Max pulled the car by the garage and Sam came out.

Zoe and Bailey leapt out of the backseat and dove for her. Lucy followed close behind and all three dogs mauled Sam with affection. "I've missed these guys," she said, burying her face in the midst of the furry gang.

Max carried the bags and Linda took the arrangement into the house. Sam followed with the dogs circling her. She gave each of them a hug. "Gosh, I'm so happy to be home for a couple of days."

Max had the food arranged and pulled out some plates. Sam glanced at the beautiful fall arrangement. "When did this come?"

"I made it today, when I heard you were on your way home. You need something festive in the house this time of year."

Sam hugged her. "It's so cute, with the mini pumpkins. Thank you."

Sam retrieved some cold drinks and they gathered to enjoy salads and wedges of dough sprinkled with garlic and parmesan, plus three different pizza wraps they cut into quarters and shared.

"So, Jeff's doctors are confident he'll be home in a couple of weeks. He's going to need to continue physical therapy and he'll have to go back for checkups, but with you and Dr. Sean close by, they're good with him coming home. He's been doing great in therapy, much better than when you guys were there in September."

"Oh, what wonderful news. He'll be so glad to get home," said Linda.

Sam nodded. "He's thrilled. He misses his dogs."

"Will he need a walker or wheel chair?" asked Max.

"No, I think he'll use a cane if he needs it, but he's been walking unassisted. He's a little slow and stiff looking, but his balance is back, so he's stable. "

"We'll help with anything you need. Just say the word."

"They want him to go to therapy at the hospital on Mondays, Wednesdays, and Fridays. So I might need a little help with those appointments, but other than that, I'll need to keep him busy. I'd like to go back to work in the shop a little. I need some normalcy."

"We're both back at work, but we don't work on Monday or Friday, so we can help with those days. How many months do they expect he'll be in physical therapy?" asked Max.

"Not sure, but they said to plan on this schedule through the end of the year. It may taper off if he does well, but they don't want him losing any ground. And I want to have a big Thanksgiving here. We'll have you guys and Jeff's family and Becky's family, plus anyone else I can think of. We have so much to be thankful for this year and I think it will do Jeff good."

"Will Ashley come?" asked Max.

"I hope so. I haven't heard from her since she went back home, but I know Jen and Charlie talk to her and she calls Jeff. I'm inviting her and Will, but I'm not sure if they'll come."

"I think Peter and Brooke may come here for Thanksgiving, so we may have four more," said Max.

"Oh, that would be terrific. We have plenty of room, but I may need help with the dinner."

"You can count on us. And I'm sure Becky will be all over it," smiled Max.

"Yeah, she will. She'll have it all planned and organized, probably overnight."

She looked at Linda. "I talked to Jeff a little about the land we're getting in the settlement. One parcel is about five acres of land between the high school and the elementary school. Jeff and I discussed it and want to dedicate the space to something beautiful and we'd like you to consider designing a botanical garden to be enjoyed by the community and visitors. We'd like to call it Cooper Gardens."

Linda's hand went to her mouth. "Oh, I'd be honored and overjoyed. What a terrific idea."

Max nodded. "I can't think of anyone better to design it. You'll have to incorporate some ideas from our trip."

"I'll get to work on it right away and get you some sketches. It's wonderful of you and Jeff to turn such an ugly event into something lovely for the town."

"We don't need the land and would rather have something everyone will enjoy. It will put Brenda's money to use for something worthwhile."

"And you guys are set on all of Jeff's medical expenses and needs, right? It sounded like Marty had it covered," asked Max.

"Yes, Marty thought of every possibility and has it wrapped up. Everything's covered, plus some. He's handled everything. I haven't had to deal with it at all. He's been wonderful."

They finished dinner and stashed the leftovers in the fridge for Sam. The dogs had quit hovering and all of them were nestled on their beds by the fireplace.

Sam made a pot of tea and they moved to the great room. "What's on your agenda for the next couple of days? You leave Friday, right?" asked Max.

"Yeah. I'll go back Friday around noon. I think I'll sleep in tomorrow and go to the shop and bake a little and visit with everyone. Do you guys want to leave Lucy here?"

Linda shook her head. "I think she better get used to being an only dog again, so we'll take her and see how she does. The three of them have become quite the team."

"I can see that," said Sam, glancing at the pile of black, brown, and golden red fur, lumped together in one big ball of dog.

"Why don't you come for dinner Thursday? We're both off, so we'll have time to cook. There's no point in you cooking for yourself," suggested Linda. "Maybe we'll ask Regi to join us."

Sam sipped her tea. "It sounds fun and I'd like to get to know her better. Molly came to dinner at Becky's twice. She's very articulate and mature, plus a sweet kid. I had fun visiting with her and Kyle. They're alike in many ways."

Linda yawned. "We better hit the road. We'll see you Thursday for sure. Come over whenever you want in the afternoon and bring the girls."

Max took her hand and helped her from the couch. "Come on, Lucy," he shouted. Lucy raised her head and extricated herself from the other two dogs and trotted to the door.

They hugged Sam goodbye and hustled Lucy into the SUV. Sam watched them drive away and turned out the lights. She cuddled into her chair, with the afghan Annie had given her at her wedding shower, and Bailey and Zoe repositioned themselves so one was on each side of her.

* * *

It was a sunny November day, two weeks before Thanksgiving, when Max travelled with Steve to Shilshole Bay to pick up Jeff and Sam and bring them home. Sam hinted she would feel better if Max accompanied them on the journey, and he didn't hesitate.

Becky drove Sam and Jeff from the hospital to the marina, where Steve and Max were waiting. Max noticed Jeff had a cane, but didn't appear to need it. He'd put on some of the weight he had lost. Although thin, he looked much healthier and stronger than he had in September.

Sam gripped his hand tight and carried a tote, while Becky wheeled a piece of luggage. Steve and Max met them and relieved them of their bags and luggage. Becky gave Max a big hug and promised to see him at Thanksgiving.

"How are you doing today?" Max asked Jeff, with a hand on his shoulder.

"I'm terrific. It feels great to be out here," said Jeff, his head ensconced in a warm hat. "Even better to be going home."

Steve embraced him in a strong hug. "You look good, Coop."

Jeff smiled. "Thanks so much for everything." Tears filled his green eyes. "You don't know what it meant to have you bring my family over. I owe you."

"That's what friends do. You don't owe me a thing. You coming home is the only thing I need." He kept his arm around him as they maneuvered down the pier.

Max stowed everything below and he and Steve boarded and helped Jeff on, holding his hands and making sure he was steady. Then they gave Sam a hand. Steve helped get them situated in the plush cabin below and then took his place at the wheel to guide them out of the marina and home.

"Linda will have your dogs home by the time you get there," said Max. "They're going to be so excited to see you. We'll have to make sure they don't bowl you over. Zoe pounced on top of Sam when she came to visit.

Linda was going to lock the dog door with them outside until you get situated."

"I'm trying to talk Sam into letting them sleep on our bed tonight," grinned Jeff.

She rolled her eyes. "Yeah, he's been trying to guilt me into giving in on my no dogs on the bed rule."

"I think she'll cave," laughed Jeff, putting his arm around her.

Steve had them back in Friday Harbor in no time. They unloaded and stepping onto the dock spotted a huge banner that read, *Welcome Home Jeff.* White ribbons with black polka dots were tied on every post and pole along the marina.

Jeff looked around and noticed all the firefighters standing along the dock, waving and shouting greetings. "Oh, man. I don't know if I can do this," he whispered to Sam. She gripped his hand tighter.

They started down the dock and Jeff waved to his friends, shaking hands as he went. Sam and Max kept him moving until they reached Max's SUV. Steve loaded their bags and hugged Sam.

Max drove out of the lot amid hoots and cheers. The street was lined with more ribbons and waving friends. Max turned and took the road to Sam's house. All along the way, people were posted on the side with signs welcoming Jeff, honking their horns and shouting, "We love you, Jeff."

When Max turned into Sam's driveway, they saw balloons and ribbons adorning the entrance. Max looked over and saw tears streaming down Jeff's face.

"You okay?" he asked.

Jeff nodded. "Yeah, just overwhelmed. I wasn't sure I'd ever be here again."

Sam hopped out and opened the garage. She and Max helped Jeff in the door and led him to his chair in the great room. "How about a cold drink?" asked Max.

"I could go for lemonade," said Jeff.

Sam started to go to the kitchen. "I'll get it," waved Max. He returned with lemonades for both of them.

Max brought in the luggage and told Sam they had stocked the fridge with some groceries and some meals people had delivered for them. Linda had also picked up his prescriptions and put them on the counter. "Now if you two need anything, you call us. We've tried to encourage everyone to leave you alone for a few days, so hopefully, you'll have some peace and quiet."

"We'll be fine," said Jeff. "I appreciate all you've done while I've been in the hospital. Tell Linda thanks for me."

"I will. We'll see you soon. Give us a call when you're ready for company." Max bent to hug Sam and hugged Jeff, too. "Do you want me to release the hounds on my way out?"

"That would be great. I'll try to deflect them so they don't smother Jeff."

Moments later, the clicking of toenails and scurrying of feet announced the entrance of the two dogs. Oblivious to Max's commands, they rushed around the corner and made a mad dash for Jeff and Sam. Zoe jumped onto Sam, filling her lap. But Bailey sensed Jeff's weakness and slowed as she went to him. She put her head on his lap and a paw on his knee.

He stroked her soft head. "Bailey, girl. I've missed you." He bent and touched her nose with his. She licked his face and he smiled. He buried his head in hers and hugged her.

Max stood watching. "Obviously, I'm not a dog whisperer. Sorry, they both ran right over the top of me."

Sam laughed, struggling to free herself from Zoe. "No problem. I don't think anyone has ever been this happy to see me."

"They aren't the only ones delighted to see you two back where you should be." He placed a hand on Sam's shoulder and squeezed. "Remember to call."

"I forgot one thing. Jeff thought it would be good if you joined us at his first therapy appointment tomorrow. Could you meet us there at ten?"

"Sure, we've got nothing planned, so I'll see you both at the hospital."

* * *

Over the next week, Jeff fell into a new routine. Max talked to Jeff's physical therapist and adjusted the machines in Sam's gym for him. He did his home exercises each day and was in physical therapy three times a week. On those days he was tired and came home and took a nap. Linda and Max took turns staying at the house with him, to give Sam a bit of a break and let her get back into the shop. It also let Lucy play with the friends she missed.

On the days Max was there he took Jeff and the dogs for a walk on the beach. It made Sam nervous, but Jeff loved it and his eyes sparkled with excitement each time Max come through the door, knowing he'd escort him.

One afternoon when Linda and Max were Jeff-sitting, Sam called and asked if they could stay for dinner. She planned to order Jeff's favorite pizza and bring it home to celebrate his freedom from food restrictions. The doctor had given the nod to allowing Jeff to eat whatever he would like, but she wanted to surprise him.

It was cold and breezy, but Jeff was determined to have his time on the beach. He bundled up in layers and Max borrowed a hat and gloves. The dogs loved it and weren't deterred by the chill or the wind. They darted along the sandy shoreline and dashed into the water, chasing and playing. "I've missed this," said Jeff, watching the three of them face each other, doing their best downward dog.

"Are you warm enough?" asked Max.

"Yep. I'm good. How about you?"

Max's face was red from the cold. "My blood is too thin from all those years in San Diego."

They turned back and Jeff whistled for the dogs to follow. As the house came back into view, fat drops of rain began to pelt them. The dogs ran ahead of them and skidded across the lawn and waited on the deck, watching. Max and Jeff were slow and steady, but finally made it back, totally soaked. Linda had been watching and met them with towels she had pulled fresh from the dryer. After the humans dried off, she used the towels on the three soggy dogs. She fed them dinner and led them to their beds by the fire.

Max and Jeff were already sitting on the hearth by the fire. She put the kettle on and brought them both mugs of hot tea. "This'll warm you guys."

A few minutes later the dogs sprinted for the door, broadcasting Sam's arrival. Linda went to meet her and helped her carry in the pizza box and another bag of food, including a couple of pink boxes.

"Hey guys. It's cold and wet and miserable out there."

"Those two plus the dogs were out on the beach, so we've been sitting by the fire."

Sam laughed. "I think Jeff loves the beach more than the dogs." She went about getting plates and silverware.

She rounded the corner to the great room. Jeff raised his nose in the air and said, "I smell Big Tony's."

She smiled and said, "I wanted to surprise you, but I heard from the doctor today and you no longer have any food restrictions. I knew you'd want to celebrate with some pizza and I brought home two pies." They had eased Jeff from liquids to pureed food in the hospital and he had been eating solid foods, but all of them were basic and bland.

Jeff turned to Max. "See why I love her so much."

She motioned them into the kitchen and they congregated around the island to enjoy a familiar, but excellent meal. "And Tony wouldn't take any money. He's honored his pizza would be your first big meal."

Jeff freed a slice and sunk his teeth into the cheesy crust. "Mmm. I need to pace myself, because I think I could eat this whole thing."

Sam asked to hear more about their trip to Victoria and both of them brightened when they described the fun they had exploring the area and raved about the hotel. "In fact, while we were there, we decided we need to plan a trip so the four of us can visit in the spring or summer. The gardens are absolutely stunning and I'd like to see them in a different season," said Linda.

Jeff and Sam agreed it sounded like a fun time and thought a trip in June or July would be perfect. Jeff suggested they aim for Sam's birthday and plan the outing.

The conversation turned to Thanksgiving. Becky had been working on the guest list and had confirmed thirty-three family and friends would be attending. She and Sam discussed the menu and Sam ordered two turkeys and a ham from the butcher shop. Becky, Brad, and their two kids would be staying at Sam's and arriving the day before to help with the meal. Linda was making a couple of salads, Ellie would supply rolls, Jeremy and Heather were bringing all the drinks, and Regi would handle the appetizers.

Jeff chatted with Ashley and she and Will were coming on Thanksgiving Day and would be staying with Jen. Sam included Rita in the guest list, since she knew Kyle was with his dad and Rita's daughter had elected to stay in Seattle. Steve and Darcy and their son Dan were also coming as Jeff's guests. After Sam's repeated urging, Annie from the yarn shop agreed to come.

"Wow, you're going to have a full house," commented Max, as he liberated another piece of pizza.

Sam smiled. "It's gonna be terrific." She rubbed Jeff's free hand. "This is going to be our best Thanksgiving."

Linda helped Sam clear the dishes and the two men returned to the great room and settled in to watch some television. "So, I'm hoping Ashley's visit is a positive one. I haven't talked to her since her meltdown with me at the hospital," said Sam, loading the dishwasher.

"Does Jeff know what she said to you?"

"No, I never plan to tell him. I'm hoping she's in a better place now that he's doing okay."

"Me, too. I don't want your Thanksgiving ruined and frankly, she needs to grow up. She's always been a bit of a brat and I think Jeff indulged her after the divorce, trying to appease her. But she needs to get over it. Let's make sure she sits by Jen. She handles her best."

"On a happier subject, you're going to enjoy meeting Max's kids. Peter is a lot like Max and Brooke resembles Lisa. He's proud of both of them. They're both kind and intelligent."

"I'm excited. A little nervous, too."

"They'll adore you. How's your mom doing?"

"She's doing well. She's good about taking her medication and adhering to the diet and exercise plan the doctor recommended. I think she knew something was wrong and was afraid it would be serious, so she put off getting checked out. She actually sent Max a beautiful card and a note thanking him for recognizing there was a problem. She apologized for not letting him check her out when she was here and told him how happy she was he had come into my life."

"Wow. That's got to make you feel good."

"Yeah. I was pretty stressed out anticipating her visit and then anxious when she was here and frazzled when she left. I'm looking forward to a more relaxing visit with her next time."

Sam retrieved the two pink boxes and opened them to showcase a gorgeous chocolate cream pie with thick curls of chocolate covering the whipped cream and a lemon meringue, with a mountain of bronzed meringue, toasted to perfection. "So much for trying to behave until Thanksgiving," said Linda.

Sam put both pies on a tray with plates and Linda followed with hot tea. Jeff's eyes widened as he admired the desserts. "Oh, man. This is like the best day ever."

"What can I slice for you?" she asked.

Max and Jeff looked at each other and in stereo said, "How about a piece of each?"

Thirty

Linda had to work extra starting the weekend before Thanksgiving to help with the demand for holiday flowers. She was in charge of table decorations and squeezed in some time to work on her creation for Sam's dinner. Max's family was due to arrive on Wednesday and all four of them would be staying at the house. Because of her lack of time, she asked Regi to help get Max's house ready and she had been tackling chores after school.

Linda was boxing the decorations for the table and had put the centerpieces in the cooler, when Sara walked into the back room. "We can finish this, Linda. You get out of here and get ready for your company."

Linda looked at her watch. She had an hour before she expected Max and the kids. "You're a lifesaver. I'll pick up these centerpieces for Sam's tomorrow."

Linda gathered her tote and put the boxes of decorations in the car. She already had placed fresh flowers around Max's house, in anticipation of guests and the holidays. "If you need me this weekend, call. I know it's always busy and I feel bad not being here," said Linda, as she put her gloves on.

"We can handle it. But, if we're swamped, we'll call. Happy Thanksgiving," Sara said, giving her boss a hug.

"Happy Thanksgiving to you, too." Linda waved and wished everyone a wonderful holiday as she rushed out the back door.

She raced home, freshened her hair, changed her clothes, and made a pass through the house, checking for anything out of order. They were planning to eat out tonight and tomorrow they'd be at Sam's, so in the near future all she had to worry about was breakfast and Max suggested they order a box of pastries from Ellie's. He planned to get them on his way to the ferry dock.

She started a fire in the fireplace and lit a few candles. As she put the kettle on, Lucy darted for the garage door and she knew Max was home. She glanced in the mirror one last time and took a breath.

She heard laughter and voices and Max came through the door. "Hey, sweetie, the kids are here." He moved to her and put his arm around her.

"This is Peter and his lovely wife, Alex. And my beautiful Brooke with her husband Mark. Linda took in their smiling faces and relaxed as both Peter and Brooke moved to embrace her.

"Dad has told us so much about you, but I'm so glad we're finally getting to meet you in person," said Peter, who had the same smile as Max.

"Yes, we couldn't be happier for you and Dad. He's so much happier here than he was in San Diego," said Brooke, hugging Linda to her.

"It's wonderful to meet all of you. We've been looking forward to this visit for months. Let me show you to your rooms and then we can relax by the fire. And don't let me forget my dog, Lucy. If you'd rather she stay outside, let me know."

"No," insisted Peter. "We all like dogs and she's a sweet one," he said, bending to rub her head.

In preparation for the visit, Linda had moved her things out of the guest bedroom and into the master bedroom with Max. She put Brooke and Mark in the blue room and showed them where they could find extra supplies in the bathroom. Linda had designed a beautiful arrangement with blue hydrangeas and white roses accented with twigs in a glass vase. She added tiny white lights wrapped around the glass to serve as a subtle nightlight.

She'd done the same for Peter and Alex in their green bedroom and had chosen creamy white hydrangeas and pink roses for them.

"So, guys, feel free to rest or unpack or whatever. Then we'll hang out here until dinner. Our reservations are at six, but we have snacks if you're hungry," said Max, as he and Linda left them to get organized.

Linda had prepared a platter of cheeses, along with crackers and fruit for snacks. Max added some chips and poured salsas into bowls. He carried the tray out to the great room to set it on the coffee table when Peter and Alex came around the corner.

"Your house is gorgeous," said Alex. "I love the view and the open style of this area," she motioned to the room and the outdoor living space.

"You'll have to come back in the summer when we can enjoy the patio. It's a wonderful spot," beamed Max.

"Yeah, Dad. The whole place is terrific. And Linda is beautiful," said Peter.

"She's even more beautiful on the inside."

Brooke and Mark came from the hall a few minutes later, followed by Linda. "What can we get everyone to drink? We've got a variety," she offered.

After taking orders, Max helped her in the kitchen and they returned with a tray of drinks. "So, tonight we're taking you to a favorite spot. It's not fancy, but the owner is a wonderful guy and he has great food. It's called Lou's Crab Shack," said Linda, handing Brooke and Alex a glass of wine.

"He has the best crab cakes and lobster mac and cheese in the world," added Max.

They visited and the kids answered all of their questions about how things were going in their lives and at work. Linda knew Peter worked at the Mayo Clinic and he explained he was in the cardiac surgery department. "How proud you must be, Max," she smiled.

"I am. They're both wonderful doctors. Brooke is working at the children's hospital associated with Vanderbilt."

"I bet that's rewarding and heartbreaking at the same time," said Linda.

"It's hard sometimes, but we have a lot of success, so I try to focus on those cases. It's easy to get attached to the children."

Alex was finishing her education and Mark had taken a position at a law firm in Nashville. "Wow, you're all so busy. I'm delighted you were able to get away for this visit," said Linda, presenting more of the appetizers.

Brooke said, "I'm glad we both have paying jobs, so it feels a little less stressful now, despite the long hours. We're saving to buy a house."

Peter and Alex had purchased a home recently and weren't done decorating and organizing. "This place looks so put together in such a short time. How did you do it?" asked Alex.

Max clasped Linda's hand. "This lady, right here. She's a master at design and sketches ideas and plans overnight."

"Oh, I didn't do much. Your dad had most of this furniture and I only organized it and added a few things. Would you like a tour?" she asked, looking at her watch. "We have at least thirty minutes before we need to leave."

Max led them on a tour of the house and they snuck outside to look at the patio and the outdoor kitchen. Despite the cold, they ventured out in the yard to admire the plants. When they came back in they huddled in front of the fire.

Once they took the chill off, they piled into two cars and headed for Lou's. Linda drove Brooke and Mark. She pointed out places of interest along the way and slowed as she approached Harbor Coffee and Books. "This is Sam's place. She's anxious to see you guys tomorrow."

"It's terrific Dad is back near Sam. They've always been so close. And I have to tell you how much it means to me that you have all of our family pictures displayed in the house, especially Mom's."

Linda glanced over at her and smiled. "Your dad will never stop loving your mom. I know that and I don't want him to stop. I'm lucky he has a big enough heart for all of us."

She parked and Max pulled in behind her with Peter and Alex. Lou's was busy, since he was one of the few restaurants open the night before Thanksgiving. He greeted Linda with a hug and was introduced to the foursome. He led them to a table and left them with four menus, knowing Linda and Max had it memorized.

They ordered a variety of dishes and shared them all. They enjoyed the leisurely meal while hearing more about Max's new job and Linda's business. While they were eating Linda reminded them she had a chocolate mousse cake for dessert. "Your dad shared your affection for chocolate and it's one of our favorites, so save room."

"I'll eat yours, if you're too full," winked Max, as he took out his wallet to pay the bill.

They took them on a short trip around the harbor area to enjoy the ambiance of the moon reflecting off the water and the stars against the clear dark sky. "It's peaceful here," said Peter. "I see why you like it so much, Dad."

They traded kids on the ride home and Peter and Alex peppered Linda with questions about her life on the island. She pointed out her flower shop. "Oh, what a cute window display. We'll have to stop by there before we leave on Saturday," said Alex.

"I'd be happy to show it to you. Our Christmas season kicks off on Friday, so we'll be changing the window and decorating trees out at the nursery. It's a beautiful time to be here. I wish you were staying longer."

"We'll have to plan a Christmas trip. Maybe next year," said Peter.

They unloaded from the cars and settled in by the fire. Max had movies on hand and Linda sliced Ellie's beautiful and delicious cake. She delivered the plates and snuggled into the couch awaiting the movie.

"I'll be gone early in the morning to help Sam. But, we have a big box of delicious pastries from Sweet Treats—that's the same shop where we bought this cake. So help yourself whenever you're hungry."

Max hit the remote and Linda got to enjoy her first Thanksgiving tradition with the Sullivan family—watching *Planes, Trains, and Automobiles*.

* * *

Linda arrived at Sam's before six the next morning. First, she unloaded Lucy and watched her bound through the open door to roll across the floor with Zoe and Bailey. They hadn't seen each other for several days and their lively play got them booted right out the back door. Next, she carted in the decorations, deposited her spinach salad and a raspberry pretzel Jell-O salad in the fridge. It took another trip to get the centerpieces and the change of clothes she brought.

Sam laughed when she realized Linda was on her third trip. "Sorry, I should have helped. Glad your ankle is back to normal."

"Oh, man. I'm so thankful to be healed and able to drive and work."

"How was your night with the kids?"

Linda smiled. "Wonderful. I was uneasy, but once they arrived it was great. They're both so friendly, along with their spouses. Max is elated they came."

"I knew you'd like them. They're terrific kids and I know they're genuine when they say they're excited for both of you. They were devastated when Lisa passed away, but were worried about Max being alone."

"They're easy to be around and it's fun to hear about their lives." Linda shifted to the boxes. "So, I'll start on the decorations. How are you doing?"

"I'm finishing the pies and plan to get the turkeys in next. Becky's in the shower, so she'll be down soon. She's making breakfast for everyone."

"Let me know if I can help with anything," said Linda, as she took her box into the dining room.

Charlie had brought a couple of folding tables to make a second dining table. Linda started with a runner on each table. She had chosen a mixture of plum, amber, and rust for the napkins and runner. She placed the large and low centerpieces stuffed with ivory, cream, and white blooms, accented with shiny lemon leaf and abstract twigs, on each runner. Then she accented the length of the runner with assorted mini pumpkins, acorns, pinecones, leaves, and gourds.

Next she added woven round placemats, followed by a decorative charger. She had picked out a mixture of glass and metallic painted chargers in plum and amber. She followed with the ivory china Sam had from her mom. She placed a dinner plate and a salad plate on top of the charger. She followed with the colorful napkins and then added her handmade place cards, which she had made by painting leaves. She placed each colorful leaf atop a tree round cut from a birch branch.

She added white votive candles in a variety of glass holders to each table. And she completed each place setting with silverware, a wine glass, and a water glass. The overall result was a rustic elegance.

Sam's dining room table was wide, but the folding tables were a bit narrow for all the decorations. Linda had her hands on her hips, frowning at the table.

Sam and Becky were behind her and had been watching her work. "Linda, the tables look magnificent," said Sam.

"I'm not thrilled with this one," she pointed to the folding table. "I'm not sure there will be room for all the serving dishes."

Becky chimed in, "They're perfect and we can squeeze in the food. Don't worry."

"The centerpieces are wonderful. They're so elegant and perfect with the colorful selections you made," said Sam.

Becky moved to the table. "Look at these leaves and little tree stumps. How cute."

"I like the look, but we'll have to get creative with the serving dishes," said Linda, gathering her boxes.

"It's too pretty to eat on," said Sam. "Everyone's in the kitchen and Becky's starting breakfast so come and take a break."

Linda joined them and watched Becky pull a casserole and a gooey cinnamon and nut bread out of the oven. "Oh, it looks decadent," said Linda.

Sam had two roasters plugged in on the counter with the turkeys and was checking things off her list. The scent of cinnamon wafted through the house and drew Jeff and Brad into the kitchen. Soon the kids, Chloe and Andy, followed. Everyone loaded paper plates with Becky's creations and they squeezed around the island to devour breakfast.

Jeff was out of sweats and wearing khakis and a dress shirt. His hair had grown and the scar on his head wasn't as visible as it had been. He was laughing and joking, sounding more and more like the old Jeff.

Although the air was crisp, the sun was shining and Jeff wanted to take the dogs for a run on the beach. As soon as they had the breakfast mess cleaned, Max arrived with his kids and they all decided to go with Jeff. Linda exchanged her jeans for dark chocolate pants and a burgundy embellished shell with a sheer burgundy blouse. Standing by the tables she had designed, she could have been posing for a cover of a magazine.

They were eating at two o'clock and Ashley and Will were supposed to be arriving before noon. Soon Sam's house was filled with all the guests she told to come early, so they could visit and snack. Football filled the big screen and Regi and Molly delivered a variety of appetizers and snacks in the great room. Charlie and Hayley picked up Mary and brought her with them.

Ellie, Annie, and Rita all came together and carried in bags of Ellie's homemade rolls and breads. Steve and Darcy arrived with their son, Dan, and a case of wines they wanted to contribute. Jeremy and Heather were laden with coolers packed with ice and drinks. The house was filled with the comforting aroma of the roasting turkeys, baked ham, and fresh baked dough.

Becky and Sam had peeled what seemed like hundreds of pounds of potatoes and had the stuffing ready to bake, along with the sweet potato casserole. Sam had made cranberry sauce earlier in the week and glancing over her list saw all she had left was the gravy.

Shortly after noon, the bell rang and Linda answered it and found Jen and Megan with Ashley and Will. "Come in, we've been wondering where you were."

"It's my fault. I was running late getting ready," said Jen. Jeff came out from one of his many visits to the kitchen to snitch samples and spotted Ashley.

She rushed to him and hugged him so hard she threatened his balance. "Dad," she said, tears streaking her cheeks. "You look good."

"I feel good," he said, taking her hand. "And how are you, Will?"

"Good, Jeff. Glad to see you're doing so well."

Sam heard them talking and looked at Becky and took a big breath. "Here goes nothing," she said, removing her apron to reveal her elegant plum outfit, and hurried out to greet them.

"Hi, Ashley," she said, testing the waters. "And you must be Will."

Will moved to hug her. "Thanks for having us."

"Of course, we're so pleased you could come. It's a long trip from the east coast."

"Yeah, but it wasn't too bad. If we didn't have to get back to work, it would be easier."

Jeremy and Heather were busy handing out drinks and made sure Ashley and Will were served and ushered them over to the snacks. "We need to introduce you to everyone here," began Jeremy, as he went around the room, making sure he pointed out all the friends they hadn't yet met.

Sam escaped back into the kitchen to finish the meal. She had everything on the tables before two o'clock and announced for everyone to find their seats. Annie and Rita marveled at the table Linda had set. "Oh, goodness, I hate to disturb it," said Annie.

Linda assured them she had taken several photos of the tables and they were meant to be used and enjoyed. She helped them into their chairs, next to each other. Mary sat on one side of Jeff and Sam on the other, with Ashley next to Mary and Charlie next to Sam.

Sam had prearranged with Max to give the blessing and as always he did an excellent job. He gave thanks for family, friends, and the abundant food, plus an emotional acknowledgement of Jeff's recovery and homecoming. "I can't remember a Thanksgiving when I've had so much to be thankful for, so I ask for these blessings and continued blessings on those around the table today. In Jesus' name, Amen."

Everyone murmured "Amen," followed by several sniffles, as eyes were dabbed dry. Slowly, Ashley moved her chair and stood. "I'd like to say something, too." She paused. "I'm so thankful my dad is home," she hesitated, "and I want to offer an apology to Sam."

Sam's eyes betrayed her shock, but she recovered with a smile.

"Most of you know I've struggled since my dad and mom were divorced. I've never dealt with it and when I came out to see Dad in the hospital I said some hateful things to Sam. I blamed her for the accident and haven't treated her with any respect or kindness, even at their wedding. I'm seeing a therapist and he encouraged me to do this today." Her voice broke as she struggled to maintain, "I'm truly sorry, Sam. I hope you'll find it in your heart to forgive me. I'm happy Dad has you in his life. He deserves the best and from what I've seen and can now admit, you're it."

Everyone had tears in their eyes as Sam rose from her chair and went to Ashley and hugged her tight. "Thank you, Ashley. That means so much and of course, I'll forgive you." Sam felt the heavy weight she carried begin to dissolve.

Jeff got out of his chair and put his arms around both of them and kissed the top of their heads. "I love you guys. All of you."

Charlie lightened the mood, "Let's eat before it gets cold. I'm starving."

Megan countered, "What's new?" The tables erupted in laughter.

The focus shifted to the feast spread before them. It took forever to pass the dishes around the table, but once the platters and bowls stopped moving a hush fell over the group. The only sound was the clinking of silverware on plates and sighs of delight as the guests tasted the food.

"Excellent turkey, Sam," said Max.

"Everything is delicious," said Regi.

Compliments were tossed about the room like pizza dough at Big Tony's. And what took days to prepare was consumed in less than an hour. When everyone was finished, Jeff tapped his glass.

"I want to say a few words. You all mean the world to me and this is a very special day for me. I'm relieved to have the worst behind me and thank each of you for the help you've provided to us over the past months. We're truly blessed to have such wonderful friends and family. And I know how hard these past months have been on Sam. She's the love of my life and there's nobody I want by my side more than her. I'm so glad I'm here and get to spend the rest of my life with her. I love you, honey."

She squeezed his hand and kissed him. And this time when she glanced at Ashley she detected a genuine smile on her face and affection in her eyes.

Thirty-One

Max and Linda squeezed in as much of the island as possible on Friday's outing with his family. They spent time at Linda's nursery and watched as Lucas worked on finishing the lights and arranging the lighted lawn decorations. Linda promised to bring them back when it was dark, so they could appreciate the outdoor display in all its splendor.

The nursery was busy with people buying live trees and cut trees and the flower shop was bustling with activity. The window had been transformed into a Christmas village. "Wow, I can't believe the shop looks so different in only a day. Your staff must have worked all night." They took cups of hot cider as they wandered around the shop, looking at the variety of decorated trees, heavy with themed ornaments. Linda noticed which ornaments attracted Alex and Brooke, and while they were chatting, had Sara box a variety for each of them to take home.

Linda nodded. "It's a tradition. This is always a big day of celebrations on the island and starts the shopping season. Next Friday is our official tree lighting and the beginning of the Festival of Trees."

They opted to eat lunch at Soup D'Jour and visited the hardware store, Jen's salon, Sweet Treats, Knitwits, and a couple of the gift shops, plus stopped for hot drinks at Sam's shop. "Peter said they're thinking about planning to spend Christmas here next year," said Brooke.

"I hope they're serious," said Max, raising his brows at Alex.

"Well, I know I am. We talked about it last night and after hearing about all the activities, I want to plan on it. I think a small town Christmas would be fun," said his daughter.

Max's eyes widened. "That would be terrific if all four of you came." Linda saw the delight on his face.

Alex added, "We're serious, we talked about it when we got home last night, too. I think it would be great. We're at my parents this year, but next year would work."

"Let's plan on it. It would be wonderful to spend some time here, so hopefully, if we put in now we can take the week between Christmas and New Year's," said Peter.

They finished their drinks and made the loop back to the cars. Sam had sent enough leftovers to feed Linda and Max for a week, so they opted for a dinner of turkey sandwiches with all the fixings and chocolate mousse cake for dessert. Close to nine they took a drive out and marveled at the entire nursery filled with cheery lights and moving reindeer, plus snowmen, wreaths, a Nativity scene, and of course Santa.

Linda glanced at her old house and noticed it was decked out in white lights. She hadn't had time to visit, but intended to stop by over the holidays and see how Ben and Sherrie were doing. The house looked very festive and inviting, which made her smile through the tears she felt sting her eyes.

* * *

After seeing Max's family board the ferry, Linda went to work and Max went home to bring in her Christmas decorations and await the delivery of their own Christmas tree.

They were in the habit of eating dinner with Sam and Jeff on Tuesdays and Wednesdays after they got off work. Sam was working a few hours each week, when Jeff was at his therapy appointments and when Linda or Max could stay with him. She was planning to go back on a more permanent basis after the first of the year.

Jeff had been hinting he would like to go into the hardware store a few hours each week. His stamina was improving and being back home made all the difference in his mental health. Most of the time he didn't use his cane around the house and he was dedicated to exercising, usually twice a day.

On Wednesday, over Sam's homemade turkey soup, they discussed the tree lighting on Friday. Jeff was determined not to miss the annual event. The lighting was at six o'clock and Max suggested they go to dinner following the festivities. He offered to make reservations at the Beach Club, where they'd have a great view of the harbor decorated for Christmas.

"That sounds perfect," Sam said. "The coffee shop is open late that night. Most of the merchants are having open house celebrations in conjunction with the kickoff of the festival."

"Yeah, Buds and Blooms will be open late and I'll need to make an appearance at some point, but dinner sounds terrific," agreed Linda. "I'm working the weekend, too."

"Do you two have plans for Christmas?" asked Max.

Sam shrugged and looked at Jeff. "I haven't given it much thought."

"I had been thinking it would be fun to have Christmas in my new house," said Max. "Do you guys want to come over?"

"What are your plans with your family?" she asked Jeff.

"I usually go to Jeremy and Heather's, but nothing is set in stone. Charlie is planning his Whistler trip over Christmas, so he and Hayley won't be here. I haven't talked to Jen. My mom will go to Jeremy's. Ashley and Will have to stay in Virginia this year."

"Regi and Megan are going to cover for Hayley, and I may work a bit, since Rachel will be gone for Christmas."

"Jen and Megan would be welcome, of course. And I'll invite Regi and Molly. Maybe we can talk Kyle into stopping by," said Max.

Jeff smiled, "Sounds fun. You guys work out the details and I'll talk to Jen and see what she was planning."

Max started clearing the plates. "Say, Sam, did you happen to bring any pie home for dessert?"

She took a sip of tea, raising her eyebrows over the rim of the cup, and pointed to the fridge. "What do you think?" she winked.

* * *

Linda had to work part of the day Thursday, but they planned to decorate the tree Thursday night. She brought home a huge wreath she had made for the front door and takeout from the Jade Garden. After dinner, they put on some holiday music and began sorting through the stacks of boxes containing her massive collection of Christmas décor.

Max hadn't decorated for Christmas for several years and had given Brooke and Peter the ornament collection Lisa had accumulated over the years. He helped Linda go through her boxes and unearthed some lifelike artificial garland, ornaments, snow globes, boxes and boxes of lights, and cheerful holiday figurines made of every material imaginable. Candles, table décor, silk arrangements, and handmade painted wooden reindeer covered every counter.

"You told me you loved Christmas, but this," he gestured to the island and the floor, "is a whole new level."

"I know," she smirked. "It's a sickness. I can't help it. I've always loved Christmas and working at the shop, I tend to collect things I admire each year and before you know it, well..."

Max smiled. He spied a sprig of mistletoe in one of the boxes and held it over Linda's head. "Uh, oh," he said, looking up. "You know what this means."

She laughed as she glanced above her. He brought his lips to hers. "We can finally put that thing to good use," she laughed and with a glint in her eye, wrapped her arm around his neck and kissed him again.

It took hours, but they finished the tree and placed all the decorations. Garland with tiny white lights draped the mantle over the fire place, the banister leading to the loft, and wrapped around the pillars in the main living area. She found a place for all her knickknacks and inserted silver and glass globe ornaments, candles, and pinecones in the festive greenery over the mantle. She carried the same theme into the dining room and accented the dark green table runner with the shimmery embellishments.

The fresh cut tree infused the house with the fragrance of Christmas and the mixture of glass ornaments and silver balls reflected the miles of white lights adorning the twelve-foot tall beauty. Linda wrapped the tree with wide organza ribbon, in pale silver, shimmering with metallic flakes. With the room dark, a fire burning, and the tree lit, it was breathtaking.

It was late, but they were wide awake, so Linda fixed some hot cocoa and Max slid *The Bishop's Wife* into the DVD player. They cuddled on the couch, the tree twinkling, warmed by a roaring fire and a soft blanket, watching Cary Grant portray an angel sent to assist a bishop struggling to build a new church.

* * *

Linda had to work all day Friday. She got a late start because of their midnight movie, but kissed Max goodbye promising to meet him at the tree lighting. She spent the day working on floral arrangements and decorating the treat table for the open house. As was her tradition, she ordered hundreds of donut holes from Ellie and had her decorate them in festive red and green sprinkles, sugars, and frostings. Ellie put them on sticks; like lollipops. Linda inserted them into floral foam and served them out of fancy vases. She supplied hot cocoa and cider along with the donut pops.

She had everything ready before four, when the open house officially began. There was a scavenger hunt and customers tried to collect stamps from all the merchants for a prize. She had all her Christmas items on sale for the weekend and from past experience, knew it would be busy.

The school choir and band were setting up to play at the tree lighting and she glimpsed Santa and Mrs. Claus roaming the street, handing out candy canes. The boats in the harbor were decorated with multicolored Christmas lights and all the light poles around the harbor were decked out in garland. The town workers made sure all the trees surrounding the harbor were adorned with lights that would be turned on when the plunger was pushed on the old time box to light the Christmas tree.

She was swamped with customers and glanced away to see Max watching the scene. He caught her eye and pointed at his watch. She looked at her wrist and saw it was five minutes to six. She retrieved her coat and gloves and scuttled from behind the counter.

"Wow, you weren't kidding about being busy."

"I know. Sorry, I lost track of time."

"Sam and Jeff are saving us a place."

He guided her through the throng of people circling the tree and stepped into a hole by Jeff. Sam handed her a warm chai.

"Sorry I'm late, I—" and she was interrupted by the band playing "Joy to the World."

They sang along to the holiday tunes and clapped as Annie was invited forward to perform the honor of sinking the plunger to light the tree. Annie was honored as a lifelong resident, leader of the merchant group, and an active volunteer in the community. The crowd shouted, "Three, two, one."

She hit the plunger and the tree was illuminated with thousands of colored lights. The trees around the harbor and in the park came to life, glowing with white lights. The crowd cheered and clapped and sang "We Wish You a Merry Christmas", while Santa took his seat in the giant red velvet chair, ready to greet the line of children waiting for him.

Max took Linda's hand and Jeff put his arm around Sam. They wormed their way through the crowd to the Beach Club. They had a perfect view of the harbor and the lights, plus the illuminated tree. They enjoyed a delicious dinner and good conversation.

As they were eating dessert, they noticed Regi on the bench, staring at the ferry dock, bundled in her scarf and a hat. The holiday lights echoed in the still gray water of the harbor. "I sure hope Cam shows up," said Linda.

"I know. I'm concerned she has so much of her life depending on this fantasy. I hate to think what she'll do if he doesn't," said Sam.

"I wish she'd forget him and invest her time in Nate," said Max. "He's a nice guy and clearly interested."

"I know they've gone out exploring the island and he took her in his boat. He stops by the shop to visit her quite often," remarked Sam.

"Does he know about Cam?" asked Jeff.

They all shook their heads. "I think we should tell him," said Max. "Poor guy, he'll be devastated."

"It's going to be a mess, either way. I hate to see Nate hurt, but I don't feel like it's my place to divulge her story. And she hasn't told Molly," said Linda. "When is her birthday, Sam?"

"It's the day after Christmas and his is December twenty-third."

"This is going to be an interesting Christmas," commented Jeff.

"She looks sad sitting out there on the bench. Jen said she always keeps her eye on the ferries docking," said Linda.

"Speaking of Christmas," Max said. "I was thinking Christmas Eve dinner would be fun."

"That'll work fine. We'll stop by Jeremy's on Christmas Day, but not until late afternoon. Jen said she and Megan didn't have plans, so they're glad to be included," said Jeff.

"Great. I'll invite Regi, too." Max shook his head, looking at her, as she sat motionless, staring at the water. "We'll see how it goes. At least Molly will be here."

The waiter brought the check and Sam swiped it out of his hand, faster than Max could react. "Our treat. We owe you about a thousand dinners for all you've done."

"You don't owe us a thing," smiled Linda. "I'm grateful we're all together."

Santa was gone and the crowd had thinned by the time they left the restaurant. Jeff and Sam hugged them goodbye and headed to her shop to check on business. Max walked Linda back to the flower shop and waited for her to gather her things and followed her home.

When they turned into the driveway, she gasped. The entire yard was illuminated. All the trees and shrubs twinkled with lights including the new miniature pine trees that lined the walkway to the house. The lawn had a group of lighted reindeer posed next to a cheery snowman with a scarf made of red lights.

She jumped out of her car and rushed to his as he was getting out. "When did you get all this done?"

"Today, while you were at work." He smirked. "I had a little help from Lucas."

"It's gorgeous."

"Well, I knew you missed your festive house at the nursery and wanted to make sure you had a memorable first Christmas in our new house."

She linked his arm in hers and turned to kiss him. "I love you more than anything. And I love my second home. Thanks for making my first Christmas special."

They didn't bother putting their cars in the garage and drifted from tree to tree as they made their way to the front door. Her wreath greeted them as they unlocked the door. A soft glow from the tree and the lights over the mantle welcomed them. Lucy was on her bed in front of the fire. Max hung their coats and took her hand, leading her to the giant noble fir.

"I could look at this all night. It's my favorite part of Christmas. I like to sit in the dark with only the lights from the tree and watch the magic of the season," she said, the lights reflected in her dark eyes.

He gently rubbed her hand and led her to the couch. They noticed a sliver of the moon in the dark sky through the window beside the tree. She leaned her head on his shoulder.

"So, you know how we haven't had time to get to changing the sheets in the guest rooms and moving your stuff out of the master suite yet?" he asked.

"Yeah, and I have to work all day tomorrow."

He reached inside his pocket and pulled out a silver box with red ribbon. "Well, I don't want you to move out, ever." He flipped open the lid and revealed a large diamond and platinum ring, sparkling in the lights from the tree and the flames from the fire. "I love you. I've been waiting for the right time to ask you to be my wife and I can't think of a more perfect night or setting."

She looked at him and smiled. He got down on his knee in front of her, holding the ring in his hand. "Will you do me the honor of marrying me? I want to spend the rest of my life here, with you."

"Oh, Max, I love you." Tears filled her eyes as she nodded, "Yes, I'll marry you."

He grinned. "Let's try it on." He slipped the shiny ring on her finger. The Art Deco style of the old European cut large diamond combined with the subtle small diamonds surrounding it and the understated filigree along the band, were perfect on her hand.

She held her hand out to admire the striking ring. "It's gorgeous." She smiled and wrapped her arms around his neck, bending to find his lips and kiss him. After a prolonged kiss, Max slid next to her on the couch.

"I can't wait to tell Sam tomorrow," he said. "She'll be overjoyed."

"When shall we get married?" she asked.

"I'm leaving all of that up to you. The hard part's over. I'm relieved you said yes."

She gave him a questioning look. "It was easy. I'd be lost without you. You're the man I've waited for my whole life. I love you and want to spend all my days," she paused, "and nights with you."

He smiled and brought her head to his shoulder, as he slipped his arm around her. She nestled into his shoulder and said, "And the best part, I don't have to move my stuff out of the master bedroom."

Thank you for reading the second book in the Hometown Harbor Series. If you enjoyed it and want to continue the series, follow the links below to my other books. I'd love to send you my exclusive interview with the canine companions in the Hometown Harbor Series as a thank-you for joining my mailing list. Instructions for signing up for my mailing list are included below. Be sure and download the free novella, HOMETOWN HARBOR: THE BEGINNING. It's a prequel to FINDING HOME that I know you'll enjoy.

All of Tammy's books below are available at Amazon

Cooper Harrington Detective Novels

Killer Music

Hometown Harbor Series

Hometown Harbor: The Beginning (FREE Prequel Novella)

Finding Home

Home Blooms

A Promise of Home

Pieces of Home

I would love to connect with readers on social media. Remember to subscribe to my mailing list for another freebie, only available to readers on my mailing list. Visit my webpage at http://www.tammylgrace.com/contact-tammy.html and provide your email address and I'll send you the exclusive interview I did with all the canine characters in my books. I encourage you to follow me on Facebook at https://www.facebook.com/tammylgrace.books/, by liking my page. You may also follow me on Amazon, by using the follow button under my photo. Thanks again for reading my work and if you enjoy my novels, *I would be grateful if you would leave a positive review on Amazon*. Authors need reviews to help showcase their work and market it across other platforms.

If you enjoyed my books,
please consider leaving a review on Amazon

Hometown Harbor: The Beginning (FREE Prequel Novella)

Finding Home (Book 1)

Home Blooms (Book 2)

A Promise of Home (Book 3)

Pieces of Home (Book 4)

Killer Music: A Cooper Harrington Detective Novel (Book 1)

Praise for Tammy L. Grace, author of The Hometown Harbor Series and the Cooper Harrington Detective Novels

"This book was just as enchanting as the others. Hardships with the love of a special group of friends. I recommend the 4 part series as a must read. I loved every exciting moment. A new author for me. She's Fabulous."

— *MAGGIE!, review of Pieces of Home: A Hometown Harbor Novel (Book 4)*

"Killer Music is a clever and well-crafted whodunit. The vivid and colorful characters shine as the author gradually reveals their hidden secrets—an absorbing page-turning read."

— *Jason Deas, bestselling author of Pushed and Birdsongs*

"I could not put this book down! It was so well written & a suspenseful read! This is definitely a 5 star story! I'm hoping there will be a sequel!"

—*Colleen, review of Killer Music*

"Tammy is an amazing author, she reminds me of Debbie Macomber… Delightful, heartwarming…just down to earth."

— *Plee, review of A Promise of Home: A Hometown Harbor Novel (Book 3)*

"This was an entertaining and relaxing novel. Tammy Grace has a simple yet compelling way of drawing the reader into the lives of her characters. It was a pleasure to read a story that didn't rely on theatrical tricks, unrealistic events or steamy sex scenes to fill up the pages. Her characters and plot were strong enough to hold the reader's interest."

—*MrsQ125, review of Finding Home: A Hometown Harbor Novel (Book 1)*

"I thoroughly enjoyed this book. I would love for this story to continue. Highly recommended to anyone that likes to lose themselves in a heartwarming good story."

—*Linda, review of Pieces of Home: A Hometown Harbor Novel (Book 4)*

Made in the USA
Columbia, SC
12 October 2023

24363904R00190